D1516020

DORIT
IN
LESBOS

T O B Y   O L S O N

Linden Press / Simon & Schuster

New York / London / Toronto / Sydney / Tokyo

Linden Press
Simon & Schuster Building
Rockefeller Center
1230 Avenue of the Americas
New York, New York 10020

LINDEN PRESS/S&S and colophon are registered
trademarks of Simon & Schuster Inc.

Designed by Chris Welch
Manufactured in the United States of America

10 9 8 7 6 5 4 3 2 1

Library of Congress Cataloging-in-Publication Data

Olson, Toby.
  Dorit in Lesbos / Toby Olson.
    p.   cm.
  I. Title.
  PS3565.L84D67   1989
  813'.54—dc20   89-13072
                                                    CIP

ISBN 0-671-68486-8

Sections of this novel have appeared in *Boulevard*,
Conjunctions, *The Gettysburg Review*, and as a limited-edition
volume called *The Pool* from The Perishable Press Limited.
Grateful acknowledgment is made.

The author wishes to thank the
Rockefeller Foundation and Temple University
for time and support.

For Paul Blackburn,
still alive in his art.

Whether we wish to comprehend the animal from the point of view of an artist or, as scientists, wish to discover the laws of its construction—light will be always thrown on the subject, and it will be a help to us, if we separate the internal shapes from the organic form as it appears to the eye. This will be the first step, and a considerable one, toward recognizing the intrinsic value of what is visible. We shall perceive that the appearance which meets the eye is something of significance and shall not allow it to be degraded to a mere shell which hides the essential from our glance. We would not wish to be like grubbers after treasure who have no suspicion that the really valuable things can be found anywhere but hidden away deep in dark places.

—Adolf Portmann
Animal Forms and Patterns

Come now, delicate Graces and
beautiful-haired Muses.

—Sappho

DORIT
IN
LESBOS

My Dearest Wave,

I cannot tell you what the Aegean looks like in the morning sun, but I'll try. It's light blue and crystalline, and where the sea deepens and the current picks up at the point, a rich blue darkening, lovely almost as your eyes.

There are rocks down under the surf close to shore; the water turns lime green there, eddies of occasional froth, and moss on the high boulders that peek out like the heads of benign behemoths in the wake's soft recession.

I've seen a few boats in the distance, only a few. Fishing boats, I think. And I've seen a school or two, moving in a mile-long drift in a vague ribbon just under the surface.

All this is by way of saying that I've a high window that looks out over the sea. I'm set back from a fingertip of peninsula, here in a small snug harbor on a small island in the Cyclades, thinking of you.

There's a man who brings food and supplies. I've been down to the village with him in a kind of two-wheeled donkey cart on a road no more than a shepherd's path, about a half hour at walking pace: small colorful flowers, their heads nudged or broken by the wooden spokes. A poor and primitive man, younger I'm sure than he looks, very bad teeth. He has enough English to make our appointments. Olive eyes, of course. And a sense of humor, I think, though I can't always tell what he's laughing at.

The village is nothing much, and very poor. But there's a small hotel there, old and colonial and with amenities, a bar and a screened veranda. I had a drink and a talk recently with a pair of Englishmen there. Outside of that, a few shops and a grocery store, a machine-repair place, two restaurants, bars, and a rough and beautiful church.

But here it's a different story. My house is high up on a sloping hillside, white stucco, small little rectangles and different levels. There's plenty of sun and light all day and only a soft breeze. Clouds pass quickly beyond the promontory, but here the butterflies can hover and the flowers only nod. The harbor is very small, and rocky for a good distance out. There are no boats close in at all, and I can see no other houses. But I fear I sit at the wrong window, Wave. It's hard to keep my head down and at work. Well, in a few days maybe. I'll get used to it all by then.

I'm halfway through a heart. At least I think I'm that far. It's always been harder than limbs are: how get life in stillness into that most vital of all organs? The anatomy is so simple, so circular and fixed. There are those washes of membrane though, pericardium, gloss of aorta, those wetly transparent sheathings fixing the capillaries. It can all be like subtle drapery, *folding* drapery. At least I hope I can render that as movement.

I know now I've made the right decision. I've come to see that clearly in the past few months, even though I know you'll think it's just another of my binges. Probably my first letters were a little crazy like that. And I have to say too, though I doubt you'll believe it, that it had nothing at all to do with her, except that her own going might have served as a kind of model to release me. This is not just another false start. Christ, Wave, I'm sixty-two years old now. I just had to get down to it.

And I am asking you for nothing this time either, only that you'll know I love and miss you. I'll keep writing, telling you about this place and how the work goes. I hope you'll stay with me, in these letters, write when you can, though I know I've no right to ask anything. I trust you're doing well. There's a check enclosed here, royalties on that last big anatomy book. I'll see that they keep coming, probably through Ross. I'll make arrangements. Do let me know if you need anything. If you hear anything. You're right, I do still miss her terribly. But that is not the reason for my leaving.

But I won't end this here, not on that note. There is more news, though it may seem very local to you and of no consequence. I suspect that on this island, at least until I'm settled in, everything I come across will seem like important news.

The two Englishmen I met and spoke with at the little bar are professional men, both quite a bit younger than I, mid-forty or so. I'd passed them in my donkey cart and seen them look out at me from the veranda. There are not many Americans in the village, at least none who are not immediately recognizable as tourists, and I must have been somewhat of a sight in my rickety cart. They smiled and I waved to them, and later on, when I passed the veranda on foot, they called out to me.

One of the two, Bayard, is a doctor, an oncologist from London, and you can imagine that we had things to talk about. I told him what I was up to, and he was very interested and a little disappointed that he wouldn't be on the island long enough to get to my little house to see some illustrations.

The other fellow, Harwood, is a lawyer, from London also. They seem to know each other quite well, but Bayard let me know that they were really on the island because of their wives' association. The women weren't with them, at the bar, but were off somewhere sightseeing.

It seems that the wives are art collectors, amateurs, they said, but doing it seriously and with enthusiasm. They'd all come over to the island for some showing or other. People were here, they said, from various places in Europe. There were even going to be a few Americans. "Where?" I remember asking. "Not here in this village surely."

"Oh, no!" Bayard told me. "There's a new museum on the other side of the island, a beautiful place supposedly. Most of the others are staying over there. A sizable crowd, I hear. We wished for a quieter venue, though I'm not sure our wives appreciate that."

At least that's the gist of his words. I remember Harwood laughing lightly as Bayard finished.

It came out in our talk that the showing was to be of British and Greek work, that there was some sense of cultural exchange in the occasion, and that the organizing principle had something to do with Realism. They called it *new* Realism. They used the term casually enough, but kept referring to their wives as the experts, the ones who knew what this business was all about. They joked and laughed about their own lack of knowledge, and I think I noted a slight hint of embarrassment that they should be involved in a business such as this at all. What they seemed to know the most about were those from the London social set who would be attending.

Bayard made note of the major texts I'd illustrated, taking particular interest in the most recent, and Harwood seemed to cling to the fact that I'd been gainfully employed in a particular way for many years. I didn't tell them what I was up to now; it didn't seem the right thing to do. And when they asked me how long I'd be on the island, I lied a little and put an ending date on it.

As we spoke and I asked them more about the show and what they knew about the other side of the island, Bayard said that if I was free I should come over with them. They had hired a boat, a large one, and there would be plenty of room. They'd not been there themselves, but they'd heard that the trip around was a quite beautiful one.

And so, dear Wave, I'll be going to a fancy art opening tomorrow evening. I only hope that my ragged sport coat won't be too much of an embarrassment. I really never thought I'd get social at all here. I'll have to guard against involvement beyond the evening. I've work to do, and can't get teased away from it. I'll write you about the opening.

And let me say again that I miss you. I know I've said it in my other letters, but they were probably crazy, as I suppose I was. I mean that craziness of disjunction and separation, of travel and unsettledness, of anticipating work and not having a place in which to get down to it. You'd love this place of mine, a house better than any in which I've ever lived. But that's probably a reflection of my peace of mind and readiness and nothing more. My heart awaits me. There it rests, on this broad table under my window and beside this pad.

Good morning or evening, Wave, whatever it is where you are. I see the blue of your eyes in the distant water. There is nothing at all that I have forgotten about you. I'll be back to you, in another letter, in a few days.

My love,
Edward

"**Y**OU MAY BE WONDERING about the girl," she said. "But he didn't mean another woman. He meant Angela. He said he missed her, but I don't really believe that. He left after all, and it was I who was left to search for her. There were never women, I don't think, just little spurts of leaving. I remember in those first crazy letters, I think he went on a little about those times."

"Where are they now?" I said.

"I think I tore them up. I was surely angry, unstrung, as you might guess. Even now there's so much that's hard to hear. That he'd never lived in a better house? There are things insensitive and even cruel there, don't you think so, Jack? I was only fifty-two then, and I'd lost my daughter."

I could hear the voice of a younger woman as she spoke my name. For everyone else it had been "Jackie" then, but for Aunt

Waverly it was always Jack, something I had not thought of in over twenty years.

We sat in the living room of the same house, on the same street in Congress Park, Illinois, and because it was summer and the curtains were drawn open, the windows up, I could see the side of my own old house over her shoulder and, through the dining room, could hear the voices of children playing in the oval park across the street. Tall Aunt Waverly, still erect and lovely, sat in a chair across from me. Her hair was gray now, but still close-cropped and loose. Her eyes might still have held that same Aegean blue.

Her telegram had reached me on the distant coast of California, of all places on the very sand of Seal Beach. I'd been up and in my studio since 5:00 A.M., going over the topographic map and water system schema. There were bruises, a good-sized hematoma at my hip, deep muscle aches. I hadn't slept much. I'd been worrying the project over in my mind and had been thinking, too, about Chen.

By seven the sun was strong in the windows, and I had put things aside and pulled my weary body to the beach. It was only a block away from my place, but far enough so that the stiffness in my shoulders and legs worked out a little by the time I got there. I'd tried to jog, but it was no good. I'd finally found a place for myself, down the beach a bit, a large rock near the water, and had sat in the sand leaning against it. It was still early enough, a week-day, and the beach was almost empty: a few men and women walking dogs, a half-dozen lazy surfers beyond the shore swells, sitting on their boards. I'd put my head back against the rock and dozed off. I think I slept a little.

Then my face felt cool, a tightening in the cut I'd gotten there. Something was blocking the sun. I turned my head and opened my eyes, and there was the messenger, in full uniform with hat, stand-ing in the sand beside me. He looked ludicrous, the buttons on his epaulets blinking in the morning light, the toes of his brightly shined shoes covered with sand. He handed down the envelope and stood and waited. I was wearing a swimsuit and sweatshirt and had nothing else with me. I turned my palms up. He looked down at me for a long moment, his face in complete shadow under his brief bill, then shrugged and turned and plodded back up the beach. I tore the envelope open and read the message. YOUR UNCLE EDWARD PASSED AWAY LAST WEEK. FUNERAL SATURDAY AT 10. PLEASE COME. YOUR AUNT. WAVERLY CHURCH.

On the way to the Long Beach hospital, I passed the complex where the thing had happened. The freeway made a long, looping curve around it, and I could see the sprawl of low modern buildings, slightly elevated, in the distance for a good five minutes as I came upon and passed it. The site, close to a hundred acres in all, was coming along on schedule. All the hill contours and paths were in, and we'd finished most of the large and trickier plantings, even had them top-dressed temporarily so we could see them in a finished state against the rest. The larger boulders were in place, each embedded in the earth, showing a low profile, and Chen's pool was completely finished. We had some flowers to do, and that would be important because we'd decided on only a few drifts as accent. It was Chen's idea, keeping the whole somewhat severe, as were the buildings, things taken off traditional Japanese settings. Chen was Chinese by his father, second generation, but his mother, a very forceful and determined woman, was straight out of Kyoto. There was a terrace near the freeway's verge, and that was giving us some problems, but the only large-scale work left to be done was a little grading and fill. We had just under a month left before the opening. They'd pushed it ahead on us a bit, something about executives and timing, and they understood it might not be completely finished by then. So long as it was presentable.

The place was to be a showcase for the business, our first really large industrial commission. We'd done small businesses, but mostly typical California estates, those manufactured ones we'd made grow up out of nothing, formulating total landscapes in Hollywood and San Diego and along the coast. We'd been in business together for ten years, and we'd done well. But now I was forty-four, Chen over fifty, and we both knew that this was the big one, that we were stepping up with it and that maybe it was about time. The project had been working itself out smoothly, at least until a few days before, when things got a little sticky.

I drove past the broad curve of freeway, the site only visible now in the rearview mirror, and headed for the off ramp that would take me into Long Beach. I was thinking of Chen, his injuries, and how I'd have to tell him I'd be going back east. We had men on the job, ones I knew we could trust, and I could keep in touch by phone as much as was necessary. Still, it wasn't a good time. The further along we got, the more important the decisions would be. I knew Chen would accept my going purely. For him family was all-important, not at all as it had been for me. In our years together we'd become more than business partners. We were friends, and I felt I was betraying our friendship just a little, betraying him. He wouldn't feel that way; I knew that, but I was still bothered.

They'd come upon us at dusk, a Sunday evening, while we were in the trailer packing things up. We'd been on the site for most of the afternoon, checking the sinking sun's shadows as they fell on the large rocks and growth clusters, using the theodolite to get a proper angle for the terrace. Then, when the sun was almost gone, we'd spent a good hour going over fixture placements, where the spots would go, angles of lighting along the periphery. We'd done it all before, on hazy days and even in the rain, but this was really one of our last shots at large corrections and refinements. Soon we'd have room only for small changes. Things were nearing a point from which we'd be unable to back off, and we were anxious to make sure we hadn't missed anything.

We'd gotten a few calls recently, not too subtle warnings, but we hadn't taken them very seriously. We'd hired minority workers mostly, Chicanos and a good many Asians, most of whom we'd used on smaller jobs with no trouble. They were the best workers that we could find, but they were the cause of the phone calls. A splinter group in the union had been fighting for a quota system. Many Anglos were losing jobs to California's recent Asian influx, and the group intended to do something about it. They were making some legal inroads, but there had been a few instances of violence with other companies. They'd let us alone when our crew was small, but this was a big job.

There were four of them, men in their middle thirties. Chen's fifty-three, but he's put in a lot of years landscaping, doing the physical part of it even after we went into business, getting down into things with the workers. And I've kept myself in pretty good shape as well, some tennis and rooting around with Chen and the others on most of the jobs. Still, these were big men, and it was clear they'd done this kind of thing before.

The door of the trailer was open. We had the lights on, and we were gathering up some contour drawings at the drafting table. I heard a rap, then a voice, and when I looked toward the door one of them was standing in it. He had a hard hat on, something in his hand, and for a moment I thought he was one of our men. He didn't say anything, just looked at us. I saw it was a wrench he held, a heavy one with a red handle. Then I heard a splashing, smelled gasoline, and when I looked to the trailer's window over the drafting table, a wash of liquid was running across it. Chen was off his stool and on his feet beside me, already starting toward the door. The man blocked it. He was smiling now, a sure smile, nothing humorous in it.

I reached for Chen's shoulder, but he was past me before I could stop him. I saw the wrench come up, the man's arm moving awkwardly in the tight space of the doorway. The wrench clicked against the trailer's curved ceiling, and before he could bring it down, Chen was on him, his arms gathered across his chest, his shoulder in the man's stomach. He hadn't gotten much speed in the short distance he had traveled, but he had been so direct and sure in his movements that the man was caught off guard. The wrench came down, hitting hard into Chen's thigh. The man grunted through the blow. Then the two of them were falling out of the doorway.

I jumped quickly after them, throwing the plastic square I held behind me toward the drafting table, and when I got to the doorway I saw Chen and the man rolling on the ground. Two of the other three were moving toward them. The fourth man, very large and in coveralls, held a gas can, swinging it and dousing the trailer's side. The can was up, a stream of gas leaving it, but his head had turned, his eyes wide, watching the two bodies as they fell in a tangle down the three steep steps at the trailer door. The two men closed in on Chen. I saw arms come up, what I thought were baseball bats in their hands, heard the sick, dull thuds as they struck heavily into Chen's body.

Then I was coming through the doorway too, my arms open. I managed to hit the two men wielding the bats while I was still in the air, banging into one of them with more force, but my fist made solid contact with the other's head. He staggered back, and I came down on top of the one I'd gotten my body into, knocking him to the ground and rolling with him. I heard a yell and felt pain, something deep in my thigh. Then I came to my feet, free of the tangle of arms and legs.

Chen was still on the ground with his man, and one of the others was on his feet again and hitting into Chen's back and shoulders with the bat, striking him once in the leg; I thought I heard bone breaking. The man with the gas can dropped it, a wash splashing out and wetting his feet and coverall legs, a thin fan of droplets reaching up to his stomach and chest. He had something shiny in his hand, and I saw his fist close around it. I moved toward him, feeling a rush of air at my temple, and jerked my head around in time to see the man behind me wind up for another pass. I caught a glimpse of a blue snaking along his thick forearm, a tattoo of an animal or something, then reached back for the man smelling of the gas, felt his first punch on my left shoulder and heard something click and saw it fall down beside us as I reached him, grabbing his shirt at the neck, and got my knee up, hitting not his groin but his hipbone solidly at the crest.

His leg gave out under him, and then we too were tangled and down in the dirt, rolling. Something hit my forehead and bit sharply into it. Then I was on my back and had my fist in his hair. He was on top of me, very heavy, quickly draining my strength away. I was sure I couldn't handle him very well, maybe not at all. Then I got my hand in the dirt and touched the object that had cut me, a thin butane lighter. I pressed down and turned the wheel, then stretched my arm out along his hips and legs.

His arm was up, and though I had his head pulled back a little he could still see down to me, his lids over half his eyes, looking along the surfaces of his cheeks. His fist was above my head, the knuckles oddly large and very distinct. Then he seemed to pause a moment to consider. I saw his lids jump up, a strange reflective look in his eyes. I released his hair. I could feel the heat, smell the burning fabric. He rolled off me then, and I rolled too, staggered to my feet.

He was dancing along the trailer's side, his shoes on fire, flames rising up from his ankles to his legs. One of his arms was aflame, his shirt receding and disintegrating from wrist to elbow, and there was a thin line of fire rising quickly up from his crotch and across his stomach. He banged into the trailer's side, bounced back staggering, his hands hitting almost tentatively at his chest and sides, then turned in a circle, dancing again. His left hand touched his temple, a ring of flame at his wrist, and then his hair caught fire.

The man who had been behind him was standing still now, watching him burn, his mouth open and the tip of his bat resting in the dirt. I reached down and grabbed the gas can and moved toward him. He saw me coming and raised his bat again, but it was too late. I had the can swinging at arm's length and caught him full in the side of his head, gas flooding down over him as he crumpled. Then he was rolling, his hands pawing at his eyes.

I looked over to where Chen was still wrestling with the first one, their moving bodies firmly entangled on the ground. The other was standing over them, his bat near his shoulder. He had been watching for openings, hitting down into Chen when he had a clear shot. He still held the bat ready, but he was no longer swinging it. He was turned and watching the burning man as well, and when I turned to look too, I saw that he was running, away from the trailer, down over a berm and heading nowhere, almost a hundred feet away from us now, the fire like a suit of fire enveloping his entire lower body and still rising, licking in a tube of flame at his waist. His hands were like gloves of fire at the ends of black and smoky arms, and he was beating at his flaming head with them as he ran away from us.

I turned back and saw the man with the bat. He was looking down at Chen. Chen was on top of the other now, smothering him with his small body. His leg came out at an odd angle at mid-thigh, flopping and useless. I couldn't see his face, but I saw his fist, his knuckles white, holding the man's collar at the throat. The man was hitting up at Chen's head and neck with force, but he was getting nowhere. Chen had him, and it was clear that he wasn't letting go.

The one with the bat turned to the other man on the ground. He was on his hands and knees now, only his head moving from side to side, his face just a few inches from the dirt, and moaning. The two of us stood still and watched him, seeing the slight tremors in his forearms. Then the man with the bat looked over at me and I at him. He lifted his bat a little, a half-threatening gesture, then glanced back at the kneeling man and down at Chen and the other. Then he looked quickly back at me again, shaking his bat. I could see the indecision in his eyes and took a step forward to test it. He lowered the bat, looked once again at the kneeling man, and then was turning. I saw him shift his weapon until he held it at the middle, like a large baton. He was running then, getting to a good speed much quicker than I would have thought, in the opposite direction from the burning man. He ran with considerable grace, up the gradual slope that led to where the raw and severe buildings of the complex looked like two-dimensional rectangles now in the dim light of evening.

Then I was running too, heading for the trailer, limping slightly, the pain in my thigh getting stronger. I made it up the few steep steps to the doorway, reached in and jerked the fire extinguisher free of its bracket on the wall. When I got back, the man was no longer striking out at Chen, and the other one, the one I'd gotten the extinguisher for, was gone. I saw the almost comic outlines of his hands and knees in the dirt, strange animal tracks. I'd wanted to hit him again, to cave his head in with the heavy extinguisher. I looked off across the landscape, but I couldn't see the burning man. I could feel my arm vibrating, the weight of the extinguisher, and I lifted it and banged it into the dirt where the man's kneeling body had been, then left it lying there and went to Chen.

I lifted him carefully away. He didn't want to let go of the man's collar. He was talking, incoherently, a mix of what I thought was Japanese—his mother's language—and English. I got him up in my arms and carried him to the trailer side and rested him in a sitting position against it.

Chen's man was beginning to get up, shaking his head, feeling at his throat. I got the fire extinguisher, went back and hit him with it, hard, the metal canister pinging as it bounced off his head. Then I went back to the trailer, got the first-aid kit, came back and rolled the man over on his face; I taped his wrists and ankles, using almost half the roll.

I tried to get Chen up in my arms, to take him into the trailer, but when I touched him he yelled out in pain. His face was bloody, his clothing torn, and his leg was clearly broken at mid-thigh. He was still incoherent, and when I checked his eyes I saw that his pupils were dilated. His nose was broken, and there was a moist rattle in it as he took in air. I thought briefly about a blanket, but it was July, and though the California dusk was cooler than the day had been, it was still warm. I edged him away from the trailer side, got him down on the ground on his back, then got the extinguisher and put it under his ankles to get his legs elevated at least a little against shock. I left him where he was then and went back into the trailer and called the police.

When I got to the hospital, Chen was awake, propped up on pillows in his slightly elevated bed. The remnants of his half-eaten breakfast were still on a tray on his bedside table. There was no one else in the room, the empty bed beside him tight in its crisp white sheets, sun falling over it from the windows at the end of the room.

Chen's leg was casted, held up from the covers a little by a system of cables and pulleys. Though the swelling had receded a little in the past two days, his face was still a mess, bruises along his neck and cheek, a black eye yellowing, and a line of stitches running up from his lip to the corner of his left eye. I reached above my own eye as I looked down at him and felt the hump of thick scab where the lighter had cut me. It was tender underneath, and I suspected some infection.

"You should see the other guy," he said, his mouth forming a painful smile, moisture gathering at his ducts.

"I did," I said. "Both of them. The burning one might not make it. They haven't caught the other two, but they've hinted that the one you dealt with is talking. There shouldn't be any trouble from them anymore. And I've spoken to Benitez too."

Benitez was our head foreman on the job. He'd been with us, on most of our larger contracts, since the beginning.

"Benitez came over here. He told me about that call last week. You know, the one he got, and then the ones some of the other men got. Nasty personal calls they were. But nothing, he said, since it happened. But what did the guy spill?" Chen said.

"They won't say at this point. But I got it that they're not worried. I figure that we shouldn't either. Don't you think so?"

"I do," Chen said. His nose was packed, and his voice, though strong enough, came out thick and muffled.

I told him about my uncle's death then, knowing I'd feel better getting it out quickly, and that I'd have to be going east, for a while at least.

"Of course," he said. "No question you have to go."

"I'll call every couple days."

"Have you talked with Benitez about it?"

"Not yet," I said. "This afternoon. I'll call Blackburn again too. I've got reservations for tomorrow morning. The funeral's Saturday."

We talked a little more. Chen was alert enough, asking those important questions that would need answers before I left: where I thought we stood, what things would need attending to. He was clearly tired, still not really beginning to recover, and after fifteen minutes or so I got up and started to leave. But Chen wasn't finished.

"My family's been coming a lot," he said. "Even my nephews have. I can count on them as gofers. They don't know shit about the business. But they're smart. They can keep their eyes on things. You know, get to the site and such. And of course there's Donny. He's only got a couple of classes this semester. He'll like ordering them around." Chen smiled again, carefully this time against the pain. "You haven't seen your family much."

"Not at all," I said.

"Watch that. It could be interesting. Anyway, it's gotta be a good thing. Seeing them, I mean. Always a good thing."

"We'll see," I said. "There's really only one left, maybe two. As far as I know." I realized that in all these years, I'd told Chen very little about my family. Only those few important facts. And that he had never pushed it.

"Go do it, Jack. It'll be all right here." He shifted in his bed, folding his hands delicately across his stomach.

I left him, thinking he looked brighter, better than when I'd first gotten there, suspecting that the talk of family accounted for it.

When I got back home I called Benitez and had a long talk with him. Things had been at a standstill for the last two days, but he figured to get started again before the end of the week. Then I called Blackburn, our lawyer, and laid things out for him, giving him my aunt's address, telling him I'd call as soon as I got in, at least before the week ended. He told me not to worry, that things were in hand. It would be a while before any court business. The insurance company would be no problem. The police were still investigating. He couldn't see how there could be further trouble, not with the current visibility of the thing.

After I'd talked with him, I got my suitcase out and packed it. Then I took a long shower, in the middle of which I decided to put the plug in and let the tub fill. The hot water was biting into all the superficial aches and the deeper ones, and once down in the bath I spent an hour there. Forty-four, I thought. I'm too old for this shit. Even though I got through it. Everything seemed in order, or in good hands, and I was satisfied. I was even beginning to look ahead to Congress Park, wondering a little what going back there would be like.

"Things started arriving a few days ago." Aunt Waverly had turned her head and was looking somewhere in a corner of the room.

"Those crated pieces first. Then, shortly after, the carton of papers and the two suitcases. He would have been eighty-two, you know. There's a letter that preceded the body, something from a doctor. And a death certificate. It only gives the cause of death, his heart, after a fall of some kind. And a brief paragraph about the circumstances in the letter. In an apartment house, I think. Somewhere in London."

"I would have thought that island."

"Oh my, no! You'll see from the postmarks. He was only there a short time. Well, two years or so. But that's a short time out of twenty. Mostly, he was in London."

"And he kept writing to you."

"He wrote. And then he would stop writing. Sometimes years went by. Checks came to the bank, from Ross, his agent, and from publishers. In the beginning I answered some of his letters. Then in a while I wrote telling him to stop. But he didn't stop. I would think he had. Years would go by. And then there'd be another letter or two. I finally stopped reading them, even opening them. You'll see. I had a new life after a while, such as it was. I don't think he ever quite understood that. He was an artist after all. Very self-involved." She smiled and laughed lightly, and I nodded and smiled too.

"I can't really hate him anymore. I doubt that I ever did."

"And Angela?" I said.

"Oh. Well, I don't even know where she is, you see. Not for a long time."

Her voice told me it was a very long time. She seemed devoid or drained of emotion about them, as if she were talking about something that was now history. I had never known what had happened there. Of course, I myself had left right after the accident, a fool thing that had happened right along the park out front, at a slow speed. I could vaguely remember the tears Aunt Waverly had shed, remembered Angela moving hysterically around me. We were the same age, and I suppose she feared for her own circumstance, the way it had become shockingly real in mine. I couldn't remember Uncle Edward's response much at all. He had been my father's brother, but he was only a vague presence in whatever memories I had.

I was completely numb through it all. I headed west and north, into Oregon, worked awhile on ranches, then had somehow found my way into the navy. After that it was college, then graduate school in architecture. I'd kept in touch for a time, uncles and aunts, but they had all died at early ages, and only Waverly and Edward had had a child. Angela wrote cards at first, but that had ended abruptly. After a while, I stopped writing. There had only been a few letters anyway. I heard from Aunt Waverly periodically, brief notes on holidays, had answered her with cards. I didn't return for funerals. It must have been over fifteen years since I'd had any significant contact at all.

"Angela was married, you know."

"I didn't know that. You didn't write."

"Yes. A quite nice man, in fact. At least he was then. We've lost contact. A long time ago. I didn't write because it ended."

"Is he close by?" I asked.

"Well, he used to be. But I'm not sure anymore." There was a slight hardening of her voice now, which I took as a guard against feeling in recollection.

"He was tough on them, Edward was. He approved of very little. And even when she left, I think he didn't see that he might have had a part in it. She was pregnant, you see. Three months or more. And he wasn't pleased that they should plan a child. They'd been married awhile, but not really on their feet yet. At least as Edward saw it. Still, I can't be sure of all the causes, for her leaving, I mean, or what part Edward might have had in it. I'm not sure even now that I understand it very well. It was shortly after that that he began to pursue, once again, what he called his 'real' art."

"And then he left," I said.

"That's right."

"And what about Angela, do you think? Was there a baby?"

"Oh, well," she said. "That's another story. An abortion, I'd suspect. She was pregnant when she left." She shifted in her chair, and a last glow from the fading sun touched in the wispy hair at her temple. "But I must say, Jack, I think I feel rather free now, finally. God! At seventy-two!"

I don't know why she gave me the box of family pictures and that first letter, but both were waiting for me on Angela's old bedside table when I got to the room. She'd said to take a little time, freshen up, and after I'd done that I took a little more time and read the letter and looked at the pictures.

There was nothing in the photographs for either of us, I thought, but remnants of a lost life. Aunts and uncles at family picnics and other gatherings, my own parents, bright-eyed, easy in their bodies. And then Angela and me. I was just about the same height as she was then. The bulk of the pictures had been taken when we were quite young, and most of them showed us among adults, in the park or in living rooms.

There was a large plaque in the park then, a listing of the dead from the Second World War, and the oval of the park itself had been lined with massive Dutch elms. Disease had gotten to them sometime after I'd left, and they and the plaque too were gone now. There were pictures of the two of us, standing at attention in front of the plaque's glass rectangle.

I found my mother's mother in one of the pictures, hazy in the background of the shot. She was heavy and wore a simple house-dress, her hair up in a bun. She'd been my only living grandparent and had died before I was seven. I had a box of photographs my-self, stored somewhere in California, and some of the pictures were vaguely familiar. But there were shots of Angela here I'd never seen before. She had grown older than she was in my collection, which ended with my parents' deaths. There were a few of her in her late teens, a couple with young men standing beside her.

The last gathering was informal, something in the late fifties by the look of things. Angela was lounging in the living room, on the couch. She seemed ready to rise and go as soon as whatever event she was restrained in was over. I thought she looked quite beautiful, stretched out with her arms on the couch back, but tense. Her dark hair was long and braided and draped over her shoulder.

There were shots of Aunt Waverly, but almost none of Uncle Edward. I dimly remembered him as the one behind the camera, the one who made the record but was seldom a part of it.

I'd flown into Midway in the early afternoon, a Wednesday, and had taken a taxi to Aunt Waverly's house, getting there just as the sun was beginning to cast its longer shadows across the park. I was stiff and a little tender from the flight, but my only visible injury was that mean cut at my brow, and Aunt Waverly quickly over-came her shock at seeing it and offered me medicine and a fresh bandage.

Once I'd cleaned up, we'd talked a little in the growing late afternoon darkness in the living room, and she had asked me if I could see my way clear to deal with Uncle Edward's belongings. She couldn't do it, she said. Not for a while certainly. And the paintings really needed to get ordered properly, at least as a start. Maybe later she could deal with them.

I told her I thought I could handle it. I knew very little about such things, the art especially, but I thought somewhat selfishly that it might be interesting. I thought too about Chen, that I'd better call him and that it wouldn't be good to spend too much time away from him and the project. I felt a little wary as well: the sticky possibilities of reconnections.

She told me there wouldn't be many people at the funeral, just us, if I would come, and a few old friends, she thought, in addition to Edward's agent. A closed casket. The fall had done things to his face.

"It's been so long," she said. "I'm not sure even that I would recognize him, not without the tattoo. He'd grown a mustache."

"Tattoo?" I said.

"Yes. An odd thing, in fact. It's in the letters."

I said of course I'd come.

"I guess we're the last of it," she said, and though I didn't really want to hear that just then, didn't feel drawn to what it might imply, I think I truly did still feel things for Aunt Waverly, things that went beyond the immediate circumstances. She was my mother's sister-in-law, and though I had not seen her in many years, I could now recognize bits of my mother's own expression and movement in her, things I'd thought I had forgotten or buried long ago.

They had been close, living house to house, had raised their children, Angela and me, almost as a joint venture. I felt she brought me some fixture in time, the way two women had been in this place in the same culture and circumstance. And she had been my favorite aunt, and that had been because she had called me Jack and not Jackie, had been attentive and personal in the way that some adults could manage because they saw children as real people. I didn't think my mother had ever seen me in quite that way. Maybe my father had, but I couldn't be sure.

I couldn't remember much in the way of particulars, just gestures in sunny places and a few snatches of conversation, but I felt a well-being in remembering them, a sense that I had felt it then too, when I was a child in her presence. Dear Aunt Waverly. I wanted to say something about Angela, that she might be a part of what I was feeling, something I could share just then, but I could tell it was not the right time for it.

I slept in Angela's room that night. It had been stripped almost bare, but for the old bed, the dresser, and the bedside table. Almost no evidence at all that she had ever been there. The room was on the second floor, to the side of the house, and before I went to bed I stood in my shorts at the window that faced my own old house, just a few feet away. I could see the glow of lights below me on the ground floor. Someone lived there, people I had no idea about at all. My own small window was directly across from where I stood, dark, the closed curtain (or was it a shade?) unclear on this moonless night. But I could imagine my own room there, the shape of it, the walls and what the sill looked like on the inside. I wanted to open the window and reach across the space and touch the glass. I vaguely remembered Angela's arm, her fingers stretching out to me across that space. Hadn't we passed notes and things? Something like that. It had all seemed like another life to me for a long time, and I was shocked at the recollection and the image. I stood there looking across to the dark window frame for a while, and then I turned and went to Angela's bed and slept a dreamless sleep.

. . .

I woke late in the morning, around ten, feeling refreshed and without jet lag, but as I shifted and slid my legs over the bedside, the results of our struggle at the trailer came back to me, a deep hurt in my upper thigh, some stiffness in my shoulders, the irritation of scratches and many bruises, and that deep laceration rising a little from my eyebrow. Not bad enough for stitches, but an annoyance. I touched my brow and felt the tenderness and swelling. Aunt Waverly had given me some penicillin that she had, but it wasn't doing anything yet.

I wasn't feeling all that bad though, and halfway through my shaving and cleaning up, all the stiffness and the pain had receded. It was ten-thirty by then, and I thought I might give Chen and Blackburn a call.

Waverly was in the kitchen when I got there. She must have heard me. She had breakfast ready: juice, coffee, and toast, and two brown eggs sitting beside a small stoneware bowl on the yellow counter beside the stove. She was dressed in a simple and light summer suit, her hair combed into careful order and a light blush of makeup on her cheeks.

"I'm going out for a while," she said, "to see about some flowers."

"Good," I said. "It might be good to get out."

I said I'd pass on the eggs. She seemed a little disappointed, but also anxious to get going. She sat with me while I drank my juice and ate the toast, munching on a piece herself and sipping at a cup of black coffee. Then she asked me to bring my cup along and showed me where Uncle Edward's study was, a large room at the back of the house. I didn't think I'd ever been there as a child. I saw her off at the front door, watching her make her steady way down the steps and walk to where her car was parked in front of the house. Nothing feeble at all, I thought. A very handsome woman still. Then I closed the door and went back to the kitchen and called Chen.

"Too soon," he said. "You only left just yesterday."

"I know, I know. Is it better today?"

"A little better. Last night was the best yet. I slept right through."

"Me too," I said.

"How is it there, Jack?"

"Too soon to know. My aunt seems okay. She'll handle it, I think. But I'll need at least until the middle of next week. What do you think?"

"Think, shit. It'll be fine. And don't bother to call Blackburn. Give me your number, and I'll keep in touch with him. I'll call you if anything comes up. The rest'll be all right too."

"Okay," I said. "The wake's tomorrow, and then the funeral Saturday. I'll try you again on Sunday. But call me here if you need anything."

I heard Chen's breath in my ear. "Don't be a mama hen, Jack. It'll be fine. Just do what you have to do."

Uncle Edward's study was a larger room than I had expected, and it had clearly served as both office and studio. It was at the very rear of the house and ran the entire width of it, a line of four large windows in its back wall that overlooked the small backyard and beyond it a slightly shabby garage and what I remembered was an alley. The curtains had been pulled back, each window lifted a little from its sill, and though a gentle and warm breeze blew in, I could smell a thick mustiness in the place and figured it had been closed up tight for a long time. It was the beginning of August now, not nearly as hot as I thought it would be in Illinois.

The room was almost empty. There were a large desk and a chair pulled up under it in the middle, two folded easels in a corner, and an old bureau pushed up against the wall at one end. Standing at the back wall, between the windows, were two wooden crates, about four by five and a foot or so deep, sturdy and well made. His work, I thought. And there were two battered suitcases beside them. On the edge of the desk and carefully lined up with its corner was a low, rectangular wooden box, one of those used to ship wine in, and right in the middle of the desk was a large manila folder.

It was after noon by the time I settled in. I'd checked the outsides of the crates for damage. I was curious about the work in them. I had only seen a few reproductions from time to time in art books and catalogues. But opening them would take some time, a crowbar or a hammer, and I was drawn to the papers too and decided to get to that first.

The wooden box contained a series of neat and organized accordion files, each marked with a careful letter, a personal code of some sort. One held bills and receipts; there were various formal letters in another. And in one of them I found two sheets of slightly ragged paper, a running list of what I took to be the names of paintings, a list of dates beside them, and beside that a listing of places and proper names. There was also a packet of photographs in the file, Polaroids, I thought from a glance at them, held together with an old rubber band. They were clearly photographs of paintings. Maybe other shots in there as well, but I didn't open them just then. The other files held what looked like important papers, things I'd have to go through, but I wanted to get to the manila folder, to what I knew would be the letters.

Aunt Waverly had put a white envelope on top of the folder. It had her name and address on it, and the return was a printed hospital name. I opened it and read the death certificate, finding nothing that she hadn't already told me. Medical language, but a heart attack, either following or preceded by a nasty fall. It was stamped with a seal. It gave his address as a place called Muswell Hill, a name I had never heard, but a place clearly in London. The envelope also contained a brief note from a doctor, also with the hospital name on it. After I'd read the certificate and the letter over, I put them aside and opened the manila folder.

There was a thick packet of letters inside, all legal size, addressed in a careful and blocky hand, and gathered together with a broad ribbon. She'd put them in order, or maybe kept them that way. They looked like a gathering of love letters, but I knew already that they weren't quite that. The one I'd already read was on the top. I checked the last one first. It was unopened and postmarked in 1977, the Muswell Hill address. The previous one was written two years earlier, in '75, and there was nothing between '77 and the present. That's a five-year gap, I thought, a very long time. I'll have to ask her about that.

I started to open the letters, then thought better of it and decided to count them. There were twenty-five, only the first nineteen of which had been opened. I went back to the front of the pile and set aside the letter I had read. Then I lifted the second one. It was fat and edged out a little from the clean slit where it had been so carefully opened. It was postmarked only a week after the one I'd read. I got up and went to the kitchen and filled my mug again with coffee. Aunt Waverly had left it over a low flame on the stove. Then I went back, sat down in Uncle Edward's chair, and read his letter.

My Dear Wave,

I would have written you the morning after the opening, but I was somehow driven by the event and had to get back to my heart again. I've plans now for the whole cavity, lungs and the thick trunk of vena cava, vines even of pulmonary arteries. I suspect there'll be some different views, studies to bring forth motion in some way, maybe even a series. I can't of course tell yet, but I think I might have some key to vitality here, what I'm after and was giving me problems. The heart itself is very close to finished. At least the elements are all there. The rest will be in washes of membrane over the whole, many transparent layers. That will take time, careful and tedious work, but with each wash an often surprising result that keeps me at it.

So, you see, I've been busy, no time at all to write to you. Tomorrow I'll be heading down to the village. I think I'll walk this time. The weather has been lovely, and I need the exercise. A box of paint should be there from the mainland. Duchamp said that paint itself was readymade, and because of that all painting was readymade aided. I wish it were as easy as that sounded. The body is surely readymade, but the aiding is a very slow and painful matter, at least for me at this time. It was all those years of illustration that got me into this in the first place. Very hard to shake free of simple representation. And yet representation, though of an entirely different order, is exactly what I'm after. Well, I've never been very good at theory, never had any reason for it. I'll just have to plug on. But let me tell you about the opening.

Bayard met me at the village dock, a long and narrow one with fishing boats on tethers along its leeward length. There were boats also at anchor and some I could see steaming into the broad harbor as I approached him. It was close to five o'clock when I got there. Most of the fishing fleet was in or coming in, and in two hours, at the time of the opening itself, I knew the sun would be sinking in. It would take an hour or more to get around the island, but it was still early, the women were not ready yet, and Bayard took me casually along the dock to where their boat was waiting, Harwood standing in the stern, with captain's hat on, waving.

The boat was large and broad-beamed, with lacquered wood decking and a high brass railing all around. Not a seagoing vessel but a touring craft. At midships, behind the wheelhouse, there was a colorful striped canopy, white wicker furniture under it: chairs, table, and a liquor chest. A bowl of fruit was on the tabletop, and Harwood had a tall glass in his hand. Beyond the canopy, in the stern, was a broad open area with more furniture, a place for sunny conversation. It was an awkward and yet elegant boat. The crew was in the wheelhouse, a small old man and a younger one, bare-chested, who put a shirt on when the women appeared.

They came down the dock shortly after Bayard and I had reached the boat and climbed aboard. They were carrying baskets, holding their long dresses up above their ankles, leaning toward each other, talking. Harwood waved, and one of them lifted her basket slightly.

The women got aboard and settled in, laughing and joking about the better shoes they carried in their baskets, and introductions were made. Bayard's wife, Caroline, shook my hand firmly. Susan smiled and nodded, a little shyly, I thought, but it's possible that the shyness was my own. They were all dressed quite elegantly, the men in fine summer suits, the women in colorful but formal dresses, and I was in my old sport coat and slacks. At any rate, we managed to settle in and speak pleasantries, and after the boat had made its way from the harbor and we found the sea was calm, everyone seemed to loosen up, and we drank and chatted and leaned back in our wicker chairs. The women stayed under the rear edge of the canopy, and we three men sat out in the stern, under the gentle sun.

We stayed in close to shore, watching the sun sinking seaward, lighting the hills and gentle valleys we passed. We saw shepherds, a few wild goats on hillsides, and passed by other small villages, children at the shoreline waving. And we passed a few ruins as well. Nothing really distinguishable as the structures they once were, but fashioned obelisks, various blocks of marble, clearly ancient. Even bits of statuary, I think, but we weren't close enough to tell.

The trip was long enough, over an hour as I've said, so that I at least began to feel that I had entered another time. This is a primitive island, as I have probably mentioned, and what cars and machinery are on it are found mostly near roads that run down its center. For the whole of our trip we came across nothing modern. It was as if we were in times that were timeless, that had been this way for many hundreds of years.

I saw it all this way at least, and relaxed in it; my cares seemed so insignificant and distant there. I'm not sure about the others, if they were affected at all. Both Caroline and Susan talked on about the opening. Harwood, it seemed to me, was drinking quite a bit and mostly stood at the brass railing looking down into the water at the boat's side. He listened to what was said and turned often to add comment, joking at times about his wife's intentions to purchase something at the show. Bayard conversed with the women, and I kept watching the shore.

They talked about those who would be present at the opening, various dignitaries and even some of the artists themselves. There was to be a good-sized British gathering, an almost equal number of Greeks. "Fewer Americans," Caroline said, "but there is that rather striking young couple we saw in London last month." Bayard was not sure of them.

"You remember," Caroline said. "He was a doctor, an oncologist, in fact, like you. What *was* his name?"

"Oh, yes, right. Janes, wasn't it?"

"That's right. Of course," Caroline said. "We saw them sightseeing the other day, didn't we, Susan."

I remember she raised her head as Caroline spoke. There was a strange and enigmatic look on her face. She said she did remember, and that was all she said. Then in a moment she turned her head to the shore, smiled, and called out to Harwood, telling him and us to look at the beauty of the sun on the hills.

The sun was indeed beautiful there, soft and slowly spreading out in the beginnings of its setting, moving down to touch the hills and low mountains at their crests. We had rounded the tip of the island by then, had come around so gradually that we had hardly noticed, and had started along the other side. And in a while it became almost impossible to see things clearly on the shore. The women had to tilt their hats to keep the failing sun out of their eyes, and we men moved to chairs under the canopy with them. But soon the sun dipped behind the hills. They were higher here than on the other side, and we were left in a subdued wash of dim light, the sea around us turned to a subtle rose. There were flickers of lights now on the shore, just a few of them, electric lights, I knew, but I fancied in their wavy glimmers that they could as well have been small torches. The sea was rising up slightly now, not into turbulence but enough to give a gentle rocking to our large craft. I saw the women grip the arms of their chairs and tense a bit. But soon the rocking left us. It did so abruptly, and I could see the last ripple of it as it rolled away below our gunwales and out to sea.

We'd made an almost imperceptible curve to leeward and had entered a large and gradual inlet. I could see the low hump of an island to the sea side of us, and when I turned and looked behind, the end of our own island was well out in the sea at our stern. What pleasant breeze there had been was now totally gone, and the water to both sides of the boat was perfectly flat and calm. Bayard got up from his chair then and went to the rail, and the rest of us rose also and followed him.

We could see more lights at the shoreline now, dim ones, and in the middle of that array a vacant area, slightly aglow, a kind of wash of red there, not unlike the wash of membrane I had plans to cover my heart with. And we were heading slowly toward it, rough structures to its sides now beginning to emerge in the growing darkness. Soon we could make out houses, a few fenced stables, all crude and extremely poor looking, their wood in this light and distance seemingly oily or oozing with slow rot. And there was oil on the water itself now, a broad continuous slick, our bow sliding through it. We could see it in the curl, yellow and faintly green, strings of sticky seaweed rolling in the foot of foam.

The closer in to shore we got, the more the wasted structures to the sides of the opening seemed to reach out and enclose us. They were to both sides of the boat now; we were entering a broad channel, but their lights did not glow brighter. They were still shadow figures, two-dimensional, set at awkward angles to each other in no rhyme or reason. And we could not see a single animal or person.

The opening seemed to broaden as we approached it, the glow emanating from it washing to its sides, lighting the hills and structures to our left and right in a faint rose hue. Then we entered the mouth of the opening, were moving through its dead and quiet channel. We could hear the labor of the boat's motors, see the crude and primitive structures at the shore more clearly: houses and grimy outbuildings, all stained dark with a kind of greasy wetness. I saw a man then on a tilted porch. He too seemed oiled and stained. He raised his arm and gestured in an aggressive way as we slowly moved past him. Then we were through the channel and making a broad right turning. We had passed into a small and completely protected harbor, and when the boat came round we saw the source of the light.

The building was not overly large, though all aglow, but in its whiteness it appeared so, no more than a half mile in the distance as we approached it. The areas to its left and right and back behind it were all steep hills, too severe for any building, and so it stood alone, isolated from its dark natural surroundings, the flat stone terrace and steps that fronted it approaching the water's edge, where a broad slab served as a place for docking. Its foundation was so low that at our initial distance it looked as if it were resting on the surface of the water at the harbor's end.

White marble or limestone, it looked like a Greek temple of some sort, two large rectangles, a high and graceful dome at its center. Its stone slab, steps, and broad terrace rose up until they reached a slightly narrower plane at an entranceway, a wide and elegant arch.

The building was lighted from below, the whole facade distinctly visible in that wash, and because the stone was white and reflective, there was a slightly fainter aura of light extending a little into the now dark night a few yards from its upper surface.

At the foot of the docking slab at the water's edge was a low stone railing, broken at its middle; it seemed to allow access to the steps that led up to the entrance, and set in the squat, thick railing's surface were fat stone candlesticks in which large torches were burning. It had been those flames, reflected light from the building shining through them, that had given the rose wash at the harbor's mouth and now reached out to us, a good distance across the harbor's still waters, a block of light that we would soon be entering.

The women had moved to the other side of the boat, and we three men leaned out from our side, watching as we moved closer. I could see there was no more oil or seaweed in the bow's wash, and when I looked up again I saw that there were other boats, moored at the stone railing, their superstructures lighted by the torches, skeletal figures standing out against the night. And there were people too, some stepping from the boats, others lounging and milling around at different levels on the steps and terrace, garments bright and multicolored in the bath of light.

Our captain brought us around, coming first to starboard in a wide arc, then back to port so that we approached the building from an angle. When he cut the engines back, we could hear laughter and talking, and there were those near the water's edge who called out and waved to us. The mate secured the boat with ropes, looping them around bollards at the slab's edge. I could hear our wake slap gently against it. The slab rose no more than a foot above the harbor's surface, and the brief gangway that the mate provided was almost on a level.

I and the others stepped ashore and were greeted immediately by a young Greek waiter with a tray of drinks. I remember that the tray was glass, circular, and with a very low edge; it was crowded with wineglasses, bubbles rising in them. I took one, as did the others, then saw Caroline raise hers to someone up on the terrace. She touched Bayard on the arm, smiled at the rest of us, and moved away. Then Susan saw someone and left us also.

The three of us lounged at the stone railing near the water's edge. Boats were arriving every few minutes now, and two large yachts had come to anchor in the harbor, their occupants ferried ashore in motor launches that appeared from somewhere in the darkness at the building's side. The night was warm and dry, and the women gave what hats and wraps they wore to attendants who seemed ever watchful, young and swarthy men in formal dress. Neither Bayard nor Harwood seemed inclined to leave my side, and though the latter left to search out a drink from time to time, he always returned with bits of gossip and laughter.

"There are a few here that I know quite well," Bayard said at one point. "But I don't see them just yet. Ah, but there's the American, Janes!"

He had nodded toward a dark-haired man who was standing and talking with two tall and rather striking women. He seemed to stand closer to them than was necessary. They were off to the side of the torches slightly, just a little bit in shadow. The man himself was not tall, slightly shorter in fact than the two women. He was touching their arms and shoulders lightly in their conversation.

"Which one is his wife?" I asked.

"Oh, neither one of them." Bayard laughed as he looked around. "I don't see her here at all, in fact."

"He seems to be doing all right," Harwood said. There was the hint of a slur in his voice now, and his gestures had become broader. Soon a light bell was rung, and people began to head toward the archway.

We entered through a brief foyer, cloakrooms on either side of it. Beyond I could see clusters of people and a bit of the broad wall in the distance at the back of the central white room. There was what looked like a triptych hanging there, something colorful and figurative, flowers with women sitting among them. Once inside, I saw that the central room, over which the hollow dome rose majestically, emptied through tall archways into the two rectangles at the building's sides. There was more gallery space there. The high walls of all the rooms were bone white, and lighting, the source of which I couldn't find immediately, bathed the paintings and watercolors hanging on them. In the center of the main room were two long tables containing bowls of cold shrimp and various other foods. There was a bartender at either end of each array, handing out glasses of champagne. The mood was festive, and though people glanced at the paintings from time to time, most seemed more concerned with their conversations, the meeting of acquaintances and those desired ones.

Bayard kindly introduced me to some people, and I passed a few words with them. Then I made my way to the walls. Many of the works were much to my taste, or at least they had things and techniques in them that I felt an affinity for. Almost all were strictly figurative, nudes and still lifes, "modern" in the way their juxtapositions were not traditional. I searched out washes, those thinly applied layers, and found them in the most photographic of the works.

As I passed from piece to piece, I began to notice the red dots appearing on the small information cards to the sides of the paintings, then noticed the formally dressed man with a clipboard, people approaching him and talking. He would nod, then move to find a work and put a red dot on the card. A good number of the works were finding buyers, and I guessed that the opening would be a success.

There had been a small piece, a slightly abstract rendering of a woman's torso, that I had liked a lot. It was well down a row of works in one of the rectangular spaces to the side of the main room, and after I had passed by every piece in the show, I decided to return to it. I nodded to Bayard and Harwood as I passed them; they were now together with their wives again, talking with two other couples whom they seemed to know quite well. Only Harwood still held a glass in his hand.

When I reached the side gallery I was headed for, I had to pass among a cluster of people standing in front of a large, rather dramatic work. Beyond them, the gallery was almost empty, just a few couples looking and talking. As I passed the last of these, I saw the woman. She was standing directly in front of the painting I was headed for, and the intensity of her posture and concentration as she looked at the work was such that I felt uncomfortable in approaching her. The painting was clearly hers for the moment, and I moved to the other side of the space and waited.

She was a rather striking woman in many ways, but the thing that struck me most at the moment was her braid. She wore a lime-green dress, a rather loose thing, open in a V from her broad shoulders almost to the small of her back. Her braid was fiery red, very thick and long, and it ran down from where it was pulled tight at her skull directly along her spine. Indeed, it looked like a spine itself, and I wished I had a sketch pad with me. I vaguely knew that this was something for me, something I could use.

Having no way to draw her braid, I watched it. And I watched the red egg of her head too, the way it turned slightly as she read the painting of the torso. Though her back was straight, she was bending slightly from the waist, her arms hanging a little forward from her shoulders, her hands in loose fists. I don't know how long I was lost in watching her, but in a while I felt someone's presence behind me, then even a movement of air, I think, as he came abreast of me and headed for the woman. It was the man Janes, the American that Bayard had pointed out earlier. The woman turned and smiled as he reached her and touched her hanging arm at the elbow. Only then did I see her face.

She smiled at him, not up at him; she was as tall as he was. I guessed she was no more than mid-twenty, but her posture and elegance were beyond her years. The man's back was to me, and I had no way of telling if he was smiling too. I saw his head move back a little in the direction of the central hall, saw her nod tentatively, her smile fade a bit. Then he took her arm more firmly, stepped to the side slightly, and brought her away from the painting.

They were both facing where I could see them clearly now. They were indeed a striking couple. She with her long waist, low and heavy hips, small breasts, those broad shoulders, and that oval face, that slash of blood red at her lips, a marking that seemed almost an insult. Her skin was tight as a drum, almost transparent, lightly freckled; his, on the other hand, seemed thick and impenetrable. He had delicate eyebrows, but eyes that were deep-set, serious and a little intimidating, and a slightly beaked nose. He was clearly older than she was, a good ten years, I guessed. I saw that he was not smiling and had probably not been doing so before. They passed by me, never noticing me, and went into the central hall.

The boat trip back had little in it of the drama of our arrival. Still, I did feel that we were leaving a certain place and going to another, one more prosaic and conventional. It was very dark, almost pitch black as we left the harbor. I could not see the mouth into it until we were abreast of that opening. And as we motored toward the tip that we would head around to get back to the village, both shore and sea were no more than a darkness, only a slightly deeper hue to suggest the separation of land and water.

Once around the point, there were stars in the sky. They had surely been there before, but I suspected that a cloud cover had obscured them on the other side. On this side, the shore was now bathed in starlight, lovely and benign as we passed slowly along it.

Harwood was asleep in one of the lounge chairs under the canopy. I saw a glint on the deck beside him, running lights in the stern reflecting up from our wake. Susan sat in a chair beside me. We'd been silent for a good while after Harwood had gone to sleep, and whenever I'd looked over at her she had been watching him, a look on her face that I could not read. It was dark under the canopy, but light enough so we could see his features, the dark hole of his open mouth, the slight flare of nostrils.

"A very pretty sight," she said. I was watching Harwood and did not know what she was referring to. I turned to her and saw she was looking toward the stern.

"I mean that building, the whole affair really. I bought a piece, you know."

"Did you?" I said. "Which one?"

"A woman's torso, a small piece. I've collected others of his."

I felt myself pulling my breath in, flushing slightly.

"He's Dutch really, with some Spanish blood, I think, though a British citizen. Vas Dias. A rather remarkable painter."

"How old is he?"

"Quite young, in fact; twenty-seven, I believe."

I wished to keep her talking for a moment at least. I was strangely assaulted by the fact that she had bought the painting. I'd had no real chance to see it after I had watched the woman. I felt it taken from me now, too quickly. I knew it was a foolish feeling.

"Do you know that Janes couple at all?" I asked.

"Yes," she said rather softly. "I know her, from the galleries, but I don't know him too well. He does the buying, I believe."

"What are their names?"

"Dorit," she said. "He's Mark. They've a place in London. It seems they spend a good deal of time there, coming over from the States."

"Is there something that she does?"

"She writes a bit, I think, or at least she used to. A doctor's wife, you know."

And so these and other words passed between us. There was more, I'm sure, but I have no clear recollection of it. I remember it was disconcerting to be conversing so near to her sleeping husband. But she seemed to know him well, knew that he had drunk enough and that we would not wake him.

After a while, Bayard and Caroline joined us again. They had been standing in the stern, watching the water and talking. We spoke some of the opening, the people and the work, and in a while we saw the lights of our village. Susan reached over, shook Harwood and woke him. He blinked a little and rubbed his eyes. His voice was creaky at first, but by the time the dock came into view he was up and standing at the rail.

We shook hands all around and said goodbye at the foot of the dock. My man was waiting, asleep in his donkey cart. I roused him and we set out. Though it was midnight, I was wide awake. It was a lovely, starlit night, the hills bright and distinct. I watched everything as we moved slowly along, and when my house came into view it was white and beautiful, at ease in its softened rectangles on the hillside.

I worked the whole night through, Wave, struggling with a spine that was a rope of hair. There's something there that I'm sure can take me farther. It was only when the sea became visible out my high window that I went to bed.

I believe I'll be working on with some intensity for a while now, so I'm not sure just when I can write to you again. Know that I'm thinking of you and that I'll get back to you as soon as I can. Be well there in Congress Park, that place that seems so very far away from me here. Still, whatever the distance, you are in my thoughts.

Forever,
Edward

I T WAS RAINING, A midsummer rain of a kind that I remembered from my childhood in Congress Park. There was nothing really specific that I remembered, just the open porch next door, the sound of the rain's falling, soft and steamy and relieving, an end of oppressive humidity for a while, and a slight hint of electricity in the air. And it was going to continue raining. At least I thought so, but I didn't say it.

We drove slowly in Waverly's small car, I at the wheel, she giving me directions that I found I did not need, and headed for Brookfield and the wake, only ten minutes from Congress Park.

"There's Saint Barbara's. You remember?" She pointed out the grammar school on the right. It had changed, new buildings and a new church, but the old ones were still there, where I had taken my first communion and attended school for eight years.

Farther down on the right, we came to the mortuary, Abbott's, the same name but now a low modern building with manicured lawn and a careful row of ferns to each side of the door. We parked right in front. It was still raining heavily, and there were no other cars in sight.

Once inside and free of our raincoats and umbrella, we stood alone in the long foyer for a moment.

"Should we go right in?" Aunt Waverly said. But then a man appeared.

"Allen," Waverly said. "This is Jack, Edward's nephew; you may remember him?"

The man was younger than I was, I thought, and surely couldn't remember me. Probably old Abbott's son, or even grandson. Times in the past were not that easy for me to keep straight.

"Of course," he said, and took my hand, then moved between us and kissed Aunt Waverly on the cheek. She suffered this with a dignity that I remembered. Then the man led us to a door and into the viewing room.

The casket rested on a low pedestal at the far side of the room, two white wicker baskets, tall and spilling with wisteria, at either side. There were three rows of chairs facing the casket. The walls of the room were covered in dark fabric. Music, quiet and forgettable, floated faintly over our heads. There was no one there but the three of us and of course Uncle Edward, in that final darkness in his metal box.

"It's early yet," the man said. "I'll leave you now. I'll be back shortly."

I took Aunt Waverly by the elbow. "Should we go up?" I whispered.

She pressed my hand against her side. "Why not," she said.

It seemed strange to be standing there, side by side, looking down into the shine of the metal surface, a slightly curved surface that gave our images back to us distorted. And it was strange too that we whispered, not in confidence but as if the three of us could be in conversation, were so close to each other and didn't need more than whispers. I wanted to reach out and touch the metal, maybe even stroke it; it seemed an appropriate thing to do. Waverly did reach out, but she only touched it for a moment with her fingertips. I looked up from the casket. Her face was placid, even a little cold. Then she turned her head and looked at me, and the coldness left, thin lines at the corners of her eyes, just the beginning of a smile.

"All in all," she said, "blaming him now seems almost foolish."

I thought she might weep a little then, but she didn't. She just kept looking at me, as if searching for something familiar in my face, something from her distant past.

I wasn't feeling anything at all for him. I thought of his second letter, and that helped a little, brought some of his vibrancy up to me, his cruelty too. But he'd written it close to twenty years before, and that recognition dulled his presence for me again.

It struck me that these two, the one cold and alone and below me, the other with heart beating only inches away, were the only two left and that I'd better do something, now or very soon, something strong before they both slipped away and I was left alone. Then I thought of Angela, their daughter. She was something, wherever she might be. California and my real life kept entering my thoughts as well. I needed to call Chen again, to find out about things. I needed to get back as quickly as I could. I caught myself glancing around the room, searching for a phone.

Then I heard a door in the distance, a rustling of fabric and quiet talking. Aunt Waverly took my arm and we turned. There were people coming in, and we were the dubious hostess and host.

Only a dozen people showed up for the wake. A man came out from a large medical publishing house in Chicago, a vice president. He talked to Aunt Waverly, said he was staying over and would be at the funeral. Though he didn't say it in words, it was clear in our brief conversation that Edward had accounted for a good deal of money earned by his company and that it was only right that he, as representative, pay his last respects. He was a decent enough man, I thought, and though he asked about Edward's estate, what pieces of work remained, and it was clear to me he'd be interested in acquiring something, he said what he had to say with taste and consideration. I took his card and told him I'd let him know in time.

The others were mostly Waverly's friends. Two women from a reading club, another from the distant past, who had known both Waverly and Edward when they were young and newly married. It was she whom Aunt Waverly talked most with, gentle gossip about those they'd known then and what became of them. I spoke briefly to the woman myself, just a little curious to know if she had been acquainted with my parents. But she didn't remember them, just that Edward had had a brother.

There were two young women there as well, students from the Art Institute in Chicago. They were quite shy, awkward in a circumstance in which they clearly had no real part. They'd come, they said, because of Edward Church's art. They had a teacher who had taught them about it. I did my best to put them at ease, talked to them about things that were going on in California. They were interested, as bright art students ought to be. They said their teacher really valued Uncle Edward's art, and that they did too. One of them said, "It's weird but very good." They said there'd be other students and their teacher too at the funeral. They were a kind of advance guard. They'd wanted to see his wife close up. I introduced them to Waverly, and she was measured and gracious with them. Fortunately, their shyness kept them from asking her many questions. She wouldn't have appreciated that.

Waverly introduced me to Fred Ross when he came in. He'd been Uncle Edward's agent and still would be that for Waverly. A tall, thin man in his seventies, he had a fit and ready air about him, and he was clearly concerned that things be done right and to Aunt Waverly's benefit. I knew he'd been Edward's agent since the beginning, almost a family friend. He gave me his card, after he had penciled in his home phone number on it. "Anything at all," he said. "At any time." I liked him immediately and said I'd be in touch before I left.

The next morning was bright and sunny. The rain had cleared out in the night, leaving drier air behind it. The temperature was in the low eighties, and there was little humidity. It had been a strangely dry summer so far, Aunt Waverly had told me. Not at all typical but very welcome.

I woke in the morning in Angela's bed a little disoriented. I may have dreamed. There was a dark harbor in my mind that I soon associated with the reading of Uncle Edward's letter. But it was more than that. Something about rising to the sight of my own old house, that window across from me. In my first moments of consciousness I felt myself as a child again, a young one and not an adolescent. Then a deep pain in my thigh brought me fully awake. I must have slept on the hematoma. I had other aches as well, that tightness in my shoulders again, a slight stiffness in my left knee. A hot shower brought me away from these discomforts. The hematoma's swelling didn't seem significant, though the large discoloration looked ugly enough. When I reached to my forehead, I could tell that the swelling there had receded. I thought of Chen as I shaved. He'd gotten by far the worst of it, and I ran the event over in my mind, looking for places where I might have done something more to help him. I felt guilty, but I could find no real evidence for that feeling. Tomorrow, I thought, Monday at the latest. I'll call again.

We ate together in Waverly's kitchen, a large breakfast this time, eggs and sausage and a stack of whole wheat toast with thick raspberry jam. The yellow kitchen walls were flooded with warm natural light.

"Last night was okay after all," I said.

"It was," she said, buttering the toast. "But nothing much is coming up in me. He has been dead to me for so long a time, at least the Edward in that coffin. The one who wrote those letters, well, I'm not sure about that one."

She laughed lightly. It was a relief to both of us. We feel so strangely connected, I thought, in our disconnection. It was as if she too had been away for twenty years. For a few days Edward was back again and would be the center, and she said she felt oddly out of place, as she had when he left and for so long after, here even in this house that she had held alone for so long. And here I am, I thought, my own old house so close by. It's been even longer. I was seventeen.

I thought of the unread letters then, something else we had in common. Neither of us had read them, and I began to understand why I hadn't pushed ahead with them. I could have. Just worked my way through all of them in the two days I'd been there. I realized then that I'd be taking my time.

There were many more people at the funeral than we had thought there'd be. Not only had the teacher from the Art Institute brought out a large contingent of students, there was a group of fellow artists there as well, names I recognized, mostly older men, lithographers and other graphic artists, and a number of painters. They seemed to have no connection at all with the institute group.

"I did put a notice in the *Tribune*," Aunt Waverly told me as we stood in the sun in front of the church. "But I never expected anything like this."

"Do you know any of them?"

"No. None of them. I recognized some names though. I'm not sure if Edward ever knew them. Could it be his reputation?"

The funeral ceremony was quiet and undramatic. Aunt Waverly had spoken to the priest. She'd wanted nothing of the usual maudlin business. The priest had stuck to the liturgy, only giving some spare biographical and professional facts of Uncle Edward's life. He made only brief mention of his medical illustration and the work that came after, just enough to place him as an important artist.

Afterward, the line of cars made its way to the cemetery, about half of those who had been present at the funeral trailing behind the hearse and the limo in which Waverly and I rode. There were prayers at the graveside but nothing else, no dirt cast by Waverly on the casket, no testimonials, and because of the briefness of the ceremony, people seemed slightly dissatisfied and milled around, standing under old trees and beside gravestones.

At one point the teacher from the Art Institute approached me, said things about how much he valued Uncle Edward's art, asked me what was to become of what was left.

"We'll have to see," I said. "I haven't begun yet to go through things."

"I hope you'll keep the institute in mind," he said. And I told him I would.

Students came up to me, as did the few older artists who had come to the cemetery for the burial. I saw a few talking to Aunt Waverly as well.

Just before the time came to leave, I saw a woman standing alone, out in the open. Her eyes met mine, and she took a halting step forward and headed my way. She looked to be close to my own age, maybe a little older, thin and athletic. She was dressed in subdued clothing, a slightly mannish summer suit, and I could see as she approached that her garments were finely tailored, expensive. She was rather short, with close-cropped hair cut in a severe style. She wore makeup, but just a little, nothing on her lips.

"Did he leave any papers?" she said. "Anything at all about London?"

She had moved to stand slightly beside me, not facing toward me. There was something conspiratorial in her voice and stance. She spoke quietly, though we were off to the side, beyond anyone else's hearing.

"I'm not sure exactly what you mean," I said. "Do I know you?"

"No," she said. "I never knew him either. Well, I *knew* him. Socially at least. I knew a lot about him." She didn't offer her name.

"I'm Jack Church," I said. "Edward Church's nephew."

"I know that. You're the executor."

I was taken back by that designation. It was not exactly what Waverly and I had decided upon. Yet the work I would be doing, had already started, was exactly that.

"That's right," I said. "Is there something I can do for you?"

"Well, it's not really me," she said. "But in a way. There is something, about the papers."

"Can you tell me who you are?"

"I'm Joan," she said. "But that really doesn't matter. I knew Dorit then."

"Dorit," I said, the mention of her name bringing back her presence in the last letter. "I guess there may be some things. I haven't had a chance to look much yet. But I know the name."

"Look," she said. "Here's my number. Would you give me a call?" She had the number ready, on the back of a business card.

"Yes," I said. "If I find anything. I'll be in touch."

She nodded, turned, and moved away from me, and when I turned to watch her, trees had intervened and I only caught glimpses of her sleeves and legs. Then she was gone.

It was five o'clock by the time we got back to Aunt Waverly's house. The sky had darkened slightly, and I suspected that it would rain again. Waverly had bought some cheese and wine, and when we got to the house she had put a roast in the oven for our dinner. We ate the cheese, some nuts from a round bowl, and sipped from our glasses. I could see she was making an occasion for us, some small way of formally noting and closing off the day. We sat in chairs in the living room, in the half darkness again, mostly in silence. I could hear the creak of the stove coming up to temperature in the kitchen. Then, after a while, she began to talk.

"A lot of things in the past few days. In fact, close to a week now. Ever since he came back. His face was ruined, Jack. But I'd already come to think of him as another person. Almost a *real* person, though not the one who left me. But he's come back now, and now he's gone again—finally, let's hope.

"Do you know what I did for those twenty years? I kept accounts. I went to book clubs, study groups, and a few art shows. I read magazines and history. I cooked careful, stingy meals for myself, the kind my mother had made. I lived like an old woman, from the time I was fifty-two years old.

"When Angela left, we didn't quite know what had happened at first. Edward was disenchanted with his illustration work then and was spending his evenings in the back room, doing that other work, what finally got him to leave. Angela was twenty-four then, and pregnant. Her husband was working long hours, making a go for them. And she would come over in the evenings with her women friends. They cooed over her, touched her stomach, talked about maternity. There was hardly room enough for me to get near her.

"She wasn't happy. I could tell that. Not at all. The women had been her friends, but now she was pregnant and things were different. She didn't want that baby, at least she didn't want to be a mother. Things had changed. She didn't even want to dress that way, you know, in the dresses designed for that. And the women too seemed odd about the thing. As if they were acting, playing some roles they had learned somewhere, perhaps from their own mothers. She was losing the terms of her life with them, her friends. Soon she wouldn't be free like them anymore. I don't know. It was all wrong somehow.

"Then one evening her husband arrived, really a very nice man, still a boy to me, and there was a blowup. Things were said. Edward came out of his study and had words with Angela's husband and with her. The women that Angela had brought over with her left. Things were patched up tentatively, though not with Edward. He was back in his damn study, and Angela and her husband went home.

"The next day I got a call from Joel. Angela had left. Then Edward left, very soon after. There's more, of course. We did try to locate Angela, at least Joel and I did. Edward was in a kind of desperate rage. Torn a lot of ways about the thing, but centrally I'd say he was more concerned about his art. What he was beginning to call his art. We tried to make amends with Joel. But there was nothing for it. Angela had simply disappeared. I think he blamed us, blamed Edward at least. Not completely. He was no fool. But your uncle had had a part in it, and both he and Joel hardened against each other in ways that couldn't be softened.

"It was, I think, and it is cruel to say, that your uncle never really cared much for Angela at all. He'd wanted a son. And it was true too that I was somewhat under his thumb. It was the way things were for so many of us, I mean women, at that time. Angela may have wanted to talk about the child, not wanting it. It was of course an impossible thing with her father. Not a subject for discussion. And he would have none of my talking about it with her either. I could have, of course, but that's what I mean about being under his thumb. He decided such things, the important things, and to keep peace between us I was silent.

"It could have been that she'd tested us, out of her desperateness, gotten nothing, and then just left. That she never contacted me at least makes me think so. That I was equally blameworthy. I can accept that. There may have been other things too, but I gave her no doorway, no place where we could enter into anything together. Then Edward left. He never took part in the search for her. Maybe she found that out somehow. That may have had something to do with her not returning.

"I tried to put it all behind me—hysterically, I imagine, in the beginning. I was very active in things I was doing. I didn't withdraw. Then, in a while, I think I *did* put it behind me. The letters that came from Edward were as if from someone I did not know at all. It's curious the way they changed so quickly, from that madness of the first few, through the ones you've read. It was as if he'd become some fictional creation, of interest to me as a character only.

"There were the checks, and they kept coming, from publishers and from Ross. I'll give Edward that, though I suspect they were only a way of separating from me, of being clean with his guilt, mechanical about living with it. And I accepted them as my due, received them as mechanically as they were sent, impersonally, to the bank. There was enough there always for me to live on. He owed me that, and I took it. Divorce was never mentioned. It was always 'Dearest Wave.' It was always 'I'll be back to you again, in a letter, very soon.' And even when there was a space of years between letters, they would start up again as if there had been no space at all, just 'Dear Wave,' and then his news and life, the life always as a curiosity that he was somehow separated from.

"And I must admit I welcomed the letters in some way for a long time, the exotic life, for me at least, in them. They were a kind of long novel, one of those historical trilogies that adolescents can get so deeply into. I didn't really miss them when they didn't come for a while, but when I got them I read them carefully, sometimes over and over. Then after I stopped reading them I was still pleased when they arrived. I'd check the postmarks, return address. I had my picture of where he was, and that was enough for me. I know it's strange, but I think it's somehow healthy that I stopped reading them. Strange, maybe, that I kept them though. But I'm beyond concern of that kind. At my age after all. Funny, what I'll miss now is not really Edward at all. That ended years ago. I'll miss the letters. It's as if the novel didn't come to its ending, though its author did."

I sat in my chair in the half dark and listened. Aunt Waverly's face was completely in shadow, and there was no place but in her words for me to read her emotion and expression. I filled in pictures, those of Angela and Edward in her pauses, filled in the textures between facts as well. She was talking mostly about twenty years before, and the pictures I had were even older than that, almost thirty. I had my memories and the two letters, and that was about all. Wasn't this like a novel for me also? Curious to think of it that way.

I could smell the roast now, could see the dark side of my own old house through the dining room window over her shoulder. I wondered vaguely about lost years, urgency, and timing.

"Do you have enough time, Jack? Is there enough time?"

T HE NEXT MORNING I began in earnest. Though it was Sunday and the day after her husband's funeral, Aunt Waverly told me over breakfast that she'd be going into the city, to a few museums and galleries. No reason to sit around and think, she said. I saw her off at nine. She'd leave the car at the train station and would be back, she thought, in the evening. Before she had rounded the corner at Raymond, I was on my way to Uncle Edward's study.

I went to the desk, sat down, and set the stack of letters neatly to the side. Then I reached into the low wooden box and pulled out a couple of accordion files at random and put them on the desk in front of me. I wasn't sure just how to begin. Then I heard a faint scraping behind me, something coming from the alley to the rear of the small backyard, a sound that seemed vaguely familiar. I went to the window and looked out. It was a child, I thought, though I could only see occasional flashes of color and movement beyond the low hedge that separated the rear of the yard from the alley. A child riding some trike or other three-wheeler. I realized then that it was not some child's sound that I had thought I'd heard. It was the sound of the scissors man, something again from back in the past. He had pedaled the alley in the forties, stopping to sharpen scissors and knives. I thought I remembered a faint bell, the scrape of the grinding wheel's turning.

I turned and headed to the desk, checking my watch as I went. It was too early to call either Blackburn or Chen, and it was Sunday too. Chen would undoubtedly have family at the hospital. I wasn't sure I should bother him, though I thought again that I'd better call before too long. Maybe tonight.

When I got to the desk, I reached for the folder containing the photographs and lists of paintings, setting the lists aside and taking the rubber band from around the stack of Polaroids. The photos were poor, dimly lighted, and many of them hazy; for documentation only, I thought. I laid them out in two rows, then counted them. There were only ten. As I was gathering them together again, I noticed that one seemed thicker than the others, and when I put my thumbnail at the corner I found that a photo had stuck to the back of the one I held. I peeled it away and laid it above the row I hadn't yet gathered up. It was distinctly different, an almost photographic rendering of a large, terraced garden. I took it to the window and held it up in the natural light. Very straightforward and distinct, I thought. And very little in the way of forced composition that I could identify. It was clearly not the whole garden, but a section of it. I put it at the bottom of the stack and set the photos to the side. Then I turned my attention to the lists.

The lists were typed, single spaced and orderly: titles and dates of execution. There were two sheets, the second ending halfway down the paper, and as I glanced at the dates I realized that it was really one list. The left-hand margin meandered a little and the sheets were ragged at the corners. It seemed that he had used the list as a running bibliography, typing the information in as he finished a work. To the right of many of the entries were names: museums, private parties, businesses, galleries, and names I could not identify. Some of the entries had "con" typed in after the right-hand column. "Consignment," I thought. I checked the last entry, just a title and a date, December 5, 1977. Nothing in the last five years, or he had stopped keeping up to date. I counted the entries; there were fifty-two.

After I had glanced over the list again, I found my way to the basement door and went down into the cellar. There was a dim light at the foot of the stairs, and I could see Uncle Edward's old workbench deep in the back of the room. I found a small crowbar, a hammer, and a couple of rusted screwdrivers, then went back to the study and got to work on the two crates.

Each crate contained five paintings, all about the same size and all on stretchers, unframed. I lined them up beside each other against the back wall, tipping them enough so that they wouldn't fall forward, and I closed the windows down to the sills, opening the top half of the double-hung glass instead, letting in a good six inches of air at the top of each frame. Then I took the rubber band from the stack of photos again and quickly compared them to the paintings. There was one for each, and then there was that other one that I had found. I stood back then and took in the paintings.

The work throughout held what I judged to be those washes Uncle Edward had talked about in one of the letters. There was a deep vibrancy in all of them, something that did not come from extremes in perspective. Most of them had at least a fragment of the human body in them, and even in the few that were close to portraiture there was at least one place where the body under the skin showed through or where the skin was peeled back, revealing the systems under it. These places had the flavor of medical illustration, what I remembered of those few anatomy texts that I had had occasion to look into, but they were somehow different, more real than that. The systems under the skin were alive here, and I guessed the effect was gained by a slight torquing of the systems, movements that brought them into a kind of alignment with the ways the body parts were moving in the paintings as a whole. And the layers of glazing had brought a shining wetness forward as well, a slight contrast between the juices of vitality within the body and the drier textures of the surface skin.

I searched along the row of paintings, looking for a heart and a braided spine, but I couldn't find anything. As consistent as the content of the paintings was, I did not think as I looked at them that they had been painted in the same period of time. There were changes, not dramatic ones but ones of refinement and attitude.

They seemed to get stranger, even riskier, to flirt in what I took to be their progression in time with a kind of surrealism, or better a kind of realism reminiscent of Mexican fresco painting. There was nothing really political about them, but a sense of desperate humanism, a statement about the power of life under the skin, a desire for the liberation of it in the face of the more studied and slightly sterile outside of the body. I felt a kind of despairing nobility in the work. I knew that it was very good. The one piece that stopped me and kept drawing my attention was a nature study.

There was a figure of a woman in the lower right corner of the piece, a nude sitting in the grass, looking at a large old tree at the composition's center. Her left arm rested across her knee, and the skin stretched over her elbow was thin enough so that I could see through it to the workings of ligament, bone, and tendon there. The tree seemed at first straightforward in its rendering, but when I got closer and squatted down on my haunches, I could see that the trunk was transparent, as were the limbs, the smaller branches, even the leaves. And under the transparency was a matrix that seemed clearly treelike but at the same time had veins, folds of fascia, subcutaneous flesh in it. Where the thick trunk separated into its first heavy limbs there were organs of some kind at the forks, woody and sap filled. The veins in the leaves were capillaries, and when I squinted and got closer I could see that even the grass the woman sat on, each careful blade of it, was transparent also, with something in it that throbbed.

I looked back at the nude woman, the way she regarded the tree, and when I studied her elbow more closely, I could see that its workings had the tree in them, bone like hickory, the ligaments like thin shavings of the flesh of raw wood.

I rose to my feet, a little dizzy. I had been squatting for a long time, and my legs were tingling. Still, there was more to my disorientation. I felt that the painting had twisted my sense of a given structure, one I counted on without knowing that I did, turned it a little, so that when I stood and got my bearings, everything in the room and out the window seemed changed for a long moment.

I went back to the table and got the list and a pencil. Then I went to one of the paintings and picked it up and turned it. There was nothing on the back of the canvas, but penciled in along the staples on the wood at the top of the stretcher was the painting's name, *Man Running*. I turned the painting around again, stepped back a little, and looked at it. It showed two women sitting in heavy chairs in a small room, and out a window and across a street there was a man in mid-stride moving quickly at the edge of the window's frame. The skin was peeled back from his Achilles tendon; all the power of his thrust as he rose for the next stride seemed contained there, above his heel as it lifted off the pavement.

I went to each of the paintings then, turned them and found the titles and made check marks on the sheets. When I was finished I moved to the desk and went over the lists, looking for some pattern in where the checks fell. There were no apparent clusters, though all the marks came late in the listing, most of them on the second page. None of the marks fell in the first ten years after Edward's leaving.

I got up for a moment and walked around the room, letting my eyes fall on the paintings as I passed along them. I didn't see one that wasn't finely finished and strong. Then I went back to the list and looked at the checks again, read through the whole list carefully. There were no marks beside the works with names of private parties and museums listed. They only fell beside those that had not been sold or consigned. That's reasonable, I thought. He'd held these back, but not, I guessed, because he couldn't sell them. I was sure they were too good for that.

Then my eye caught two titles on the second page, paintings done in the mid-seventies, only a year apart. They both had the same title, *Dorit*, with the numbers 1 and 2 after them. The first was followed by "British Museum," the second by the name of a private party I didn't recognize. They aren't here, I thought. Neither had a check mark beside it.

I put the lists aside then and reached for the stack of letters and read the next four, short letters, written in the year following the first two. There was little more about the island, the view from his window. They were full of technical matters about drawing and painting, about the difficulty of getting started. There was no reference in them to the opening he'd written about in the second letter and no mention again of the British people. He had been immersed in the beginnings of his work, in uncertain ways at this point, and there was nothing I could find in them to move me forward.

The seventh was another long one, on different paper, and when I checked the date and postmark, I saw that it had been written a full year later and that its return address was in London. I went back to the previous letter, but there was nothing out of the ordinary in it, no hint that so much time might pass before the next one. Then I checked through all the letters to see if I had confused the order, but everything was in place. I checked my watch. It was one o'clock in the afternoon. I had been at it for four hours.

I got up, moved past the paintings, and went to the kitchen. There was some roast beef left from the night before, and I found bread and mustard and made a sandwich. I smiled to see that Aunt Waverly had laid in some beer, and I opened a bottle and sat at the kitchen table. I could hear the voices of children in the park again, just faintly over the hum of the refrigerator, the tick of the clock. I decided then that I would give Chen a call. I went to the phone and began to dial, then changed my mind and called information, getting the number of the Art Institute in Chicago. I couldn't remember the teacher's first name, but I had his last. He wasn't in, and the secretary wasn't too helpful, but when I mentioned Uncle Edward she paused for a moment, then asked me to repeat myself. Then she got interested. I made an appointment for the following afternoon. I wasn't sure just what I might be told, but I knew it was time that I try to learn something more about Uncle Edward's work.

I washed my glass and plate and put them in the sink drainer and returned to the study. Light was coming strongly in the windows now, and some of the paintings were brightly illuminated. I wasn't sure about the effect, so I went to the wall and gathered the paintings and put them back in the crates. I selected the five that I thought might be the best, at least the ones I liked best, and put them together in one of the crates. Then I went back to the desk and read the seventh letter.

My Dearest Waverly,

I cannot begin to explain why I have not written to you in so long a time. Sufficient I hope that you will not harden completely against me if I say it has been the work during this past year, the struggle in it and its hold over me. The island became a place of such isolation, an aloneness lived in by my spirit too comfortably, that after a while I became suspicious of the health of it. I was working intently, it's true, but there came a day when I heard a chance word while on one of my now less than monthly visits to the little village, a political comment, and I realized I had lost the world completely. Two years, Wave, and I had literally spoken no more than a few sentences to anyone.

I'd solved things, taken a few beginning steps to get me where I was headed—I still don't actually know just where that is—but I realized that I was at serious risk of losing even that.

And so I did not write. I wrote to no one, in fact. I see now that I was barely able to keep up with the accounting. But that, I trust, has been at least some sort of bond between us. I trust that the checks continue to arrive on schedule. I understand, as I have for a while now, that you can't write to me, can't go that far in forgiving. I don't expect it. Possibly I don't even want it. But I will continue to write to you, and I believe, now that I'm back in the world, that my letters will be more frequent, at least without such a large void between them. But I was, I believe, ill in a way. Was it the illness of the artist, I wonder, one starting out past mid-life, trying to in some way catch up? I can't be sure. Maybe this is just melodrama.

I left the island two months ago and have taken a flat in London. Well, not London proper, but here in Muswell Hill, an almost suburban community (but more charming than that) a very short distance from Hampstead Heath. I've plenty of room. Not as much as my island house, but a large apartment on a second floor, a bright, sunlit studio out front facing north onto the street. I hear children playing, an occasional car or dog, but not much more. The street is a cul-de-sac, and from early morning to noon I can work without annoying interruptions. And I've been out and around too, have spent time at museums and galleries, even went to the theater a few times, enjoying the crude, lower-class comedy that they have here all the time.

And the work goes well. What was beginning to close off into illness on the island has, in the short time of my stay here, begun to open up. I've not left the body, but I've begun again to sketch from the living model, and I've been doing nature studies too, trees and even flowers. I do them outside, in a park not far from here, one I can walk to, and it isn't much of a trip to the art class that I attend two evenings a week, just for the model.

So that's the way things stand. I've not really been social since I arrived here. I've avoided that. But to have people around I can talk with—the grocer, my fellow "students" at the drawing class— this has been just enough for me to begin feeling healthy again. And I've one *great* piece of news, but to get to it properly there's a story.

I was at the Tate two weeks ago. I'd made plans to spend most of the day there. I'd been working very hard and I needed the break, and besides it's a place any artist must visit thoroughly, such a wealth of material there that I had only seen in art books.

At any rate, I'd been browsing for most of the morning, and I decided to take lunch in the museum cafeteria. I found a table set off a bit in a corner and proceeded to munch at a salad and to glance through a catalogue of Mexican art that I'd purchased. At one point I looked up and saw someone who seemed familiar, a woman alone at a table near mine. She must have felt my gaze, because she looked up also. We recognized each other at the same time, I think, and she rose and took her tray and came over to me. It was Susan, Harwood's wife, one of the couples I wrote you about who were at that art showing two years ago on the island, the ones I shared the boat ride with.

We talked, she telling me about Harwood and the Bayards, the other couple, and I saying something about how my work was going, how I'd arrived in London only a short while ago. It was a brief but pleasant conversation, and it ended with Susan inviting me to a party on the upcoming Saturday. Just a few couples, she said, about twenty people. I might enjoy meeting them.

I believe I told you that Harwood is a lawyer, but I never suspected that he might be such a successful one. At least by the look and location of his house he is. It's a large town house on Sloane Square, an exclusive neighborhood indeed. I could see light through the curtains of the large bay windows on the ground floor as I climbed the broad stone steps, the shadows of people moving behind them. There were five couples and two single men and a woman present when I entered. Susan greeted me at the door, and I saw Bayard nod and wave to me, smiling in a far corner of the large room. He was standing beside an elegant marble fireplace, leaning against it, talking with two other men. Caroline, Bayard's wife, approached me as soon as I had crossed the sill, took my hand, and touched me lightly on the shoulder.

"How good, how fortunate to see you, Edward!" she said, and moving between the two women, I was taken through the room and introduced. All of the other couples, like the Bayards and the Harwoods, were collectors, all the men professionals, doctors and lawyers and an architect. The younger of the two single men was an artist, a name I had heard of when we were introduced. He looked at me with a curious expression, but he was friendly enough, asking me appropriate questions about my work. The other man was a gallery owner, and it was clear to me from the outset that the young artist was with him, at least professionally. The single woman was an American, from Milwaukee, I think, and we passed a few pleasant words about the Midwest. I wasn't quite clear about her connections to those present, though she seemed to be spending time talking with the young artist. They were about the same age, I thought, thirty or a little older than that.

The party continued along in a relaxed and congenial way. There was much talk about art, conversations peppered more with financial considerations than aesthetic ones. People continued to arrive, and in a while the room was comfortably full. Some had taken places on couches and in chairs, and the rest of us stood, talking, moving from the food that was laid out to the bar and into other conversations. I had some pleasant moments with Bayard and Harwood. I remembered them, even from our very brief time together, in a warm way, and we even spoke a little about our boat trip and the opening two years ago. Harwood allowed that he had had a little too much to drink that night, but as he said it I noticed he gestured with a freshly filled glass in his hand. I saw too that Susan was watching him.

"And your work is going well, I hear," Bayard said at one point. "Susan and Caroline have talked!"

"Yes, it *is*," I said. "I'm very happy with the progress I'm making."

"Is there anything one can see?"

It was not Bayard or Harwood but a voice at my elbow, a tentative one, and when I turned slightly I saw the gallery owner standing there. I was about to answer, when over his shoulder I saw a vaguely familiar face, a man standing in the doorway at the far end of the room. I couldn't place him at first, then I saw the head of a woman, a spill of red hair, entering the doorway beside him. Her face was turned slightly away from my vision, the thick hair like a rich monk's cowl spreading over her broad shoulders. I knew who it was then. Something about her posture, the way she leaned slightly forward as if expectant, was unmistakable.

"Yes," I said, lowering my eyes to look at the gallery owner. "I've a good many, in fact. More than I have room for."

Dorit and her husband had entered the room now and were moving, with smiles, to someone they seemed to know quite well. I noticed that it was the artist, the American woman standing beside him. Dorit leaned over and put her cheek against the artist's cheek, her hair brushing his shoulder, her face lost to me in the

formal kiss. Her husband—I remembered his name as Mark now
—was smiling and talking to the American woman.

"Is it possible that I could see something? Could you bring something in?"

"I've photographs," I said. "And there are a few smaller pieces
that are easy to carry."

He took out a card then, wrote an appointment time on the back
of it, and handed it to me. It was only after we had chatted a little
longer and he had moved away, only after I saw the looks of pleasant affirmation on Bayard's and Harwood's faces, that the possible
importance of what had just transpired reached me.

"You were quite cool!" Bayard said. "Do you know what he is?"

"I know his name," I said. "I've seen the gallery listed in the
Times."

"About the best you could link up with these days," Harwood
said, a slight slur in his voice now, something that I remembered
from our boat trip so long ago.

I *had* been cool, but it was unintentional. It was the couple's entry
into the room that had thrown me while we were talking. I wasn't
sure why; there was just something about this woman Dorit, something that drew me in a way that I didn't as yet understand. It was
only later on in the evening that I had the opportunity to meet the
couple, to look at them close up, and to talk a little.

They sat on a couch beside each other, I in a chair across from
them. Bayard was there also, in a small upholstered rocker beside
us. He'd made our introductions and had started things off by
telling me that the two were real Londoners now, expatriates from
the other side. Dorit sat rather primly, straight and a little stiff
against the cushions. She had gathered her thick hair, tucking it
back behind her neck, and her hands were together in her lap. The
slash of red that I remembered had been her lips the last time I'd
seen her was now a softer rose. Her eyes were a little milky, a faint
green, and her lashes and brows were so spare and blond that they
could not halo her eyes or set them apart from the rest of her face.
This rendered them vulnerable and seemingly unfocused. Still,
there was a drama that I remembered in the high and prominent
cheekbones, her oval and narrow face. I watched her as I could,
though it was her husband who did most of the talking. He was
leaning forward a little, elbows on his knees, and in his position he

seemed slightly smaller than she was, though certainly in no way as vulnerable. He was dark, had heavy features and a slightly beaked nose. His eyes were crystal clear under his strangely delicate brows, always tightly focused, even probing.

"That's right," he said. "All the way from San Diego. Too much flying back and forth for consultations. I've taken a place at Bart's. Besides, I like the art over here."

Bayard laughed. "He'll clean the good stuff out, if we don't watch him. Bart's, Edward, that's Saint Bartholomew's Hospital."

"An old and awkward place," Janes said. It was a joke, but his eyes seemed serious.

"Come now, Mark, it's our most venerable." Bayard smiled.

Mark turned toward him and nodded. "As long as there's enough cancer."

There was a slightly awkward moment, and I took the opportunity to speak to Dorit.

"And you?" I said.

"She's with me," Janes said. "There's plenty here, isn't there, Dorie?"

She tipped her head back slightly, raised a hand, and with her finger traced the sharp arc of her cheek.

"Yes," she said. "Well, I write a little. I can do that here just as well." She smiled, looking at me, her thin lips parted, showing the edges of small, almost translucent teeth.

"What is it you write?" I asked.

"A kind of journalism. Just bits and pieces of things."

"She had some articles in San Diego. Isn't that right, Dorie. Maybe you can get into something like that here." He had turned around in his seat and was facing her, almost excluding us from the conversation, watching her intently.

"I suppose so," she said. "Yes, maybe I can."

I had the feeling that their talk was a rehearsal of things said before in exactly the same words. His voice was completely devoid of any interest, and her answers mechanical. Bayard looked at me fleetingly, shifting in his seat.

"Well, time enough," he said. "After all, you only just arrived."

"That's right," Janes said, turning back toward us. "Plenty of time."

It was only later on in the evening that I had the opportunity to speak with Dorit alone. The party reached that point when everyone had spent time with everyone else, however briefly, and people began to return to those they wished to spend a more extended period with. I'd managed to speak with the gallery owner again, but we'd made our appointment, and there really seemed little to say until that time. Our talk was brief and a little awkward. He avoided asking me about my work, and I could only muster a few opening questions about his business. I hadn't spent much time talking with the young artist and the American woman, and I felt I wanted more. After all, we were the only artists there. But Dorit was talking with the two of them, their heads slightly together, and it seemed inappropriate to break in. Mark Janes was gathered with Bayard and another doctor around the fireplace, in animated conversation.

The walls of the room were hung with expensive paintings and prints, and when I glanced down the hallways that ran off from it I saw other pieces, each individually lighted by an inset ceiling fixture. There were tables in the hallways, and these held ashtrays and bowls of fresh flowers. I was sure the halls were open to the party, but I decided to check with Harwood before exploring them.

"Well, of course, old man!" he said. "Susan would die if she thought you'd missed out on anything. At the very end there, on the right, that's the gallery, what Susan calls it at least." The slur I had noticed earlier was gone, and it struck me that he was a very careful alcoholic.

I explored the hallway on the left, leaving the room he had mentioned for later. Here all the works were lithographs and other kinds of prints, each one choice, I thought, and each contemporary, mostly figurative, but some abstracts in the bunch. Checking the titles and names written on small cards mounted below each work, I perceived the collector's attitude. All the abstracts were earlier works of artists who were represented by later, realistic work, Abstract Expressionists who had come around, I thought. Though there was material that I liked, there was a certain coldness in the collection as a whole. It had all been chosen too methodically, with too much consideration for value.

When I entered the main room again, I automatically looked for Dorit. I couldn't find her, and I headed down the other hallway, the one that ended at what Harwood had called the gallery. The hall was empty, but I heard a faint cough from what I took to be a room at the end. When I entered the doorway, Dorit was standing there alone. She had a hankie in her hand and was holding it to her mouth. When she heard me, she dropped her hand quickly and turned toward me and smiled, her eyes moist. She had been crying, and though I feigned ignorance of it, I thought it must have something to do with her husband, possibly even with London, with finding herself suddenly here.

"Hi," I said. "Getting a breather?"

"Hello! Yes. Well, just looking around. A fine collection, isn't it?" She raised her arm in an awkward gesture, as if changing her mind in the middle of it, so that her hand fell back to her side before it even reached her hip.

"Fine enough," I said. "Have you found something you like?"

"I like this one." She turned and lifted her hand again, this time the one that held the handkerchief, and gestured toward the small painting in front of which she stood. I came around to her side and looked at it with her. I remembered it. It was the same woman's torso that she had stood before at that opening on the island two years before. I remembered that Susan had purchased it, how that had bothered me.

The painting was subdued and rather dark, very little in the paint itself that reflected light. The stance of the torso was traditional, posed in a standing posture, hip slightly slung, the left arm elevated as if holding something, an urn or a vase, and though it could have been called a realist piece, the flesh was more mottled and suggestive than was usual. It had a stonelike quality to it. It was as if it had been a larger painting, one in which the whole figure and its gesture had been present and had then been cropped like a photograph so that only the torso remained, no head, arms, or legs, just the stubs of their beginnings, and the feel of such cropping caused the torso to seem to stretch out, to reach for its members somewhere outside the canvas and frame. It was extremely sexual, though there was really nothing lifelike about the flesh at all.

"I know why I like it," I said. "It's the missing parts. I'm trying something analogous." The last wasn't true at all; I knew it as I said it. But before I could stop myself, I had told her what I was after, things about the life of the body under the skin, ways to reveal that, make the inside real on the outside. I finished by saying that I'd like to paint her, and then felt an immediate awkwardness. All the words seemed to be out before I could check them. I'd had no idea at all that I was going to speak to her in that way.

When I had finished, looking mostly at her arms and shoulders as I spoke, I raised my head to her face. She was looking at me intently, but with a complete openness in her milky eyes. It was clear she'd been listening to every word that I had said. Then she smiled and nodded.

"That would be lovely," she said. "But, you see, my husband. I doubt that he would understand. I mean he'd *understand*, of course, but doing it might be difficult. But we'll see; maybe sometime. But what you say is so interesting. I think you've explained to me why I like this painting!"

She turned from me and looked at it again. I turned with her and noticed the small card below it.

"Do you know him?" I said.

"Why, yes, of course!" she said. "He's here!"

And that, Wave, was the end of it. The party wound down after that. I went around and said my goodbyes to those I had spoken with, making sure to say a word to the artist about how much I liked his painting. He accepted the compliment with grace, the young American woman standing beside him looking up at his face. Though I didn't approach the gallery owner, who was deep in conversation, I did manage to catch his eye for a moment, enough to smile and nod and raise my hand in farewell. Both Susan and Caroline, whom I had spent almost no time with, said they regretted that and hoped we would get together again soon.

"Maybe at the Tate!" Susan joked.

Bayard shook my hand warmly, said we should plan to get together for lunch. In the tangles of my goodbyes, I missed seeing Dorit and her husband again. When I looked around the room, they were gone.

It was a few days later that I went to the gallery. I took four small pieces with me and some photographs as well. The day after the party I had checked around and discovered that his was indeed one of the most respected small galleries in London. He specialized in realistic work, the most advanced of it, at least by those artists who were quite well known. But reviews that I read in the library also suggested that he was not beyond adventure, taking on a few artists who were unknown quantities. The reviews of their works were mixed, but each one, even when negative, showed respect, a respect that seemed to have as much to do with the gallery as with the painter.

The long and short of it is that he agreed to take me on. He looked at the four small pieces carefully, and he went through all the photographs, using a magnifying glass on some of them and referring back to the works I'd brought with me as he did so. His questions had to do with dating, how the works related to one another, both in subject and in technique. He agreed to take the four paintings I'd brought, and we made another appointment, this time for him to come out to my studio. He didn't say anything about a show, private or otherwise, but I had a suspicion that that might be just around the corner. At least I hope it is.

So, Wave, I've entered the marketplace! It's nothing that I'd given much thought to so far, but I must admit to feeling some real pleasure in the prospect. Now all I have to do is keep at it. I've plenty of ideas and feel that the work will be coming now at a good pace.

Oh, and Caroline called me the day after I went to the gallery. She'd gotten the word of my success. (There seems to be a quite active grapevine here.) She's invited me, together with the Harwoods, for cocktails in celebration this coming Saturday evening.

Well, this has been a long letter indeed, and about all there is to say for now. I will, absolutely, write to you again soon, let you know how things go at the gallery and at the upcoming party at the Bayards'.

Though I know you cannot forgive my not writing to you for so long, I hope you *do* know that it didn't mean that you weren't in my thoughts—guilty thoughts, I admit, but ones of longing too. I'll forever miss you, Wave. Be well, and think of me kindly if you can.

Yours, as ever, and forever,
Edward

H OW LONG IS TWENTY years? It depends, I guess. For Edward, the way things appeared to be starting out at least, it was probably a fairly short time. He had seemed to think he was older, maybe too old, when the letters began, but now he was intensely interested, a little overly enthusiastic even, like a much younger man. I had to keep remembering that he had been sixty-four when he wrote the last letter. I could see the years getting started, that quick rise to a measure of fame, which it was clear he welcomed, at least the beginning of it, in this last letter. I wondered how he felt near the end, what that would be like when I got to it.

I suspected that for Waverly it was a different matter entirely. Though I had no real sense of what her years had been like, what the days and hours in them had been like, I was sure they had been slow, leisurely, at times probably excruciating. There was no sense that she had started her life over once it was clear that Uncle Edward was not returning. She must have known, at some point, that the letters were as much a vehicle of permanent separation as they were one of connection. What a weird connection, I thought. He just wouldn't let her go. But the letters were brutal, so often completely unaware of whom he was writing to and the occasion of the writing. Could he be asking her to take pleasure in his new life, his rich associations? Was she a confessional of some kind, or a waste dump? And I suspected that she too was culpable. I wanted to ask her more about this, but I wasn't sure yet just what the questions would be. It had been book clubs, shopping, a few short trips that she had referred to, a few friends, always casual ones, nothing that she could stick herself into and begin again. I suspected too that there would be no way that she could articulate that.

She was smart and aware. I thought of her as a lovely and still desirable woman, yet there were places of disconnection that seemed part of who she was, had possibly always been part of her. Psychology, even of the deepest kind, was just not a reasonable avenue into her. I'd have to look elsewhere for answers, and I dimly knew that I'd have to be aware as well of my own part in it all. I was feeling myself sucked back into a life that I, like Edward, had left a long time before. We were both back now, but I, unlike him, was aware of being back. I had feelings in that house, ones that went beyond the simple presence of my old house next door. Thoughts of my childhood, of my parents, even of Angela, were coming back to me. I was falling in love with Waverly, my favorite aunt, all over again.

She returned from the city before nightfall, carrying packages and an overloaded purse. She was animated, anxious to take things out and show them to me, but I could see lines of tiredness and care at the corners of her bright eyes. She'd brought me something, she said, and made me face away from her and close my eyes while she unpacked it.

"Now turn and open them," she said, and her voice was the same one I had heard before, so many years ago. I did what she asked and saw her standing there and grinning, her arm extended, a small, thin object in her palm.

It was a penlight, made of brushed silver, with a small silver pocket clip at one end. Thin and very easy to carry and with a bright, narrow beam. To search things out, I thought, or to study something closely in an otherwise dark space. She'd found it at an architect's shop, she said. She thought it was something I could use in my work.

We talked in the evening, over a light dinner, and though I asked her about the letters again, trying to get some better sense of what it had been like for her to receive them, she was tired from her day in the city and said she didn't really have the energy to go into that right now.

"But you can see how he was writing like an Englishman. It got so quickly foreign. And the way he quoted what people said. As if he remembered word for word. They didn't seem like real letters at all, if that means anything, like writing *to* someone. I think I felt I was overhearing them. You know? It got very odd. I guess it began that way, in fact."

I told her of my plans for the following day, that I'd be going to the Art Institute, my first real step in getting Uncle Edward's estate in order.

"That's good," she said. "If you're lugging things, why don't you take the car?"

I agreed to that, and we talked on a little further, mostly about my landscaping. She seemed very interested and asked many questions, but soon she was suppressing her yawns, and I got up and kissed her good night, thanking her again for the gift.

I spent most of Monday morning going through Uncle Edward's papers. I read over the death certificate again and the brief note from the doctor. Edward had died in London, but whether at home or in the hospital I could not tell. It was clear he had had his attack and fall at home. The doctor's letter confirmed that. The certificate and the doctor's stationery both named a hospital, Saint Bartholomew's, the same place Edward had written about, where Mark Janes had taken a position eighteen years earlier. Why there? I thought. Surely there must have been something closer.

Sorting through the papers, I came across a bank savings account book, various rent and utility receipts, a checkbook, and a packet of letters, most of them addressed to galleries and museums and to a bank in Brookfield, the town close by, where Uncle Edward's wake had taken place. The savings account book and the checkbook bore the imprint of a London branch in Muswell Hill. The final entries in them were not recent, a check written and a deposit made, both in 1977, close to five years before. I checked back through the utility receipts and found that the payment dates came right up to the present, to the end of last month. Check numbers and dates and amounts of payment were entered on each of them, in Uncle Edward's careful hand. But in '77 the check number series changed. He must have switched banks, I thought, and searched through another accordion file for statements. Envelopes containing statements and canceled checks were there, but nothing past 1977. If he had changed banks, there was no documentation of that here. Seven hundred pounds was on account in savings, another hundred and fifty in checking.

I looked carefully through all the rest of his papers. There was not much really, considering they covered a twenty-year span. There was a neatness and order about them, a mechanical spareness that suggested Uncle Edward had not dwelled excessively on such things. The letters from museums and galleries were mostly ones that expressed interest in Edward's work. He had not kept copies of his responses to them, or at least I could find none. In among the letters was a thick envelope containing royalty statements and a few check stubs forwarded by Uncle Edward's agent in Chicago. I put the envelope beside the bankbooks and folders. I would have to contact the agent, the London bank, Edward's medical illustration publisher, probably follow up on some loose ends I might find in the museum and gallery correspondence. But that was not much really. Edward's affairs seemed to me to be in good shape. Once I got seriously down to things, I should be able to finish up not later than the end of the week. At least get things in good enough order so that Aunt Waverly could manage them.

It was eleven by the time I'd finished up and made a list of things to start with when I got back from the Art Institute. My appointment with George McHale, the teacher there, was at 1:00 P.M. It was eight o'clock in California. Late enough, I thought, and went to the kitchen phone and called Chen at the hospital.

"The burned one died," he said. "Perez was here."

"Who's Perez?"

"One of the cops. He still couldn't say what the other one spilled. But he assured me that we shouldn't worry. They've been keeping an eye on the place. Donny saw them. But only for a while, and they don't get in the way."

"How is he?"

"Donny? He's okay." There was laughter in his voice. "I think he kind of likes this business."

"How about you, Chen?"

"Hell, I'm doing fine. The leg's coming along properly, the butchers tell me. And the rest will be okay too. I'll have the same face."

"I don't know how quickly I can get out of here," I said. "Possibly by mid-week, but I doubt it. Surely by the weekend."

"Don't worry about it, Jack. Christ, with the nephews, Donny, and Benitez, the place is covered with watchful minorities. I've got them running back and forth at all hours."

It was good to hear the strength and humor in his voice. And I knew he wasn't covering anything up. It was not Chen's way. The fact that I was dealing with family matters was completely justifying for him. Things could have been in deep trouble, even gone to hell, and he'd insist, and in a moralistic way, that I stay with it until I was done. When he said that things were in hand, I knew he was telling the truth.

"How about the job?" I said.

"We're still on schedule. Benitez put the men on overtime, but only for a couple of days. It was enough to catch up. He says he figures a week's room for fuckups. That's just a little tight. There's still a hair's slack in the budget. We can stretch it to at least twelve days with a little more overtime if we need to. Should we?"

"Of course," I said. "You make the decision."

"Or I'll call you."

"Right. But if I'm out or something, just go ahead."

"Right," he said. "Hey, Jack."

"What?" I said.

"Get the fuck back to business."

When I'd made the appointment with George McHale, the woman had given me directions to a side door, a place where I could park close to the building. I arrived there at one on the dot. I'd reached the city a little early and had driven along the lake, coming in from the south side, in the face of that skyline that is like no other. I'd had time even to drive over the river, get a good look at the Wrigley Building.

McHale was waiting at the door of the side entrance, and he helped me carry the crate of paintings up steps and down a brief hallway to his office. He didn't actually work for the institute, he told me on the way. He had a kind of adjunct job, actually for a few years now, teaching a couple of courses, figure drawing and beginning painting. He was a short, wiry man, in his early forties, and I could see his scalp through his mouse-colored hair as we moved along, holding the crate of paintings between us. There was an edge of vulnerability about the way he looked, but it was quickly undercut by his sure and sunny enthusiasm.

When we were seated in his office, I handed the list of paintings across the desk to him. He was watching the crate, glancing at it from time to time, clearly anxious to see what it contained. He spread the list out in front of him and put on his glasses.

"I'm just getting started," I said. "And I thought if you could give me some sense of things, could answer a few questions?"

He nodded, not looking up, slowly running his finger down the list, then moving to the second page, stopping here and there. I sat back in my wooden chair and waited, and in a while he put his hand palm down on top of the list and looked up at me.

"Okay," he said. "Now let's open the crate."

We took the paintings out and leaned them against the wall, in a place where there was good light and where we could see them from our chairs. He didn't sit back down though but squatted briefly in front of each of them, leaning forward, even moving a little to the side as he scanned them. He looked very closely at the one with the figure and the tree.

"I like that one a lot," I said from my chair, and saw the back of his head move as he nodded emphatically in agreement. Then he came back to his desk, sat down, and looked at me again.

"Okay," he said. "Now what can I tell you?"

"Well, first, are the names familiar, can you tell if the list is complete? And what about the private buyers? That, and maybe some idea about value. I'll be getting in touch with galleries, maybe even some sort of appraiser, but I need somewhere to start out. I don't want to go in completely cold."

"You can forget about the galleries for information, I think."

"Why is that?"

"He had some problems. Two instances, as I recall. Really, just typical gallery fuck-overs, but he withdrew completely, took everything back. And from that point he refused to deal in the usual way. He'd only sell privately. He accepted shows, but that was it.

There was a woman in Wisconsin who wrote a monograph about it. At the university. She died a few years ago."

"Would that account for this careful list?"

"Oh, no. There's nothing odd about this." He tapped the list with his finger. "But what *is* odd are these check marks you've made. Are all of these of about the same quality as the ones here?" He gestured toward the five paintings.

"I'd say so."

"You see, I know the one with the tree. It's been reproduced in catalogues; one of the others too. And I think I know *all* of the ones on this list that aren't checked. But I don't know any of the others you've checked. Are these the ones you have?"

"That's right," I said.

"Well, you see, the tree one and that one at the end . . . Let's see." He looked down at the list again. *"Presence Unknown.* That's the name." He got up quickly from his chair and went to the painting at the end of the row and squatted down again and looked closely at it for a few moments, then returned and sat down.

"These two have been reproduced, I mean photographed. They've appeared in places—catalogues, art books. They're pretty well known, especially in Europe. He never did gain much of a reputation in the States, not much at all until quite recently, though he had one for a long time among artists. But you see there are no names or anything to the right of them on the list. Must mean he never sold them, only showed them. And as I've said, I don't know any of the others you've checked, the ones you have."

"Can you say what you think this means?"

"What it means," he said. "You know these five are first rate. What it means, I think, is that he held the very best ones back, at least the ones he thought were. It means you've probably got the best of what he did. Some odd things though. First off, there is nothing at all after '77."

"Could it mean he quit painting then?"

"Oh, Lord no! Not at all! There's been a rush of things on the market, especially in the past two years. Very strange and startling things, I hear. But I haven't seen any. They've been going only to private parties, a good number in America, but in England too. That's really the odd thing, that there is nothing about them on the list."

"Can you say anything about those two paintings with the name Dorit?"

"Well, sure. Of course. There's one in the British Museum. I know that one. And then there's this second one. We have it here."

"You have it *here?*"

"Right," he said. "I can show it to you. We purchased it through a dealer. He probably got it from this person here." He put his finger on the list.

"There's one other thing," he said. "You ought to know. That one, *Presence Unknown.* He did it quite a while ago, close to ten years. It's been worked on again, and quite recently, I'd say."

I heard his words and his enthusiasm in saying them. But I wasn't at all sure what they might mean to me.

"Not faked in some way, I hope?"

"No, no, no. I don't think so. It's not really changed. Just the texture of the glazing, a kind of feathering out into older surfaces. Maybe he'd had the wrong mixture, and it had faded. Or maybe some bad tubes. That can happen. So he worked it up again, to get the shine back. I'd have to study it, maybe get some help. But I'd guess, for sure, that it was him. Why would anybody tamper with it?"

"I guess so," I said. "So what does it all come down to?"

"What do you mean?" he said.

"What kind of worth are we talking about here?"

"Oh. Well, that depends. On how you go about it, you know. Sell them as a group, go through a dealer, or do it individually on your own. There are other ways too. But I'm sure it's safe to say that there's not a single Church here, at least in the ones you've brought, that would go for under a hundred thousand. And that's *very* conservative. Some, like the tree one, for example, for considerably more than that, maybe two fifty. I mean what *you* could get for them, not what they'd sell for on the market. That side would be harder to figure."

I didn't know what to say, so I didn't say anything, just let the figures sink in. He said it was very conservative, and if I were even more conservative I'd still come to a figure of at least a million dollars. I wondered what Waverly would think of that.

We were out of his office then and heading along a broad hallway down in one of the basements of the institute. We passed doors with heavy locks on them, windowless rectangles set flush to the wall. He was slightly ahead of me, moving quickly, looking back as he spoke.

"A big Impressionist show is up now. That's why it's in storage. Usually it's out. By the way, you asked if the list is complete? I think it must be, to '77 at least. As I'm sure you know by now, he was a very organized man."

He stopped at a door near the end of the hallway, took out a key, and opened the heavy lock. Inside the cool, windowless room there were two tiers of metal racks extending from wall to wall, like broad library stacks, plenty of space to move between them and remove the paintings and prints that stood in rows, upright and in a clear order. A large digital device of some kind was mounted to the right of the door. Temperature and humidity, I thought. McHale checked it somewhat automatically after we had entered. There was a desk in the room and two easels, heavy ones, their legs spread out, ready to hold selections. McHale went to a small card catalogue, pulled out a drawer, and fingered through the entries. He found what he wanted in a moment, located the right stack and headed down it. I waited in the open area, leaning against the desk.

"Got it." I heard his slightly muffled voice from well back in the stacks.

It was not a large painting, no more than two and a half by three, but he handled it with great care, two hands on the frame, as if it were heavy and awkward. He got it to one of the easels and put it in place, then gripped the easel with both hands and shook it slightly, making sure that it was steady and firm. Then he stepped back from it, feeling for the desktop behind him, and perched himself on the edge.

"This is the second one," I said.

"Yeah," he said. "Number one's in the British Museum."

The painting was a realistic rendering of a nude woman standing beside a desk that was very much like the one I stood beside as I looked at it. I was sure, remembering Uncle Edward's descriptions in his letters, that she was Dorit. She had those prominent features, milky eyes, long, narrow torso, and her hips flared out dramatically. Her hair was red, tight, and pulled back from her face. Broad shoulders and small breasts. She was standing very erect, not at all at ease, and there was something artificial about her posture, as if she had just forgotten that she was posing and had lost the casualness that the pose suggested should be there. There seemed no expression in her body at all, but in her face, slightly turned, her eyes on the desktop, there was plenty of it. The slash of her red mouth was enigmatic, the tense beginning of a smile or maybe a grimace. Her eyes seemed to bulge out slightly, lime green, with the hint of a sparkle in them.

There was a window behind her, in the center of the painting, and out of it I could see a street lit by tall, old-fashioned lanterns, people moving along the sidewalk, one of them running, a slightly emaciated man with dark features and of average height, a figure I remembered from one of the other pieces that I'd examined.

It was night. There were shadows in the room. The background was dark and moody, but the figure and the desk were untouched by the shadows, almost as if they had been lifted from another circumstance entirely and embedded here.

I wasn't sure at first what it was that she was looking at, a thick ropelike object snaking gracefully across the desk's surface. Then I saw the small red ribbon at the end of it and knew it was her braid. I looked at the back of her head and could see the slight bunching behind her ear, the place where the braid had been severed.

I moved from where I was leaning and went closer. The figure beside the desk in the painting seemed to move too, to lean away from the darkness behind her and begin to step away from the desk, get free of what she was looking at there. I could see then that *that* had been the awkwardness in her posture, the tense readiness to move away, countered by the focal draw of the braid.

And it was not really a braid at all. Only when I was very close to the painting could I see this. It was a spine. *Her* spine, I guessed. And it was rendered with an anatomical certainty that was clinical and very sure. It was in its sheath, but that clear tube of membrane was made of transparent hair. I could see through it to the spine itself, but I could not separate it from the spine. There were places where the hair insinuated itself into the spine, winding among the disks and vertebrae, and I saw as I studied it that the hair was indeed braided into the tissue, in such a way that the two were inseparable, linked together in some perfect way. I looked at her eyes, but even up close I could not read the expression in them, nor in her mouth. Only the desire in her body to move away was clear to me now.

I looked closer into the shadowy background. There was a small

picture hanging on one of the walls, a photograph or a small painting of a woman, her features very particular, even familiar. The
same particularity was in the running man's face on the street in
the far distance. It was a face I did not know, but one that I thought
I would recognize again.

"Symbolic, do you think?" McHale spoke softly from somewhere
behind me.

"No," I said. "I don't think so. Maybe encoded."

"Exactly," he said. "Something special, don't you think?"

"It is that."

"Well, I think it's magnificent," he said. "I came upon him, you
know, close to fifteen years ago, when I was in art school. Really a
chance thing, a couple of pieces from a small group show in London. I was just browsing in the library. Then I began to search
things out, but there was very little, occasional pieces and almost
nothing written about him, only a couple of brief references in
obscure reviews. I even got hold of the medical books he'd illustrated. I think he's a very special painter. Do you think I could
come out and see the rest?"

He asked the question very tentatively, and it would have been
easy to turn him down. But he had been a real help to me, and I
was moved by his enthusiasm and desire, things that made plenty
of sense to me as I gazed at the painting. Uncle Edward was indeed
a special painter. Though what was here had a distanced and tortured quality that was not so different from the circumstance of his
letters, here the qualities were all in the painting and clearly not in
the painter. I was looking at Dorit's face again, and I answered him
without moving my eyes from it.

"Sure," I said. "Why not."

Driving back on the expressway, I missed the turnoff that would
take me north to Congress Park. Part of the reason was the fact of
change and my too easy assumption that the area was still familiar
to me. But there had been plenty of building in the past twenty-
seven years. What had been farmland was now suburban housing
projects and industrial parks. Even the crossing highways that I
passed, the ones that I had known by numbers, now had names,
futile humanistic nods to suburban sprawl. Futile for me at least. I
knew I could never see these communities as other than raw and

temporary. Congress Park, Brookfield, and the other older towns had a history, for me a personal one, but one too that was real. Parts of the far west beyond Chicago were as old as the city itself. We never thought of them as suburbs in the modern sense. They were not dim satellites around a vibrant center, not like these projects I was passing by.

But I might have seen the turnoff still, had I not been figuring. I had first gone through the numbers McHale had suggested, and any way I looked at it, the ten paintings would have to come to at least a million dollars in value. Probably a million and a half was more like it. I said the figure aloud but couldn't get it to sink in. Surely it could mean nothing to Aunt Waverly. If anything, a burden. What could she do with it: give it to one of her book clubs? She could give it to me, of course; I might be her only living relative. But this brought Angela to mind, and I began thinking of what the money might mean in that case.

It was only when the new suburbs had thinned out and the still remaining far west farms began to appear that I recognized I was miles beyond the expressway turnoff I should have taken. I slowed and took the next one, figuring I would head a little north, then find something to take me back east toward Congress Park. Once past the cloverleaf with its new broad lanes, the road turned into a secondary byway running along farmland, a rural route number that I had no memory of at all. The fields I passed were lying fallow. I could see crops in the distance, and beyond that occasional buildings, probably small towns along the railroad that headed west from Chicago to some distant terminus. The road was narrow, two lanes, but in good condition, and there were few side roads coming into it. I moved at a good pace, Aunt Waverly's little Ford running smoothly at fifty.

Then I caught the car in my rearview mirror. It may have been behind me for a while. I wasn't sure. It was back a good distance, but moving up, a station wagon, I thought, maybe an Oldsmobile. I slowed down a little to let it pass. There was nothing coming up in front of me. The road was straight and flat, and I could see ahead for a good distance. But the car came up close behind me and made no move to come around. I slowed a little more, checking the road in front again. Then I felt the jerk, the heavy thud as it hit me. It was just a kiss, but enough to set the little Ford swerving. I fought the wheel, hit the accelerator, and looked in the mirror again. The car was closing. The windshield was tinted, and I could not see the driver. He hit me again, harder this time. Then instead of coming in for another whack, he dropped back a little, blinked his lights, and put his left-turn signal on.

I was still fighting the wheel, hitting the brakes a little, then the accelerator, getting the Ford under control. I was down to thirty miles an hour. There was no chance to outrun the bigger car, and I could see no turnoffs in the immediate distance, no buildings, nothing but fallow fields on both sides. I reached under the seat, then jerked open the glove compartment as I bumped along the narrow shoulder, bringing the Ford to a stop. Nothing, not even an ice scraper. I moved the gearshift to reverse and checked the door lock buttons.

The station wagon pulled off onto the shoulder with me, staying a good six car lengths back. There was still nothing I could see through the tinted windshield, and for a few moments there was no movement from the car at all. Then I saw doors open on both sides.

Two dark heads appeared, and at first I thought they were black men, then recognized that they were wearing ski masks. They came out from behind the doors, and I saw that the one in the road had something in his hand, not a gun but a dark small club of some sort.

The one on the driver's side moved down to the edge of the shoulder as he approached the Ford's rear. I lost him from the mirror, but didn't reach out to adjust it. I felt it was the other one, the one with the club, that I'd have to worry about initially. I felt strangely calm as they were approaching me, remembering what had happened at the trailer a short time ago. I'd handled that, and I could handle this as well. I still had my left hand on the wheel, and I could feel the pain in my tight grip and had to concentrate to loosen it a little.

I had no real sense of their efficiency. But I didn't think both of them coming at me was a smart move on their part. I had the car running. They could tell that, and the one down on the sloping shoulder was not in the best position. They can't be professionals at this, I thought.

When the one on the roadway reached the Ford's passenger

door, he lifted the club up, a small wooden bat with a black handle, and tapped twice on the glass. I could feel the presence of the other one just back of the driver's door, to the side of my head.

I reached across the passenger seat and rolled the window slowly down. He put his hand on the frame, keeping the one with the club in it slightly elevated and held back.

"Show me your hands," he said.

"What did you say?"

"I said show me your fucking hands!"

"I can't hear you," I said, speaking softly, as if I were at a greater distance from him.

I could see his belt buckle, his gloved fist with the bat in it, his fingers tightening on the doorframe. He was back a few inches from the side of the car. Then his head came down and into view, his masked face looking in at the window.

I had my left foot against the driver's door at the frame, and I pushed off, reaching out and grabbing for the mask. I got him above the nose, a finger hitting his right eye, my fist gathered in the fabric above his forehead, a clump of hair under it. I yanked in and down, banging his face into the doorframe, and at the same time hit the accelerator and jerked the wheel with my free hand.

The Ford lurched back, the front end coming around, down and over the shoulder. I heard a thud and a yell from behind me on the shoulder side. The club had come in the window now, and the one I held by the hair was trying hard to swing it. It hit the dash, the soft fabric on the inside of the roof, my thigh with a weak swing. I kicked the gearshift into drive with my right knee, then hit the accelerator and drove down off the shoulder and into the fallow field.

There was a small ditch at the verge of it, and when I hit it the masked face bounced into the doorframe again, even harder this time, and the club fell and clattered against the dash. I let him go then and got both hands back on the wheel.

The Ford luged down at first, coughing, sinking into the soft soil, and I eased back on the gas pedal to get a purchase. The wheels spun, then slowed and grabbed in the earth. I must have been going no more than five miles an hour as I moved away, straight out into the field.

I looked in the mirror then and saw the man who'd had the club that was now rattling around on the floor beside me. He was rolling in the narrow ditch, flailing, reaching for his face. The other one was up, staggering a little, looking at the Olds, at me, then over at his companion. He made his decision then and started running back along the shoulder and in the direction of the station wagon.

I was about a hundred yards away when I saw him turn from the shoulder and enter the field. He only made it in for a few feet, the rear end of the heavier car catching in the ditch, the wheels spinning and sinking in and the front end vibrating and lurching as he gunned the motor.

I was halfway across the field, could see another road, its sloping shoulder in the distance, when the man got out of the car and slammed the door. He stood and looked in my direction. Then he turned and headed along the ditch to where the other one was, now out of my sight.

B Y   T H E   T I M E   I   W A S   O N   my way to Congress Park again, I'd decided not to call the police. At first I thought I would and had kept my eyes open for the first gas station. I'd found one at the edge of a small village no more than a few miles from the field I'd driven across, and had pulled in near the building and parked beside the lighted phone booth.

I checked the outside of the car, finding only a few scuff marks on the rear bumper, and while I walked around it I thought of how Aunt Waverly would receive the news. Though she had that sure air about her, seemed always in control, I questioned what was going on inside. She might be much more fragile than she appeared.

I went to the phone booth and stood in front of it and knew I wasn't going to call. Instead I called Aunt Waverly, telling her that I'd gotten slightly lost, that I'd be back shortly. I asked her if she needed anything and told her I'd get the juice and milk. Then I opened the passenger side of the car and found the club. I hefted it and looked down at it; nothing special, just a piece of hard wood with a black tape wrapping. Then I saw the dots of red at my knuckles, others falling and joining them. I reached to my forehead and felt the wetness and closed the door again and went to the gas station men's room. I dropped the club in the wastebasket and looked at my face in the mirror. The cut was open again and oozing blood. I held paper towels over it, pressing them in, until it stopped.

Driving back, I thought about what had happened. The men hadn't carried guns, didn't seem to know exactly how to go about the thing. They'd probably followed me from the Art Institute, really unsure if they would find a place to come down on me as they had. They had no way of knowing that I would wind up in the country that way, on an empty road. They hadn't had much of a plan. Then, too, it was possible that they had nothing at all to do with the paintings or with me in any particular way. They could have just been road robbers, though that didn't seem likely, given Aunt Waverly's inexpensive car. As cool as I'd felt through the whole thing, I hadn't been cool enough to get their license number. I couldn't even remember if they'd had a plate.

If I called the police, they could guard Aunt Waverly's house, but that was about all they could do. I wasn't even sure that the car had been an Oldsmobile, and I could give no very helpful description of the two men. And Waverly's was an active neighborhood, the houses close together, plenty of children playing in the park. As long as one of us was home, I couldn't see them coming at us there. They'd surely *think* I'd called the police, and that was just about as good as doing so. It didn't seem reasonable at all that they'd try the house.

But I recognized too that it was something more than all this. I didn't want anyone else involved just then. I wanted Uncle Edward's affairs in order first, feeling that in some way they were mine until I let them go. I decided I would get the paintings out of there as soon as possible, get them somewhere safe. I'd have to make some calls as soon as I got back.

When I arrived at the house, Aunt Waverly was in the kitchen, putting a meat loaf together. It was five o'clock. I greeted her and spoke briefly about my trip to the institute, said we'd have to talk some things over this evening. She said okay, after supper. I peeked into the bowl of pork, beef, eggs, and bread crumbs. Her hands were deep in the mixture. I pushed against her, putting my face close to her hands to catch the smell. She laughed and elbowed me away.

Then I went and got the crate of paintings out of the car trunk and carried it up to Angela's bedroom, put it in the corner against the wall beside the bed, then went down to Uncle Edward's study and got the other crate and carried it up there as well. I'll sleep with them, I thought. That should be safe enough for now.

It was five-fifteen by then. Probably too late. But I went to the living room phone anyway and tried the office number on Fred Ross's card. He was in, just getting ready to leave, he said, but he listened cheerfully and with concern.

There was a museum in Downers Grove, he said, not far away. It was small, but it had sufficient storage. He knew the curator well, and besides, any place would jump at the chance to store the stuff. They'd figure a bird in the hand: maybe they'd get something out of it for their permanent collection. But even if not, the future publicity, if only a few words in their newsletter, would help with fund-raising. He said he'd call tomorrow and make arrangements.

"How about now?" I said, telling him I was getting worried about the humidity in Uncle Edward's study.

"Sure, why not," he said. "It's not that late yet."

I asked him about his arrangement with Uncle Edward. I'd found no contract among his things.

"There wasn't any," he said. "Really, I haven't done much in the last ten years. Nothing at all, not even correspondence, since '77. I used to keep in touch with him about the illustration royalties, a letter, a call now and then. That was a straight ten percent. Mostly it was just a matter of sending checks to Waverly's bank. I had to send him contracts every so often, but that petered out pretty quickly after he gave up the illustration entirely. The checks have been coming straight from the publishers for a while now. I get accountings."

"Did he have an agent in London?"

"Not that I know of. No, I'm sure he didn't. He was a tough customer about such things, at least he became that way—not too trustful. It was only that we had been together since the beginning, you know. He trusted me. For all I know, he handled things on his own in his last years."

I thought I had all I needed and didn't think it made any sense to call the medical book publishers, but I asked Ross about it anyway, just to be sure.

"You're right," he said. "Nothing they can do for you. But if you need anything more, be sure to ask me. I'll do what I can."

He said he'd call me back in an hour, one way or another, about the Downers Grove museum.

"I called the agent," I said, when Waverly joined me in the living room. I'd already poured out a glass of sherry for her and was fixing a bourbon for myself.

"It's time to get the paintings out of here, to somewhere with a constant control on temperature. I don't know about such things. Maybe humidity can hurt them."

"Oh," she said. "I guess that's good. Anyway, Fred's a good man. He was with Edward from the beginning."

"He'll call back," I said. "Later on tonight."

"You had a call," Aunt Waverly said. "A woman. Joan. I didn't catch the last name. The number's on the pad."

"Did she say anything at all?"

"No. Nothing. Just asked if you could call her."

I finished pouring my drink, said I'd be right back, and went to the phone in the kitchen. The number was there. I looked at it for a moment, then got my wallet out. It was the same number, the woman who had handed me her card near Edward's grave. I reached for the phone, then changed my mind. A little later, I thought, and headed back to the living room.

"It's a lot of money," she said.

"Indeed it is."

We had finished our meat loaf, salad, and boiled potatoes and were sitting in the living room again. Though it was almost completely dark, Aunt Waverly had not turned the lights on. I remembered that preference, the way she liked to enjoy the slow fading for as long as it lasted.

"Do you have any use for it?" I said.

"No, not that I can think of. No. Not at all. How about you?"

"Me neither." And we both laughed lightly and smiled at each other. I could see the dull shine on her teeth, but most of her face was in shadow. She got up then and went to the far corner of the room and turned on the floor lamp, clicking it down to the dimmest bulb. Then she returned to her place, a small wing chair, uphol- stered in dark crushed velvet.

"But what about Angela? I mean if we could find her."

"I can't think about that, Jack. And it's been too long. He stayed in touch for a while, her husband, but that was over long ago."

"Do you have a number?"

"A *phone* number? Of course I had one, but I can't imagine that it's any good."

"It may be something," I said. "Worth a try at least."

She sat for a moment. Then she shook her head slightly and got up and left the room. I could hear her in the distance, opening drawers, shuffling through things. She was gone a long time, and I got up and fixed myself another drink. I had half finished it by the time she came back.

She didn't sit down but stood in front of me, a wrinkled piece of paper in her hand. Her face was distant, even austere, but I could see a moistness at the corners of her eyes. She hadn't worried the issue too long when I'd asked her for the number, but now I could feel what I thought was a sense of distant and undefined longing coming out in her. I looked away from her face and took the paper and put it in my shirt pocket. Then I got up and moved to her, let her put her arms around and hold me. I couldn't tell if I was hold- ing her, or she me.

"I fear it's been too damn long, Jack." Her voice was clearly vulnerable now, in a whisper, and slightly choked.

"Shush now," I said. "We'll take it slow and easy."

We spent a while talking about Angela then. Her opening slightly to me seemed to allow for that. There had been that barrier of formality between us, but it had softened some, and I think part of that had to do with our just getting to know each other again. I tried not to probe too much, just let her attempt to articulate the quality of things around the time of Angela's leaving. What kept coming clearer to me was Uncle Edward's part in the thing, a cer- tain rigid passivity that was hard for her to characterize but seemed crucial. It was not what he did but what he didn't do, both in act and in emotion. "She had lost him long before that," Waverly said at one point. "But she didn't know it, I think. And she didn't know how to reach out when the time came. Not that it would have made any difference."

"And with you?"

"Oh, well. It was her *father*. She had me, you know. Though in a passive way."

"But can there be some explanation for why she didn't keep in touch? With you, I mean."

I'd pushed it a little too far, and I could see that it was all she could do to keep control. Her fingers lifted, her nails touching into the chair arms. I knew she didn't have an answer, though she seemed ready to speak. And then the phone rang.

"Stay here," I said. "I'll get it in the kitchen," and I pushed up from the chair.

It was Fred Ross calling back. He said he'd reached his museum man.

"He's very enthusiastic. Both from the purely aesthetic end and because it can be good for the museum. Down the road at least, if he can let the news out at some time. Even just that they were stored there for a while."

"When?" I said.

"Two o'clock tomorrow afternoon. He'll come himself. If he doesn't hear from you, he'll be there."

I got the man's name and number, thanked Ross for his help, and hung up.

Aunt Waverly had come to the kitchen while I was still talking. She had taken teacups out and put the kettle on.

"It's all right," she said, as I turned from the phone. "I didn't realize it could feel so raw after all this time. But I'll handle it."

"Of course you will," I said.

After we'd had our tea, talking only, then, about the deal Fred Ross had made, that I'd have things ready for him the following afternoon, Aunt Waverly said she thought she'd go up, maybe read a book.

"Do you want a last look at the paintings?"

"Not now," she said. "Maybe tomorrow. Are you going to call that woman?"

"Yes," I said. "Right now, I think."

She got up from the table, came over to where I stood, and embraced me again. Then she headed for her bedroom. I sat for a few minutes longer, finishing my tea, then checked my watch. It was close to ten. Almost too late, I thought, and got up and went to the phone.

"Joan?" I said. "This is Jack Church."

"Oh. Hello, Mr. Church," she said. "Thanks for calling back."

"Is there something I can do?"

"Well, yes, there is, as a matter of fact. I'd like to talk with you. Could we possibly meet somewhere? Maybe you could come over here?"

"Where are you?"

"Oh. In Riverside. Not very far."

"I know it," I said, and took down the address as she carefully spoke it. I would see her the following afternoon, at five-thirty.

After I'd hung up the phone, I crossed to the kitchen sink for a glass of water. As I turned the tap, I could feel the events of the day close in on my arms and shoulders. It had been an active day, and I was tired and ready for sleep. I'd have to be up early in the morning. I wanted a good few hours of work on Uncle Edward's leavings before the museum man came at two.

Across the sink from me I could see through the window to a window in the kitchen of my own old house, and I remembered how Waverly and my mother had opened the windows in summer and had called across to each other while they were both cooking or doing dishes. The window tonight was dark, a heavy shade drawn, and there was nothing at all to see.

Then suddenly a light came on behind the shade. I saw a figure —a woman, I thought—moving. The shadow grew larger, then stopped, the outline of a torso and head, standing directly across from me. I reached out and carefully raised Aunt Waverly's window. The one on the other side was open a bit at the bottom. I heard water running, a faint clatter, and then a quiet humming. She was doing the dishes, singing to herself. Mother, I thought, feeling my eyes begin to fill. Then I lifted the glass, my hand wet from the water that had overflowed it, and drank deeply. I reached out again and carefully lowered Aunt Waverly's window. It's certainly all gone, I thought. Forget it.

T HE LETTERS THAT COVERED the next ten years, though full of social gossip and talk of Edward's rise in the London art world, were strangely devoid of any breadth or richness. I read them slowly, resting briefly between each one, but I could not make them capture in any way the span of time they covered. There had been the war in Vietnam, all the upheaval surrounding the turn of the decade, but the letters seemed immune from all that, their concerns so very separate. Then again, I thought, he'd gone from sixty-four to seventy-four in those years. No wonder that his concerns were elsewhere, as he tried to make his way so late in his career. Only then did I put his age against the years, recognizing that he had been born right at the turn of the century.

There were fifteen letters in all, and only three more after that to cover the years between '75 and '77, when the letters ended. It was after the twelfth one in that succession that Aunt Waverly had stopped opening them.

I'd gotten a sharp knife from the kitchen and slit the edge of the thirteenth letter in the pile and read it through carefully before I'd finished the preceding ones. I guess I expected something special, as if Aunt Waverly's decision would somehow be figured in the letter itself, but it was just another in the series, in no way different from the ones I'd looked at. He seemed to be working very hard and intently, but only on occasion did he speak of his painting, and the enthusiasm for talk about it that I'd noted earlier on now seemed turned to privacy and reticence.

The first few letters, spaced apart by long periods of intervening months, all began with those heartfelt apologies to Aunt Waverly. He'd been busy working. He was sorry. How could she forgive him. But then, after a while, that stopped. Even the letters' closures, occasions where he had before made mention of their relationship, began to change. They were slowly turning to documents, almost like journal entries, an autobiographical record, and as this happened they lost that quality of discretion that previously had taken some account of whom Edward was writing to. He wrote of himself and his life, intimately at times, and it was becoming increasingly clear that it was a very separate life, one that had nothing to do anymore with Waverly's at all.

He was getting closer to the Bayards and to Susan Harwood. Harwood was drinking more heavily than before, it seemed. Though Edward remained on the outskirts of the city, still in Muswell Hill, he came in often to cocktail parties and art showings.

"They're really quite lovely people when you get to know them. The women especially. And I've had very good talks with Bayard; our medical connection has been constantly fruitful. Harwood is always congenial; it's fun to be around him, but superficial. The drinking gets in the way of anything deeper. The class thing is a problem for me at times, it's true. The world's changing, politics and the war. But they seem to drift above it all in their privilege. Very hard to get them to talk seriously about such things." This was in '69, November 3.

Outside of the parties and art events, there were no other people that Edward had associated with intimately. I looked for mention of Mark and Dorit Janes and found some. They'd been present at various occasions, but always among large groups of people, and there'd only been room for superficial conversation. He'd spoken to Mark about medical illustration, but that had led nowhere. He noted that Janes was distant, slightly arrogant, he thought, or at least so immersed in his work that he had little interest in anything else, but for his art collecting, something that he seemed not to take very seriously in any aesthetic way. It appeared to be a lark to him, like some sport that he had taken up to get a little exercise, a bit of entertainment to the side of what was important. And there seemed another cause of his distance as well, an edge of bitterness between him and the Harwoods. Still, he attended their parties, almost as if he wished to make his unfriendliness known to them. There were only a few occasions when Edward had spoken to Dorit, but I noticed that these were always written of with great care and attention, as if even the most casual conversation was pregnant with some meaning for him.

He remained with the gallery that had taken him up initially until 1970. Though he wrote only occasionally about his relationship with the gallery and its owner, it seemed to be a good one. He seemed satisfied with the way things were going. Work was getting sold and he had had a one-man show, a small one but one that was well received. There was even a review in which he was called a new and important painter. "At my age," he had written. "New?" He was sixty-eight then.

Then all of a sudden things had collapsed. He was cold and slightly guarded as he wrote about it; bitter, I thought. The gallery owner had pressed him on the exclusivity of their arrangement. Edward had sold a few paintings on his own, and the gallery owner wanted commission and wanted Edward to stop selling privately in the future. There was talk in the letters about a contract, even some hint of a lawsuit.

It was after that that the content of the letters began to change, though I couldn't be sure that his falling-out with the gallery had anything to do with it. It may be that he was still socializing, still seeing the Bayards and Harwoods and going to parties and openings, but he stopped writing about that. He turned to mundane daily events, and to things around him that he was watching closely so that he could take them into his paintings, and though he didn't really speak of his art in any detail, my guess was that he was moving more exclusively into it, as if the stakes were rising and he was committing himself to it in an increasingly serious way.

I was reading the last letter that Aunt Waverly had opened. It had been written early in '72, and he was talking about two related paintings that he had plans for, when I came across a passage that brought me to a stop. I went back and read it over.

"We met again for a drink the other evening near Piccadilly, and it was there that the idea came to me. Dorit was strangely at odds with herself over Mark's absence, as if she both wished for it and feared what could happen without his control over her present. It was something about her face, carriage, and gesture in that quiet turmoil that touched me, something I knew I could do things with. He'll be back in a week, and I'll hope to see her again before that."

I looked back through the letters that preceded the one I was reading, but I could find no mention at all of other meetings with her. That was very curious, as I couldn't imagine Edward leaving such a thing out. I read on in the letter, a long one this time, and well beyond the middle of it I came across a passage containing the names of the paintings that he had spoken about earlier.

"I don't usually have titles in advance, but this time it seems right. The names came to me with the impetus, Dorit's look and manner, and I suspect that they, like her, will drive the paintings to their completion. I'll call them *Drunk in Absence* and *Presence Unknown*."

I continued reading, and after two pages in which he wrote about the café, what Dorit was wearing, and the way she moved and gestured, he made reference to an emblem that hung from a chain at her neck. It was something her husband had given her just recently, and it represented something else, a tattoo that he had given her, or seen to her getting, shortly before.

I read the passage over again. There was something shocking in the way he reported the intimacy of her telling him these things, his casual manner, and I was sure now that things had passed between them that were not in any of the letters, at least an under-standing of some kind, even though it may not have taken shape in words.

"I asked her if I could borrow the emblem, a curious piece in-deed, and I myself now have a tattoo, the emblem's figures in miniature, somewhat secret behind my left ear. My hair covers it, but I know that it's there, and I suspect I'll incorporate it in some way in these paintings. I'll include the figure at the end here, just for its curiosity."

There were two more pages before the letter ended, statements of enthusiasm about getting down to work, a few occasional words of closure, and then the emblem figure.

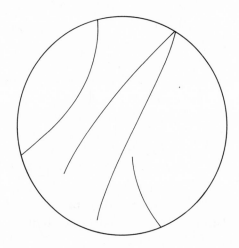

I read once again the first letter that I had slit open, then slit the next one and read it too. Neither had any reference to the meeting or the paintings in them. I looked ahead to the next one and noted the date, the sixth of April, 1975, three years after the one that had contained the emblem figure. I didn't open it but set it and the others to the side.

Aunt Waverly had stopped opening the letters, and I could understand why. The tattoos and the talk about Dorit were an intimacy that she was being asked to share in, but with no sense at all on his part of how she might be hurt. It would have been a terrible insult were it not so inappropriately presented, so openly and without regard. It must have been then that she had seen herself as only an absence to him. How odd that the tattoo should identify him for her now.

I reached for the list of paintings and checked through it. Both of the ones that Edward had spoken of in the letter were there, and both had check marks beside them. They were dated as finished in early '73.

I got up and went to the crates I'd slept beside the night before. I'd carried them back down to the study at seven that morning, after coffee, when I was ready to get to work. Both paintings were in the crate I'd taken with me to the institute, and I recognized immediately that *Presence Unknown* was the one McHale had thought had been recently touched up.

The paintings were the same size, just a little smaller than the Dorit one that I had seen at the Art Institute, and I looked for a good place to display them. Though it was getting on to 10:00 A.M., the sun hadn't yet reached the back windows of the house, and I wanted them well lighted. I finally decided on the bureau. It had a wide, low surface, three drawers below, where Uncle Edward had stored illustration supplies. It was against the white wall at the end of the room, and there was nothing hanging above it. The house was quiet. I wasn't sure whether Aunt Waverly was home or not.

When I had the paintings in place side by side, I stepped a few feet back from them. I remembered them only a little from my examination of all the works a few days before. There were human figures in both paintings, the events of one taking place in a room, the other set in a landscape on a sloping piece of ground in a park, I thought, trees, a narrow pathway, a few pieces of metal furniture, the kind with twisted filigree woven thickly into the arms and backs. Then I noticed that something was wrong and went to the chest again and reversed the paintings' order, placing *Drunk in Absence* on the left, *Presence Unknown* beside it. It was now a diptych, even more forcefully narrative than I had thought.

To the right side of the canvas in the left-hand painting was a reclining nude. She was sitting in a tattered, overstuffed wing chair, her feet up and crossed at the ankles on an ottoman. There was a table in the center of the room, a window above and behind it in the back wall. Both were familiar to me, objects that I thought were the same as ones in the Dorit painting I'd seen at the institute, things in Uncle Edward's studio in Muswell Hill, I supposed.

The room in the painting was quite dark, though it was clearly daytime. The window framed a scene that I could not clearly distinguish from my distance, but there was sun and light out there. I could see a dark place on the wall to the side opposite the figure, and when I moved in closer I thought that it was the picture of the woman I'd seen in the painting McHale had shown me. The figure was hazy and small, but I could make out her dark complexion and hair. She seemed slight, even a little sickly.

Because of the light that came in at the window, there were large, hard-edged pieces of shadow falling across the room's elements, sectioning off the focal nude from the other things in the room with an effect that was almost cubist. When I concentrated on the hunks of shadow themselves, I saw that they were not formed in a natural way. The sun at the window didn't quite do what it ought to have done, and the shadows formed an abstract composition, a fractured surface floating over the primary one. Though they were deep shadows and the whole scene, except for the brighter light at the window, was a dark and somber thing, I could see that they'd been arrived at through the use of many layers of glazing and that the objects in the room, including the figure, had not. This caused the shadows to detach themselves. They seemed to float a little away from the canvas surface, to shimmer on the verge of motion.

The figure's head was washed a little by the sunlight entering from the window, which caused the shadows falling across it to be notably sharper at their edges than elsewhere in the work. Her face was an enigmatic thing, and it was hard to keep the negative spaces on the same plane with the positive, to see her face as a whole, let alone have a clear feeling about its expression. But I thought it must be Dorit. I thought, even, that I could make out a hint of her braid where it butted thickly into the back of her head, though her head was turned slightly to the side and there was a darkness there.

A shadow cut on an angle across her forehead, through one eye and down her cheek. Another split her lips at an impossible angle, causing almost a snarl, but it could have been a half-thoughtful smile as well. I couldn't tell, but I did think of the painting's title and thought it was important. It could surely program the painting, and there was the fact too that Edward had made the work only after deciding upon it. There was indeed a feeling of absence in the room, and drunk was a good name for her enigmatic expression. I myself felt an almost drunken uncertainty as I studied her.

Given the position of the window, the way the light and shadow fell from it, there was a thin, cloudlike circle extending from the woman's head, up behind her and around the window. It just missed taking in the picture that hung on the wall, but was so close to its edge that it set it off in dramatic contrast. The picture seemed left out purposely, and though I could not see the features in it well at all, I thought I felt some longing in them, almost a physical reaching out, as if at any moment the picture might move on the wall, slide to the right and slightly upward, to come into the light of the vague cloud.

I realized that there were other objects and conventional points of interest in the room. There was the posture of the reclining nude as well, the way her hands fell, the rendering of her limbs, and when I factored the rest out and looked with care at them I saw the subtle art, the supple roundness and the actuality of the flesh tones, even the blemishes, the realism of nails, and the way the fingers intertwined, covering her sex in a modest, almost classical way. But all this, when I looked at the painting as a whole, seemed perfunctory. Only her head, that shadow cloud, and the window were of importance. It was indeed an absent, lonely room, and all the attentions in it were focused elsewhere. It was like a prologue, important only as an introduction to what followed it, and I suspected that this was its singular power and that without the other half of the diptych it would be a very moving thing all by itself. But I had the other half.

I moved up close and looked in the window frame in the first painting, then checked its contents against the second. They were not exactly the same, but it was clear that *Presence Unknown* was essentially a painting of what appeared out the small window framed in the background in *Drunk in Absence*. It was the same park in both, the same perspective and photographic framing. The path and the metal furniture were there, and there were even figures present in both. But in the window there were elements that were replaced by others in the painting on the right.

In the window in *Drunk in Absence* there was a nude woman sitting on one of the metal chairs, her position similar to that of the primary figure in the heavy wing chair. She was present also, much larger, of course, in *Presence Unknown*, where she was the central figure. In both, she was leaning back, her head slightly turned, intently watching something to the other side of the composition.

In *Drunk in Absence* her legs were extended out before her, slightly separated, her heels resting on the ground. She seemed to be looking down the pathway that wound from thicker trees, up into the clearing where she was sitting. There was a woman moving along the path, a slight figure, wrapped in a raincoat that she held closed across her breasts with both hands. Her legs and feet were bare, her dark hair roughed up and gnarled, as if recently rained on and still damp. There was no way to tell really, but I suspected that she had nothing on under her coat. Her head was up, her expression, though it was hard to judge given her relatively small size in the window frame, seemed anticipatory. She had a smile on her lips, and her eyes seemed bright.

In *Presence Unknown,* she was not there, at least not on the path. There was a man there instead, farther back than she had been, still among the last trees of the forest he was coming out of. He was dressed in a careful suit, and he carried things, a broad leather case of some kind in one hand, what looked like a small painting, hanging along his leg from his fist, in the other. Though he was still far down the path, his head was turned in the direction of the reclining figure, and he seemed to know she was there and was heading for her. His stride was long and very certain. It was not that he was hurrying to the woman but that he was sure of himself, knew exactly where he was going.

Back even deeper, in the woods behind him, was another figure, a very shadowy one, light in leaves mottling its features so that it was hard to tell if it was a woman, the same one who was coming along the path in her raincoat in the window frame, or someone else entirely. The figure wasn't moving but was standing, half hidden behind a tree trunk. One of its arms was elevated, and it had something in its hand. It could have been a bit of rope, a paintbrush, even a hard weapon of some sort. It could also have been a braid. Whatever it was, it seemed to be pointed at the back of the man as he strode purposefully up the path.

As I looked at the tree limbs and the leaves that partially obscured the figure, I noticed that there was something there, configurations that I recognized and knew in a moment were the same that I had seen in Uncle Edward's tree painting, human sinew and passages of circulation slightly under and married to the physiology of natural growth. I moved from the branches and leaves at the figure's head, letting my eye roam through the other trees, shrubs, and grasses that laced the entire composition. Everything was animated in the same way. Only the figures and the hard metal of the furniture were free of it, conventionally what they were.

I studied the two figures on the pathway carefully and for a long time. They were small, the details of their clothing very hard to distinguish perfectly with the naked eye, and there was a distance at which, as I moved very close to the painting, my eyes would unfocus before I could pick enough detail out. In a while I turned from the painting, stepped back, and had to reach up and rub my eyes.

I needed something, maybe a pair of Aunt Waverly's reading glasses or a magnifier of some sort, and I started to leave the room in search of that. But then I thought I'd better look where I was first.

Nothing seemed likely. It was a very spare room, no cabinets or drawers, and the desk was really a trestle table, a slab of thick wood supported by heavy legs. There was a closet in one corner, and I went to it, but it was empty. Only the bureau on which the paintings rested was left. It had a small drawer and two larger ones in it, and I searched through them, finding various miniature instruments, small pointed brushes, metal knives, and tweezers. In the broad bottom drawer were sheets of transparent plastic of some kind, pencil markings on some of them. I lifted one to the light near the window and saw a drawing of an organ, thick veins and arteries running from it. Leftover transparencies, I thought, leavings from Edward's medical illustration work.

I returned the transparencies to the disheveled pile and reached back in the corner of the drawer, finding two small leather packets, the kind that unfolded and had pockets on their felt insides. In the one was a series of graduated needle-point brushes, and in the other I found what I was after, ten circular lenses, each in a small pocket of felt, all about the size of a monocle. There was a small handle in the packet as well, a finely made clear-glass device about six inches in length, with an empty glass circle at its end, a fixture into which the various lenses could be snapped.

I lifted two of the lenses in my fingertips and looked through one of them. The grain of the wood on the bureau top came into sharp focus, and this focus became even sharper and more detailed when I checked the other. I affixed the second lens in the handle, noting the small number 4 etched at its edge, and moved close to *Presence Unknown*.

I had to change lenses from time to time as I examined the surface of the painting, bringing things into clear focus, seeing just how detailed the work had been. Only with the number 10 lens, one that I could not look through for very long, was I able to see the brush strokes in the smallest elements in the painting, and then not all the time. In places there seemed a final level of miniature detail that the lens could not reach.

I moved over the surface with care, saving the figure of the seated nude for last. I could not determine where the touching up that McHale had mentioned started, though I guessed it might account for an almost indistinguishable lightening in the glaze over the nude figure. But that could have been part of the original intention. I couldn't be sure.

The nude was in the sunlight, clearly the same woman as in the other painting, clearly Dorit as I had come to know her from Edward's descriptions in the letters and from the painting at the institute. Her hands rested on the metal arms of the bench. Her extended legs were spread out a little at the thighs, something caused by the way the backs of her legs were pressed against the edge of the bench seat, and on the broad surface of her left thigh was a construction of some sort. I could see it faintly as I held the lens over it, something that was reminiscent of what Edward had done with the braided spine on the table in the other painting.

I changed the lens in the handle to a stronger one again, and when I got it at the right distance from the surface I could see the construction clearly. It was indeed the same kind of thing, but there was more to it than I had expected. Here the twisted leaf and tree sinews under the transparent surface of skin were forming figures, two nude bodies intertwined, their limbs running off into extensions of fascia and other damp tissues and vessels. The central bulks of the figures were clearly vegetable, but at their edges they were gradually transformed into the appropriate anatomy of the woman's thigh.

They could have been sleeping, adults together in an embrace that followed sex, but they could as well have been children. Though their anatomy was distinguishable, the turn of buttocks, flows of musculature in arms and backs, there was something fetal, not yet fully formed, about them. Both had short hair. Their faces were turned away. It was not clear if they were male or female.

I moved the lens up to look at the seated woman's face. It was the same face as that in the other painting, but here there were no shadows cutting through it. Where the other had seemed fractured, the face in this rendering was whole, though slightly dreamy in its expression, what I could see in the eyes unfocused, though the gesture of head and neck seemed to me intense. I looked hard at the face but could read nothing further in it.

Then I scanned over the entire body again, making sure that I had missed nothing important. When I reached the hands, I studied the way they rested, half gripping the arms of the metal chair.

I thought they were beautifully rendered, expressive but enigmatic. She could be getting ready to push against the arms, to raise herself from the chair and walk to the path. But it was also possible that she was preparing to grip the arms tighter, to somehow steady herself and stay where she was. Her fingers were long but not delicate, each nail pared back to finger's tip. Then I noticed something about the nails themselves and got the strongest lens again and put it in the handle.

Now I could see the texture of cuticle, growth lines under the surface of the nail's transparency, even the slight burrs the file had missed. And I could also see the slight discoloration across the nails' surfaces, a color change that melded gradually in, changing slowly from a deep pink to a lighter one. It seemed to be caused by the sun, by the way the nails' curves caught it. I moved the lens back slightly, and the edges of discoloration were pulled to a tighter focus. They were letters, and I could read them clearly now, two words, enough letters for each nail. *Find Angela.*

April 6, 1975

Dear Wave,

Very soon, as you know, in a matter of months only, I'll be seventy-five years old, and I've been driven in my work these days as if that made some difference. But I don't feel it that way. Even those increasing attendant difficulties that age brings, that you'll find out about too in your time, aren't really a bother to me. If there is any rage and disappointment, it's that I might have begun too late, that I am owed more work than I can ever accomplish. Water under the bridge though.

Whole weeks have gone by in which I have seen no one. I can hardly remember eating, my brief trips out for supplies, qualities of weather. I'm wearing glasses finally, typically farsighted at last, and that's a difficulty. My painting requires very close work, and I find I have to adjust the canvas constantly against reflection, rest my eyes too often, just when I need constant attention to the most careful details.

I write on this late afternoon, free finally from headache and that constant hangover from too little sleep. And I *can* write because I have finished a painting, a difficult one, and have no desire now to go on, to enter yet again into this obsession of mine that always feels a little like a sickness. At least not for a while.

It's Sunday, and this morning for the first time in weeks I heard the church bells ringing a few streets over. I finished the painting on Friday and have been out and around since then. A walk in the park, dinner at a restaurant among the welcome voices of other people here in Muswell Hill. Then on Saturday I went to London, to galleries, even to a pub for lunch and beer, and spent the early hours of the afternoon strolling among shops of women's clothing, things of mild interest but nothing to bring me fully back to the world again.

It was in front of one of these shops that I bumped into Susan Harwood. She said she had called and called and couldn't reach me. There was to be a dinner party that very night, a joint effort with the Bayards and others, something at the club. They were throwing it in honor of Vas Dias, the artist I've mentioned before, the one I had met at previous gatherings over the years. He had received a major commission from the government for a public work of some kind. She asked if I could still make it, and since I was already in London I said I could. I'd not been answering my phone, I told her. I'd been busy.

And there was other news too. Mark and Dorit Janes were returning to the States. This was news that brought me up rather short, and I was made to feel a further discomfort in the way Susan delivered it, pointedly and watching carefully for my reaction. It had been weeks since I had seen Dorit, in times when Janes had been away, and yet her presence had been with me, in my work and the thoughts and considerations that it had engendered.

"Going back?" I remember saying, unable to keep a certain feebleness out of my voice.

"Yes," she said. "Very soon now. He's taken another position, I believe in California."

I think Dorit had been very close to agreeing to sit for me, regardless of Janes' wishes, but I had not pressed it in those times of our meetings. Just her presence for a brief time had seemed enough to get me started, and I was driven enough to work ahead, sustained by that. But when I heard of her leaving, I realized in the moment just how much I did want to paint her in the flesh and realized too just what it was that I thought to capture in the act, something I knew I couldn't get from memory.

It was her uncertainty, something that infused much more than her glance and speech. It was in her body, the way she moved and gestured, even in the ways she chose for her hair and makeup. I knew it would even be there in the way she stood, would pose for me. I saw it as a dynamic thing, a potential for motion that was totally implicated in indecision, a connection of emotion and body that I thought to capture through that analogue that held me, has held me from the start obsessively, the placidity of body's surface against that other power, more primal, just under the skin.

Susan blinked at me over her glasses. I said I'd see her at the party, how good it was to see her.

The club was what I took to be a typical men's club, a number of small rooms full of heavy Victorian furniture, tall windows hung with heavy fabric, and a musty smell that seemed the result of poor ventilation. It was an elegant enough place, and the large ballroom in which the party was held was graced with a few large and quite beautiful Oriental carpets. Most of the chairs had been moved out, a few well-spaced and plush couches remaining for those who wished to sit.

I could see the place was quite full of people when I arrived and stood in the broad doorway at the room's entrance. Just inside the door was the owner of the gallery I had been associated with. We could not really avoid each other and were able to pass a few civil words. The guest of honor was standing with a group of people clustered around him, near the center of the large room. I saw Bayard there and Caroline and, a little off to the side, the slight woman who had been with the artist at Harwood's party where I had first met him and at every other circumstance in which we had chanced to meet. It had been over ten years since our first meeting, but I could not see much difference in the look of either of them. He still had the bright eyes of someone on the way up, though he was already quite near the top, and she was still a little shy, uncertain of herself. Her dress had changed though. She wore her clothing closer to her body. It had a more tailored look to it and seemed less of a display now than a protection against visibility. Beyond the group, close to the rear wall of the room, I could see Dorit's hair moving as she turned her head. Janes was beside her, and they were talking with another couple.

I went to the cluster of people, greeted Vas Dias and congratu-
lated him, shook hands with Bayard and with Harwood when he
saw me and came over to say hello. We chatted pleasantly, and in
a while I removed myself and went to the bar at the side of the
room to get a drink.

I felt her fingertips on my shoulder a moment after the bartender
had handed me a Scotch, and when I turned and saw her thin
smiling lips, those watery green eyes, I moved against her before I
could check myself, took her elbow in my palm, and reached out
to kiss her.

I'd startled her. I had never so much as touched her, and her
head jerked back a little involuntarily, and my lips brushed the side
of her nose. We both laughed then, like adolescents. She was
blushing, and I felt heat rise up in my own cheeks as well. I didn't
turn to look beyond her, though, to check to see if anyone had
noticed my furtive kiss.

"Well!" I said. "That was very odd."

She laughed lightly, lifting her rather pointed chin, but her eyes
remained in mine.

"Not so," she said. "You must have heard that we're leaving."
She began the statement as part of our light play, but her voice fell
to a sad seriousness as she reached the end of it. On the surface
her words were a non sequitur, but just a little deeper they contained significance that I dared not reach for just then.

"Let's go away from here?" she said. And in her words and the
way she shifted her body, tossed her head slightly so that her loose
red hair bobbed and brushed her cheeks and then settled, I held
that uncertainty that was the thing that moved me most about her.

"Away?"

"Just to the other room." She smiled. "There are paintings."

The room was crowded by this time, and when I scanned the
gathering I could not find Janes anywhere.

"This way," she said, touching my arm, and I followed her to a
smaller doorway at the room's side. We entered an alcove and from
that moved to a room a few feet away. It was a library of some sort,
heavy wooden bookshelves lining three of the walls, the other
hung with a few old portraits, dark and in need of cleaning.

"Well, here they are." She laughed. She was working at it now,
not really part of her laughter at all. Then she turned away from

the paintings and faced me again, her eyes washed with a thin mist.

"I tried a number of times to call you." It was clearly hard for her to hold my gaze. "I'd decided to sit for you as you'd asked me to. Funny, that it took me so long to decide."

I knew it really wasn't funny. Certainly not now. She had not mentioned Janes as having any part in her decision.

"You're leaving. When are you leaving?"

"Oh. Oh, in a week or so. Mark's taken a good position in Los Angeles. Well, near it."

"Is it hard to leave?"

She shifted on her feet and turned in a somewhat awkward way, facing the wall and the dour paintings. I saw a tightness in her broad shoulders, the way her knees locked under her knit skirt. She didn't speak for a while, but I think she knew her next words all the time.

"I don't know," she said. "Really. I just don't know."

"What is it that you don't know?"

"Anything," she said. She was in the middle of some kind of gesture, one that I could understand only when she completed it. But she wasn't going to complete it. I could tell that. The gesture would dissolve in her uncertainty about it. She didn't really know what she felt, not even what it felt like to be frustrated in not knowing. The half-completed gesture was not really enigmatic. It was a clear capturing of an absence. It was what I wanted. To at least paint it.

"But do you want something?" I said.

She paused again, still looking at the wall, then turned away from it and looked at me.

"I think I want my life. But I don't know. I don't know what that is. But I *did* want to sit for you."

"I can tell," I said, trying to lighten the conversation, to remove that unsettling tension coming from uncertainty. I smiled, but it was the wrong thing to do. I'd not lightened things but just made light of what she'd said, and her words had been very serious. Her face fell a little, a clear sense of pain and misunderstanding in it, and she looked away from my face. I waited a few moments.

"Dorit," I said, and realized that it was the first time that I had spoken her name to her. I'd even avoided it in those times when we'd been alone together. "I didn't mean to joke. I'm sorry. Come here."

She turned her head back and leaned a little in my direction, her feet still in place, an awkward and painful motion, and I moved without hesitation and took her in my arms in brief embrace. I felt her hair cover the whole side of my face, the small loop of her earring hit my lips. My hand came to the quick rise of her hip near her long thin waist. I gripped her there firmly, and then we separated.

Her eyes were even more watery than before. Her pupils seemed to be fighting for focus. She was looking at me, but I could read nothing decisive at all in her expression. It was not anxious or even sad. Certainly it was not desperate, and it struck me that she found herself in situations like this often, circumstances in which she simply didn't know what she felt, or even how to feel, and that she had learned to adjust to the discomfort that this brought her, had found a feeble way to slightly disassociate herself from even having feelings about her uncertainty. It didn't work for long. She was back again in a few moments, her eyes finding the distance, her face expressive now and in pain.

"We do have a few days still," I said. "If you could come to my studio, I could at least take a few photographs. It isn't the same. But I could work from them, and it would be something at least."

She didn't hesitate at all this time. "Oh, yes!" she said. "That *would* be something. Wouldn't it?"

We went back to the larger room and the party then. Dorit was excited, a little impetuous, but in a few moments I saw her face change, and when I looked where she was looking I saw Janes. He was standing alone at the far side of the room, and I thought he had seen us enter. But he made no sign, and soon his head turned and he moved to conversation with a couple who were standing near him. We parted then, she turning back after she had moved a few feet away from me, smiling brightly.

I went around the room then and entered into conversation with the others that I knew. I had a brief talk with Vas Dias. Bayard and I chatted. I saw Susan watching me from a distance at one point, but I was unable to disengage myself at the time, to get to where she was and speak with her. She had a strange look on her face, and I guessed that she too had seen Dorit and me enter into the room.

In a while the party began to wind down. The crowd thinned a little, and there were people standing near the doorway, chatting, holding their coats over their arms. I myself was ready to leave, when I spotted Dorit and Mark standing alone across the room from me. They were faced toward each other, but they didn't seem to be talking. Soon Dorit turned her face away, looking at the remaining clusters of people. Her eyes found me in a while, and I saw her lift her hand from her side in tentative gesture. Janes was looking at me too then. I started to move toward them, feeling it would be awkward to turn away. Then I saw the gallery owner approaching them from the side. I pulled up then, and when he reached them and engaged them I turned away.

So that is my brief story, longer in fact than I suspected it would be as I started writing. Any letters in the months between this and my last one would have been a bore. There has been nothing in my mind really but my work, the details of it, how to solve this problem or that one, and I've been so immersed in it that I couldn't have written at any rate.

Maybe there will be more paintings under way soon, though even with the promise of Dorit photographs it's hard for me to think so. Just that matter of feeling I've drained myself completely with this last one. But then I've been here before. That exhaustion after birth, though I hesitate to push *that* metaphor.

Until my next letter then.

Love,
Edward

I MET A SWISS LANDSCAPE architect once, when we were together at a conference in San Francisco. I had an interest in what he was doing, expansive things that went against the grain of current concerns. He did gardens like those you could still find preserved on estates in the British countryside, eighteenth-century affairs in which nature seemed allowed to run its course. It was a philosophical matter then, but it was not that way with him. His had more conscious art in it, attempts to recover the violence in such growth and through it a kind of beauty.

But as a person, he was unlike the drawings and colored sketches he showed me. A large man, Germanic looking and slightly awkward, romantic, very gentle. We ate somewhere near the Esplanade, and he took great pleasure in his crab and lush California salad—avocado everywhere, crisp varieties of lettuce, and artichoke.

"We eat very good in Switzerland," I remember him saying. "But we don't eat exactly like this." He had a bright glow in his eyes, watery whites and his pupils blue and shining.

And he told me a story, for no other reason, I think, than that it was fresh in his mind and that he was still moved by it. We'd had a few drinks and we had eaten late. It was after a particularly good seminar on golf course landscaping and how problems faced and handled there could have application in other settings. It had solved some things for both of us, or at least had suggested some solutions, and we were both feeling up and very loose after it.

The story was about his father, who had had his eightieth birthday just a few months before, and how he, Hans Jurg, a man in his late thirties, had made a plan for a trip with his father, just the two of them, ten days driving through the Swiss countryside and into Germany and Belgium.

When it came time to set out, his father was not all that well, had come down with a slight flu and was a little weak. But they went anyway, stopping at times for more than a night at small inns so that his father could rest on the porches or stay in bed late, in order to get his strength back. And when they did stay longer than a night, Hans Jurg would spend some time exploring alone, keeping his own counsel and pondering what it meant to him to have this opportunity of time alone with his father.

His father didn't talk much, but that didn't matter, not to either of them. It was enough to share things, dinner, tea in the evenings, time spent together at some church or ruin near a lake. His father was a small man, a retired professional of some sort, as I remember, and rather frail. He'd been wiry, tough, and athletic in his youth, and I remember Hans Jurg saying that the loss of his strength bothered him and that the way he handled that bother was to dress tightly and very formally, to avoid situations in which his weakness would be apparent, and to hold himself erect, which took some effort.

"He always wore his hat square on his head. He remained—a little too much, I believe—very within himself."

And halfway through the span of their journey, on a rainy afternoon, they came to a country inn that had nothing available for them but a room with a double bed. This would have been no problem for either of them, but his father had slept fitfully the night before and they had had too busy a day of traveling and sightseeing, and his father was quite tired. But there was no alternative, and after Hans Jurg had seen his father to bed at seven in the evening, he went to the inn's common room, smoked, drank hot tea, and looked through the local paper. He was tired too though, and shortly after ten o'clock he himself retired. The bed was big enough, his father was quite small and sleeping near the edge of it, and Hans Jurg was able to slip in and settle himself without disturbing him.

Then, in the night, at a time he wasn't sure of, he was brought awake by a sound and by something touching him. He remembered turning as he came to his senses, feeling his father's hand slip from where it had rested on his shoulder, hearing his father speaking words that were indistinguishable in some dream but were clearly words.

He thought to reach out to his father, to shake him gently and rouse him from his dreaming, but he didn't do so. There was nothing anxious in the words at all. It couldn't be a bad dream. And so he remained still and silent. His father was facing him from across the bed, his arm extended out above the cover just inches from Hans Jurg's body. The fingers flexed once, taking in a loose handful of blanket. The words began to come more intermittently, and when they stopped he heard his father breathe deeply, then exhale in a low humming snore as he slipped back into deeper sleep. He could see his eyelids flutter in the faint light, his nostrils flare out a little and then settle. He watched his father's face for a long time, and the more he looked at it the more his eyes became accustomed to the dark, until he could see it quite distinctly. A rosiness had risen in his cheeks, a healthier color than had been there for the past few days of their trip, and Hans Jurg felt an edge of anxiety leave him that he had not known he'd been carrying. There even seemed a slight smile on his father's thin lips, and the deep creases at the corners of his eyes were in repose. In a while, Hans Jurg felt his own eyes closing, but he didn't turn away. He fell asleep facing his father in the bed.

They finished their trip without further incident, always managing to find lodgings in which they had separate rooms. His father's health seemed to come back to him, increasingly, after the night they slept together. When they reached home again and parted, they shook hands formally at his father's door. His mother was not in but had left a note and food on the table.

It was the following Sunday, two days later, that he went to his parents' house for dinner. His wife was with him, and they chatted about their trip, things seen and done.

"You know," his father said at one point, "I had the strangest experience one night. It was a dream. That night we shared the bed, you remember, Hans Jurg? Well, I dreamed I was sleeping with my wife here, your mother, and we couldn't get to sleep and were lying awake talking. It was a very long conversation, very detailed, and at one point in it I was moved to reach across to you, Mother, and touch you, to say something. I didn't know at all just what I was going to say, but when I touched your shoulder I just said, 'I love you,' and then we just went on with our quiet conversation, as if I had not said it, as if it was nothing special to say at all. I remember too that I was smiling, and though in the dream I could not see your face clearly in the bed across from me, I somehow knew that you were smiling too.

"And that was all of the dream. But then I woke up. It was still dark. I didn't know the time or where I was at first, but there was Hans Jurg in the bed across from me, and his posture as he lay facing me was exactly your posture, Mother, in the dream. For a moment I was confused, not sure just who this was I was sleeping with. The posture was really exactly the same as in the dream, and it took me a few moments to know it was Hans Jurg and not you."

I remembered Hans Jurg and his story, the conference and those few bright days in San Francisco, as I drove the miles in Aunt Waverly's car to Riverside. Hans Jurg had said that the point of the story was not in the dream but in the talk of it afterward. Never had his father spoken such intimate words in his presence, not before the trip and not since, either. He'd come to think of the dream as a kind of positioning, an accidental one, so fortunate, in which his father had found a place where he could speak, could say the things he really felt, have them out in a story about a dream, a place that was unaccounted for, without apparent cause, only something to be wondered about as an interesting experience.

California seemed strangely in the past now, even though it had been less than a week since I'd left. I was constantly coming back in my mind to Chen and the job, surprised that I had almost forgotten about them. And I was sure Hans Jurg and his story came back to me, as the woman's shadow figure in the window across

from Waverly's kitchen had moved me, because I had entered back
into the place of memories that I had thought were behind me. But
it was not only the physical reminders, the park where I had played
as a child, my own old house, so close to Waverly's. It was my aunt
herself, the way my mother seemed embodied in her, and it was
Edward too, for though he was dead he was coming alive again for
me, his letters and now the paintings filling what I had thought
could only remain an absence in those years since I had last seen
him. He was never a vivid and rounded presence even then, more
a kind of vague power and influence, and I couldn't be sure how
much of what I now held of him was something new. Still, it was
as if the thread that had been violently broken with my parents'
death and with my leaving was spinning out again, making that
web to span the distance of twenty-seven years and thereby reach
to connect me to a kind of continuity, a complex linking up of what
had been and what now was.

But I had not returned to my parents yet, only that shadow figure
as reminder of my mother. I could only vaguely remember my
father in his garden, and I had not really looked across to that other
backyard in order to evoke him. He had taken great pride in his
vegetables. A gentle man, I thought, softer than the image I had of
Hans Jurg's father. The matrix that the thread reached back into
seemed closed around Aunt Waverly, the only place, with Edward
dead, where the past could literally live, and in her vibrancy I was
somehow stopped from moving back beyond her presence.

But what of Angela, I thought. What could the matrix be for her?
That could take me farther back, even to the place of those snapshots Aunt Waverly had given to me so quickly after my arrival in
Congress Park again. Once past the shock of seeing it, I knew that
Find Angela was almost an order, or at least that I was bound to
take it as such. What it might have meant to Uncle Edward when
he made the painting, or touched the message in later, still remained to be discovered.

The curator from Downers Grove had arrived promptly at two in
the afternoon in an oversized van, a helper in coveralls with him.
He was younger than I would have thought, perhaps thirty-five,
friendly, but very workmanlike and serious when he saw the boxes
of paintings. I gave him Uncle Edward's list, and though he studied
it, he made one of his own, in a careful hand, checking stretchers
and canvas surfaces as he moved slowly through what was there.

Two of the paintings had shallow cracks at their corners, faint white lines of canvas showing through, and he showed them to me, making notes of their condition beside the names and numbers on his list.

It took him close to an hour to go through and recrate the paintings, and when he was finished he helped and guided the other man in loading the crates into the truck. I walked outside with them and watched as they carefully roped the crates securely against the foam rubber that lined the van's interior walls. The curator then had his helper wait beside the truck and went back with me to Uncle Edward's study, where he sat at the desk and wrote down his museum hours on the back of his calling card. He'd brought a contract with him, and making his list of paintings he'd used a carbon. He signed both of them, then watched as I did the same, handing me a copy of each document before he left. I told him I might be over tomorrow or the next day.

Riverside was an old and wealthy community, the flavor of which I recaptured immediately as I passed over the bridge crossing the Des Plaines River from Lyons and entered its winding streets. I'd driven a grocery truck for a small German meat market on the Lyons side of the river when I was in high school, and all our delivery business was to these large and sprawling brick and frame houses, to maids in white uniforms in back kitchens. The streets were a rich maze of turns and circles, and though the houses were close together, there were large old trees and hedges, and each seemed off in a private world of its own.

The house I was looking for I found with very little trouble, surprised a little at my memory of the various twisting streets and dead ends. The place was deep into the community, in a section of it that contained more modest dwellings than those with a view of the river. It was a dark brick building, two story but so broad and heavy that it looked like one. A long drive ran at its side, passing the house and ending at a large three-car garage to its rear. The dwelling was fronted by an ample brick porch, with overhanging eaves and brick pillars, and when I parked in front and got out of the car I could see brackets for screens on the porch's wide stone railings and along its vertical supports.

She was waiting at the door when I got there. I saw it open a little as I walked up the deep brick side steps from the drive, and she came out, small and lean as I remembered her, in a lightweight tailored suit, the jacket unbuttoned, showing the fabric and cut of the rather severe tan shirt that she wore under it. I thought her hair had been recently cut, tight around her head, even shorter than it had been at the cemetery. Her brows were rather thick, and her mouth had a slight natural pout to it. High cheekbones and broad, placid forehead. She was quite beautiful, actually. She seemed in very good shape, and the cut of her skirt and her fine burgundy heels showed off her narrow ankles and firm calves. I thought she must be a businesswoman of some sort. She was close to fifty, but she had the body of someone not yet forty.

"You've come," she said. "Right on time. Come in."

I followed her into a deep quiet living room, light flooding in from both the porch behind us and a graceful row of windows at the rear of the house, beyond the large archway that led into a dining room. The two had been separate rooms at one time, but they'd been opened to each other, creating a large living space. It was close to the beginning of dusk, and the sun was sinking, but the windows were old leaded glass, and the light was softened as it passed through their wavy surfaces. Two floor lamps had been turned on. There were soft shadows spreading across rich Oriental carpets, deeper ones cast by wing chairs and dark tables.

"I used to deliver groceries here," I said.

She had excused herself for a moment, then returned pushing a small glass-and-copper cart with liquor bottles on the bottom shelf, a variety of glasses on the top.

"Here? To this house?" she said.

"No, not here. But in Riverside. A house a couple of doors down, I think. But that was a long time ago, almost thirty years."

"I wasn't here." She handed me a glass of bourbon. "I must have been in Madison then."

I heard sounds from the rear of the house, from what I guessed was the kitchen, then the whisper of a door. Another woman came into the dining room, and I pushed on the padded chair arms to get to my feet. Her hands came up as she moved toward us, motioning for me to stay put.

"Oh, that's all right," she said. "I'll just be a minute."

She was taller than Joan, but just as lean, a little younger, I thought, her hair long and blond. She was wearing old, worn Levi's and a blue shirt and slippers. She crossed in front of me and moved to Joan's chair.

"Excuse me," she said. "Is it four fifty?"

"No, five hundred," Joan said. "Then, when the timer goes off, you shut it off completely and let it sit. But wait. Let me introduce you."

When the woman, whose name was Marilyn, was gone, Joan and I settled back in and sipped from our drinks. We were each waiting for the other to begin, but we were in no hurry. It was cool and pleasant in the half-dark room, and I could hear no sounds from the street at all.

"You knew Dorit," I said.

"Yes," she said, her glass clicking against the table as she set it down. "When I was abroad. I was involved with a painter then. We were in the same circle. Not the same circle actually, but the same when it came to art. And involved isn't right either. He was gay, you see. We more or less escorted each other. In those days, even in the art world, in London at least, things weren't all that open. I knew Mark as well. But Dorit better."

Her last sentence was a little tentative. She had quickly given me a lot of information, and now she seemed to want to hold back a little. There was a lilt in her voice, which, like her body, seemed younger than it ought to have been. But a quick certainty too. It was as if she spoke in the way a woman of her age ought to speak, knew what that sounded like and did it, but behind it was a toughness and a smartness, a worldliness that let me know that there was really no coy nonsense about her. She wanted me to know this. It was the way her expression often ran aslant of her speech. A way of letting me know that she was making constructions that were far more whimsical than she herself was.

"I've read about you," I said. "At parties."

This brought her up a little, but just slightly and for a moment. Her face clouded, then cleared again.

"There were letters, then," she said. "I do remember him writing them. Actually, Dorit told me. His wife kept them? All of them?"

"All but the first few."

"Well, that's why I wanted to see you, actually." She had a way of turning her glass while she spoke, just enough to get the ice cubes to rotate. They caught the remaining sun, blinking faintly, spots of light at times on her cheeks and arms.

"Not the letters specifically. But whatever information." She put the glass on the rosewood end table beside her chair.

"You see, Dorit and I had a brief thing in London. Just before she left. I thought, when she came back, it might continue. But then she moved in with Edward."

It came at me very fast, information that got ahead of what I knew of his life so far in the letters. In a way I didn't want to hear it, wanted control of the pace, more leisurely, as I'd been having it.

"Moved in with him?"

"That's right. She came back in six months. They'd separated, and she'd found a job as a copy editor or something. She seemed to go straight to him. Initially for the painting, I guess. At least that's what she said. At the time. I saw her once at the Bayards', tried to get started with her again."

"When was all this?"

"Well, not all that long ago, actually. Let's see." She tipped her chin up slightly, looked into a dark corner of the room. "Late '75. And early into the next year. I came back here in '76. Only six years ago! My, it does seem longer than that."

"But why do you think they broke up? Was it you?"

"You mean Mark and Dorit. I would have liked to think it was me. Then, at least. I probably did think that a little. But no, it wasn't that. And I don't think there were other women either, except for Susan. It was a different kind of time then, and I'm not actually sure what Mark's feeling about such things might have been. He *was* possessive, even controlling. I wouldn't see it as experimentation either. Something deeper than just sex. She was desperate for something. I don't really know what it was."

"Do you mean Susan Harwood?" I remembered things in the letters.

"Oh, yes," she said. "They kept it very secret though, and it was only a few times, I think. Once Dorit told me, I could see it in her. Susan, I mean. It was before us. Quite a while before, even before they moved to London, during their visits there. *That* may have been experimentation. And Mark knew about it, Dorit told me, at least about the first time. I don't know if he found out that it continued for a while. I think it bothered Susan more than Dorit."

"What is it you want from me?" I said.

"Actually, I don't know." She lifted her drink again, held it, rotated what was left of the melted ice, sipped from it, and put it back down on the table. "What I want to know is what happened to her, what it was like with Edward, where she went after that.

You know, actually, I fell in love with her. It was infatuation, that's sure, but I still think of her. She was mysterious. There were things about her that I need to know. I have a need to know." She laughed lightly. "Isn't that the way they say it?"

"I haven't gotten that far," I said. "In the letters, I mean. But maybe there is something there. The letters stopped coming in '77 though, only a year or so after you left."

"Oh," she said. "But it may be an important year. You know, I did write once or twice. To Muswell Hill. But there was no response."

"Do you think that's odd?"

"I don't know. We were never on bad terms, I mean afterward. I may have been a little starry-eyed, but I wasn't pushy. I would have thought she might have written."

"Do you know anything at all about a tattoo? A little figured circle?"

She had lifted her glass again and looked into it, and when she heard my question she almost dropped it.

"My God!" she said. "How in the world! How did you know that? Yes, yes. Deep in her thigh, and when she spread her legs . . . " She caught herself and looked away, and I could see the deep blush rising in her cheeks. I too was unsettled and spoke quickly again.

"On *him*," I said. "Edward. It's in one of the letters. I mean a drawing of it."

"Oh. Oh, no," she said. "Could it be the same one? I'd certainly like to see that."

We were both quickly energized and shocked, and neither of us spoke for a few moments. I lifted my own glass and drank from it, the bourbon warm now, and she saw me and got up and took my glass. Then she turned her back and worked at the cart, and when she handed the fresh drink to me we were both in control again.

"I'll send you a copy," I said. "I can get it copied." She had returned to her chair, sat down again, and crossed her legs.

"Mark had seen to her getting it," she said. "I don't know what it was about, though I think it came when she was involved with Susan. But it could have been just a lovers' thing. I think Dorit knew, but she wouldn't speak about it. And he too had it?"

"Yes. Up behind his ear. He said his hair covered it. But we can't be sure it was the same, can we?"

"Not until I see it," she said. "I'll remember."

We sat silently for a few long moments, trailing our own thoughts out of the room and to other times and places. It was quiet beyond the room still, then I heard a faint sound, something hitting against metal from the kitchen.

"What more can you tell me?" I said. "About her and Edward, about anything."

"Well, I can tell you how it was for the two of them—Mark and Dorit, I mean. Really, I can't tell you a lot about Edward. I knew his paintings. They were strange; very beautiful, I think."

"Go on," I said.

"Well, Edward had a very dark side. At least I saw him that way. Not a dangerous side, but as if he had a very separate and private life, one that there was no possibility of entering. I've known painters who have had that. But his seemed more intractable and secret than the others'. I don't think it had all that much to do with his age, though he did seem to see himself as a late starter, you know. And that clearly bothered him. He was really so much older than the others.

"Then, too, I saw Dorit after they were living together, but I couldn't get a thing out of her about what that was like. I *do* know that living with him hadn't cured her, if that's the actual word for it. She remained as she was before that, uncertain and a little disconnected. So I can't really tell you much more about Edward. He seemed kind enough. Certainly he was serious about things. It was no simple lustful older-man business, I don't think. It was more complex than that between them."

"What about Mark, then? You were going to tell me about that."

She was about to speak, when I heard the faint call from the kitchen. She got up then and excused herself.

The sun was almost completely gone now, and as it faded, the lights in the room seemed to grow brighter, casting broad circular shafts on the carpets and the chair arms. I could hear muffled talking from somewhere in the rear of the house. Then I heard her steps, the door opening, and she came back again and went to her chair and sat down. She took a cigarette from a silver case on one of the low veneer tables, lit it, then caught herself and offered me one. I shook my head and waited for her to settle in. She drew at the cigarette, looked at it and put it in the ashtray.

"It started a good year before they left London for California. At least that's when I began to notice it. I'd been watching them closely, interested in Dorit as I was. And I was seeing them often too, mostly at parties but at times for dinner. Mark was seriously interested in the work of Vas Dias, my artist friend, and there were many circumstances in which we were together. Dorit was not really as interested as Mark was, though I think she had started out that way. But she had a different taste now, one that of course ran finally to Edward. Maybe it was the strangeness of his work that drew her, or maybe just some mild vanity in his initial interest in painting her. I'm not sure.

"At any rate, it wasn't too different from circumstances I had seen before, actually, things we've all seen before, I guess. I began to notice that he was responding to superficial things in her, behaviors that bothered him or at least, in the beginning, began to make him feel a little uncomfortable. It may have been repetitions in her talk, subjects about which she tended to use the same verbal constructions, vocabulary he saw as not earned but as borrowed artifice. Actually, I'm sure it was also things in her way of movement, because I clearly saw his growing reactions to them. She always moved with a kind of uncertainty, even made the smallest gesture with it, and to me this was very clearly a part of her character, deep-seated and fundamental. But for him I think it slowly became mannerism, even something she did consciously and on purpose, to put a certain face before the world.

"I've always thought, and I still think, that something actually very simple to observe, but quite interesting at the same time, happens in such circumstances. It's really that he simply fell out of love with her and then became desperately enraged, as if it were her fault, as if it were she who had caused his loss. What's interesting is to see it happen as a spatial matter, what the many effects can be, and to wonder how it happens exactly, what actually comes first.

"It was as if he'd gotten some physical distance from her, had pulled back in the way a camera might, and once he got that far away there was no real chance of returning, moving close again. The things he saw, the ones that I saw caused him to look slightly away or press his lips together and narrow his eyes, were things on the outside of her now. They may have been just manifestations of who she was before he'd moved back, but now they were surfaces, as if a costume and a script of set lines, a barrier preventing him from seeing the person who was behind them. And all this seemed the beginning of a kind of transformation, a kind of shift and turn of focus.

"In the first few times that I noticed, his expression and movements had an edge of desperation in them. He would interrupt her, take her arm too quickly, before, in her profound uncertainty, she was actually ready to move. I thought it was that he felt he could strip these seeming superficialities away now that he saw them, was bothered by them for the first time. This didn't work, of course. It only had a way of exaggerating what was bothering him, because he was calling attention in himself to it.

"Then after a while his desperation seemed to leave him. He pulled back from her even more, became rather cold, almost objectively observant. I think it was somewhere in that pulling back that he both lost his love for her and regretted it, and came to blame and resent her for the loss as well. What might have been love changed to anger, from loss of possession. Maybe the two, love and possession, were always joined with him. I think that's true, but I can't presume to know it.

"I could tell that she felt this pulling back and its attendant change in their relationship, that it made her nervous, and that her way of handling this nervousness was to guard herself, and the only way she had of doing that was to avoid decision, to move even farther back behind those things she sensed he was watching. And so the things that had bothered him became more exaggerated, actually *did* become mannerisms much of the time, but mannerisms that were manifestations, a little larger than life, of who she actually was.

"Then finally I could see that being bothered shifted to a kind of straightforward dislike and disengagement. He despaired of either reentry or change. He became almost neutral, accepting. But this acceptance seemed to be a recognition that for him she now *was* the superficialities that he had first noticed in her, that they were an inextricable part of her, and that he was really through with the whole thing. He was through with loving her, with relationship, and this drew him even more into his possessive stand. He needed now to own her, to control that object that was now a shell that had contained her in their way of being together previously.

"Then too there were those of us who noticed it all. Dorit of course noticed, but I don't think she understood it, and I think it's very possible that his removal, in giving her the same vantage on him, may have brought her to the same place where he now was. Oh, I think she did still love him then, but I think too that she was finding things out in him that were a disillusionment for her, sur- faces as well, possibly, ones she probably blamed herself for a little but ones she hadn't known of before. And I think she actually feared, more than came to believe, that they were the real him.

"They *were* both very uncertain people. I really have to stress that. Maybe he was even more uncertain than she. I mean he was probably less aware of himself and the consequences on others of his behavior. He couldn't see his uncertainty and because of that acted as if it weren't there. Very successfully, in fact. But one could see it, in his overinsistence on control, both of himself and of Dorit. She was, as I've said, mysterious, and part of the mystery had to do with the way she lived in her feelings. Not that she was hyster- ical, though at times she was that, but rather that her feelings could have a way of pushing her beyond reason, beyond consideration. A little wild, I guess you could say, instinctual. *Just* a little, and I may exaggerate that. It's the thing, actually, that really drew me to her, and maybe I was a little blinded by it.

"There were those of us who noticed it all happening, saw how their way of being in places together was not the same as it had been, and one of us was Edward. Susan Harwood noticed it. 'What's happening with them?' I remember her asking me once, and I remember her words clearly because of her tone when she spoke them, a little expectant, pleased almost, and I knew which one of them she was after or had been with even before I learned it as a fact from Dorit. I think Caroline Bayard noticed it too. At least I remember her watching them. None of the men noticed anything, except Edward. It was not that he was so perceptive about people, by any means. But he had been infatuated—no, it was more like inappropriately interested—for a long time.

"At any rate, he began to move closer to her. I watched that carefully, but I could see no lust in him. He was close to seventy- five and she was closing on forty. There could have been that. But not then, I don't think. Maybe later. Then it was the way she moved and looked. I think he saw her as a painter saw things, was drawn in deeper by the nexus of exaggeration in her, didn't see it as surface at all. You know his paintings? Something about the inside on the outside. What he was always after in his work.

"Then Dorit and I got together finally. Actually, it was just before she and Mark left London for California, a few weeks before, and in the last week we didn't see each other at all. She was going to Edward's studio then, getting her picture taken."

Through the whole story Joan had been sitting back deep in her chair. The end table was close beside it, and she could reach her drink or light a cigarette without shifting her posture. But her hands had moved, her face had been animated, certain, distanced and very close to the events she told about. As I watched her, heard her, I felt myself doing the same things that Janes had done in her telling. At times she seemed all mannerism, all surface, and I found myself not liking her very much. But this didn't last. The story and its twists and turns held me, and even the noticeable lilt of her voice, the repeated constructions and words, didn't get in the way. After a while I didn't even notice them much. Often the story did not seem like a story at all.

"I don't know what else I can tell you," she said. She had leaned forward now, stretched a little, extended her fingers and ran them slowly back and forth along the chair arms.

"When exactly did you leave?" I asked.

"I think I told you that. In '76, close to the end of the year. They were living together then. In a pretty committed way, I think. They were together earlier, of course, when she came back from California, but then I think she left for just a while, then came back again in earnest." Her hands relaxed, and she settled back in the chair.

"Will you tell me about the letters? If there are any? And send me that tattoo drawing?"

"Yes," I said. "I'll read on when I get back. Or tomorrow. I'll call you."

She nodded. A brief smile started at the corner of her mouth, but it didn't come up.

"But maybe a few more things, if you've got time?" I glanced toward the back of the room, in the direction of the kitchen.

"Oh, that," she said. "It has to sit and cook awhile, after the gas is off. There's time. Marilyn's taking care of it."

"Okay. Well, what about Edward's being from Congress Park, you from Madison and now here?"

"Nothing at all," she said. "Coincidence. Edward and I talked about that, that we had come to London from almost the same place, and near the same time, but just briefly. He kept mistaking it for Milwaukee. He didn't seem to want to get into it, actually. He'd put that life behind him, I guess. What is his wife like?"

"Waverly? She's my aunt. You know, it's hard to be clear. She's seventy-two years old now. A remarkable woman, after all these years."

"Quite a bit younger than him, I guess. But not as young as Dorit."

"When did you last see him?" I said.

"Oh, I can remember that," she said. "I was getting ready to leave. Actually, I mean. I must have even had my tickets. He was getting on toward eighty, I guess. He and Dorit had a party, just a gathering of a few people, out at that place of his in Muswell Hill. I remember it because it was the first and only time I'd been there. I doubt that anyone had before then. I knew it was the last time I'd see her. Actually, he couldn't have been that old. Perhaps seventy-five."

"If it was '76, then he was that old. He was born at the turn of the century."

"I didn't know that," she said, and looked up to a corner of the room again, thinking. "The Harwoods were there, and I'm sure the Bayards too, as I remember. I, and a woman friend of mine, and a few others. Vas Dias was there as well. I remember because I welcomed seeing him. He'd been away, in Greece or somewhere, as I recall. And we'd not been seeing each other much before that either, not for a while at least. As he got up there, his reputation, he didn't need our formal guise. I'd stopped needing it too. I'd come out, you see. Not announcing anything. We didn't do that then, not there. But I was no longer pretending.

"I hadn't seen Dorit or Edward either for quite a while. They kept to themselves. He must have been active in painting her then. It was shortly after their breakup. Well, actually, 'breakup' is too conventional. You know, I think it's even doubtful that they were sleeping together when she first moved in. At any rate, she went back to California and Mark. I saw him once while she was gone. He was quite distracted. But then she came back, moved in again for what seemed a permanent thing. The party was a way of noting that, of being open and public about it. Ostensibly it was for his daughter though. She was staying with them. That was the last time I saw either of them. I left London shortly after that."

"His daughter? Are you sure?"

"Yes. Well, maybe she was his stepdaughter. Is that possible?"

"Was her name Angela?"

"Well, no. Actually. That doesn't come to mind. But it could have been. It's not too clear to me. I remember what she was like though. Not her look, I don't mean, though I think like him, but that her hair wasn't in good shape. Dark, I think. And she was small. Worn or tired, I guess. I don't remember that she had much to say to anyone. Not sullen exactly, but close to that. Maybe just tired. I was watching Dorit, I'm sure you see. Not much time for anyone else." She smiled faintly, remembering.

"Okay," I said. "But she was staying there, with them?"

"That's right. I think that's right. But I never heard anything about her again. I left, of course."

I wanted to ask more. I couldn't really think it had been Angela. Nothing that Joan said was particular enough to go on. And I doubted that asking things further could jog her memory. She'd been very good with memory in our talk, and I thought she was clear about what she remembered right then. And yet I think I knew that it *had* been Angela. She was too sharp to remember that part wrongly.

"How old do you think she might have been?"

"Oh, I can't be sure. But I guess around forty, close to that. Younger than the rest of us, I'd say, except for Dorit, of course. Maybe they were the same age. I seem to remember that, feeling odd. But I can't actually be sure. I really don't know."

That would have been her age then. Both of us, she and I, had been born late to our parents. They were in their thirties when they had us, at least Edward and my father had been. And Joan had said too that she was small.

"Dark hair?" I said.

"Yes, I do remember that."

"Do you keep in touch with anyone at all from those days?"

"No. No one."

"Not your artist friend? The Bayards, Harwoods?"

"Oh, no. That was all past long ago. I too was an artist then, or was trying to be one. God, I tried it for a very long time, almost fifteen years." She spoke a little wistfully, then smiled. "Absolutely no talent at all. Just enough to kid myself. And when I finally made myself discover it, I left. London, the country, everything. All of it behind me. Except Dorit, of course. I couldn't quite shake that. I've been in the stock market since then. Actually, I'd dabbled in it all along. I'm very good with that."

I could see how she would be. She had a very sharp, very mechanical mind. And she had imagination too, but a tough and analytic one.

We were silent for a moment, each of us catching the smell of the roast as it drifted in from the kitchen. She lifted her glass up, now only an inch of amber liquid sloshing as she rotated it, and looked slightly to the right of my head, focusing, I thought, on the wall behind me. There was nothing there but a bookcase, and it was too dark now to see titles on the spines from where she was. I too looked beyond, catching the wave of some dark branches beyond the leaded glass windows. I had one more thing to ask her, but I wanted to be sure to put it the right way, not to frighten or confuse her. And not to imply anything. She'd need an open mind. Just maybe she knew something she didn't know she knew. I, myself, had no conclusions at all, nothing as yet even to begin to fit it in. The smell of the roast was faint, but very rich, too rich somehow for our conversation. I thought I should get to it. She wouldn't be wanting to talk much longer.

"Mmm," she murmured. "It's come out. It'll have to sit now for a few minutes. Could you join us?"

"That's very kind of you," I said. "But no—no, thanks. I have to get back. There's just one more thing though."

"Yes, okay. Another surprise? You seemed surprised by his daughter, if she was that." That faint, quick smile came to her lips again, her brows rising a little.

"It could certainly be." I laughed. "But I wonder for whom."

Her smile broadened, and she shook her head a little, a residual gesture, I realized. She'd recently had longer hair and was still tossing it.

"That's something," she said. "Go on."

"Well, it's just that I wonder. Is there anything at all that you can think of, anything let's say secret or shady. I don't know. Illegal maybe?"

"That *is* a surprise," she said. "But what can you mean? About what?"

"I don't know," I said. "Possibly to do with Edward's painting. Near the end, that is, before you left. Or maybe even something with the two of them, him and Dorit. Just anything."

She looked beyond me again, considering, thinking back. I saw her blink once, scanning, moving through things. She took a long time, taking the question seriously and in a measured way. I had my own answer ready. I was not going to tell her about the two men in the station wagon. Finally she turned her head a little and looked at me again.

"I've been thinking," she said. "You know, I seem to remember that there *was* something. It's just a vague feeling I have. I've thought, but I can't catch it. Nothing illegal. That's not it. But like a secret. Something that might have had to do with his daughter, and at the party. Someone else involved, and I think it had something to do with Dorit too. What could it be? But maybe then it's nothing. The years can play funny tricks, as can such questions."

"I've known that," I said. "But not for a long time."

"Why do you ask?"

"No real reason," I said. "Just something about the letters. I don't know. As you said, maybe it's nothing. Just the past in some way."

"I don't know," she said, tipping her head slightly, thinking back again. "There could just *be* something. Some thing. I just can't get it."

And that was the end of it. Marilyn entered the room, tentatively, just as we finished talking.

"It's ready," she said, a slight question in her voice.

Both of us got to our feet then, stretching a little, moving from leg to leg. I smiled and said goodbye to Marilyn, then put my hand out. Joan took it; her grip, as I expected, was firm and certain. She'd held back nothing, I thought.

"Will you call, if there is anything?" she said. "And send the illustration? I'll keep thinking about your question. We can talk again."

She left me at the door, and when I reached the car and had gotten into it, I looked back under the overhanging eaves. I thought she was still standing there in the doorway, but it was dark now, and I couldn't be sure.

It was under a half hour's drive back to Congress Park and Aunt Waverly's house, but I decided to take a long way around, to wind through the streets of Riverside and Lyons looking for houses where I had delivered groceries. There was plenty to think about.

I hadn't told Aunt Waverly about the two men in the station wagon, and now there was other information, far more important, that I felt I'd have to keep to myself as well, at least for a while. What good could it do to tell her about Angela, even though it had not been all that long ago in London. I couldn't even be certain that it had been she. Joan wasn't really sure. And yet I knew it was she and knew also that I had no real right to keep the information from my aunt. And it was possible too that Waverly might know something, something that she didn't know she knew, and that telling her what Joan had said could open that up, give her a way to the information I needed. I didn't know what I needed, but I was stuck and surely needed something. I felt that time had stopped somehow. I'd been there almost a week, had been busy with the letters and the paintings, had looked over bills and bank statements. Still, I'd accomplished close to nothing. At least I felt that way. And it was time too to be getting back to California, to Chen and the project we were involved with. I'd better call him again, I thought, and couldn't remember just when it was that I'd last spoken to him.

I moved past large set-back houses with long driveways and heavy old trees reaching their limbs out over well-kept yards. I even pulled up in front of a few of them, picking up vague details. But I couldn't get myself into that grocery boy past of mine just then. It was this other past that had me. So I left off, drove back to Ogden Avenue, and headed west.

Aunt Waverly was below the front steps, to the side of the porch, when I drove up. It was quite dark now, but she had the porch light on, and I could see her clearly as she poked among the hedge of bushes below the front windows. She heard me close the car door, rose up from her bending, and put her hands at the small of her back and stretched, then she raised her right arm and waved. She had her robe and slippers on. I checked my watch. It was nine o'clock. She waited until I came up the walk before speaking.

"It's a damn squirrel," she said. "I had the door open, and I heard him. He's got a cache or something. Nuts, I suppose. I wish they'd stay in the damn trees."

"He might bite you," I said.

"Oh, Jack! Don't be silly. It's a squirrel!"

"Nevertheless," I said, and she looked quickly at me, saw my smile, and began laughing. I laughed with her, then moved over to the bush she'd been poking up under and squatted down. It was dark under the bush, though the porch light lit the tips of its upper branches. I felt around tentatively, until my fingers hit something. I closed my hand on the objects and brought them out. They were three nuts, pieces of earth and leaves stuck to them. I held them in my palm and showed them to her.

"Dig around a little more, will you?"

"Right," I said, and squatted back down again, Waverly standing behnd me, leaning over my shoulder.

"Get up under there good. They like to twist the branches around, make a little pocket, then dig a shallow hole."

I found the place she meant, a gnarled nestlike thing, a small indentation in the ground under it, and dug a little with my fingers. Just under the surface were more nuts. I brought them out, piling them on the grass at Waverly's feet. In the fourth handful, I felt something scrape the pad of my thumb. It was not nutlike, and when I brought my hand out, I stood up beside Waverly, where the light was better. I had two nuts, but something else, something shiny.

"What is it?" she said.

"I don't know."

I moved toward the porch, and we looked again. It was a child's ring, a small little thing, just a metal band with a glass stone, slightly greenish, round and like a pupil.

"Oh, those buggers will grab anything!" she said. "Probably belongs to a child in the neighborhood, but who knows? I'll ask around tomorrow. We look for squirrels, then nuts, then we find such a thing as this. Those sneaky little buggers. Could you mess the nest around a little, Jack? Really, I wouldn't mind, but they can make such a racket in the night."

I went back and reached up under the bush and ran my fingers like a rake through the twists and gnarls. Some were quite tight, almost woven, and I had trouble separating them. But I got it good enough in a few minutes, and then we went into the house, Waverly closing the door and throwing the light switch beside it.

"Have you eaten, Jack?" she said.

"Well, no, actually, I haven't."

"Well, I didn't wait," she said. "I was out most of the day, a little tired, and I felt I shouldn't. There's cold cuts in the refrigerator, if that's all right."

"Of course it is," I said. "I'm not very hungry."

I went to the kitchen and made myself a sandwich. There were a few beers left in the refrigerator, cold to the touch, and I opened one. Before I sat down, I went to Uncle Edward's study and got a pad and pencil. The stack of letters was still resting on the desk where I'd left it. But the room felt empty with the paintings gone.

Back in the kitchen, I sat down and started the sandwich and beer and made some notes. I could hear Aunt Waverly in the living room. She was listening to the radio in the dark. It was turned down low, but I could hear faint laughter, the voice of Jack Benny, I thought. One of those old-time radio shows. I looked up, across to the kitchen window. I could just see the top half of the window in my old house across from it. The light behind the drawn shade there was dim, and I could see no shadows behind it.

My list was brief, but each item struck me with its possibilities: call Chen, try Susan Harwood and the Bayards, contact Angela's husband, copy tattoo for Joan, call McHale. Then I got up and went to the front door. It was dark in the living room as I passed it, only the faint light of the radio dial visible. I thought I heard a quiet snoring. Aunt Waverly was asleep in her chair. I opened the door quietly, closing it with the same care behind me.

A light breeze had come up. It was a warm night and a little humid, and the moving air felt good as it stirred the hair on my arms. The stars had come out, lighting the walkway, the car, and the park beyond it. I moved to the side of the car and looked into the park, the same one that I had played in as a child, but the stars were too bright for me to imagine the vanished plaque in some darkness, the other configurations, of flowers and shrubs, that I remembered.

Halfway up the walk to the house, I paused, hearing something. There was a slight rustle in the higher branches of a tree near the porch of my old house across the way. My parents had sat on that porch in the summer. I could almost see them in their chairs, enjoying the warm summer night, the shadows of the now gone elms just a few yards away. Then I heard the sound again and looked to my right. The bush near Aunt Waverly's steps was shaking slightly, the tips of the upper branches quivering where the starlight touched them. The little bugger's back again, I thought.

I GOT UP AT SEVEN IN the morning and went down-stairs. Aunt Waverly was nowhere in evidence, but there was a pot of coffee over a low flame on the stove. I poured a cup, then pulled a kitchen chair out and sat down. It was Wednesday, a full week now since I had left California. It felt like a much longer time, and still I wasn't finished here and wouldn't be for a few more days. I'll call Chen as early as seems reasonable, I thought. Try London too, and see if I can get that copy made for Joan.

I was lifting my cup for a sip of hot coffee when I heard some-thing, a rustling or shaking, then the scrape of metal below me, then a dull clunk. I got up, taking my cup with me, and went to the basement door, opened it and called down. Her answer was muffled and far away. I moved to the foot of the steps and saw Waverly, back in a far corner of the room. She was bending over something, her back to me.

"Hey, what's up?" I said when I'd reached her. She was rummaging around in a wooden box that she'd clearly gotten from a pile of boxes that were stacked beside the old, unused cistern. She'd lugged it to the surface of the workbench. It was cool in the basement and a little damp.

"Oh, nothing," she said. "I couldn't sleep after five, so I decided to get started on this place."

Started with what? I wondered. She had turned to face me and was wiping her hands on a white rag.

"You know, I never really did get into this. Oh, I had some junk hauled away, some of Angela's old broken toys and such, but mostly this stuff's been down here for twenty years or more. Look at these tools of Edward's. They're all rusted up."

There really isn't much down here, I thought. The place was dusty, but even after all this time there was a certain order: things in boxes, screws and nails in jars affixed above the workbench. Both Edward and Waverly had been orderly people. Most of the floor was empty of objects. She had a few boxes, six or so, gathered on the workbench around her.

"But look at this," she said. "I seem to remember this." She reached the object out to me. There was a smile on her face.

"Lord, yes," I said. "I remember too. How in the world did it get down here?"

It was an old worn fielder's mitt, moldy, but when I lifted it to my nose I could still smell the neat's-foot oil in the pocket. I thought I remembered losing it one summer. It came back to me as I held it that it had been a hard loss.

"I found this too," she said.

What she held in her hands now was a smaller, more solid object, something I didn't recognize immediately, even when she handed it to me. It was a small box, wooden and square, and with a convex enameled cover. I took it into the light of the bare bulb above the workbench, wet my finger, and rubbed the dust and dirt from the surface. The cover held a little picture, a seascape with a house on a promontory, a sliver of sandy beach, high waves breaking over rocks along the shoreline. It could have been California, but the house had a European flavor to it. I thought there were lights in the windows, though the scene was of a sunny day. It was Angela's. I recognized it, and with the recognition came back memories of the two of us sitting up in her room, showing each other our possessions and talking secretly about our plans for the future. We had been no more than seven years old.

I prized the lid away. It was stuck down, and I had to work a fingernail into the crack to get it open. Inside were a small key chain, a metal pig, an Indian penny, two miniature soldiers, and a bull's-eye mib. I remembered each of the objects. They had been mine. The box had been Angela's though.

"I don't remember any of this," Waverly said.

"Who knows," I said. "It's been a long time." But she must have taken them, I thought. I could not remember losing all of them, but was stirred by the penny and the mib. Both had been favorites. She took them and had squirreled them away for some reason. It was hard to figure, but I couldn't help thinking that it might have something to do with her leaving. Something could have been going on with her even then, something to give a hint of her eventual leaving and what would become of her. I thought it might be time to tell Aunt Waverly of the possibility of her having been in London with Edward just six years ago. But I held my peace. It might be too long ago now to make any difference. I wanted to read at least another letter first, to find out if he had written anything about their daughter.

"Doesn't this bother you? Going through all this old stuff?"

"I wanted to see if it would, I guess. I felt good, even though I couldn't sleep anymore. So I thought I'd give it a try. At any rate, it's about time I cleared things out. But no, it's not bothering me all that much, I guess." She smiled and flushed a little. "Well, most of it anyway."

I thought she might go on, but she didn't. She just continued to rub her hands absently with the rag. Then in a few moments she looked up at me, her eyes bright and a little moist.

"I'm glad you came, Jack."

Later, after breakfast, Aunt Waverly returned to the basement and I got a pad and pencil and began making calls. It was nine o'clock when I started, and though I was at it until past eleven, I had little luck.

I tried Joan first, on the chance that she might have remembered something, but there was no answer. I didn't really expect one. It was a workday, and both she and Marilyn struck me as people who would be up and out early.

There were plenty of Bayards and Harwoods in London, but there was nothing near the square that Uncle Edward had mentioned in his letter, and no doctors or lawyers listed under either name. And there were too many listings for me to try calling all of them.

I tried Saint Bartholomew's Hospital in London and found that Bayard had indeed worked out of there. He'd died three years before, and the woman I spoke to could give me no information about his wife. At first I thought she had information but was holding it back. Something to do with propriety. But as I talked with her, it became clear that she would be as helpful as she could. She just didn't know anything. I asked her about Mark Janes, if there was any record of his being there. She found his name in an old directory, but she could find nothing in the way of a current address. Then I gave her the name of the doctor who had signed Edward's death certificate. I had to wait while she checked it. It took her a long time, but when she came back on the line she said she'd found him. He was not staff but did some medical work out of the place, though not really too much. She'd been unable to find a record of Uncle Edward's death. That wasn't odd, she said. It was recent and could be waiting still to be filed. If I could call back in a week or so.

Then I got information again and tried for Uncle Edward's number in Muswell Hill. There was no current listing. That was curious, and I pressed the operator, finally reaching her supervisor, a young man who did what he could, finding an old listing for Uncle Edward at that address. He said I should try the business office if I needed to pin things down to exact dates. They should have the proper records. I tried that and learned that the phone had been disconnected in '77, close to five years before. I pressed on, trying for Dorit's name and Angela's. They had nothing current for either, though an old one for Mark and Dorit, under his name only. I managed to get the current number for the Muswell Hill address and gave it a try. It rang for a long time, and I was ready to hang up when someone answered, a man with a thick accent, not British. He'd lived there for six months, but he knew the place had turned over a lot in the past few years. He didn't recognize Uncle Edward's name when I mentioned it.

When I was finished I went to Uncle Edward's study and looked over the death certificate and the doctor's letter. He'd died in London, that was sure, and there was specific mention of the Muswell Hill address. I checked the return addresses on the cartons containing the papers. The address was there as well, printed in carefully on each of them.

I went back to the kitchen then. It was after eight in California by that time, late enough to call Chen.

"It's taking longer than I thought," I said. "But surely by the first of next week at the latest, maybe even Sunday if I can make it."

"Is it because of trouble?" He sounded much stronger than when I had last spoken with him, and I felt my spirits rising.

"There *is* that," I said. "Some bits of confusion at least. But no. It's really just the details. Things I don't know about yet. I've never done anything like this before."

"You'll get it done. Everything's going along good here."

"What about our schedule?"

"Yes, yes, yes," he said. "Donny and Benitez, what a pair! Donny's running back and forth. Keeping the nephews going too. And Benitez comes almost every day. We go over things in the evening."

"How about your bones?"

"Not so old, these bones," he said. "It's healing pretty quick. They've got me in a chair and figure I can get to crutches pretty soon. Most of the swelling's gone. Maybe one Zapata scar is all. Shouldn't be too bad really."

"You'll look meaner."

"I don't need to. I'm like a patriarch as it is. Got Donny and the nephews on the run!"

He asked me a few things about what was going on, but he didn't press it. Just general questions. It was his way of offering whatever help he could give without actually offering it. Just letting me know that he was there if I needed him. It was his family thing again. He wouldn't pry into my business unless I asked him to. And yet I remembered how open he'd always been about his own family matters. At least with me he had. And I felt some privilege in that.

"I might have some questions for you when I get back," I said. "Some stuff I'm not figuring too well."

"Whatever," he said. "We can talk. But just make sure you give yourself enough time."

"I will," I said. "I will."

I sat in the high-windowed room in the small museum in Downers Grove. It was two o'clock in the afternoon. I could hear the faint peck of a typewriter down the hall. Light came in the windows, an airy sodium glow from the parking lot. The last two letters rested on the empty desk, and beside them I'd placed Uncle Edward's list of paintings, now dog-eared from the wear I'd given it.

I'd left Aunt Waverly after lunch, taking the page from Uncle Edward's letter that held the tattoo illustration with me, as well as a stamp and an envelope. There was a copy center on Ogden, and I'd had the piece in the mail to Joan before one o'clock. Waverly had quit her work in the basement before I left and had gone up into the attic for more rummaging around. She seemed relaxed with doing these things, but I couldn't help feeling that she was searching for something. The sky had darkened with rain clouds, and many of the lights in the house were on as I drove away.

The paintings had been uncrated and stood in racks that were newer but very much like those at the Art Institute. The circumstance reminded me of McHale, and I knew I ought to call him soon. I'd promised him a look at the other paintings.

I got up from the desk and went to the racks and checked behind each stretcher, finding dates and titles. There were six pieces done in the years between 1970 and 1977. The two Dorit paintings had been done in those years as well, as had a few others on the list. It had been a very prolific time for him, all of it after he had started his involvement with Dorit.

One of the six was the first painting that I had examined, the tree piece, and early in '73 were those two startling pieces that I'd looked at carefully, *Drunk in Absence* and *Presence Unknown*. Of the three remaining, there were a landscape and two interiors, both with figures. The list named two other landscapes near the same time. Their titles were similar to the one I had, and both had the names of private parties beside them. I decided to look at the landscape later, and removed the interiors from the rack and placed them against the wall behind the desk.

Again I was in Uncle Edward's studio with the figure I had come to know as Dorit. She was present in the nude in both paintings, in the one on my left standing at a window looking out and in the right one reclining again in the heavy chair.

I was aware that the paintings might be related in some formal way, and I stepped back to judge if they were parts of a single narrative. But there was a difference in the light in the room and in their moods. In the one where she stood at the window, her left arm over her head against the frame and her face in profile, the room was lit with a glow of bright sun coming in through the glass. The other painting seemed to be capturing another period in the day, a time close to dusk, and the room and its objects were mostly in darkness, only the chair and the figure in it pushed forth from the canvas, slightly haloed in artificial light cast from a floor lamp close to the chair.

I compared the figures, continuing to look for some story in their different postures and the moods suggested by them, but there was nothing that I could find. Dorit at the window held that same hesitancy in her posture that Edward had painted before, that he had talked about in his letters, but the eye was thrust away from that posture, following her attention to where she gazed, out the window and down to the street below it. She was turned so that neither her face nor her breasts were visible, but he had captured the hesitancy in her back, the way her braid fell beside her spine, and in her buttocks and legs. It wasn't clear if she was leaning against the frame, pushing toward the window glass, or was beginning to push away from the frame, starting to turn her head and body, possibly as a result of fear or disdain, away from the scene she had just witnessed below her on the street. The curves of her body were beautifully rendered, almost sculptural, her stance close to classical, but he had captured its potential motion, an ambivalent one, and there was an unsettled edge of contradiction in the work. It was very hard to know how to feel about it, what its tone was.

Dorit in the chair was another matter. She was almost completely at ease there, leaning back, her legs spread slightly apart, hands resting on her thighs. The light that bathed her was strongest around her head, neck, and shoulders, fading a little as it descended, until it reached her feet, the right one almost lost in shadows on the dark rug. There was only a slight bit of tension in her, that in her neck, for though she was fully reclined in the chair, sinking into it, in fact, her head was lifted from the cushion, her face tipped down a little so that her eyes were not visible, and her neck, a certain tightness and definition of tendons along its sides, seemed to have worked slightly in the effort of pulling her head away from the cushion. She was looking down at her lap, or at least it seemed so, and when I looked there too, I saw that her stomach was slightly distended, rounder than I remembered it from the other paintings. But her right hand on her thigh was forming a kind of gesture, and she might have been looking where her index finger seemed to be pointing, along her thigh to her right knee.

I looked beside her knee, peered between her thighs to see if there was any evidence of the tattoo, but it grew dark there and I could see nothing, at least not with my naked eye. The knee itself was prominent, made slightly larger than it should have been by a shaft of light striking against its slick hardness. Even without the use of Uncle Edward's magnifying lenses I thought I could see that there was something going on at the knee, but rather than looking more closely right then, I turned again to the other painting, moved closer, and looked out the window Dorit was standing beside.

The man was there again. At least he seemed to be the same one I had seen in the other paintings. Who else but Janes? I now thought. And yet I couldn't be really sure of that, not as sure as I was of Dorit.

He was moving along the sidewalk, against the flow of pedestrian traffic, and though he was looking directly in front of him, there was something in his expression, in the way his shoulders were set, that suggested that he had just moments before turned his head back from looking up at the window where Dorit stood. His coat lifted a little from his back, and though the group of pedestrians moving toward him were walking quickly as well, there seemed more urgency in his stride, as if he were somehow getting away from something, perhaps from the sight of Dorit herself.

I looked back at her at the window, thinking that it was his gaze that had caused her hesitancy and ambivalence, but I couldn't be sure of it, and I looked to the street again and studied the moving crowd. There was someone behind them, a vague figure standing off the sidewalk on the grassy verge. I moved closer, knowing I would have to get the lenses out to be certain of her, but as sure as I could be that she was Angela.

She was facing the building across the street from her, her head up and her eyes looking over the heads of the passing walkers. It was clear to me that her eyes were on Dorit and that it was her look that had caused Dorit's tension. I looked at the man again, unsure of him now. Could it be Edward himself? I had what I thought was a pretty clear image of Janes, but I recognized that I had gotten it almost exclusively through Edward. And my image of my uncle had been fixed so many years before and had not clearly come back to me. And even at that he might have changed a lot over the years.

I went around to the desk and got the packet of magnifying lenses that I had brought along with me, opened the folds, and snapped the number 5 lens into the holder. Then I returned to the painting and studied the features of the figure carefully, but I still couldn't be sure of him. I checked the edge of the stretcher for the title, *From a Window*, which told me nothing. I checked the other one as well, *Soon Committed*, and that seemed more promising. Both were dated 1977.

I went back to the desk and inserted a stronger lens, then went over the surface of the painting in a thorough and methodical way. There was nothing on the fingernails this time, nor in the various shadowed structures around the figure. I found the tattoo, very faint but distinguishable, up on the inside of her right thigh. Only half of it was visible, given the spread of her legs, but it was clearly the same figure as that in Uncle Edward's drawing.

When I'd finished with the room and the body's surfaces, I came to that knee where I thought she might have pointed, then squatted down and moved the lens close up to the painting's surface. I needed something stronger, and I went back and clicked in the number 8 lens and returned again. I had to move the lens in, then slowly back again, to get the focus. I kept losing it but finally got my forearm against the stretcher side and steady. Then I had it.

The knee, like other body parts I'd seen in other paintings, was transparent, and given the body's posture in the chair, it formed the shape of a dome. Under the skin of the dome, what I took to be the accurate anatomy had been painted in. The patella was there, the various ligaments, tendons, and softer tissues. But they, like the skin covering them, were transparent. There were lines of faint capillaries running through the patella, faint swirls that I took to be the structure of cartilage, and at the patella's edges there was a faint feathering out, a change in coloring, from flesh tones to a very light rose that caused the impression that the patella was floating, as I thought it should be, encased in its anatomical mechanics. I leaned back, turned my head away for a moment, and rubbed my eyes. I wasn't sure just what the feathering meant, but it seemed to me that it could mean that the painting had been touched up, like the one McHale had identified that way at the institute.

Then I looked back again, my head at a slightly different angle, and I could see that the patella was a cloud, or a light aura that looked like a cloud, under a dome that was probably the sky itself. I put in the strongest lens then and looked into and through the cloudy patella, and the circumstance below it revealed itself.

The scene was of a roadway somewhere in what looked like country, a dirt road, I thought, running straight between flat fields that lay fallow, the spikes of the remnants of last spring's crops poking up in ragged rows. The soil was almost black. It seemed to have been raining, and the road glistened slightly. There were two cars parked along the road; both had pulled to the shoulder that descended sharply for a few feet, ending in a shallow irrigation channel, then opening out into the stubby and wasted fields. The doors of the car to the rear were open, and there were two figures standing, one on either side of the car. They had just reached the front fenders. The one on the roadway carried a blunt object in his hand. Both of the figures wore ski masks.

I felt something sting at the corner of my eye, and when I lifted my hand to my forehead it came away wet. I moved the lens and brought my hand into view. My palm was covered with fresh blood, and I knew that the cut had somehow broken its scab. I moved back from the table, holding my palm up, watching the blood trickle through the creases, a line tracing in a skin line onto my wrist, and jerked my handkerchief out of my back pocket, then dabbed at my forehead and face. There was a wastepaper basket in the room's corner, and I went to it and turned my bloody hand over and shook it, then reached down, still holding the handkerchief to my face, and squeezed the remaining blood into the balls of thick white paper at its bottom. When I brought the handkerchief away from my face it was covered with blood, and I could feel the trickling on my forehead begin again.

I took my shirt off, being careful to use my fingertips, then I pulled at my T-shirt, staining it where I touched it, and brought it over my head and into a ball. Then I wiped the rest of the blood off my hands, found a clean white spot, and pressed it hard against my brow. I stood in the middle of the room, the ball of fabric pushed into my face. I could feel a slight vibration in my legs. I kept my eyes closed, and just stood there and pressed.

After a good long while, when I thought it might be safe, I carefully brought the ball of white fabric away, turned it to find a remaining clear surface, then dabbed tentatively at my forehead, cheeks, and eyes. The blood had stopped flowing, and I ran my fingers carefully along the line of cut, finding it was dry. I put my shirt on then, throwing the bloody T-shirt into the wastebasket, and went on stiff and shaky legs back to the table and the painting.

I lifted the lens holder again and peered through the disk down at the figures and fields, looking carefully at the cars this time. They seemed to me to be British. I was sure at least that they were not American made. I thought that the rear one, a station wagon, might be an English Ford, the one in front a Rover. They were at least foreign, and though they looked new I didn't think that they could have been made in the eighties. I guessed the middle to late seventies, but I was uncertain about that judgment. They were not like the cars I'd been involved with, not the same make or age at least.

Nor were the fields beside the roadway any replica of the one the two men had attacked me near. But the road was of a similar size and straightness, the fields certainly fallow, and the two men moved in the same way as the ones who had approached me. They both wore ski masks, and one had a club in his hand.

I was sweating now, and I pushed back from the table and rested the lens in its holder in front of the painting, then moved around the room, stretching my body and shaking my wobbly legs, touching occasionally at the now dry cut line above my eye.

In a while I went back and squatted down and looked into the scene again, just to make sure. Nothing had changed. There was the road, the fields, the cars, and the men. The windows on the rear car were dark, and I couldn't tell if anyone was in the driver's seat or if there were others in the car, and I could not see through the windows of the front car either. I looked across the fields on both sides of the roadway and thought I could see figures that might be hills, even mountains, in the distance on the right. I checked the few trees that were visible, but couldn't distinguish what kind they were. I kept looking, moving my eyes over the situation, but there was nothing else. What you see is what you get, I thought. And I could do nothing about it.

I must have paced the room for a good ten minutes after that. I thought I would put the painting away, gather up my things, and leave. I would go back and tell Aunt Waverly what I had seen. Then I thought maybe I could call Chen. But then I might go back and look at the painting again, study both paintings, try to figure something out. Maybe I had missed something, some explanation or other. I found myself stopping in the center of the room, looking over at the closed door, then back at the painting, then back at the door again. My legs were tense now. My body was shivering slightly with indecision.

And it came to me as I stood there, halfway between motion and stillness, that I was like Dorit in my posture, was caught between things as she had been, both in the paintings and in Uncle Edward's descriptions of her in the letters. I think I laughed then, catching myself before the laugh got too strong a hold on me. I shook my arms at my sides, rose up a little on the balls of my feet, and jumped up in place, bounding a few inches off the floor, lifting my arms up from my sides, extending them, and rotating them in small circles. I can't be sure how long I did this, but in a while I stopped it, let my arms hang down at my sides, and rolled my head slowly in small circles, getting the tightness out of my neck and shoulders. I stood still in the center of the room then, no longer glancing uncertainly at the painting or at the door. My eyes fell on the letters, and in a while I went back to the table and sat down.

Dear Waverly,

Dorit has returned, and I'm painting her in the flesh now, no more those flat photographic images to deal with. I'd done some work of value with them, but it couldn't be the same. And I think I knew a frustration even before I began. There was that still coldness in them, no more than a hint of those hesitant gestures that had drawn me. An energy within the stillness of hesitancy, something that was constantly with me even in her absence, so that the photographs seemed to mock me, a pale and stilted image of what I knew.

But she is back in London now. They are separated, Janes somewhere in California in a new position, a hospital as I gather, but a plan for private practice as well. She can't speak much about it yet, and though I'd wish to fancy that the reason for their separation and her return has something to do with me, I know I think that it's otherwise, though unclear to me, and I suspect to her as well. So far at least. She's even more unsure in her manner than she was before, and that's a sadness on the human side. But for the painting there's an added energy now, as if her body were a mix of catalytic power and held-back desire. If not desire, some fundamental ambivalence. Each step or move, each comment, has a tortured reserve behind it, a constant measuring, as if everything were the last important thing, could make all the difference in her life.

I'm putting her up here in Muswell Hill until she gets settled, can make some decisions about the immediate future at least. I think she knows that the separation is permanent. It was, after all, her decision and not his. But she can't really acknowledge this yet, can't really believe, I think, that she could have been capable of a decision of such finality. And so she speaks of it, in that very halting way she can manage, as if she had no real part in it. She'll have to wait for choice as if it could come to her from the outside.

Having her stay here was at my insistence, really a selfish thing. I can watch her, paint her almost anytime. It's our agreement. She will sit for me as long as she stays, and I admit I haven't and will not aid her in deciding to find some situation, work or otherwise, that might remove her from me.

And I have been encouraged in ways I did not anticipate with her. There have been times after sitting or in the evenings when the tension has lessened and what might seem to others as an awkwardness has drained away from her, at least enough so that the zone in which we found ourselves was almost placid. We have talked then, language and movement fluid, her posture not so much between things as in them, in the talk itself, this place, and in reminiscence and gossip. We've really very little to reminisce about, it's true, but we have our little private jokes, those few times in crowds or over drinks in private where our special little perceptions have been the same.

And these specific times are entering into the paintings now. They are not there when she is sitting; then it's all that tension that I'm after, that hesitancy that I can't find another word for. But I know her a little watching her, know that over tea or a drink later she'll relax a little and be different. So it is now no longer her look and movement only that I need. It's relationship's specifics as well, and I feel I dare not lose her presence or I will lose what now is integral to painting her.

We've been one month together, and I've convinced her that it's time to come out a little, if for no other reason than to avoid twisted

rumor. To this point we've remained private. Still, it's clear that the
word is out. Everyone knows she lives here with me. It's a good
idea to articulate things in a public way. That's what I've told her.
To let them all know that our relationship is really professional, no
more than an agreement between friends. We should have a get-
together of some kind, in the near future. She's not really contacted
anyone. Things will be awkward. But I've convinced her we can
get beyond that. It will make a difference too, getting her separation out and stated. But this last I have not mentioned to her. Nor
have I mentioned my own fear of any change. It seems the only
way though. I could lose her by nurturing her uncertainty, and
could lose her force in the painting as well. The painting is very
strong right now, and I need more time with it. I can't say how
much, but there is no end in view.

What it is exactly I'm not sure. Something bordering on music? I
mean I can't hold her in my mind well enough without her presence. Oh, I can do that, but the central, crucial element is missing.
As with music, that difference between mute humming in the
memory and the mechanical sound wave vibration, here it's the
eye on the actual flesh in still movement. Well, I despair of explain-
ing it. That I might make some myth or other out of her, inflating
everything in order to make my paintings better. I can't know. But
I feel younger and stronger, not like a father but like a vibrant
master now. When I look at her I feel that my whole life is just
ahead of me, that I can paint her forever and always with a freshness.

But why do I say all this? It's that she's surely a part of the
paradigm of all I've come to see as my mission. Not to inflate the
thing, but that I am driven to those places under the skin, to make
them actual, to operate on the assumption that there is something
just below the surface that is the real explanation, animal, im-
printed, pantheistic, in everything. And in Dorit it seems almost
always ready to ooze out, to become the skin's very surface, so that
the inside will become the outside, right and perfectly symmetrical
at last. Oh, what a vision I have of that, not quite a visual one just
yet. I've seen it in the morgue when I was illustrating, saw bits of
it in surgery, but I was on the wrong track entirely then. Does it
sound mystical? It isn't. It's real life. For me at least: It's what is
driving me.

Drinking water out of the sink tap the other day—there's one in the corner of the room I call my studio—I heard her shift behind me in the chair. It was a whisper of skin against rough fabric, hardly even a sound at all. Yet in it was the choice involved for her in movement, the hesitation just preceding it, the slight sigh of regret in the cushion afterward. She had moved but gotten nowhere. As if a door had been opened from a choice of many doors, and beyond the door had been just a series of other choices, other doors, with no real anticipation of anything other than the same thing beyond. The water splashing in my palm as I held it under the tap, the sound close to my ear as I lowered my head to drink, had made me question that I'd heard anything at all, and I turned my lips away from the flow of water to look over at her.

She was where she had been, naked, her broad shoulders flat against the cushion, her arms along the chair's arms and her legs crossed and extended out before her. But her face had changed, almost imperceptibly. Her thin lips had risen at the corners a little in a moody smile, the milk of her green eyes had lost its tentative focus. She was looking over at me, had raised her chin ever so slightly. Her hair was loose and thick and touching her white shoulders. I could see her small, separated breasts, the rising column of her neck, her delicate ears.

"Edward," she said. "I don't know really what to do."

"What you're doing," I said, bringing my head up from the tap. "It's really quite lovely."

"Don't joke," she said. She meant to say it sharply, but she was incapable of such conviction in her speech.

"It's about men," she said. "And about women too."

The words seemed to come out of her without any effort, but I could tell she'd been working at them for a very long time, had worked to find a time and place, a situation in which she could speak them, and had finally arrived at it. I imagine she had rehearsed saying them and that they were the actual words she meant, not some euphemism or diversion or encoded statement. She didn't mean sex or circumstance, or some other actuality, some way of proceeding in the world outside of her self. She meant, I think, how it was that she should feel. She didn't really know that. She simply didn't know.

I made love to her then. I reached and turned off the tap, then wiped my mouth with my arm and crossed over to the canvas. I had taken up the brush, filled it, and was ready to begin again,

when I looked at her. Her mouth had opened a little, not in surprise or anticipation but in a kind of half wish, a thought that
maybe I could answer something, some little part of something.
And I saw her eyes too, then recognized that she was responding
to something that was in my look, something different from the
brief words of our conversation.

Her eyes tried to focus on me as I moved from behind the canvas
and went slowly toward her, opening the buttons on my shirt with
one hand, vaguely aware that I still held the loaded brush in the
other. They couldn't get me easily. They swam a little, occasional
sparks of a deeper green in them, but still a milky lime green glazing them. Light in the wispy filaments of her downy brows. Only
that long thin nose of hers seemed fixed and certain. Her chin
trembled. I think her hands tightened their grip a little on the chair
arms.

I had my shirt off and was on my knees when I reached her. I
kissed her knees, watching her face as I did so. I must have held
the brush out and up to the side. Her head came down a little,
away from the chair back, watching me. She uncrossed her ankles,
moved her feet back, opening her legs. I saw our strange tattoo
well up in her thigh. She watched me look at it, then moved her
hand from the chair arm and touched my ear. I held her right knee
and kissed the inside of her left. She made a sound, in some language, deep in her throat. I was still watching her face, her half-
focused eyes, the slight flare and then recession of her nostrils.

Then I saw a tightening in her neck as I moved closer to her in
between her legs. The inside of her thighs touched my shoulders. I
could smell her now, and for a moment her eyes clouded, then
became crystalline and clear. I don't know why, but they reminded
me of the Aegean. I saw the tendons in her neck as her head
moved. Her eyes left mine, rising upward, showing their milky
whites. Her head pressed back against the chair cushion. She may
have been seeing the ceiling fixture, an edge of the sink, I don't
know. I had my mouth on and in her then. She was like a sea to
me, like tasting the sea. I wasn't sure at all just where she was.

I don't know how to come back to you from this telling. I'm no
youth anymore, and she's quite young enough to be my daughter.
Maybe I'm alive to myself these days in my painting, and maybe
the future seems to me like a slow, constant opening. But I know
it's not true really. I'm on the way down, the way outward from

my life. She's really just beginning. She's late in that, it's true, but once it's all settled she'll have unlimited time. It's as if we are passing in opposite directions. Something like that. I don't really know.

This intimacy has caused, as far as I can tell, no negative alteration in our relationship, though it is not at all tentative. The relationship isn't tentative either, but of that pure, almost instinctual kind that seems to need no mental understanding for its sustenance. I mean, I don't feel I know her in a way that can be spoken of or explained rationally. I'm coming to know her better through painting her, a knowing that has a selfish product to show for it. But our talking is still, and I fear always will be, exploratory, a delicate examination for both of us of what the other might be like. It is more for me to find that out, I think. I'm clear enough to her, but she's still a mystery to me. She's told me she's been with women, but told it to explain that it has not really helped her. The issue is there for her, something to find out about women and men. Painting her keeps me at a distance, and that bothers me, because the paintings themselves are reaching down and out to something. It may be in time that things will slowly alter, but I've a gnawing feeling that that's not so. I can only follow now, like a younger man might, as if the future held my life and not the past.

Yours (until another time),

Edward

I HADN'T NOTICED STORM or wind, but when I reached the small museum parking lot I saw the scattered twigs and leafy branches, the one good-sized limb that had ripped away and come to a shuddering rest at the lot's curbing. It was only six o'clock, but the sky had darkened, low clouds were scudding, and there was that edginess of electricity in the air. Wind hit at my shirt sleeves, a few cool drops of rain struck against my neck and forehead.

Driving back, I realized that it must have blown hard and for a while. There were cars with hoods up and breakdown lights at the shoulder along the roads that would take me back to Aunt Waverly's. Gusts came up from time to time, and even the old and heavy oaks were waving their branches. I passed downed power lines, could hear through my closed windows the sound of faint sirens in the distance.

He'd called her eyes Aegean green, or at least had been reminded of those waters in seeing them, and I remembered that in the very first letter he'd spoken of Aunt Waverly using the same comparison. What would she have thought and felt had she read this letter? It was a cruel thing to imagine. I had read all the others, in a different context and at a greater speed. Still, there was nothing in the ones I'd read and set aside, though they covered months and years, that might have prepared her for this one. She had what seemed to me to be a correct sense of things, that Edward's writing had become impersonal, at least grown free of their relationship. It had indeed become a record of some sort, a diary. But to think of it that way seemed kinder to me than he deserved. I didn't like him much right then. Still, the cruelty present in these revelations was only a part of the context in which he was addressing his wife, and there was an almost perfect innocence in the writing that suggested he was totally unaware of that at all. Was he an old fool taking up with a young woman? Without the painting, that might have been the case. But the painting seemed to save it, saved at least my interest in it from that.

It was all very strange, and my feelings and understandings vacillated, not least about Aunt Waverly. I wanted a rage in her where there seemed only a vacancy of feeling, but I think I somehow knew that it would have to be the rage of a younger woman. She'd been steeled over the years. Maybe she was just too experienced now for that. And there was something else. Although I could not really understand Edward, couldn't make his mind and feelings clear in the context of his writing, I thought I could understand the draw of Dorit. She was becoming a fascination for me as well. I held her through Edward. And while I questioned his perceptions and self-knowledge, about Dorit I trusted him, even though I knew how tenuous that trust should be.

When I called the number Aunt Waverly had given me, I got a grocery store. Then I tried the number on information, had them trace it back through their records. They found the place and the new number, and when I dialed it a woman answered. At first she didn't know what I was talking about, but after I'd repeated the name and said that this had been close to twenty years ago, she thought she remembered something from the deed, asked me to wait, and went to get it. It was almost seven by then.

I'd gotten back. It was still spitting rain, darker out than it should have been, but the clouds had slowed down and the wind gusts had weakened, though their force was evident in quick, occasional whippings in the squirrel's hedge below the living room windows. Waverly had put the porch light on, and strong smells of something cooking reached me from the kitchen as soon as I entered the front door. The living room was dark, but I could hear muffled sounds from above. I found her in the attic. She'd cleared things away, and that thin rectangular device that I remembered dimly from very long ago was set up in the center of the low room.

"Quilting," she said. I was standing at the top of the steep stairway, looking up at her, my chest at a level with the attic floor. Dinner would be ready by eight. I descended and went to the kitchen and called Joan. There was no answer. Then I called the number in Wheaton, a town not far away.

It was not Joel Fitz, but Gerald—his father, I suspected—and the woman I spoke to remembered something dimly about Milwaukee, the construction trade. She thought they'd built the house. It was in good shape still. Everything tight and well made. She had raised her children there, all four of them, and now even had a grandchild, and her husband was good at keeping the place up. It took me a while to get free of her talking, and in the middle of our conversation she remembered something—a fire, she thought. I asked her if she knew its source.

"Oh, no," she said. "Somebody owned it for a while between us. It was never mentioned when we bought it."

"How do you know, then?" I said.

"Well, it was something in one of the bedrooms. We took a wall down a while ago—you know, the children got too old to be sleeping in the same room, and we needed to expand and such. It was the wood up in the ceiling. Joists I think you call them. And in the wall too, a little, I think. Some charred beams. Not so bad that we had to replace anything. But a fire, I would say, definitely."

There was nothing else that came to her mind, and as soon as I could, I got free of her and hung up, then lifted the receiver again and called information in Milwaukee. There was an S. Fitz, a Joel, and a Fitz Cement Company. I called the Joel, and a teenage boy answered.

"We're all the same family," he said. "My father isn't here. Maybe you can still reach him at work."

"Is your mother in?" I said. "Do you have a sister?"

"You mean Saphia? No. She doesn't live here. My mother's not alive." His voice had cooled a little, become slightly guarded.

"Thanks," I said.

I tried the cement company, got someone who might have been a secretary, and was asked to wait. I waited a long time, and when she came back on, she said that he was gone.

"It's after seven, you know. Really, we close at five-thirty." She said I could reach him in the morning.

"Can I make an appointment?"

"Tentatively," she said. "He's very busy. You'll have to confirm it. In the morning."

I left my name. She said she'd pencil me in for three o'clock, telling me yet again that I'd have to call in the morning.

I hung up and then tried Joan again. It was seven-thirty, but still there was no answer. I could hear Waverly moving around in the attic. There was still time, so I tried California, working my way up scattershot from San Diego to areas around Los Angeles.

I found him, to my slight surprise, in Long Beach, not really far at all from the site that Chen and I were working on. There was no home listed, but there was an office number, and with little effort I got the address of the place as well. It had one of those bastardized Mexican names, half Spanish, half high-tech, some sort of office complex, I thought. It was nothing that I'd heard of. There was just the address, number, and name, Mark Janes, with an M.D. after it. No mention of a specialty or other association. I tried a few more places in the area for a home address, but only a few, and with no luck. Then I heard Aunt Waverly's footsteps on the attic stairway.

She took the business of the two men on the road without much shock. That didn't really surprise me. I'd come to know her again and to remember the way she had been years before, a very strong, measured, and even person. She was tough, in fact, and like me, I thought, someone who guarded against revealing feelings that would show her as vulnerable. She had her tender places, no question about that, and I still thought there was a very large tenderness about this whole twenty-year affair, her loss of both daughter and husband. It was just under the surface, but the surface itself was under control, and that control was central to her character. Still, I held back the possibility of Angela in London. I knew I'd have to get to it soon, but not just yet. And I held back too about the painting, the transparent knee, feeling that that was really nothing I needed to tell her.

We were sitting in the living room again, after our dinner of hamburger casserole, something she had cooked often when I was a child and a dish I liked a lot. The lights were lit this time, but on a low illumination. I could see her gestures clearly enough, but there were shadowy places on her chest and brow. Her face would come into the light at times, but when she leaned back in her chair I couldn't gauge her expression.

"But the paintings are safe now," I said. "And I don't think there's anything to worry about. I can't even be sure that they were after them. Maybe it was coincidence."

"I doubt that," she said. "But I don't care. There's nothing here for anyone. What could possibly be here?"

"And they'll have to think I contacted the police. I can't believe they'd try anything here."

"There *isn't* anything here."

It seemed an odd thing for her to say. She had said it with such insistence. But then she had been at work both in the basement and in the attic, and maybe she meant it quite specifically, that she had found nothing at all that had important meaning for her.

"The tattoo," I said. "The one behind Edward's ear? Did the figure mean anything to you? I've come across it in his letter, and it's an odd thing."

"No. Nothing at all," she said. "It was very clear there though. He'd rendered it quite accurately in that letter. But no, nothing. Just some lines in a circle."

"There's one other thing," I said. "Something that is going to shock you. I'm hesitant about it."

"Don't be," she said. "There's not much that can shock me anymore."

I could see her hands move slowly along the fabric of the chair's arms. I thought she was probably accurate about that in a general way, but this was going to be different. It had to come at her from out of nowhere. She couldn't be prepared for it.

"It's about Angela," I said. "Something you don't know."

I saw her shift in her seat. Her hands came to rest, flat on the chair arms. She didn't seem tense, but she seemed ready.

"About Edward too."

I couldn't be sure of her response, but I think her head may have nodded slightly.

"It may be—I'm not absolutely sure of this though—but it may be that Angela was in London for a time, that she saw Edward there."

"When?"

Her voice seemed small, as if it was back in her throat, the word only reaching out an inch beyond her lips.

"Not all that long ago," I said. "Possibly in '77. At Uncle Edward's studio in Muswell Hill. Maybe five or six years ago. The date's unsure. So far at least."

"What makes you think it?"

"That woman Joan. The one at the cemetery. She knew Edward. She was there around that time, in London."

I think she started to speak, to ask or say something, but she hesitated, and I continued.

"But that's all I know so far, just the possibility of her being there. Joan wasn't sure it was her, but I think from what she said that it probably was."

"And what was she doing there?" She had herself together now, though a little tentatively. Her words were slightly measured, overly controlled.

"I haven't a clue," I said. "Just a visit of some kind? I can't say, and I did ask Joan a lot of questions. I think I got about all there was to get from her."

I wasn't going to tell her about Dorit's tattoo, nor that they lived together. She didn't really know much about Dorit at all, not from what she'd read. Only his fascination with her. It would all probably have to come out in time, but I'd told her enough for now. I wasn't entirely sure I'd gotten all that I could get out of Joan. I kept feeling I might have been at a loss for the proper questions and because of that had missed whole areas of importance.

"But I'm going to talk to her again," I said. "I've been trying to reach her. Can you think of anything that I could ask her?"

"Yes," she said. "Ask her how she looked, if she seemed well."

She broke down a little then. She swallowed the end of her sentence, and I saw her head lower a little, her shoulders begin to shake almost imperceptibly in the shadows. I wanted to get up and go over to her, but it seemed the wrong thing to do just then. I was as much with her as I could be. I had no real part in this grief. She'd handled it all by herself for twenty years now, and it seemed right and proper that she handle this new piece of it on her own terms.

I sat and waited, and in a while she pulled herself together. I saw her shift her position in the chair, and then she spoke.

"Thought I was mostly past it all," she said. "I guess not, not completely."

"There can always be something," I said, not knowing really what I meant in saying it, but feeling it as part of my own recent experience.

"Thanks, Jack. I mean for all the time. And now," she said, shifting in her chair, "how about a little cocoa?" She laughed, aware of the way she changed the mood so quickly, and shook her head.

I laughed too. It was not only the change of subject but a strangely comic acknowledgment of the way we'd taken refuge in the past since I had been there. The food she'd cooked, the penlight gift, the pleasure she must have seen in me when she'd called me Jack.

"Crazy woman," she said as she pushed herself up out of the chair and got to her feet.

"Can I help?" I said, rising also, stretching.

"Of course, my dear. You remember how good it was? I still can buy the same stuff."

"Well, let's get to it," I said, crossing the room and following her out. "You know, it *is* a bit chilly for a summer's night."

I AWOKE THE FOLLOWING morning at seven and went down to the kitchen immediately, still in my pajamas, and called Joan. There was no answer. Aunt Waverly was nowhere in evidence, and I thought she must still be in bed. Then I heard those sounds again above me and realized she was already up in the attic. As on other mornings, she'd made coffee, and it was fresh and warm over a low flame on the stove.

Then I tried Fitz Cement. Though it was still early, the same voice answered that I had spoken to the previous evening. Again, she had me wait. When she returned to the phone, she told me that three o'clock would be okay.

"Be prompt, please," she said.

Then I tried Joan again, perfunctorily, and with no real hope. I'd tried her the night before, after Waverly and I had our cocoa near ten o'clock, and hadn't reached her. I let the phone ring for a long time, then hung up and headed for the attic.

She was standing with her back to me, working at the stretcher, checking its rigidity, fiddling with the braces at its corners.

"Plans?" I said. I was halfway up the steep steps again, my head just above the opening of the attic floor. She turned and looked down at me.

"Not really," she said. "I just thought I'd look it over. But maybe; you never know." She was wearing a housedress, a kind that seemed no different from ones I thought I remembered her in all those years ago. It had that flour-sack flavor, pale blossoms on an off-white background.

"Can I use the car?" I said.

She smiled down at me. She seemed a little worn, and I guessed she hadn't slept too well.

"No. That's okay. I won't be needing it at all today. I'll be here."

"Not all day," I said. "Just for a while. I'll rent one for Milwaukee." We had talked about Fitz Cement, my finding it and my intention to go there, over our cocoa the night before.

"Not at all," she said. "No you won't. You'll use my car. I don't need it, Jack." I remembered her sternness. There was nothing at all disapproving in it. Her statement was not really an order, just a plain comment of fact, one that brooked no alteration.

"I remember *that*," I said.

She laughed lightly.

"But I won't be long," I said. "I'll be back for lunch before I head out again. Can I pick up anything?"

"Well, yes, as a matter of fact," she said, touching her fingers lightly over the small sharp-pointed nails that lined the stretcher borders. "Some of these are bent, some broken. It needs repair. Could you pick some up? There's a place on Ogden." She worked briefly on one of the nails, wiggled it until it came free, then handed it down to me.

"I'll see to it," I said, waving it up at her in my fingers, then I turned and stepped back down the attic stairs.

It was raining again, though it was warm now and absolutely still, the rain falling in thin silver threads not strong enough to make the wipers necessary. The streets were shining with it, yet by the time I reached Ogden Avenue and headed east toward Riverside, some sun had broken through. There were fallen limbs in yards, branches tucked against the avenue's gutters, but nothing here even of the mild severity that I had noticed on my way back from the museum the day before. The sun grew bright, and I had to swing the visor down, but before I reached the turnoff to Riverside, high clouds had come in again, heavy white ones this time, without that stormy darkness at their edges. Still, the gently falling rain picked up a little, though I was sure it wouldn't last for long.

I had no idea what I might do when I got to Joan's, but I felt I'd better go there, see if there was a car, find out what I could. Her not answering the phone seemed all wrong to me. She'd said nothing about going away and had really led me to believe that she'd be available, both for questions and for those answers that I might give her, things I might find out about Dorit.

When I reached the house, I passed by it once slowly. The shades were up, but it was dark on the porch and I couldn't see in at the windows. No lights. It was dark enough, what with the cloud cover, so that I would have seen them. There was a car well back down the driveway, close to the garage doors at the rear of the house. I passed by again, then pulled to the curb two houses down. There were no cars on the street, and the house I parked in front of looked empty.

The rain had almost stopped again, and only a few drops wet my shirt sleeves as I moved along the sidewalk and turned into Joan's driveway. I passed the steps to the porch and strolled to the car. The door buttons were down. I could see through the passenger window that the hand brake was engaged. I went back to the stone steps and moved up to the covered porch.

The screen door was closed but not latched, and I moved to the window beside it and put my hand up and looked in. I could see most of the living room and the dining table and chairs through the broad archway beyond it. The windows on the other side of the house were a little fogged over, but the outlines of trees were visible in the backyard. I moved to the next window. From there I could see the open door to the side of the living room, a hallway wall beyond it, leading, I thought, to where the kitchen was.

I went back to the screen door and opened it, then took the inside knob in my hand. The door was open. I didn't hesitate but entered the living room, letting the screen close silently and easing the heavier door back against its frame. There was a light burning, a very low-powered bulb on a table lamp beside one of the overstuffed chairs, the one Joan had sat in when we'd talked. I stood still and listened. I could hear nothing at all at first. Then I heard something very distant, voices, I thought, in a faint scratchiness, their volume almost beyond me.

I thought I should call out and announce myself, but I decided against it, feeling awkward at the possibility of my loud voice. I felt my empty pants pocket, wishing there were something there, though I had no idea at all of what it might be. Then I moved quietly through the room and the archway.

After a few steps, I could see into the kitchen, the edge of sink there and a stove, could hear the dull hum of the refrigerator motor.

It was a modern kitchen, Formica counters and a quarry-tile floor. There were dishes in the sink and on the counter beside it, bits of dried food, a carton of milk and two glasses with an inch of some colored liquid in each of them. It struck me suddenly that they were the glasses Joan and I had drunk from when I visited with her on Tuesday. Was it Tuesday? I wasn't sure just then. It seemed a long time ago. At the back of the kitchen was another door, open also. It led into a hallway, windowless and dark, with two doors at the end of it, a little light falling on the hallway carpet.

I moved down the hallway, then hesitated, hearing the voices more distinctly now. I held my breath for a moment and listened. They were surely voices, a radio, I thought, the sound coming from the room a few feet beyond me to the right. I stayed where I was, not wanting to move forward yet, somehow knowing I was going to find something very bad. I could hear birds now, then a sharp click from what I guessed was the porch. I held my breath again, then heard steps descending, then a faint whistle. There had been no knock, and I realized that it must have been the mailman or some delivery. Then I moved the few steps to the bedroom and entered it.

The two of them were lying on the bed together in the small, rather severe room. Marilyn had a robe on, a Japanese wrap, callig- raphy and bits of green and red bridges, and figures crossing them, some standing in small formal bowers on sleeves and in the folds that fell along her legs. Joan was beside her, her left arm fallen from the bed so that her palm looked up at me from the floor. She was naked, though a triangle of blanket covered her hips and breasts.

They were both on their backs, eyes closed, heads resting on pillows. Their postures suggested sleep, but I knew that they were dead. Both were very pale, and in the crook of Joan's extended arm I could see the darkness of postmortem lividity.

I stood at the foot of the bed and looked around the room. Everything seemed in order, no sign of struggle or scuffle. There was a half-empty glass of water on the bedside table and a small tube of colored pills, more than half empty, the cap resting beside it. I thought of suicide and knew immediately that I did not believe that.

I moved to Joan's side, reached out and pushed the button turning off the radio, then leaned over and looked down at her body. Then I lifted the corner of the blanket and pulled it away. I could see her flattened breasts and stomach now, her hips, sex, and legs. She had been in very good shape for a woman her age, not much fat and only a few delicate lines at the corners of her eyes. Not worry lines, I thought, at least not now.

I looked across her body to Marilyn's. The robe had fallen open a little, and I could see her navel, the beginning of hair at her crotch. A younger woman, maybe ten or more years younger. Her hair was thick and blond. There was a slight rip at the corner of her mouth, a small cut of some kind. Her lips were slightly parted, and I could see bits of lipstick on her teeth. Her face had some expression in it, but nothing that I could understand. Joan's face was drained of all that animation that I remembered, and the loss of it caught in my throat for a moment.

I went back to the foot of the bed and stood there again, my arms at my sides, looking down at them and thinking. I could lift the phone and call the police, I thought, the thing they call a Princess phone, right there beside the radio and pill bottle and cap on Joan's side of the bed. I stood there for a while, thinking that but not imagining it, just looking at the phone.

Then I went back beside the bed, took the blanket at its edge and replaced the triangle over Joan's body. I started to turn, then stopped and reached down and pushed the button on the radio. The voice came faintly back, the weather report. It would stop raining in a while. It would be sunny and pleasantly cool tomorrow. It was Thursday, nine-thirty in the morning. Very early for mail, I thought, then took my handkerchief out and rubbed it over the radio button that I had touched.

I turned from the bed and the two women and made my way quickly through the house and out to the front door. I opened the door, running my handkerchief along its frame, and then wiped the knob. I could see the mail jutting from the box screwed to the frame, bits of a newspaper and a magazine. Without stepping outside, I reached beyond the screen door and took the mail out and shuffled through it, holding it awkwardly in a fold of the handkerchief. My letter to Joan was there, and I folded it and shoved it in my pocket, then put the rest of the stuff back into the box. Then I reached around and wiped the screen door as I had the heavier one.

I went back toward the bedroom then, stopping in the kitchen, where I washed the two glasses that Joan and I had drunk from and put them in the drainer, feeling ridiculous as I did so.

Then I entered the bedroom again and stood at the bed's foot. They lay as they had moments before. Almost alive, I thought. How very close to life they look, only those few little things that make them dead. I looked around the room again with care, but I could see nothing of significance that I hadn't seen before. I thought to do some searching, but quickly decided against it. What, after all, would I be looking for?

I left the house then. There was no one on the street, and I went directly to Aunt Waverly's car. The rain had stopped completely, but the sun had not yet made its way through the clouds again. When I got back to Ogden, I found the place Aunt Waverly had told me about and bought her an abundance of small nails.

She took the news in her stride. There was really nothing else for her to do with it. But she did have a stake in it, or at least seemed to feel that way. She said this outright. She hadn't known Joan, but Joan may have known Angela, and even at this distance in time, that was something. I told her it was suicide and that it was better that we just not get involved with it. It had nothing at all to do with us. I told her I had learned it from a neighbor. And in fact, now that I was back, I thought it might not concern us at all. Even if it wasn't suicide.

"I almost wish you hadn't found it out," she said. "It can only be a frustration. What is there to *do*? It was all pretty much behind me. Now it's back again."

"I don't know," I said. "But I'll see Fitz this afternoon. Maybe there is something. Information of some kind."

It was clear she had no hope for it. We were standing in the kitchen, both watching a pot of water come to the boil. Four freshly peeled potatoes rested in a cluster on the drainboard of the sink.

"Then I'll do the turnips," she said. "Will you get back for dinner? We can use some of this water for coffee, instant."

"Good," I said. "I could go for that. I'll see him at three. I should be back in time. Unless eight or so is too late for you."

We sat down, our cups on the kitchen table in front of us. It was raining again, that same quiet summer rain, thin lines of water streaking the window above the sink just enough to obscure the pane. I couldn't see the window of my old house across the way. It was still only eleven in the morning.

She dropped a block of sugar in her coffee and absently stirred it. Her eyes were on the rain-streaked window, unfocused. I looked where she was looking, but there was nothing but the blankly opaque glass.

"It may continue for a little while," I said. "But they say it'll be nice tomorrow."

She didn't nod or look my way or in any way acknowledge what I said. Her face was slightly drawn. There were straight pins, a cluster of them, ready in the edge of the short sleeve of her housedress. Her hair was pulled back with a bone comb. A few wisps had come loose, thin filaments along her cheek and ear.

"Poor woman," she said. "Poor women."

F ITZ CEMENT WAS LOCATED in an area that had probably been well away from the city of Milwaukee when it set up for business. The buildings were at least fifteen years old, white cinder block with simple corrugated tin roofs. There was a fenced-in yard to the back, six cement-mixer trucks in it, and a small new parking lot in front of the modest complex held about ten cars. The place was close to the road, closer than it should have been, it seemed to me, but that was because the road had been recently widened, an island now down the center, and the city had started to reach out that way, various fast-food joints and raw new shopping centers, small industrial complexes, sticking up along the road's new length.

I parked on the gravel in front of a small building that was clearly the business office, and when I entered the door I could tell by the carpeting and the leather chairs, the new filing cabinets and desks, that Fitz Cement was probably doing quite well or at least putting that face before the public. There were three secretaries in the place, and the one at the front desk greeted me, got up, and showed me to a couch. She was in her early thirties, and there was something about her ease that suggested she was more than just a worker, probably a relative of some kind. She went to the door at the back of the outer office, knocked twice, and entered immediately. When she came out again in a minute or two, Joel Fitz was with her.

He was a thick man, not very tall and a little overweight, but powerful through the chest and shoulders, and he moved lightly on his feet. His hair had receded, and there were tight lines at the edges of his eyes. I knew we were close to the same age, but he felt older to me. I suspected it might have something to do with the weight of that past I intended to enter with him. The matter felt almost historical to me, and I think his initial hesitancy once he knew who I was and why I was there came from a similar feeling. I could tell from our first words that that life was over for him and that he didn't much care to go into it again.

"How's Mrs. Church?" he said. "I mean with the old man's dying and all. Is she set up okay?"

He had taken me a few blocks away, to the new Holiday Inn. Work was still going on in the parking lot. Two pieces of heavy machinery, closed down already for the day, shone brightly yellow in the afternoon sun. We could see them from the window of the bar. We sat at a table. There were a couple of workmen at the bar itself. Otherwise the place was empty.

"She's handling it," I said. "You know, there was almost no contact over the years. But it hasn't been easy. Things have come up. About Angela. That's why I wanted to talk to you."

"I don't know," he said. "I haven't . . . "

"Has anything odd happened? I mean in the last few weeks or so? Maybe before that?"

"I haven't noticed anything. But what do you mean, odd? I don't know what you're getting at." He had an odd look in his eyes, and he shifted his large bulk in the booth.

"I don't know either. To tell the truth. But anything strange? To do with the family?"

"No," he said. "Nothing." He said it too quickly, and he looked at me curiously again, a little wary. "What family? Didn't you just say they had little connection? Weren't there letters or something?"

I was getting off to a bad start with him, and I tried to begin again.

"I'm not being clear," I said. "It's just that there was an attempted robbery. It seemed to have something to do with Uncle Edward's death, his paintings, and I just thought something might have happened here too."

He relaxed a little, folding his large hands together on the table. "I can't imagine why. Do you know how long it's been? We're talking almost twenty years."

"Right," I said. "Really, it's probably nothing. It could have been nothing. To do with Edward, I mean."

We sipped at our beers, glanced over as others entered the lounge. I was thinking of a way to start in again with him, but he spoke first.

"You're her cousin, right? I remember something bad had happened. You'd left a while before we met. Your parents, was it?"

"That's right," I said. "An automobile accident. They were both killed."

"I'm sorry," he said.

"It's been a long time for me too," I said.

"Well, maybe you can understand, then. I don't quite know how to start. She just left, you know. I was very raw then, about a lot of things. And really it's only about ten years ago that I got it clear for myself. Maybe I could handle it then because I had another family. It had been unfinished business for me before then. Not ever knowing why she left, you know?"

"In addition to Saphia?" I said.

His brows went up, and he blinked at me. "How did you know that?"

"I talked to your son," I said. "To find your number."

"He's not really my son. He's my sister's. I took him in when he was just five, after her divorce. She's dead now."

"It's an odd name."

"Her middle name. She took it on when she was thirteen. That was Angela's idea, that name. She had my mother's first name."

"You mentioned another family."

"I mean the boy. I never did remarry. And Saphia. People to care for. My mother lived with us. It was something to do, you know. People to live with and care for." His eyes drifted from my face, changing their focus as he looked out the window and into the parking lot.

"You said you know why she left now. Can you say why?"

He brought his eyes back. "Right," he said. "It was women. She had an interest in women. Flatly, she was a lesbian."

"Are you sure that was it?"

He shifted in his seat, but not out of any discomfort now. He was ready to get into it a little, and he was just settling himself to begin. I wanted to know more about Saphia, but figured it was best to let him get to it as he could.

"She was pregnant," he said. "It was that that fucked it up completely; brought it to a head, I guess you'd say. It was the early sixties, you know, and it was Congress Park. We're talking pretty conservative—socially, I mean. Not like now. It would have been heavy with her parents. To put it mildly."

"Do you think with Aunt Waverly it would have been?"

"No. You're right. I should have said with him. I liked Mrs. Church. A very bright woman. Sensitive, you know, and tough. Still, she was under his thumb."

"So, she was pregnant," I said.

"Right. She always had girlfriends. Christ, it's so obvious to me now. But then . . . So, anyway, it really threw her. She refused to tell her parents. I think she could see a real splitting off from her friends—the women, I mean. That having a child, going through it and having it, would bind her in a way she hadn't bargained for. Really, she got kind of hysterical about it all. The doctor, some bumpkin we were going to, told us it was all natural. A lot of women get that way the first time. She knew better. But I didn't."

"But was that all of it? I mean, I always thought her parents, Aunt Waverly at least, were pretty understanding. It seems out of proportion somehow."

"You're right. But not Edward Church. I don't want to get psychological about all this, but he resented Angela in a way, I think. She got in his way. I've always thought that's why he left. I mean, he could do it after she had left. Nothing to hold him back then."

"That's pretty cruel," I said.

"To *say* it is, I guess. I don't know about those things. But I think there's truth in it. And didn't you say there'd been no contact with her—Mrs. Church, I mean? That he didn't keep in touch? Were there no letters, nothing?"

"There was business," I said. "He had money sent to her account. Only a few letters."

"Recently?"

"No," I said. "Nothing in the last five years."

He leaned back in the booth, relaxing a little, his left hand making little circles on the slick wood beside his half-empty glass.

"And what about the child?" I said.

He looked intently at me, searching, I think, for accusation in my voice and face. But I was beyond that kind of thing and really wanted only information. He must have seen that. His eyes lost their tight focus, and he was looking to the side of my head, remembering.

"I think now that she was getting ready to go by the end of her third month. She began to show. Not really much, but she had to tell her parents she was pregnant. And that closed her in, I think. She felt that way. It could have been good, possibly even worked out, with Mrs. Church, but Church himself got strange. A little like she was. I can see that now. The idea of a grandchild, seeing that manifested physically in her. Maybe he too had been ready to leave and didn't need any of that right then. But that ripped it for her. She stopped seeing her friends. She even seemed happy and free of it all for a few weeks. Then I came home one day and she wasn't there. I never saw her again."

"Still, it all seems a little strange to me. I mean the cause of her leaving."

"You're right," he said. "There's more. But I think it's more about why she didn't come back than why she left."

"What do you mean?" I said.

"It's Jenny. Saphia, I mean. She had her brought to me when she was born. I don't know from where. She left her with one of her women friends, and that one handed her over. She's retarded, you see. Severely so, and I just don't think Angela could ever have considered dealing with that."

"But your son," I said. "I thought he said she lived away from home."

"She does. But not alone. She's close to twenty now. Way too much for us to handle. I've got a woman, a nurse, living with her."

"Is that why you never told Aunt Waverly about her?"

"That's right," he said. "You won't, will you? I didn't think it made much sense. To burden her in that way, I mean, without a husband or daughter."

"I won't be saying anything," I said.

There were people at the tables around us now, laughter from a group of construction workers at the bar. The place was filling with the early happy-hour crowd, but there was enough leather and heavy carpeting in the room to absorb much of the sound. Still, he leaned forward a little before speaking again, put his elbows on the table between us. The cocktail waitress brought us two more beers. He sipped at his, wiping his mouth on his shirt sleeve. He was dressed in workman's clothing, though he owned the business. Jeans and a blue work shirt. I figured he'd be a good boss. No nonsense, but fair. I thought of Angela and thought he'd probably been a good husband to her, as good as she could accept.

"The kicker may have been the drugs," he said. "The women she ran with."

"I don't get that," I said. "In Congress Park?"

"Oh, there was plenty. If you got with the right people. The wrong ones. Mostly pills, what they now call speed, and tranquilizers. I knew about the pills but was stupid about it, believing her when she said she got them from the doctor. Now, having seen a little over the years, I'm sure she was doing more than that. Marijuana for sure, probably even cocaine."

"And never another word?" I said. "Once she left?"

"No. Absolutely nothing. I called the women, the ones I knew a little. But they didn't know anything either, not even the one she left Saphia with. I think they told the truth, that she went off on her own, not with any of them.

"We were living at my mother's place then. In Wheaton, near Downers. Pretty near where you are. And then it was just Saphia and me. And in a while my son joined us. I mean my sister's son. I've adopted him. Maybe it was six years or so. We moved here, and then I got this place."

"And wasn't there a fire at one time?"

"A fire," he said. "You've certainly learned some things. How in the world did you hear about that?"

"It was just chance," I said. "Getting in touch with you. I called the number Aunt Waverly had, managed to get your old place. There was a woman. They'd done some renovation."

"Yes, there was a fire," he said. "So long ago. It was really nothing, but a serious scare for me. She started it—Saphia, I mean. My mother was out for just a few minutes. It was after that we got a woman to stay with her. She really couldn't be trusted alone. Then, after my mother died, we moved here."

"She wasn't hurt?"

"No. Nothing like that. But she could have been. There's a danger of such things. Her mind, you know."

"It's odd that those women knew nothing at all about Angela," I said. "Where she went."

"Well, it was more than just the circumstance—her pregnancy and the drugs and all. She had it wrong in her head, something wrong. I have never understood. Not completely. Her father. Really, it doesn't seem that odd to me now."

I left him at the table. He said he'd have another beer and then head home. No reason to go back to work now. It was already five-thirty.

The traffic was heavy, and even when I reached the expressway there was little letup, not until I cleared the outlying satellites of the city. Seeing him had not been a bust exactly, but as I went over things, I realized that he had added very little to what I already felt I knew. Some particulars of her leaving, not really very particular at all. There was only the drugs, something Aunt Waverly hadn't mentioned and I was sure had no knowledge of. It was nothing I would tell her about either. What difference could it make now?

There was Angela's daughter, of course, Saphia. Something startling and new, but only if I mentioned it. And I knew I wouldn't do that. Not because I'd said I wouldn't; the fact of her went beyond such promises. But she could only be a burden now. His holding the knowledge of her back from Waverly seemed right to me, something kind, actually. That she be left without a daughter and with that. He'd done the right thing, even though the idea of doing it might seem wrong. I realized I didn't know just where she lived, though I was sure from the way he spoke of her, the way his son had, that she couldn't be far away, probably in Milwaukee or at least nearby. She was close to twenty now, he'd said, but twenty had a certain fragility in this case. I could imagine her, in some protected bed or space, but I knew it was useless to think beyond that. I guessed there was nothing much left of her.

It was six-thirty by the time I got to the Chicago side of Milwaukee. I held it at sixty, slow enough to stay in the right lane. Angela seemed a dead end to me now, at least that part of her life between her leaving and her possible reemergence in London. Fitz had been no link at all. There'd been those women, but he'd been unable even to remember their names. Maybe Joan had had information. It was the only thing I thought she could have had. And not something she had held back from me. It was something she hadn't remembered. And they, whoever they were, had killed her to keep her from telling me. Or maybe they only thought she knew something, and maybe it wasn't even that they had killed her to keep information from me. It could have been somebody else entirely. Even suicide. Then again, maybe she *had* told me. Maybe they had been too late in killing her.

I tortured it all, only catching myself and stopping it when I was approaching the fringes of the suburbs I was headed for. It wasn't doing me any good. The next step had to be action, no more paintings or letters. It had to be Los Angeles and Mark Janes. He seemed the only remaining possible link just then. But Los Angeles was other things as well. Chen and the project, that whole real life of mine. Maybe there was something *he* could tell me, something from the outside that could help put the inside in order.

I reached Aunt Waverly's house just before eight and found her in the kitchen poking the tines of a long fork into the roast on the stove. A large pot sat beside it, wisps of steam leaking at the rim of the cover.

"Just in time," she said. "Mashed turnips and potatoes." She lifted the lid, letting that old aroma reach me. It was another favorite, something I hadn't smelled or tasted in years.

"Was there anything?" She was moving the spoon slowly through her tapioca. She had her eyes down, watching her fingers on the handle. We had eaten dinner in the kitchen, and once we'd settled into it I'd raised the subject, but she had lifted her finger, said, "Wait till after," and what talk there was had been about the weather, quilting, the few calls she had received while I was gone. McHale had called from the Art Institute, just checking in, wondering about the paintings and where they were. He'd said he'd be out of town for a while, that he'd call again as soon as he returned. And there had been a call from Ross as well, just to see how things were going and if there was anything he could do. He said he was working on a final accounting of Uncle Edward's affairs from his end of things. I tasted the tapioca, stirred the milk in my coffee.

"No," I said. "There was nothing. He's got a whole life there. She's well back in his past now. He didn't know a thing."

"I didn't expect so," she said, looking up and across to me now.

"He has a good business. And a family."

"Good for him," she said, a slight smile twitching at the corners of her mouth. "Good for somebody at least. He was a decent enough man, a boy really at that time." She paused, looking down again, considering.

"In the beginning I blamed him, of course. I couldn't blame *her*, not right away at least. I don't blame anybody now. Not even Edward. Maybe I should blame myself though."

I wanted to correct that. I couldn't feel that Waverly was to blame for anything. But I knew too that I was back twenty years again, and even with what information I'd gathered, I really couldn't know for sure. She was my dear aunt again. I knew I couldn't really see her clearly and objectively. I also wanted any last things I could get about Fitz before he too got tangled in memory.

"But do you think now that he had anything at all to do with it, with her leaving?"

"I've been over that," she said, "a long time ago, and again since you've come here. No, Jack, I really don't think so. I think it was all from her. The going, I mean. The impetus? Well, Edward was involved in that. I'm sure he could have acted somehow, but I can't imagine the way. I've thought to blame myself, tried even to do that in the beginning. But what could I do? I never could find any way, clearly, that I was the cause. You know, she simply left. Joel called us. She was just gone. We were all stunned by it, and we never really did get any story of it straight with him. I mean those little particulars about her leaving that could mean something. All our first force was spent in trying to find her. Our talk with him was mostly mechanical. About the police reports and such. They'd been married such a short time. Only a few years. And he had been busy making a way for them. We hadn't even gotten to know him yet."

"I'm going back," I said. "Just for a while. To Los Angeles."

"Of course," she said.

"It's the work," I said, "the job I told you about. Things are at a point very near the end. I have some careful things to do. But I'll be back. Take care of the rest of this. The paintings and the rest. In about a week."

"I've never been to Los Angeles," she said. I thought she would continue, but she didn't.

"Is there anything I could do before I leave?"

"I don't think so. You've done a lot so far."

"It doesn't feel like it," I said.

"But you have, Jack. Just coming here is good."

"You know, I haven't seen the old house yet," I said. "I'd like to do that."

"They're gone now," she said. "I haven't seen any lights the past few days. Maybe when you come back?"

"Right," I said. "That would be good. Do you know them?"

"Not very well. Really, not at all. There's been some turnover through the years. I knew the first few pretty well, but I haven't been in there for a long time. They're pretty private people. Working people. Not unfriendly, but not social. They've done some work, I know, inside. I don't know what."

"Do you think of them, my mother and father?" The words caught in my throat. It was a surprise to me, both the asking, the words just jumping out of me, and the way my eyes hurt a little when I said them.

"Of course I do." She must have caught something in my voice. She'd brought her head up from the tapioca and leaned a little across the kitchen table toward me.

"At first those quick stabs for a while. And not a little while; almost seven years. And then your uncle and Angela left, and I had too much, really, to feel about. But after that, after that softened a little, they came back to me, much more strongly once the shock of it had softened. You know, things we did when you were little, the picnics in the park. They were neighbors too, as well as relatives. Your mother and I were the best of sisters-in-law, you know. We really came to see things in a similar way. But Edward and your father had a rougher closeness. They were not the same at all, but still there was something for them in being brothers. And then you two were born, so close to the same time, and your mother and I, well, we became as close as two young women with children could be in those days. They were good times, those early years."

"You know," I said, "I could hardly remember them, at least

until I came here. Now I've been thinking of them. Mostly what they looked like, how they stood, and all. I've been missing them. Maybe for the first time, at least without that shock you spoke about. I mean, to think of them in a focused way, without craziness, the pain of the accident, to miss them. I wonder what things would have been like."

"Your father liked to garden," she said. "Edward was always in his study. I'd talk to him about his flowers and such, over the back fence. He had a way with gardening."

"I know," I said. "I think I remember that. Maybe that's why . . ."

"I'm sure it must be, Jack, why you do what you do. He would have liked that."

"I hope so," I said. "I mean I would have hoped so."

She smiled then, hearing me work at the tense.

"I know how it is," she said. "It's hard to get it right."

Later, I sat alone in the living room in the dark and sipped at a weak bourbon. It was close to eleven, and Aunt Waverly had gone up to the attic again to work at the quilting frame. She'd only worked for a while, and shortly after I heard the end of her sounds up there, she'd called from the head of the stairs, saying she was going to bed.

Once again I felt it was time to take stock, to make an inventory of discoveries and questions, and I ran through things, stopping in a few moments, realizing that the more I noted, the less I knew. What I needed was action, not lists, and there were two clear courses of action waiting for me out west. There was Chen and the site, and there was Janes, and while the two had nothing to do with each other, they were linked for me. They were out there and away from this, and they were both things that could only be gotten at by doing something. No more sitting back and letting it all happen, not for a while at least. First thing in the morning, I thought, Friday morning. I'd be back home on Saturday. I downed the rest of the watery bourbon and headed for the stairs.

Aunt Waverly had ordered the room, changed the sheets, and when I slipped naked between them they felt cool and a little damp in the recent rain's humidity. She'd left the window open slightly, and the thin curtains lifted a little into the room. I reached my toes out, touching the footboard of Angela's bed, then I pulled the covers away, got up and went to the window.

I could see the frame and the dark glass when I spread the thin curtains. The shades were down on the other side, though, and there was no way to see in. They're away, she'd said. I tried to picture what my room had been like on the other side. I could see the L of the banister in the hall, the room's shape, even the look of the furniture and its placement. It was all extremely clear to me for a moment, vivid, as if the screen of memory were a clear window, no longer clouded over by wishes for revision. Then I thought of my parents on the lower floor. It was late at night, and they would be coming up to bed soon. I could see the way they sat in their chairs, the placement of their hands and arms. But then I felt the loss of them, and memory darkened the vividness.

I went back then and crawled between the cool, damp sheets. For the first few moments I thought I was going to find it hard to get to sleep. Things ran piecemeal through my mind. But I was tired, my mind was tired. It had been one hell of an eventful day. And shortly after recognizing that, I felt the numbness of sleep; thoughts scattered and distinctions crumbled away.

In the morning I called and made a reservation for the following day, a flight that would get me into Los Angeles around two. Given the time change, I wouldn't have to get to the airport before eleven.

I'd slept in and didn't make it down to the kitchen until after nine. Waverly had left the coffee on that low flame again, and I couldn't hear her anywhere in the house. I took my cup and went to the front door. The car was there. Just as I was turning back into the room, I saw her at the edge of the park, coming along Raymond. She saw me too and lifted the newspaper in a wave.

"The boy missed me this morning," she said as she turned up the walk. "I've been to the little store on Ogden."

It was a good long walk, ten blocks or more, and her face was flushed.

After coffee and some cereal, I called the hospital in Long Beach.

Chen wasn't in the room, and I had to hold for a long time before he came to the phone.

"Crutches," he said. "Cane in a few days. I'm staggering around. There's some infection, and they're keeping me for a while longer. But I'm what you call ambulatory, getting used to these wooden pins. We can get out there."

I told him I'd be in the next afternoon.

"Everything in order?"

"Not quite," I said. "But near. At least there's nothing that can't wait. Things I can do out there, in fact."

"Good enough," he said.

I spent most of the afternoon at the museum in Downers Grove, going over the paintings once again. I looked at each of them and checked it against the list. I wanted to place what I had in some order before I left, and I didn't linger over the works, just dated them again for myself, made sure of the knee and fingernails and the recent touch-ups McHale had pointed out.

When I was finished, I set the paintings back in their racks and went to another room and made copies of all the letters. I left the originals along with the paintings at the museum. The director provided me with a secure locked drawer in the same room where the paintings were stored, and he was even careful to give me an itemized receipt. He inspired a lot of confidence, and I thought I could be sure that what I was leaving behind would be safe. I knew Aunt Waverly would be safe also, but I called Ross from the museum, telling him I'd be gone for a while, asking him to check on Waverly. He too inspired confidence. He'd done what he said he'd do, and he said this time that he would call her tomorrow night, after I left, would get out to see her, take her to dinner. I left the museum with the stack of Polaroids, the letter copies, and the one original letter that I hadn't opened yet, and driving back, I felt some confidence that I was leaving things in good hands.

That evening Aunt Waverly and I talked about what still remained to be done, both of us recognizing that we couldn't make a sure and comprehensive list yet. As some things got settled, others came up.

A few letters had come from Ross, final accountings from the major publishing houses that Edward had done work for. There would be ongoing royalties, for a while at least; some, from the standard anatomy texts, might go on for a long time. There were still a few things hanging.

"He's something," I said. "To be so quick about all this. He's been working."

"Ross is a good man," Waverly said.

There was nothing he had been able to find that remained out on consignment. He hadn't really been in touch with Edward's painting for a very long time, but he had ways to check. There *could* be things, but he didn't think they'd be major. He'd found out that there had been some significant activity on the European market in the last few years, and I remembered McHale mentioning that. All the recent deals he'd traced had been direct, and there seemed no loose ends there. He wrote that he would see to a new contract, one that would shift everything over to Waverly, with him remaining as agent. We could expect copies to go over within a week. He said he thought he'd been thorough in his accountings. They hadn't been too complex. The major, the only real issue now was the paintings, to trace them and make sure they were all accounted for, then to figure out what to do with them. Uncle Edward's list seemed complete enough, but there could be drawings, sketchbooks and such, that might turn up. Ross thought it was a little odd that there had been none of these among the belongings. It came to me that there was no reference to that kind of thing in the letters. "But then," Ross wrote, "maybe he didn't do that much. Or maybe he destroyed them if he did." He wrote that he'd do what he could, check those places he knew of in London. There would be no agent's charge for any of this. It was the least he could do.

Aunt Waverly showed me a pile of letters, various feelers and outright requests. People wanted the paintings, galleries would represent her, museums were interested in seeing what there was, with intention to purchase. There was even something from the museum in Downers Grove, the gift of a membership, one for Waverly and one for me. "Subtle enough?" I said, and Waverly laughed. And there were letters from private parties too, individuals who would be very interested in buying something.

We went over the whole pile of correspondence together, checking things, figuring returns, loose ends, things to be done. There was nothing really that couldn't wait. We worked up a standard letter to send to those who requested a look at the paintings, made a list of names, agents, museums, and private parties. I made my own list, the names and addresses of individuals. None were familiar to me. There were a dozen or so, and I checked them against Uncle Edward's list. I'd made a copy of that too, leaving the original in the locked box at the museum. Not one of the names appeared in both places.

"I can't really think yet about the paintings," Aunt Waverly said. "That fortune. Maybe when you come back."

"There's no rush at all," I said. "If they want them now, they'll want them later. But speaking of fortunes, don't you think it's odd that there was so little money on balance? I mean, the worth of all this, and yet no significant money at hand, no bonds or certificates either. Could he have spent it all?"

"That was like him, Jack. I know it's odd, given his carefulness and all, the way he ordered things, but he had no sense of money. When it was there he spent it."

"Still and all," I said. "Will you keep any of the paintings? It's been strange to me that you have nothing here at all."

"There was one," she said. "Of all things, a portrait of me. It just came one day, a long time ago. I kept it against a wall for over a month, I think. Then I had Ross take it and sell it. It was just another insult in a series of them, those letters, though of course it wasn't that for him—Edward, I mean. It was a crazy thing, not the painting but the gesture. I was getting beyond all that then.

"Before you came, I thought I wouldn't keep anything in those boxes, wouldn't want them. But now? Well, I just don't know. Maybe I should."

"Let it sit," I said. "When I get back."

At ten o'clock Aunt Waverly excused herself and went up to bed. I had an urge to ask her to linger, feeling that we should say something important to each other before I left. But I knew there was nothing of that kind. We were in some texture together, something that was still spinning out, and there was no possibility yet of stepping back to comment on pattern.

"You'll leave late?" she said. "Around eleven? We'll have a nice big breakfast, a brunch." She put her hand on my shoulder.

"That'll be very nice," I said, touching her fingers.

After she'd gone, I sat in the living room, drinking a last cup of coffee. She'd left the windows in the front of the house open a little, and a light breeze pushed at the edges of the curtains. I was restless, not tired at all, and when I'd finished the coffee I went out the front door and took a long walk, circling the four block-long parks that formed the whole of Congress Park, this old community that I had been part of twenty-seven years before. Not all that much had changed over the years. At least I didn't want to see those things that had.

There were new houses set among the older ones, and the parks themselves, now no longer elegantly shaded by those massive Dutch elms, had plastic play devices in them, not many but enough to ruin my memory of their feel. Back then the whole community that lined the parks had taken them on as an almost family effort. There had been tended flower beds, a flagpole at the end of each, and of course those simple wooden-framed plaques commemorating the war dead. The plaques were gone. There'd been the wake of other wars, ones of little popularity. The old folks on the blocks had no part in any communal present, and the younger families that had moved in over the years had other kinds of concerns.

To the far end of the row of parks, the neighborhood had deteriorated slightly—overgrown yards, houses in need of paint—but at Aunt Waverly's end, the place was still a good circumstance in which to live.

After I'd made my circuit, I returned and stopped at the far edge of the park that had been mine, across from Aunt Waverly's house and my own beside it. I looked over to the wooden porch of my old house, to the darkened front windows. I scanned the porch railings, the pillars that supported its roof. I could see nothing at all that was not familiar, though I knew that my memory of the place was probably faulty. I hadn't really thought of it in many years, but I'd been thinking of it, picturing its rooms and stairways, the turns of its banisters, ever since my arrival, my return. I knew I needed to see it again, to go inside it, use it to draw up memories with which to reconstruct things. I wasn't sure just why I needed that, but I knew I did.

I was feeling sad in my leaving, feeling almost that it was like that first leaving so many years before. That was foolish. I knew that. But it didn't feel foolish. It was a proper sadness somehow.

Then I thought of Chen, of my real life. I looked away from the house and made my way across the grass of the park, passing the place where I judged the plaque had stood. There was no evidence at all that it had ever been there.

The curtains were drawn across the window when I entered Angela's room, and I could not see through them to the house on the other side. I started to move toward them, then realized that I had done the exact same thing the night before. I felt truly foolish, knowing I was cooking up emotion, trying to find a way to construct a memory of leaving that could stay with me, be poignant in the future. It was a stupid and sentimental thing to be considering. If there was a past for me here, it was still in the future, something possibly very real, a thing I could go after. All I have to do, I thought, is find a passage, any passage, just so long as it is something tangible.

T HE FLIGHT TO LOS ANGELES was quick and easy. We got up out of O'Hare on time. The sky was clear and calm, the seat beside me empty. And I had a good deal to think about. I went over all of it again, but casually, trying to put the pieces into some pattern. I knew I did it only to gather it, make it somehow manageable, a way of putting it behind me for a while. I was heading west, and it was Chen, the site, and what other things might await me there that got me looking forward. But then, without my intention or even care, pieces of my family in the past began to come back to me.

I had a small garden, a narrow plot beside my father's, terraced a little where the yard sloped, the earth banked up with pieces of wood and stone, small gravel walkways that I could only move along by putting one small foot in front of the other. My father helped me with my plantings, all those hearty flowers he was sure would grow, the few vegetables I insisted upon. But he let me alone with it once I learned a little. Angela and I worked in it, even tried a small irrigation stream once, but without success.

And there was my father in his white suit. He was dressed totally in white, shoes, socks, and tie, even a white hat as I remembered it. Some occasion or other. We were on the front porch of my old house. Angela, Waverly, and Edward. My mother in a yellow dress with yellow shoes. It was raining, a soft spring rain, steam rising up from the sidewalk. We were standing on the porch, close to the wet railing, protected under the flat wooden roof, watching the rain.

And other things, each coming back to me like vivid cameos. Things that were cropped off and jettisoned from their places in the flow of other things, those negatives that might have surrounded and influenced them, like photographs possibly, or scenes in a perfect play, plotless, but for the tone and feel of it, some peaceful drama in which everything had a good ending.

And then the accident, the impossible heavy thud and give and rend of steel, just a block away, at the quiet, benign entrance to Congress Park. Uncle Edward holding me with some effort. I was as big as he was by then. Wrestled me to the ground even, and Aunt Waverly standing over us, her hands across her breasts tightly, a look on her face that told me. Impossible that it could have happened. And from then on the world itself was impossible, unreal, until I left.

Angela drew back. She must have seen in me some fear in her own life made real, that she too would lose her parents, perhaps wished for it, less suddenly but just as finally as I had lost mine. I had somehow made it happen ahead of her, making it possible, actual, no longer a dreadful piece of dreamwork but something she could do.

And I think her pulling away from me was the last straw somehow, that she in some way let me go, so that I *could* go. It was not that we were really close, not since we'd entered adolescence. Our crowds were different. We went to the same school but seldom saw each other. It was more that she made me feel that I was no longer who I had been, that the matrix of our association had died when my parents died, that I was no longer in the family that she had been close to me in. She would be making her own move before long, but I didn't know that, and her last separation, the one that could get her going, was from me. She didn't know it either, of course, but she freed me as she would free herself.

Aunt Waverly tried, but I took her attempts as a shift that pushed me away from her. She was no longer my Aunt Waverly but was trying to be a kind of mother to me. That too was impossible, and I lost both of them in the bargain. Of Uncle Edward I could bring little back, just a shadow figure who was only becoming who he was for me now, as I studied his paintings and the letters, someone I had never really known before I'd left. I'd found Aunt Waverly again. I was finding Uncle Edward. But the figure of Angela was still unformed and missing for me. I was not even sure that what I was working on was a puzzle, that should I find her she would form, with the two others, into something, a thing important and revealing, for me, take form in my own life in some way. And then there was Dorit, the trail leading in her direction. She was the figure I was moving toward, in various odd ways. And I felt I might be getting closer, even as I headed west. It was a job of work. I had sense enough to know that I hadn't lost that yet, that I could *do* something. And I would do it for Aunt Waverly and for those others now, Joan and Marilyn, to make some sense out of their dying and my possible implication in it. There was nothing that I could have done about my parents', but I could try to do something about theirs.

By the time I'd gotten my luggage and waited a little for a rental car at the L.A. airport, it was three o'clock. I wanted to get to the site while the light was still good, so I headed down the coast, past the exit that would take me to the hospital, and drove to the off ramp that was closest to the complex. I was a little jet lagged, awkward in the flow of freeway traffic. Though I'd been gone for only ten days, California felt strangely foreign to me. Even the air was odd, softer than in the East, and I was struck by the difference in vegetation, drifts of lush bougainvillea along the embankments, those tall, feathery palms. I drove slowly and in the right lane, not wasting time but careful and with both hands on the unfamiliar wheel.

When I reached the raw, new buildings at the site's center, I got out and stood still for a moment, taken back by the silence, the absence of cars in the white gravel lot. There was no heavy equipment moving, and all I could hear was the deep, distant drone of traffic from the sweep of freeway. Then I remembered that it was Saturday. Things must be moving along on schedule, I thought, no overtime.

I walked up the brief, low berm that fronted the central administration building, a rectangular structure, plenty of glass and a postmodern entryway, severe and serious but with a hint of Gothic filigree across its broad entablature. They'd wanted something both monumental and efficient looking. It hadn't worked too well, for me at least, but I thought the god of electronics might be pleased. The facade said money, but in a very cool and nonaggressive way. Chen had laughed at it, shaking his head.

From the crest of the berm at the building's doorway, I could see out over a good portion of the job, at the distant perimeters of which the sprawling rhythms of embankment edging the freeway's bend had now been cut and back-filled and planted. Only various low shrubs lined it, scrub pine and juniper as antidazzle, so that the whole complex could be seen for a good long time from the freeway's gentle curve as it passed by.

All the larger trees were in, dwarf palms mostly, and I could tell by the color of the earth that most of the acreage had been seeded. Even the plugs of beach grass were in, securing a hill that both Chen and I had been particularly concerned about. We'd wanted a place that seemed wild and a little uncontrolled somewhere on the site and had planned an acre of sandy soil at a point on the datum line, gentle slopes like those found edging the sea, plantings of lavender, rugosa roses, scotch broom, and dusty miller. We weren't sure if the climate and situation would allow for it, and it had been risky to go with perennials. We had a backup plan but were hoping for success from this one. It looked good out there, but I knew it would take a while before we could be sure of it.

I turned slowly, holding my hand up against the sun, and let my eyes scan carefully over the whole section of landscape that I could see from my vantage. Chen's low boulders were in place, as was most of the rest of the hard landscape, gravel walkways that were carefully raked, creating slow twisting ribbons among berms and shallow mock valleys. This was Chen's way with things, to get enough large particulars finished so that we could see places, imagine what had to happen in the interstices between them. He was a careful planner, as I was, but unlike me, he was always willing to change the plans, even drastically, as things moved along. The resolutions of our arguments about such things had good results. I brought convention and care, he impression and risk. I'd been to the university. Chen had learned things through family and heritage. The relationship had worked for us, and it was working here.

There was a light breeze pushing the few low palms, and their shiftings did things with the eye, getting the ribbons of gravel pathways to seem organic, to be waving slightly as the palms were. It made the landscape more complex than it really was, more expansive. The eye stopped in places, and the whole didn't need to be taken in with a single look. It was as if the site could have a story, one that could be read. Maybe there were events particular to it, more tonal really than narrative, something having to do with feeling about the work that took place in the buildings and what *that* might feel like. As things grew up, the impression would be changed a little, the pathways become less dramatic. I wondered if the buildings would lose their aggressiveness as well.

I found only one thing that seemed off to me, that section of terracing at the freeway's verge that we'd been messing with almost since the beginning. We'd initially decided on the terrace movement, a rather severe one, steps of grass and various wildflowers coming down the embankment at the freeway, growing lower and toward the centroid as it moved inward, something that would be seen clearly from the buildings but would be of little visual significance from most other places. Once we'd cut it in, it had seemed tricky, too much of a surprise for those who parked in the lot near the administration building, and we'd chucked it, got the men to doze it out. But then we'd put Chen's pool in, and even though we'd hidden it down behind elevations, it had quickly become too focal, and we'd put the terrace back to balance it. I could not see the pool's edge from where I stood, but I knew its place. The terrace, though we'd softened its angles, seemed to push out toward me from the freeway's verge. We'll need something there, I thought, but not that. I decided I'd better take drawings and plans with me to the hospital.

When I reached my block in Seal Beach, I saw that the gutters and the grass between the sidewalk and the street were covered with scatters of palm frond. They'd clipped the trees, and when I'd parked and turned the motor off I could hear the grind and whine of the brush shredder a few blocks away. The clipping was an every other year event, which I'd forgotten about. The last time it happened, I'd managed to spend most of my time working at the small office Chen and I kept in the city. We used the place mostly for presentations. We had a good projector, a conference table, and a fridge and stove in the wall. Chen, like me, had a more serious work space at home, a studio built onto the back of his house in Eagle Rock. I'd built mine to the side of my little house, over the garage that I'd had constructed at the same time. It had skylights and high windows, and I hadn't cut any corners. There was a good library, a large drafting table, a bed and comfortable chairs, and the right lighting in places where I needed it.

Seal Beach was no longer a quiet community. On weekends the sidewalks got plenty of traffic, but it was not enough to bother me. The houses along the street were low and a little ramshackle, built mostly in the twenties and thirties, and not all of them were well kept. They'd gotten very expensive though, and there were owners who rented or just used the places as beach houses. But there were some of us who'd been there awhile. I had a few real neighbors. But mostly I liked living there because it was close to the ocean. I walked the beach almost every day, at least for a half hour, and there was always that salt tang in the air to give me pleasure.

Carrying my two small suitcases, I went to the garage door and unlocked it. I could get to both the house and the studio that way, but before I made a choice for either, I opened the door of my old Porsche, got in, and gave it a try. The starter groaned for a moment, then quit, the battery dead. I took my suitcases and went into the house, walked straight through to the bedroom and put them on the bed. Then I went through the rest of the place, opening a few windows and raising venetians. I went up to the studio then and got copies of the project plans out, took them to the drafting table and looked at them, making sure that everything I needed was there. I slipped them into one of the large flat artist's carrying bags I kept for that purpose. Before leaving, I lifted the phone from its cradle and called the gas station. They said they would send someone out right away, but I told them the morning was good enough, before ten o'clock. I'd had them out many times before. The little Porsche was fifteen years old, and it had been giving me ongoing trouble for the last two. It was a joke with Chen, though a gentle one. The car was a fine piece of machinery still, and Chen liked it a lot. I'll have to get something more reliable soon, I thought, maybe after we finish the project.

The whine of the palm shredder was louder when I got back to the rental car. It was Saturday, and they'd be quitting soon, but sure as hell they'd start up in the morning. I'd better be ready to give up sleep early.

Chen was sitting in the solarium, leaning back in a chair, his crutches resting against another one beside him. He had his glasses on and was reading a gardening magazine, and when he saw me he started to rise up. I lifted my hand as I approached him, smiling. He was smiling too, half because he'd tried to rise, forgetting his condition, but also out of his obvious pleasure in seeing me. There were still some nasty bruises on his face and along his neck, and the line where the stitches had been, running from his lip to the corner of his eye, was red and apparent. Most of the swelling was gone though, and his coloring was much better. Some of my own lingering aches came up in me when I saw him, and I recognized how they had been almost totally lost to me while I was in the East. The cut along my brow had remained tender, but I'd often forgotten that it was there, surprised when I touched it absently with my hand.

"Limbs and torso in good shape," Chen said, still smiling, lifting his arms like a child imitating a bird. "Only this," and he knocked his knuckles against the cast that rose almost to his hip. It made a dull, hollow sound. He'd rapped it pretty hard. "At least a month before they take it off. But they'll be putting the rubber plug in at the bottom early tomorrow. Then it will be the cane."

"Chen," I said, and then sat down in the vacant chair beside him, reached out and took his hand, squeezing it and pumping it up and down.

We didn't get right to the meat of things. It was not Chen's way to do that, and the fact that we'd been apart for close to two weeks meant that he'd take even longer with formalities, those words of reacquaintance before beginning. Early on, when we'd first gotten together, I'd been impatient with this, always wanting to push ahead, to get down to business. But in a while I grew to like it, to see the reason in it. It was a way of centering, both in oneself and in the situation. Then, when that was accomplished, one could feel focused, really ready, and the work could go on without digression. In the beginning I'd just waited, impatient for him to finish, but in a while I saw the sense of it and began to use it as I thought he did.

"Really spectacular, these past few days," he said. "They've a garden here. Thoughtless, but the administrator's wife is involved in flowers, has even tried orchids. The air has been crystalline. The flowers make the little square plot beautiful."

"Are they for the patients?" I said.

"Not necessary. My family brings what's needed. But now that I'm ambulatory, I can get out to the place. We had a little talk. She was showing it off to friends. And you, Jack, what was it like in the East?"

It went on like this, five minutes, maybe ten. I told him about the funeral, a little about the paintings and the letters, but I stayed clear of the more serious matters, the deaths, Angela and Dorit.

I told him about Congress Park, what the parks themselves were like now, what I remembered of them from my past. I said I'd have some photos to show him, some things I wanted to ask him about.

"You've been to the site?" he said, when he was ready.

"Right. About two hours ago. It looked very good."

"Benitez has stayed on top of things."

"How about the other?" I said. "Has anything come up?"

"No. Nothing yet. They seem to be still looking into it. Do you think it's right? Out there at the site, I mean?"

"Have you been out there?"

"Yes. Two days ago, with Benitez. I'll bet it's that terraced piece you're thinking about."

"Right as usual, Chen. What do you think?"

"I think we should yank it out again. Do something else, but I'm not sure what."

I got the plans out and spread them on the large Formica table. There was no one else in the solarium, and we were able to dig into things for a good fifteen minutes without interruption. We tried the terrace in a few other places, tried cutting it out completely, replacing it with various other shapes and contours, but we found we couldn't decide on anything.

"We'll just have to go out there," Chen said in a while. "See it at the right times of day, figure it against light and vantage."

"Tomorrow would be best, I think. Sunday, and no work to get in the way. Can you get out of here tomorrow?"

"Yes," he said. "I can get Donny. Let's say we meet there at four?"

"Right," I said. "Unless it rains."

"Unless it does. Why don't we speak by phone at two."

After we'd settled things, we sat and talked for a few more minutes. Then the nurse came in and told Chen it was time he got back to bed, got his leg elevated again. I was ready to show him the photographs when she entered, and Chen suggested that I take a look at the garden. There were lights out there, he said. Then we could talk a little more.

I didn't go to the garden but made my way down a staircase and out a fire door that opened onto the parking lot. It was almost dark now, close to eight o'clock, and a light breeze had come up, pushing a little at the palm fronds, high on slender trunks that lined the edges of the blacktop. I leaned against the building's side and went over things.

I'd not thought much about Congress Park, Aunt Waverly, and what I'd left behind in the East since I'd gotten back. There'd been the shock of return, the feeling that I'd been gone for a long time and that California was a slightly foreign place. And then, too, I'd been working the project over in my mind since returning and seeing it. I'd let it slip while I was gone, known it was in good hands. But it had quickly become a focus again once I'd seen its clear successes and minor problems. Now, talking to Chen, I found myself at ease about things. We'd been through the worst of what could happen, and the rest would be easy going. I felt a dull nostalgia, knowing I would probably be heading back east again before long, wanting really to be here to see things through for a while. Yet in the time of my stay I had things to do.

I thought once again about the letters, one still to read, about the paintings and the Polaroids I had in my jacket pocket, the tattoo illustration, and about Dorit. I'd be searching out Mark Janes the next day, trying to find some way to him; not to reach him—that should be easy enough—but to figure out some plan of approach, considering that I didn't know quite what I wanted from him. I wanted information of some kind. That was all I knew. But getting information had recently led to things that were shocking, and it was possible that my vague searching had been catalyst to these things, that I was in some way responsible. I'd have to go carefully, but I wasn't quite sure what careful going meant. McHale came to mind, and I felt an ominous surge as I thought of him, something odd about his strong desire to see the paintings and then going away like that. I shook it off, realizing that I was assuming far too much. His life was not the one that I was looking into. He wasn't living for the paintings and the rest, as I had been. Still, I'd ask Aunt Waverly to call the Art Institute. Or maybe I'd give them a call from home.

In a while I turned and went to the door and up the stairs to Chen's room. He was tucked in his bed, clean sheets and a faint smell of disinfectant. His leg was elevated, resting on some kind of stiff pillow over the coverlet. He was sitting up in the bed, the pile of plans spread out over his stomach and legs.

"I've checked it again," he said as I entered the door. "I think we'll need the aerial shots and the countour drawings, just to make certain before we make a move. There should be copies out at the trailer."

I pulled a chair over close to his bed and sat down, but it was too low, and I stood up again.

"Good idea," I said.

"That's right. Can you get my copies? There, over there in the bag in my closet. I've got them marked up."

I got the large sheets, and we went over them for a good half hour, suggesting other possibilities to each other. We were both pretty certain about the problem at least, and I thought that our on-site view and a look at those other renderings the next day could only confirm it.

"Now," he said, when we were finished. "What's this other thing?"

I took the plans and put them on the empty bed beside his own, separating his from mine into different piles and getting the tattoo illustration out of my bag. I talked as I ordered things. I told him a little about the paintings, enough about the letters to suggest Uncle Edward's history and concerns. I left Dorit and Angela out of it. That was a long story, and I wanted to get his opinion on the photo. I think I also felt that even he might be in some danger if I spoke of everything. It was as if the whole business were a kind of disease, and those who received too much of it had possible trouble coming. I did mention the deaths, just that they had happened, so he would have some sense of why I found the matter serious. I don't think I needed to tell him that. The fact of family made it all serious enough for him.

Instead of showing him only the one photograph, I handed him the whole stack. He went through them quickly, then started through again, moving slowly, pausing for a long time over the ones he found the most interesting. He made two stacks on the cover over his thighs. I noticed that he put the one I wanted to ask him about in the larger pile. Then he took the smaller pile up again, shuffled through it, and pulled out two. They were ones with Dorit in them. He held them up and turned them toward me.

"These are some paintings," he said. "Your uncle was involved with her?"

"In a way," I said. "Yes, he was involved. He was seventy then, maybe a little older."

"You can tell it," he said. "It's in her skin and gestures, habits of his hand. Who is she?"

"Well, that's a whole other story, Chen. Just a woman to me so far. But someone I'm getting more involved with too now. I don't really know. He spoke of her in letters, but I haven't finished them yet."

"Take your time," he said.

I reached over and took the larger stack from the cover and searched through it until I found the landscape shot. Then I handed it across to him.

"It's this one," I said.

He put the others down and held the Polaroid I'd given him up in the air a little, turning it slightly to remove the glare and get it properly into the light. He looked at it for a long time, then lowered it face down on his chest.

"Could you reach me my glass?" he said.

I thought he meant his water glass and got up and went around the foot of the bed to get it.

"No. The magnifier. It's in the closet, a little box on the shelf."

I went and found it and brought it to him. He put it on the cover beside the faced-down picture and opened it. It was lined in soft velvet, a finely wrought metal handle with a thick circular lens attached to it inside. He took it out, then lifted a felt rag from the box and held the magnifier up in the light and polished it. Then he dropped the rag and lifted the picture up again and studied it through the lens, moving it back from him a little, then bringing it closer, almost against the lens surface at times.

I thought of Uncle Edward's lenses as I watched him, remembering the strange discoveries I had made with them, and though I was anxious for him to speak, I knew I had to give him all the time he needed. He took a very long time, turning the photo in various ways, moving his lens. Finally, he put the picture down on the white coverlet and carefully replaced the lens in its box. His eyes swam and took a moment to focus when he looked at me.

"It's a pisser," he said. "Extremely accurate, but luminous at the same time. This uncle of yours, he was a very fine painter. Do you know the place? Is the light here in any way accurate?" He tapped the photo surface with his finger. "The color surely isn't. This turn of growth in the corner, that's chamomile, grows like this near the Aegean. I've only seen it at garden shows and in books, but good books. The color here is off."

"I don't know. It's a Polaroid," I said. "The Aegean begins to sound right though. But I wouldn't have thought such formality there. And what about the size? That's really the thing. And who might have done it? Can you make anything out of that?"

He picked the photograph up again, studied it for a while without the glass, then took the glass out of the box again and looked through it for a few more moments.

"Could be a number of people," he said. "Depending. If it's Greek or Italian. And depending most on how old it is. If it's Greek, and it does have that touch, then it's just slightly derivative, Italian influence."

"Why do you say Italian? I'd guess it's Greek. I mean of Greece. I don't know the architecture."

"That's the point," he said. "If it's Greek, it's not one of the few famous ones but a very good one, no doubt. Maybe an apprentice. But that depends a lot on the age, and it's very hard to tell because the current surfaces, the berms and contours and of course the plantings, are recent—some of it is at least. The centroid is still the same, I think, I mean original, but there have been changes. You'd have to be sure it's not Italian."

"Let's go with that for a while. Say it's Greek. Can you figure anything about size or expense, maybe location? Anything like that?"

"Well, I'd say it's pretty high up, surely above heavy timber shade. All these plantings need plenty of sun, as far as I can make them out. It's cropped, of course. I mean the painting is. He cut out a section of it for the painting. And, too, it's far bigger than what is there."

"How big?"

Chen turned the photo so we both could see it. "The house would be up here. At the top," he said. "But a good distance up. You see this trail, its turn? There'd be another, a much larger and broader one, way back. This one is an echo. That larger one most probably cuts up and levels near the house. Maybe hooks into a sweep of drive. Gravel, probably. And in the foreground and at the foot too, it's starting to open out. I think this was done in the middle of the place, looking up toward the house. I'd figure a good ten acres running back behind him, where he stood when he painted it, but more to either side. He may have been *off* to the side somewhat, catching this wash of north light. It was surely done in the afternoon. If he did it on site, that is. I can't believe he did it from a photograph. But then I really can't be sure. Possibly fifty acres of garden here. Because of the terracing, as you've no doubt figured, the ascent is steep. It cost a lot to do. All of this was excavated. But as I said before, age is an issue. The elevations are clearly very old, I think. The last century? It could be a site on top of a site that is very old, so probably the major cost was well in the past. Possibly five to ten years of new growth here though."

"That would be right, I think. Do you think it's all indigenous?"

"Oh, yes," he said. "No doubt about that. Oleander, hibiscus, begonia, bougainvillea. Even this stuff—it's ilex, very ancient Greek stuff."

"And would some of the stuff be large when he brought it in?" I knew the answer to that. I was reaching now, asking for information that I really didn't think I needed. But Chen had so much knowledge about such things that I thought to drain him, learn everything I could.

"Nothing need have been too large. No, not at all. Most of this is not easily transplanted when it gets big. You know that. It all looks pretty healthy, well kept. There's a thing I wonder though."

"What's that?"

"Well, this was a very big job, as I've said. And I can't imagine anything so expansive, except for public things, along the Aegean, those islands. Why would your uncle take on such a thing, even if he just bought it? I mean a painter of his kind. From these other photographs. Why such artifice? Those islands seem good enough as they are, congenial to what he was doing. But then I've never been there, you know. Just books. Still, it's curious to me. This extravagance. Like time and money to burn. Do you think he might have just painted this at some public place? That might explain it."

I took the photograph myself then and looked at it. I saw it in a new way since Chen had been talking about it. I could get what he meant, could even imagine the large expanse beyond the frame now. Could Uncle Edward have made such a painting at someone else's place, a public garden? There was nothing at all in what I'd come to know of him to suggest that was reasonable. There had been those times when he'd painted on site in that park near Muswell Hill, but that had been long ago. And I knew I'd come to think of the photo, its inclusion with the rest, as yet another message. I knew I didn't want to let go of that. This and all Chen's information stopped me. I couldn't get beyond it to any judgment.

"I don't know," I said. "I'll keep it all in mind."

I thought to press Chen further, but I could see that he was getting tired. It was ten o'clock, and we'd been working at various things for a long time. I knew Chen had a way of putting a face on things. He was probably more tired than he appeared. So I got up and stretched, feigning tiredness in myself, and suggested that we give it up for the night.

"But might I keep this photo until tomorrow?" he said.

I was taken back by his question, not really sure just why. It had something to do with contagion, some vague fear that if I left it with him, he'd be vulnerable. I shook off the feeling, gathered the other photos, and left the landscape picture on the coverlet. Then I reached to the other bed and got the tattoo copy, brought it over, and placed it beside the photo on the cover over Chen's thighs.

"Maybe you can take a look at this too," I said. "It's a tattoo of some kind. An enlargement. My uncle had it in one of his letters."

Chen looked down at it, then touched the edge of the white paper, squaring it up with the edge of the photograph.

"Tomorrow," I said. "I'll call at two."

"Good," he said. "You look tired, Jack. Get some rest."

"Okay," I said, realizing just then that I was indeed tired. "You too, Chen. Hey, it's good to see you. You're coming along. Can I do anything?"

"Nothing, Jack," he said. "Just get some rest. Gotta be sharp tomorrow."

I left him, turning to wave when I got to the doorway. But he wasn't looking. He'd taken the photograph up again and was studying it through the lens. I went down the back stairway to the fire door and opened it. A breeze had come up strongly. The slender trunks of the palms were bending slightly, and I had to hold my coat across my chest to keep it from blowing open. I crossed the lot to my rental car, and before I reached it, it was raining.

It was still raining in the morning, a gentle though persistent rain. It had rained intermittently through the night. I'd awakened at 3:00 A.M., vague and restless in my own bed, had thought I was in Angela's and had risen and gone out to the front porch. It was not raining then. There were stars and a slice of moon, large clouds scudding at a good pace in from the ocean. Before I reached my bed again, rain was tapping against the panes.

Now the sky was a dull slate gray. As I made coffee, I could see rain in puddles on the cement of the fractured walkway that went to the alley from my kitchen window. The cut fronds scattered in the gutter out front had banked against the little runoff, and there were places where small waves washed over them. It was nine o'clock; I'd slept late, but it was a quiet morning. They'd not be shredding the leavings for a while now, not until they dried out, until it stopped raining.

By the time I'd showered and shaved, it was close to ten, and I made some more strong coffee and then called Chen. His voice sounded strong on the phone.

"Doesn't look good," I said. "They give rain on the radio until tonight."

"I've heard it," he said. "How about we make it the same thing tomorrow, the same business. You can call me around two o'clock?"

"Sounds good. But I thought I'd drop in tonight for a visit. Is the plug in?"

"No need, Jack. I mean you're welcome, of course. But the family's coming over. It's my son's birthday. We wouldn't be able to work any. They're fixin' to plug me in an hour or so."

"Which one?"

"It's Donny. He likes to be called Don now. Can you believe he's twenty? We're getting older, Jack."

They'd called me Jackie, back those many years ago in Congress Park. I'd liked it that Aunt Waverly had called me Jack, had seen me growing up before the others had.

"I can understand that," I said. "Don sounds better. We could be older."

"Soon enough," he said, with a laugh in his voice.

While I was dressing, I heard someone pull up out front and went to the bedroom window. It was the station. The man who'd come was the owner's son. He couldn't get the Porsche started with a jump, fiddled under the hood for a while, then figured he'd better tow it in.

"Could be the cable," he said. "But I'm not sure. I need the machine."

I told him I didn't need it today. I'd get back to him in the morning. I watched as he hooked it up and pulled down the drive. He was very careful with it. I think he liked the car about as much as I did.

By the time I got to the office complex, the rain had cut back a little, but there was still enough of it to make a raincoat reasonable. I'd decided against a jacket but had put a tie on before leaving the house. Since the meeting with Chen was off, I really had nothing to do, so even though it was Sunday I decided to begin with Janes, to check his office.

The place was relatively new, a half-dozen buildings set at rather arty angles around a square with a number of shops at ground level. Sleekly expensive little shops for the most part, though a few were places of service for those who worked in the buildings. It was hard to believe that the place contained medical offices. One might have guessed business, technical stuff, computers. Only in California, I thought.

The square was entered from the street, down a broad sidewalk lined with dramatic plantings, various Eastern ferns in hard-edged metal planters in a severe row, petal-shapes to the overhanging lights along it. Once in the square itself, it was the shop fronts, a few benches and fountains, glass doors as entrances into the office buildings; only two of the six were more than five stories high. I figured the buildings' architects for the landscaping, a package deal. They'd chosen display at every turn, and the stuff would take plenty of tending before too long.

At one place an archway passed between two of the buildings. This led to the back of the complex, where there were entrances off the parking lot, some with the names of medical offices over them. It was clear they didn't want patients entering through the square itself, at least not those who needed help, wheelchairs, walkers, and such. There were ramps in the back, an ambulance entrance. They'd designed the place to keep the sick and disabled out of sight, not to unsettle the ones who came for other reasons, who would spend money in the shops, make healthy business deals and decisions.

I found Janes' name in the middle of the listings in the lobby of the building I knew was his. He was on the top floor, the only one there, though most of the other floors had two or three firms listed. Most were medical or medically related, a few labs and one photographic studio. There was even a medical illustration firm. Unlike Uncle Edward, I thought: this one dealt in lasers, exotic photomicrometry, microscopic reproduction.

While I was studying the listings, I felt a breath of air behind me, the door opened, and there was a jangle of keys. I turned and saw the uniformed man at the same time that he saw me.

"Hi," he said. "All closed up. It's Sunday. Only some overtime in the labs. Anything I can help you with?"

He was a young man, no more than mid-twenties, I guessed. And he looked better than the job he had as watchman in this place. His uniform was extremely neat, as was his hair, even his nails, I noticed, as he moved to the desk between the elevators. There was nothing on the desk but a phone, a small pad and pencil.

"Oh, no," I said. "It's just that I was checking out Dr. Janes. Something I need to see him about. Thought I'd give it a try anyway. Even though it's Sunday."

"He's not here," he said, as he settled into the chair behind the desk.

"Well, it's Sunday," I said.

"No. I mean he's gone. About three weeks now, I think. Vacation. You could check tomorrow. The office is open. Let's see." He found a key on his ring of many keys and opened the desk drawer. "There's a number. Emergencies, et cetera. Somebody taking his cases."

"That's okay," I said. "I can check with the office tomorrow."

But he had found his book, located the number, and was writing it down on the pad. He tore the sheet off and handed it to me. He'd printed Janes' name carefully at the top. I took the sheet, thanked him, and started to leave. Then I thought since I was there I'd give him a try.

"With a place like his, you wonder why he'd need a vacation."

"Yeah." He laughed, clearly welcoming the conversation. "Huntington Harbour. You know, he's got a driver brings him in from there. Every day of the week. What a life." He shook his head, smiling.

"That's a long haul," I said. Huntington Harbour was not too far from my place in Seal Beach, and I was a little shocked by that and by the quickness with which I'd gotten the information.

"Not too," he said. "But he comes in real early, before the traffic. I usually work graveyard. Go to college. And I see him every day. And he's not driving. How can that be bad?"

"What are you studying?" I said.

"Criminology. Mostly the research end of it."

"Can it get you a driver too?"

"Oh, God no!" He shifted in his chair and laughed again. "But maybe as good a brand of whiskey as he drinks when he gets home."

"Beside the pool."

"He doesn't have one. Just a boat and a fine patio."

"You've seen it?" I said.

"Me? No, not me. His driver told me about it. Sometimes the guy hangs around here, just waiting to take the doctor to the hospital or whatever."

"Drives a fine car, does he?"

"Yeah. But just a town car. Not his. It's a rental deal. The driver and the car both. Must cost a small fortune."

"Hertz?" I said.

"Oh, no, nothing like that. I don't even think they do that. It's a small place. Fredricks, I think the name is. Yeah, Fredricks. It's only a few miles from here."

"What a life," I said, smiling back at him, and left.

I found the place through information, using the open phone booth between two of the buildings, and made the call. They were open, and I drove over. It was toward the ocean, still in Long Beach, an outfit that dealt in limos exclusively, short-term things mostly, weddings, proms, and such. When I told the woman I was interested in something long term, she brightened up. I gave Janes' name as a reference, saying I'd forgotten his exact address. I didn't recognize the street name she read off his card, though Chen and I had done considerable work in the early days in Huntington Harbour, a fairly wealthy community of good-sized homes, the finest of which fronted the harbor itself. If Janes did have a boat, his was probably one of those. It shouldn't be hard to find.

I left and went to a small diner that I knew nearby. It was twelve-thirty and still raining, intermittently now. There was no clear sign yet that it might be clearing, though; still plenty of cloud cover.

I lingered over a sandwich and had a second cup of coffee. I wasn't sure just how to continue with the matter, but I knew I was going out to find Janes' place, to see it at least. I'd have to figure what to do when I got there. Maybe he would be home. Then I'd have to decide about approaching him. Even more, I wondered what I'd do if he wasn't there. I couldn't just let things sit until he got back. I'd have to find some way to move ahead.

It struck me as I sipped my coffee that I could just stop the whole thing right there, finish up what remained with Chen on the project, go east and settle things in Congress Park, then come back again and take up my own life. Forget Angela and Dorit. But even as their names came to me, I knew that I couldn't think to do that. I was too deep in it now to let it go like that. It all felt a little like a game, a bit unreal now that I had left Congress Park behind. But

Angela at least was no game. I felt a responsibility to Aunt Waverly to do what I could to find her, find out about her anyway. She could be dead, I thought, but even finding that out felt necessary. Even as I turned her in my mind, a figure without any clear delineation, only that picture I could construct from memories of her as a child my own age, an adolescent, lost as I was then, it struck me that it was not she, really, but Dorit that I was after. It was the power of the paintings and the letters that was pushing me. I thought I'd better read the last letter soon. I knew I might need its information, though I was finding out that the letters didn't always tell the truth, at least not a truth I could count on.

But I knew as well that that was really not it at all. I simply needed the textures again, needed that slow unfolding of Uncle Edward's life, that partial reconstruction of those years I'd thought were lost to me. Somehow, through the whole crazy complex of things, I was making up my own past, bridging a twenty-seven-year void. How odd that it all centered on Congress Park, though so little about it was of that place. And I knew too that it was the last letter and that I was putting off that ending.

It was three o'clock by the time I got to the edge of Huntington Harbour, where I stopped at a gas station and found the street I was looking for on a map. It was a short, curving street, no thoroughfare but a broad half circle that started and ended close to the same place. You wouldn't go down it to get anywhere else. You'd have to be heading for one of the few houses on it, places that were set on large parcels of land, no one in sight of any other, each protected by its particular landscaping.

Janes' was at the farthest end of the curve, set back and down just a little on what passed for a hillside below the street. From the curb where I parked, I could see only his rooftops over the slope. The yard leading down to the house was heavily overgrown, large trees, eucalyptus that required a lot of care and cleaning up, and a variety of thick evergreens. The drive curved sharply down, twisting and moving out of sight where I guessed the garage would be.

I sat in the car for a few moments, knowing I'd have to find a better place to park. People didn't leave cars in the street in Huntington Harbour for very long, and I didn't know how long I'd be. I started up and drove along the curve, and half a block down I came to a house where construction was under way. A huge wing was being added, but because it was Sunday there was no one on the site. The foundation was half in, and there was a pickup parked near a mound of earth, a small flatbed trailer with a black tarp over it, pieces of lumber sticking out in places. I pulled my rental car into the newly cut driveway, close to the side of the pickup, and got out and locked it. It would do, I thought. Then I made my way back along the street to Janes' house. There was no sidewalk on his side, so I walked along the other. I wore my raincoat and carried my case, tried to look businesslike.

When I reached Janes' narrow drive, I crossed and turned into it without hesitation. It curved slightly as it fell a little, enough so that the house itself was obscured by the trees and tended shrubs that lined it and created a dense pattern over most of the property, a frontage that I judged at a good hundred feet, a substantial piece of land for a house on the water. The lot was really fairly shallow, and in moments I reached the turn of the drive and came upon it, a low-slung modern affair, its central entranceway marked by a mansard roof, with two blocky wings running from either side of it.

I went up the short brick walkway to the door. A row of glass panes flanked it, and I could see right through the house, down a kind of closed courtyard, quarry brick and skylights, wide French doors opening at its sides. At the end were glass doors wide as the courtyard itself, and beyond them was a patio, a small stone fence and gate, then a common boardwalk, and beyond that the broad finger of Huntington Harbour that served as a docking for houses that lined either side of it. I couldn't see much of the harbor. There was a boat, what looked like a good-sized yacht, docked directly across from the house, obscuring my view. I started to turn, then caught movement and stayed put. A man came into view with a hose in his hand. He entered the gate in front of the house and proceeded to drench the patio bricks with water. The hose ran out behind him, through the gate to the boardwalk.

I stepped back from the door and made my way on the crannied stone path that led around the left wing. When I got to the front, I saw that the whole length of it was patio. There were roses in large tub planters, a few fake Greek statues of very good quality, and a couple of heavy stone benches and tables. The man didn't hear me. He was washing the bricks, spraying the benches and tables. He'd left a bucket and a long-handled squeegee leaning against the gate at the entrance to the boardwalk. I moved toward him through the

planters, and soon he saw me, shut the nozzle down, and spoke. I
saw he was sizing me up, checking my briefcase.

"Can I help you?" he said.

"Maybe," I said. "I'm looking for Dr. Janes."

"Oh," he said, shaking the nozzle at his side, keeping the drib-
bles away from his leg. "Well, I don't think he's around, not for a
while, I mean. But I don't know really. I work for the Harbour, do
the boardwalk." He pointed the hose behind him. "Some people
have me do their patios. But I don't really know them. You missed
Louie, the gardener."

"He was here," I said.

"Right, yesterday. But have you checked Janes' office? That's
where I send my bill, not here. Somewhere in Long Beach."

"Oh," I said. "I'll do that. Thanks."

I started to turn, then stopped.

"Is that his boat?" I said.

"That's it." The man turned and looked at it. "Hasn't been out
for a while."

"Well, thanks," I said, and I turned and headed back around the
house. I checked the windows as I went. I could see the little decals
on them, notice of some burglar alarm company.

When I got back to my car, I opened the trunk and looked in. It
was empty. I lifted the mat that covered the spare tire and pulled
the iron out and the jack. Then I got in the car and rolled the
bottoms of my pants up a couple of turns and did the same with
the sleeves of my shirt. I took the tie off and opened the two top
buttons of the shirt as well, and turned the collar under. Then I got
back out, left the raincoat and briefcase on the seat, and, taking the
jack and iron, headed back to the house. I thought I must look like
a strange workman, but I was sure I no longer looked like a busi-
nessman. I'd messed my hair up, hoping that might help. The rain
had quit completely now, not even a few drops anymore, and
though there was no sun yet, the clouds were thinning and it was
brighter.

When I passed the house beside Janes' I could see through trees
that the man with the hose had moved along. He was washing the
boardwalk itself now. I turned into Janes' drive again and headed
for the wing that I hadn't seen. I'd noticed no heating or air-
conditioning units on the wing I'd gone around, and I figured
they'd have to be on the other side. There was no walkway where

I was headed, and I had to move into recently turned soil. I could feel the slight sink of mulch and peat under my shoes. There was nothing at all special about the landscaping, but I noticed that the evergreens were healthy. They'd been transplanted at a pretty good size, something that meant they'd needed a lot of care to sustain them early on.

There was no central air in the place, just a couple of large window units. If there was heat, it had to be electric, no heat pump or other device in view. I checked the first window unit. It was set in where the window had been opened, caulked carefully around the edges. I looked behind me before trying anything. There were trees between me and the yard of the next house, but they were thin, and anyone who was looking in my direction would be able to see me. I saw no one though, and didn't hesitate.

I checked the sides of the window that came down on the top of the air conditioner. There seemed to be nothing there, no wires, and the window hadn't been screwed down. Using the tire iron, I broke the caulking and pried the window up a little. It gave, and when I got my hands under it, it slid up with ease.

I didn't pause, but climbed up on the unit and crawled in through the window. When I hit the floor I headed immediately for the front door. The button box was there, set into the frame. The red light was on and constant. I checked the wall beside it, figuring that must be the place. There was a narrow door there, a closet, I guessed, and I opened it, pushed the few thin coats aside, and found the central box. On that one, near the bottom, there was a green light, nothing blinking. I stood and looked into the closet for a moment. I didn't know all that much about alarm systems, but I'd seen enough to figure that I hadn't tripped anything getting in. Still, he could be connected up somewhere to the police department, some silent alarm. It struck me that I was doing something a little crazy, a thing I really didn't need to be doing. At least I didn't need it in any reasoned sense. I could wait or contact Janes in some other way, find out what there was to learn later. But it was too late for that now. I was in there, and I didn't figure to get out until I'd found what I could. I closed the closet door then and began looking through the house.

I started with the room where the air conditioner was. It was clearly a guest bedroom, everything neat and in order, the closets empty. After I'd pulled the window down over the unit again, I headed to the kitchen and the living room. There were plenty of windows, and I tried to keep myself out of sight of anyone who might chance to look in, stayed close to the walls, even got down on my knees when that was impossible.

I found nothing at all in the master bedroom, just a few medical journals, an unopened pack of cigarettes, a closet with a dozen or more suits in a neat row. I looked under the shirts and underwear in the dresser, but after I'd checked a couple of drawers, I gave it up. Then I headed for the one remaining room in the place, which I figured must be the study. I remembered a skylight in the roof at that side of the house, and I didn't figure there'd be much in the way of windows where the room was located, at the edge of the right wing of the house, the corner near the harborside patio.

The door of the room was locked. But it was not a dead bolt, and using a kitchen knife, I managed to get it open easily. Inside, it was dark. There were drapes pulled across a line of high windows on the patio side, and a dark-green shade covered the skylight. I left the drapes alone, got a chair and climbed up on it, reaching to slide the shade from the skylight. Even though the sky was still overcast, plenty of light flooded in, and as I looked around the room from my slight elevation on the chair, I could see that I might not even have to turn a lamp on.

The place was indeed a study, with walls of bookcases, a large wooden desk, file cabinets, a couple of chairs, end tables, and lamps. The desk was against a wall, and on that piece of wall was a large bulletin board. I climbed from the chair, put it back where I'd found it, and went to the desk and sat down. I looked at the section of wall in front of me and knew quickly and with a shock what I was looking at.

The entire bulletin board was covered with neatly pinned up pictures. There must have been fifty of them at least. But one of them, near the center, caught my eye immediately. It was a photograph of a painting, one that I knew pretty well by now, the rendering of Dorit that was in the Art Institute in Chicago, the one with the figure looking down at the spinelike braid on the table.

As I let my eyes move across the rows of photographs, I could tell that all of them were pictures of Dorit. Some were photos of Uncle Edward's paintings of her, a few that I hadn't seen before, but I could tell by the way of the figure that it was she. But there were also numerous photographs of her in the flesh, all of them, I thought, taken when she was younger, younger than she had been when Uncle Edward had painted her.

In the very center of the top row was Dorit in a wedding dress. She was standing straight, a rather vacant smile on her face, and where her hands met at her waist, another hand was gathered in them. There had been another figure in the photo. It must have been Janes himself. Their wedding picture, but he had cut himself out of it.

I unpinned four of the photos of paintings, put them on the desk pad, and decided to risk the lamp. In the new and brighter light I could see that they were not snapshots but professional photos, and when I turned each of them over I found that they had been cut out of what must have been museum and gallery catalogues. One had the name of a gallery on it, below Uncle Edward's name and the name of the painting. I pinned the four back up, leaned across the desk, and looked more closely at the others. A good percentage of what was there seemed photos that had been taken in America, in the Midwest, I thought. Most were outdoor shots, Dorit in parks and yards, dressed casually or formally, each posed and taken with some care. I thought I could see in her way of standing, a slight discomfort and hesitation in both look and body, the things that Edward had seen, that had drawn him to paint her. She never seemed quite at ease in the pictures. Her smile, when it was present, was caught at just the wrong time, shortly before or just after she had composed it for the click. At least that was how an uninformed eye might see it. I thought I knew better and that timing was not the issue. It was just the way of her smile. She was always like that, between things, hesitant, never quite where she was.

Her hair grew into a braid as the pictures progressed. It was long in all of them, but it had been "done up" in what I took to be the earlier ones. Then any hint of a permanent disappeared, straight red hair, free at her shoulders, done in a braid or a tight bun, severe around her angular features.

Among the later pictures were ones that had clearly been taken in England. In these, the shots had also been trimmed to include only Dorit. There were those interior shots in which she couldn't be isolated completely, pictures at gatherings with other people close around her or in the background. I guessed all of these were taken in London, very possibly at some of those art gatherings that

Uncle Edward had written about in his letters. There were pictures in Victorian public rooms, and I saw paintings on sections of walls behind her. I searched closely for other familiar faces, hoping I might find Joan, even Uncle Edward, but there was nothing there. It struck me as I searched that I wasn't really too sure what Uncle Edward might look like. It also struck me that seeing the actual Dorit ought to have moved me in some way, at least to compare her to her presence in Uncle Edward's paintings. They were not realistic paintings, but the only thing apparent was how accurate he had been in catching what might be called an essence. Though there were differences, to be sure, there were no fundamental surprises at all.

At the bottom of the bulletin board, at the end of the last row of pictures, was a frontal shot, a photo of someone who was not Dorit. I'd missed it on my initial glance and had only looked closely at it as I moved methodically through the rows. I thought I knew who it was the moment I caught it, but I leaned closer over the desk to make sure. She was older, older than Dorit was in any of the photographs before me, at least forty years old, but she was still Angela. I remembered her. There were things in her face that suggested that wasted image I had been gathering, had constructed ever since I had spoken to Joan and to Angela's former husband in Milwaukee, had been gathering even from Aunt Waverly. She was smaller and more compact, leaner than I remembered. Much of that was simply age. She'd still had her baby fat when I left Congress Park. And she was darker too, a feel of toughness to the skin on her face and arms.

The picture was a bust shot only, no depth of field, and though there were outdoor figures behind her, there was not enough focus to place them, even guess at place. Her face seemed recently tanned, her dark hair was short and hooked back carefully on one side with a barrette. It was a black-and-white photograph. She was smiling, but in a restrained way. She seemed very in herself, certain and cool.

I unpinned the picture and turned it over. There was writing on the back, only a few words, *this is Angela,* and that was all. I held it in my fingers and looked down at it for a long time. Then I looked back at the wall of Dorit photographs. What is it that Janes is doing here? I thought. I could hear the faint songs of birds outside, a wash of sea against the pilings at the dock a few feet away. In a moment I jerked back a little. What am *I* doing here? I'd lost track of time and was no longer sure of its passage, how long I'd been considering the pictures and Janes' motives. He was hooked by her, that was clear enough, even after all these years.

I pinned the picture back in place and started going carefully through the desk drawers. As elsewhere in the house, everything was neat and in order. I found paper, pencils, some bills and professional correspondence. Then, at the back of the central shallow drawer, I found a large manila envelope, thick with something rigid inside. When I got the envelope out and on the desk pad, I saw that Janes' name and address were on it. It had been mailed to him, and I checked the return address, a box number in Athens, no name above it. I checked the postmark. It had been mailed to him in July of 1977, five years before. I started to open the clasp, then heard a noise somewhere in the house, a steady pounding. It stopped, and I realized that someone was knocking at the door. I sat still, then heard the knocking again, louder and more insistent.

I got up from the chair, left the room, and made my way down the hallway to a place where I could see through the glass panels to the side of the front door. Someone was out there, a man in uniform. I saw the sleeve of his right arm, something thin and official looking in his hand. He knocked again and called out. "Overnight express!"

I couldn't open the door. There was the alarm and also the possibility that he might realize I was not Janes. I too called out then. "Just a minute."

I turned and made my way quickly to the kitchen and opened the refrigerator. There was very little in there, but I found what I was after, opened the ketchup bottle, and shook it until I had a good pool of the thick red liquid in my palm. Then I started back toward the front of the house, and before I got to the door I lifted my palm and smeared the ketchup over my brow, feeling the scab there, and along the side of my cheek. I got my face close to the window at the doorside, then tapped on the glass with my hand. The man heard the tap, looked over, then stepped back a little in shock.

"It's okay," I said loudly. "Just a shallow cut." I used my ketchup-drenched hand to hide my face, realizing I must look a mess to him.

"Could you put it under the door?" I said.

"It's registered," he called out automatically, but before I could speak again, he said, "Okay, I guess. Go take care of it." Then he bent down and slid the thin envelope under the door.

It was nothing, just a letter from his broker announcing a special deal that had come his way. It was personalized, but clearly enough he'd sent it out to all his more important clients. I'd stained it with the ketchup, and decided to take it with me when I left. Seeing my face in the mirror as I washed the ketchup off in the bathroom, the strangeness of the bloody cycle came to me. I'd been cut with Chen at the trailer, the cut was opened again when I'd looked through the knee in Uncle Edward's painting in Downers Grove, and now I'd faked an opening, here as a criminal myself, a burglar in Janes' house.

I went through each of the rooms before leaving, made sure that everything was as I'd found it. The only things I took were the overnight letter and the manila envelope that I found in Janes' desk. Before I left the study, I reached inside the envelope and took out the contents. There was a brief handwritten note and a dark leather journal. I put the journal aside and read the note.

"Dear Mark," it said. "Your letters found me in London, the recent ones, just a few weeks ago. You see that I'm no longer there. You must stop writing. You ask for explanation, say that you need me. It can't be, Mark. I send the enclosed. It may hurt you, but I hope it will stop this finally. It's all I have to explain with. Please, don't write again. Dorit."

I put the letter aside and opened the journal. There was a blank page, and then on the next the handwritten prose began. Though there were places for date entries, none had been put down. It was no real journal or diary but a long prose passage, a letter, very neat and careful. I wanted to read it right then and had to force myself to close the cover over, put it and the note and the ketchup-stained letter into the envelope. Then I took a last look at the wall of photographs and reached for the lamp switch and turned it off.

Darkness flooded into the room, and when I looked up to the skylight, I saw that the sky was no longer overcast. There were a few faint stars visible, still day stars. It was not dark yet, but it was getting there. Early dusk was beginning. I'd been in the house for a very long time.

I got the chair and pulled the shade back over the skylight. Then I took the envelope and made my way to the guest room window.

By the time I was outside and among the evergreens, I could see evening lights in the house across from Janes'.

I walked back to the car, carrying the jack and the iron in one hand and the envelope in the other. In ten minutes I was out of Huntington Harbour, on the freeway and heading north. It was seven-thirty. I figured I could get to Seal Beach, be home again by eight.

Gentle Wave,

How the years have passed us by now, very much like your quiet name. Dorit has given birth to a son, Andrew, still a babe in arms as I write this letter.

How shocking it is that I should be a father, seventy-seven years old and alive again in this issue. I'd thought that painting had become my life. But to have a son, a wish that I'd buried deeply. All the surfaces of the world seem changed, though it comes to me too late.

I've held him in my arms sometimes, though not enough for me in these passing months. I have not held a child since Angela, and that's apparent in my awkwardness. Dorit can see it and withholds him, fearful, I guess, that I should not manage it. He's a delicate child, angular features like his mother, but with none of that uncertainty of bearing that's been hers, the very thing that drew me to her in the first place.

And she has changed since his arrival. No longer placidly beside herself, nor does she falter anymore. She makes decisions in her daily rounds and acts on them decisively. She seems at peace, no longer driven to indecision, in no way anymore the image I have rendered so often in the past.

And how can I state it without that mix of emotion I feel in doing so: Angela is here also. I write it down and feel myself reeling still in its articulation, though it has been for long enough now that I should be a little used to it.

I'd like to find myself in Greece and free of Muswell Hill. That was our plan, Dorit and I, to return again to that island on which I first saw her. I've been painted out in London for a while, I think, and Dorit, clear that she's a new self, knows there is nothing now that she cannot leave behind. She's thought of writing again, a thing she can do anywhere. And there have been her problems with Janes, his insistence that he have her back, and leaving London can help put a stop to that. And then there is Angela, our daughter, Wave, and my new son. And all this pushes us to think of leaving.

They are in the park now, the three of them, Andrew bundled and shaded in his carriage. I am sure they sit beneath a tree that I have painted. Angela may have been a figure there, though I did not recognize her as I formed the composition. Fruit, mineral water, hot tea in a thermos, curls at the corners of the coverlet. The white sheets on the bed behind me are severely crumpled, stained in places. It's a naked bed. I've tossed in it. The one in the other room is tightly made and mitered. They have a paisley quilt, too good for a picnic.

Wave, I think it must be a world of cruel justice. Late last night I was awakened to little Andrew's whimpers. I threw my covers back, came to my elbows. She was already passing, which one I could not tell, in a white nightgown, then back across the doorway holding him. I could see the orb of his little head held in her palm against her neck, gleam of a ring or bracelet. I heard the bed creak. He was between them then. I think there was quiet cooing. The sticks of my empty easel accusing me, in starlight through the archway. They have made a homestead in my studio. I'm as thin as a skeleton. Where can I begin?

Dorit went back to the husk of her marriage and then stayed away. Janes was adamant, but so was I, I fear. It was too soon to rush upon her freedom. Janes refused the divorce, then went along with it, then quickly regretted it. It was enough, I think, that he could focus on me, that simple sense at first of the older man (elderly man?), his own manhood assaulted in that way. It didn't help that I was an artist, nor one who had finally earned substantial sums of money.

But she stayed away, and it was inevitable, I see now. First with Joan, a young American woman I might have written you about. She was in the Bayard-Harwood crowd, a painter herself, but really a traveler with painters. That was short-lived, but passionate. And it was something that when she did come back had begun to center her. I did not want to see it then.

And we made love together, desperately for both of us, I think. For me because I'd come to need her beyond the painting, for her as a last attempt at it. I knew the tattoo on her, deep up in her thigh, that figure I'd taken on behind my own ear, duplicate of the emblem she had worn. She revealed that it was Janes' work, a thing he had forced on her. I've studied the figure on it, but without success.

But that Janes should have forced her in that way, to something she said she didn't want then, nor tell her its meaning. A kind of strange bondage. It's a matter beyond curiosity, so aberrant as to make us fear him, what he might be capable of. I set out to pursue that matter, though awkwardly, in thinking about it; to tell him after all that I had seen it on her, so intimately there, and had taken it on myself, to settle things once and for all with him. But Dorit would not allow it. He's made constant attempts at contact in the months we've been living together, letters that Dorit has mentioned but will not show me or speak of in any detail. Nothing really threatening, she's said. Still, I cannot shake the feel of trouble in the thing.

Then Dorit was pregnant. Then Angela arrived. Wave, it was so simple, on a street in London, one of those rare days when sun pushed the greens out and the sidewalks glistened, after a night of spring rain and a stiff wind that cleaned the air of smoke and humidity. She just walked up to me, to both of us, in fact.

I didn't recognize her at first. She had blocked the sidewalk where the two of us were passing. She was smiling, a rather cold smile, as I remember it now. She volunteered nothing. Just stood there in the way. And it was only when I knew her that she stepped forward, took my arms firmly in her hands and leaned into me, her head against my clavicle briefly, then pushed back, still holding me, at arm's length, watching my face, keeping me from moving to her.

We ate lunch together. She was staying with friends, she said. She had appointments. She would call.

And she didn't call. And I had no address or phone for her. It had all been very fast. We'd talked of nothing really, just the places where she had been, their names but no particulars. There were many of them and many jobs too. Generalities of what the years had brought her. Nothing at all about difficulties, though she didn't look too well really. But I had no way of knowing about causes.

She said that she knew of me, not that she had followed things in any way but that she had that kind of knowledge in her circle, many circles as I constructed it from her clipped comments. That she had seen occasional references to my work from time to time.

She watched Dorit as she spoke and at times looked steadily at her stomach. Dorit was not clearly pregnant yet, but she was living in it, and I think I saw things pass between them, what I would have called womanly things then. Maybe she could see it in Dorit's face, as I thought I had come to see it. I didn't even learn how long she had been in London.

She has changed, Wave. But what could I expect? She was no more than a girl, and she's a woman of forty or more now. I don't even remember her birthday. She has changed to a kind of person I could not have expected, even had I had expectations. That I didn't accuses me, of course, and though I am old I am not too old for such regrets. Still, they are formal ones, and that feels like a kind of insanity to me. I am old enough to welcome that as the way things are or have become in me, to take it for what it is. Changed, so that she is capable of a measured acceptance of me as her father, and what she has done to me does not seem a term in any way of malice. She is well beyond that, as I hope am I.

Whatever the complexity of causes in her leaving us so many years ago, there is that one thing at the heart of her that relieves us all of blame. We could never, any of us, have known or dealt with it, though I believe you could have, had you known, better than Angela or I. I don't even know it now, but I think it has something to do with character, that of an underlife below the surface.

Then after a while she simply appeared again. Called me in Muswell Hill, came over, and before I knew much about what was

happening she had moved in. We've come to a certain understanding since she's been here, and it is because of that that I write you
this letter.

We'd like to come home now, Wave. We won't call. That would
not be in fairness to you, and it is true too that Angela at least
needs a little time. So we have thought to wait just a while, until
Andrew is old enough to either leave alone with Dorit or to bring
him with us, all four of us to come then, back to Congress Park for
a visit.

Can you find a way to answer this letter? Can you give us the
time we need? It has been so long now, Wave, what can a few
months mean? But we'll all come if you will have us. Please, do
write. Let us know that we are in some way welcome.

Yesterday I saw them in the same park in which today they are
having their picnic. They had my son out of his stroller and down
on the blanket in the grass between them. It was warm, and they
had stripped him of his clothing. They may have done so in order
to change him, but I can't be sure. At any rate, he was naked on
the coverlet, his little arms and legs, so white and slowly moving
in the air, little graceful kicks and reaching out. And what he
reached out for in his play was Dorit's braid, thick and fiery red.

She was on her hands and knees, her head extended out and
over his twisting body, the braid hanging down in the air toward
him. Angela had the braid in her fist, was waving it, the filaments
of its slightly tufted end, which he reached up for, tickling against
his fingers, teasing them, pulling away. She too was looking down
at him. He must have been smiling, as she too must have been, as
Dorit surely was. I couldn't tell though, for I could see none of their
faces. I thought I could hear his laughter, little squeaks, the punc-
tuating language of their quiet calls and cooings. It could have been
a quality of the gentle wind in the leaves near me though. I couldn't
be sure of it.

But there was one thing I was sure of, and that was of closure.
Theirs was a different world from mine, one at a fundamental dis-
tance. It was not a term of the physical space between us, nor that
I was outside of their activity and only watching it.

In their simply patterned dresses, Angela's matching scarf, the
rings at Dorit's wrists, the way their arms brushed against each
other in their movements over the baby, Dorit's braid like a spinal
cord in Angela's fist, in all these simple things and gestures there

was a world of women only. And there was Andrew, my own son, growing even as they played their game with him. He'll enter a different world from mine, I thought. He'll live in another century.

I left them then, but I didn't set out to do the shopping that was my day's job. I went back and mounted a fresh canvas, thinking I would paint something from memory.

Write to us, Wave. Let us know that even if we are not all that welcome you will at least accept us. Wait a little while and we will be with you, though not as in the past, before very long.

Your husband,
Edward

T HAT NIGHT I DREAMED of my mother and father and the day of their accident. Not the accident itself, but the morning, before their leaving. I could not be sure how much of the dream was memory, what parts a construction of my recent days in Congress Park with Waverly, how much that simplicity that dreams can be made of, the day's residual, a wish that things had been otherwise.

At any rate, Chen was in the dream. He was in my father's chair, but he was not rocking. He wore his cast, his leg extended out before him. I was on the floor, a child, naked but with my own mind, uncomfortable in my exposure. Chen looked down at me, accepting, and I was soothed by his expression. Women were talking, Waverly and my mother and some others, I think, in another room in the house. My father stood beside the chair, and in the dream I thought he should have wanted Chen to get out of it, to give it back to him. But there was nothing in his behavior to suggest he wanted that.

He stood, legs crossed at the ankles, his hand on the chair's high back. He was looking above my head at some corner of the room. He was gazing not blankly but intently, and I thought there must be something there.

In the dream I could imagine the whole house, remember every room, closet, and piece of furniture. Each fabric and wood texture seemed a part of me, a thing that could never, in any world, be changed.

I remember I turned to where my father was looking, knowing before I did so exactly what the corner of the room was like. I was waking up from the dream as this happened. There were voices of my mother and Waverly, of the other women entering the door behind me, something about its being time to go. The thing in the corner where my father looked was just beginning to come into my view as I turned my head. I opened my eyes from dreaming, found myself on my side, the tube of rolled plans, an empty glass, and the thick manila envelope I'd taken from Janes' on the dresser to the side of my bed.

Though Uncle Edward's last letter was a revelation, I didn't experience reading it as such. I think I'd been convinced, from my talk with Joan, that Angela would appear. Nor was the child a shock to me, though I was curious that Joan had said nothing about Dorit's pregnancy, though perhaps she hadn't known. The only shock was one of regret, both that it was the last letter and that Aunt Waverly hadn't opened it. It had been written five years before. I'd have to tell her about it, but I wondered what difference it would make now. What might Edward have thought when he'd received no response? Wouldn't he have called, at least written again, to find some way of knowing whether Waverly was all right?

Janes and the tattoos were an ominous note, and I was relieved that I had not found him when I'd gone to his house in Huntington Harbour. I thought of the paintings, the *Find Angela* message and the one with the men in ski masks under that transparent knee. The paintings predated the letter by a considerable time. But they had been retouched, McHale had been sure of that. What could have happened to Angela, in those five years, so that Uncle Edward had wanted her found?

The Porsche was running with its old verve as I took it up the on ramp from Seal Beach, brought it up to fifty, and got myself into the middle lane, heading to the site in Long Beach. An hour after I'd gotten out of bed, they'd started with the palm shredder, and I didn't know the Porsche was back and fixed until the man from the gas station knocked at the front door. He was smiling, and I could see over his shoulder that he had washed the car, even shined the hubcaps.

"Runs like a charm," he said.

We talked a little as he handed over the keys, but the shredding was so loud that we both had to shake our heads. We could hardly hear. We shook hands, and he left with the man in the tow truck who had followed him out. The sun was bright in the street. The rain had cleared the air, and it was a perfect day.

I went over the letter a few times in my mind as I moved from lane to lane through the final remnants of the long rush hour traffic. But I could figure nothing else just then. Uncle Edward's writing had been strained, and he'd written as if his reader would have knowledge that could fill in details, both of fact and of feeling. It was as if he was overwhelmed by facts and feelings, and he could only write his letter as an outline of them.

The early morning dream was still with me, a vague troubling in my mind, and I was anxious to get to the site and see Chen. I had called him around nine o'clock. Donny who liked to be called Don was with him at the hospital, and he said he could get his father to the site by eleven. I fixed eggs and sausage for breakfast, the noise of the palm shredder mixing with the sizzling in the frying pan, and I was on the freeway by ten-thirty.

Chen and Donny were already at the site when I reached it, and I had a strange, brief shock when I first saw them. Chen was sitting on a yellow kitchen chair in the roughed-out square of the parking lot, his thick, casted leg extended and white in the sun, the rubber plug at his heel resting in the gravel, and Donny was standing beside him, just a little like my father in the dream. They were facing away from the buildings, both looking out across that hundred acres toward where the curve of freeway marked the farthest limits of the site.

Donny turned and waved as I pulled the Porsche in beside his car, and by the time I'd gotten out he'd come over, bright-eyed and smiling, his hand extended and taking mine.

"Dad's much better," he said. "Look at that!" He pointed over at him, and Chen raised a black cane in the air and shook it. He called out something, but I couldn't hear him.

"Cane," he said, as we approached his chair. "I can hobble pretty well with it."

"You must be a good patient," I said.

"Not so!" said Donny.

"Shut up, Don," Chen said matter-of-factly, and Donny shut up.

We had until three o'clock before they wanted Chen back at the hospital. I thought that was plenty of time, even though Chen refused to be carried and we had to walk slowly on either side of him as he hobbled along, making his way to the trailer. We had some boards out where gravel and stone would be, and in most places the walkways were in, but it was awkward going for him, his cane tip sinking into soft earth from time to time.

The trailer was still parked where it had been two weeks before, a few hundred yards from the parking lot and buildings, down-slope and in the direction of the freeway. I found myself looking for remnants of our struggle as we approached it—the gas can, marks of some kind on the ground—but there was nothing, only some lines of a fresh raking before the door.

"Scene of the crime," Chen said, as we helped him up the few steep steps. There didn't seem any good response to that, and Donny and I kept silent.

We worked at the plans and contour drawings for a good hour, at times even getting down from the trailer, moving to places of literal vantage. It was Monday, and the men were back. Benitez had them gathered far off in a corner at the perimeter, working with hand tools, raking and planting. The two yellow dozers were silent, close together and near them. They'd be used again, but intermittently. It was a time I liked on a job: men almost as gardeners, working with hands in the earth, in this case creating the garden. In the distance, the freeway was humming, but it was a constant hum and in time became almost subliminal. Light glinted off the roofs of the moving cars occasionally in the now hazy sun.

New growths were spiking up from various drifts, and we could easily see what the finished product would look like in a few places.

All the largest berms were in. There would be little room for significant change from now on. And yet it was clear that there was something wrong with the view from Chen's reflecting pool, still something awkward in the way that distant terrace entered the sight lines.

"Do you think it could be the sun today?" I said, knowing as I said it that it was a lame enough possibility.

"Many days like this," Chen said. "It isn't that. Something else entirely."

"It seemed goofy even in the rain," Donny piped up.

Chen hobbled around to face him, his cane tip sinking precariously into the fresh black loam beside the promontory we were standing on.

There were a few gently banked wooden paths running through the site. We'd cut them into contours in the land, to keep them close to invisible from the building complex and the freeway. The one we'd followed moved gradually up in a slow turning, then ended abruptly, a slightly wider wooden platform at its terminus. We'd made the platform only large enough to accommodate a few people. Chen had conceived of it as a space for contemplation, no place for a crowd of visiting executives to be courted.

The decklike promontory was very close to the edge of the pool but up above it, a good twenty yards or more, and such was the pitch we'd given to the land that ran down from our feet that I felt we were almost hanging out over it.

We'd cut the platform beyond the uppermost crest of a berm behind it, etched it down a little so that the earth to either side and behind was high enough to conceal anyone who might stand there. It had a private feel, as well as a sense of openness: that view that extended from it, out across the pool, the broad expanse of acreage, a few rolling hills and staggered palms as accents, and then in the distance at the freeway's verge that place of ultimate focus, the terrace we were concerned about.

The platform seemed to be in full view of the pool. One felt that it was the large eye of the pool that was the watcher, that it was looking up at you, or at least that there was some gentle reciprocity involved. From the promontory itself the pool was not entirely visible, its complete shape not totally apparent. From where we stood it might extend out a bit to the left, might have a tributary of some kind. And the slabs of stone under the surface of the water were not wholly in sight either. The same embankments that protected the platform and gave it its privacy cut across the viewer's peripheral sight lines. The pool could see all of us, but we could not be completely sure of it.

This had all been Chen's idea, a way of attenuating the viewer's look at the edges, a prevention of total containment and focus. It was better that way for contemplation, he had told me. The gaze could open out a little, remain slightly loose. "Avoidance of closing down in narrow concentration" is the way he put it, laughing at his own words. What you see is not always what you get, he had said, even though they'll think it is when they're at work up at the buildings.

If Chen and I had any disagreement in conception about the job, it had to do with the way he tended to think of the place as something for the workers. We had talked enough about this, and it was I who had argued for a slightly broader perspective. Although the workers were the ones who would be in the presence of the place most of the time, the visits of others, the view from the freeway, and that vague articulation in which this was to be a showcase for the company were also important considerations. The last was vague in the way we'd received it from the company in consultation about our bid, as a kind of statement of gestalt, almost that the buildings and the landscape were to be a gesture. Not so much that anyone would look at the place, not in any particularity at least, but that the whole would create a presence. And even that presence, its influence, wouldn't be something those involved over time would talk about specifically. It would just enter into influential feelings about the company, its wealth, complacency, and dynamic sureness.

Chen had been impatient during the consultation, but in a way that only I had noticed. He'd not participated actively in the talk. And I remember afterward he'd shaken his head at the way all the young men in suits had referred to things like "nuance," "lifestyle," and "corporate identity." I think he found the clearer reason in all that, probably better than any of us, but felt that it could be gotten at with less sloppy philosophical fuss by simply thinking of the workers as a paradigm for the whole business. If it could please them, it could please anyone. At any rate, conceptual difference had little effect on practice, in this case at least, and we'd been together on most everything that had to do with action.

We stood on the brief wooden promontory and considered and talked more about the pool and terrace. The terrace was far enough away, we thought, and thought the problem had to lie in the contrast between its rather severe articulation and the smoother berms and gentle land contours to both sides of it.

"Maybe when the growth gets thicker on the steps," Chen said, "moves it away from that sense of a final angle of repose it has." Then he grunted. "But that is surely bullshit I'm talking."

Donny was silent as our talk grew technical, and soon he excused himself and moved back down the path toward the parking lot and buildings.

The haze lifted a little, extending the pool's shadows, altering the hard-edged configurations of the slabs below the water's surface. The changes were very subtle and gradual, always some measured steps behind the more dramatic shifts provided by the lifting haze, the brighter sun, the few clouds that drifted down toward the sea from those low, soft mountains in the distance.

Watching the pool and the world beyond it made me feel it as a soothing analogue to my human insides as they related to the commerce of life outside me. The pool responded to the outer world, but in a slow and measured way, a calm way, and it was clear in watching it that there were limits to how the change in outward conditions could alter it. Even though from our vantage we could not view the whole of the pool or be absolutely sure about its circular shape, we could feel that it had its own dynamic, an elastic one that altered to suit those things it was confronted with, but one that could never be stretched beyond its own integrity. It would always be itself, a mysterious and slightly vague self, to be sure, but a distinct one nonetheless.

To fill the pool, we had lifted the slabs and put them in with a crane. Chen himself had run the thing. We'd had to find a thick cushion for him to sit on. The crane had a high and spacious cab, one made for a large man, and I had watched Chen stretch up in the seat to look over the system of hand levers so he could see clearly out the broad window. It was really like a picture window in the living room of a house, and even the sides of the square cab had large glass viewing ports set into them.

We had put the water in the pool first, and Chen had lowered the slabs with great care, slowly introducing them through the surface and below it with no more than a quiet wash rolling to the edges as he settled them in. It had taken him the whole day, from early morning to nearly sunset. Many rocks and stones of varying size had been needed for the primary layer, but probably no more than twenty for the surface one. And a third of these were very large. I'd counted six truly massive pieces, giant rectangles, each over two feet in thickness.

Chen had lowered the pieces in and settled them just once. There had been no readjustment. He'd made drawings, over many weeks after the pool was dug and flooded. He'd looked at it, in various kinds of weather, photographed it. Initially, it was like a dead, pupilless iris looking up at the sky. The ground for a good distance around it was relatively flat and empty. It was only after the pool was filled and finished that we'd dozed the surroundings, adding hill contours, paths, and the viewing promontory.

We'd ordered the slabs a week after the pool's concrete bottom had been given its final coat of sealer and the drains and circulation system had been thoroughly tested. Chen had gone to the quarry himself, and because of the care and time he'd taken in supervising the digging, surface preparation, and flooding of the pool once we'd worked together to lay out its placement and that of the terrace, I was sure he would be gone, considering varieties of rock material and shapes, for most of the day. But he was back in no more than two hours.

"That was quick," I said.

"Not wise to linger over life's creating," he had joked.

The slabs were delivered two days later and were stacked in large and small roughly symmetrical piles, like massive cairns, around the pool's perimeter. Then Chen had taken more pictures and made additional drawings. He hadn't measured, just used his cheap Polaroid and a large sketch pad. He even brought an easel over, and I would watch him, at lunchtime or at dusk, even once in the very early morning, standing at his easel close to the pool's side, on various higher places, even at the freeway verge, far in the distance. From there the pool was almost beyond his vision altogether. But he could see the upper edges of the rock cairns over hill contours if he placed himself properly. He wore his San Diego Padres baseball cap at all times, even on rainy days, and he had taken on a loose white navy jumper from some thrift shop from the time we'd dug the pool and begun the cementing. It was one that had been worn by a senior first-class petty officer, an engineer. There were five hash marks on the sleeve.

Then the time came for him to place the rock into the pool. The crane arrived the day before, new and yellow, the long thick phallus of its boom bright in the clear afternoon sun. We'd got it positioned on its broad tractor treads as close as possible to the pool's side, maybe thirty yards away, enough room to give the boom its proper play. It was a large, chunky thing, one made for very heavy work, and we'd been sure to chock up the treads firmly. There'd been some initial hassle about Chen's running the thing. A driver came with the rental, but once Chen produced his union operator's card, bringing it out with considerable flair, things were settled. I was sure the card was a counterfeit. Chen never belonged to that union.

The crane arrived on Friday. By that time, everyone involved in the work was ready in anticipation of the day of placement, even though Chen hadn't advertised it and we'd seen it was best to schedule things for the following day, Saturday, so that it wouldn't disrupt the work week. Our schedule was not all that tight then, but it would be getting there soon and we couldn't afford too much in the way of lost time.

Even though he started the crane's engine up around 6:00 A.M. and it was a weekend day, half the crew was present around the pool, drinking coffee out of paper cups, talking and eating doughnuts. By seven there were more, and as the day progressed I believe I saw every workman there for at least a while. Some of them stayed the whole day.

Chen's entire family came out: Donny, the cousins and their wives and children, even his mother and father, his wife and her mother, and his older son, Sam, who drove up from San Diego.

They came with lawn chairs and beach umbrellas, and they spread blankets out over the dark, raw earth beside the pool. There were enough of them, twenty or more, as I remember, that when they'd spread out and settled, they covered a good chunk of ground, almost a quarter of the space at the pool's edge. Some of the children were quite young, but there was not much running around. Someone had obviously instructed them, and they stayed mostly on the blankets, close to their parents, playing games with little bone and wooden objects that I hadn't seen before. They brought a lot of food too, large metal coolers and straw baskets, paper bags with breads and the stalks of vegetables poking up out of them. They passed around cans of soft drinks and clear bottles of good Mexican beer. They even set up a couple of hibachis, and wisps of smoke carried rich scents of various meats and fish cooking throughout the day. I saw Chen wave down to them at times, from his high perch in the yellow cab, and Donny brought him a paper plate heaped with food at one point and a quart of mineral water. Chen never left the crane, but he took numerous breaks over the course of hours, time to eat and time to parade along the catwalk that circled his metal cabin, to get another view of things. As the day moved along, some workmen joined Chen's family on their blankets, and there was much gesturing and heated and friendly conversation.

Much of Chen's early work went quickly, and he had covered the bottom of the pool with the smaller pieces of rock and stone by the late morning. We'd kept Benitez, our foreman, and a few other men on the job to help in loading and adjusting the chunks of rock in the crane's jaw. Chen would come out of the door of his cab and call down to them, waving his arms and hands and giving directions. He wanted the larger pieces for the lower layer loaded with their edges down. That way he could slice them into the surface of the pool quickly, with very little if any splashing. When he maneuvered them on the bottom, he could adjust them and get them flat or at an angle or in some cases so that they would be seen from above the surface as thin cutting edges.

When the crane's jaw broke the pool's surface, heavy ripples would wash away from it, and there'd be audible lappings and a darkening of the earth at the perimeter, then a recession, and the sun would quickly lighten and dry the edges. Once the jaw was below the surface, we could see a deep turbulence, and the pool would rock slowly like a heavy sea offshore as Chen pulled the cable taut, moved the boom carefully, and pushed the submerged jaw against the rock pieces, adjusting their placement.

He seemed to involve himself in no careful deliberations at all while he placed the primary layer. Only as the pool's slightly concave bottom filled did he have to make decisions, those having to do with adjustments of the final small slabs and rocks, some little care in etching them in at the edges. It was as if, I remember thinking, he were placing the raw materials of a mind or a personality, a set of untested emotional possibilities, and that these things were by their very nature haphazard.

In the beginning we had a clear sense of the stone matrix, because there were few rocks to start with and we could hold it in our memories until the water cleared again, could then take the newest elements into our understanding of what the matrix was. It was of course a different one for each of us, given our various positions around the pool. Though we looked at the same thing, the water refracted vision drastically, depending upon position, the particular slant of the sun at different times.

But as Chen filled the bottom of the pool, with each addition— given the difference in the three-dimensionality of the stone, the water's density, the changing sky—the reappearance of clarity after the rock entered and the water settled again seemed to reveal change that was geometric in its alteration. It became not one more rock added to a sum of rock, a thing we could with some effort fit into what our minds held, but a new thing entirely. It was like a building up, from a slowly disappearing bottom, of a system of memory, one in which elements dropped out, and in their loss altered the system itself, so that their absence was indeed a presence, had as much impact as they might have had they been there.

Near the end of Chen's placement of the lower level, I believe most of us lost contact with the thing entirely. There was just too much light, of different kinds, too many varying qualities of shape and shadow. It seemed a pure morass of energy. You could trail a movement of a pattern for a few feet, sometimes take it to the pool's very edge, but you couldn't tie it into the larger whole. The moment you saw its way of linking up and began to follow that, you'd lose its beginnings, the things that gave a kind of reason to your getting where you were, and nothing would make what might be called sense.

I remembered a game I used to play when I was a child, over thirty years before in Congress Park. I played it with Angela, and Aunt Waverly would play it with us at times, though we'd practiced and were better at it than she was. It was called My Grandmother Went to Boston, and in the game players would alternate, name an object of some kind, and the winner would be the one who could remember the longest chain of objects. My grandmother went to Boston, and she brought back a fishbowl. And then the next player would announce the same prologue and add something, a grand piano possibly, then Waverly would add a hat pin. And then it would be my turn: My grandmother went to Boston, and she brought back a fishbowl, a grand piano, a hat pin, and I would add a brown scarf, and then it might be Angela's turn again.

I always won the game, as I remembered. I had a method. Angela had one too, though less effective, and she would grow angry and frustrated at times, and Aunt Waverly would have to scold her. Hers was a simple alphabetical one, just remembering the first letter of each item, linking them. I called mine "The Forest."

It was a very clean and ordered forest, and there was a place in it that I could see vividly as a clearing. At the perimeter of this clearing one could make out a thicker stand of trees, and through the branches of one of them the vague outlines of a dark house were visible. The clearing was only a few hundred feet into the forest, and if I looked back, away from the vague house and in the direction from which I had come, I could see the forest brink, close enough to get to if there was any trouble, and I felt secure.

The clearing itself was shaded by well-spaced trees, thick elms and a pair of weeping willows, as I remembered, and the ground in the clearing was mossy, a dry, healthy moss that felt soft and comfortable to the touch. A wide stone trail meandered gently through the clearing, and there were a few granite boulders at the edges of the trail, marking its turnings.

The objects rested on the trail, all pointing in the same direction, lined up and always linked together in some way, very still, placed there with care, awaiting movement, one that would take them to the dark house beyond the stand of trees. It was clearly the house of my grandmother, who had returned from Boston with so many objects that she'd had to leave them on the trail against the time that she could get some help in moving them through the thicker woods and to her door.

I remembered my grandmother only very vaguely, my mother's mother. I never really knew her, but what I regretted when I thought of her was once again my mother's death and not hers. She died when I was only six years old. But had my mother lived until I was old enough to want to know things, I could have asked her, could have reconstructed her mother's life, found things out about the old country. Once again my mother's death and my father's, that attenuation of my past. I understood the urge, at least a part of it now. Why it was that I was driven into the past, in search of Edward and Angela, that unfamiliar past of both the dead and what might be the living. Congress Park was itself an old country now, as separate and foreign as that, but growing closer and possibly somehow attainable in reality.

A small palomino pony, its tail like a thick braid. It stands still in the gravel. Its hooves glimmer. With thick neck slightly extended, its soft muzzle touches the metal ring at the top of a large birdcage. There's a squirrel in the cage. It looks not at the pony but away and downward, to where a black fireplace poker, one with a fluted handle and a hooked tip, rests at an angle in the white stones, its hook elevated and leaning on the lip of a white wicker basket, on the far side of which, where the path turns a little, there's a boxing glove, one of its long laces loose, coming up from the path and draping over the basket's far edge. The glove is palm up on the path, and driven down through the leather and into the stone stands a flagpole with a golden eagle at its tip. No flag, but enough blue to make a pair of pants stands out stiffly in the air where the flag should be, the lower leg of the pants arching downward in a tubular curve like a stovepipe and touching the hard, curved handle of a stone pitcher. Distinct drops of red liquid hang in the air. Fallen in a line from the pitcher's spout, they'll land on a cardboard paint box, rectangular and brown, the letter *E* on its corrugated upper surface, then splash beyond it to be absorbed in the weavings of a green Christmas wreath of twisted bows and pine cones. One of the twists has come loose, and a still growing and spiky green appendage snakes out to where it takes hold of the squat leg of a small cast-iron stove. The curved door of the stove is open, and a paisley shawl spills out of it and licks, where it hangs down into the gravel, the broad wing of a dark enameled bird.

My grandmother went to Boston, and she brought back a small palomino pony, a squirrel in a cage, a black fireplace poker, a white wicker basket, a boxing glove, a flagpole, enough blue to make a pair of pants, a stone pitcher, a cardboard paint box, a green Christmas wreath, a cast-iron stove, a paisley shawl, a dark enameled bird.

Then the next item would come, or the next one, and I was never quite sure just when it would begin to dissolve. The landscape always remained the same, each tree, each constant shadow, turns in the path, that vague house in the distance. But a thing on the path would give way. What was it beyond that birdcage, between it and the wicker basket, some kind of thin object set at an angle? But then only the shadow of some object, and then only the white stone of the pathway. And beyond that now there was something blue possibly, and as I held to the pony, to his extended muzzle, parts of his compact body would come away. He'd have no tail to begin with, or she had none, there'd be a crack in the stone pitcher, the bird at the end of the wreath would fly away.

I was sitting on one of the blankets among the cousins and their wives. The children who sat beside us had long ago lost whatever taste they might have had for the proceedings, and though they glanced at the pool from time to time, looked up in mild curiosity as the crane's gears clattered and meshed, they were intent on their games and the strange bone and dicelike objects that they played them with. They would cast the bones repeatedly, directed in some way I could not figure by the numbers that appeared on the dice. They said things, quietly, to each other, but in a way that made it seem as if they were performing some ritual utterance or other. Strangely guttural sounds, not in any language that I could identify. The cast bones made no apparent configurations, and the sometimes joyful or disgusted exclamations bore no relation to the figures of the castings that I could make out.

Then I caught a flutter of cloth and saw Donny rise quickly to his feet. He stood, leaning forward a little, and gazed intently into the pool's surface. Then he moved away from the gathering, stopped at another place, and scanned the water again. I noticed that others were doing a similar kind of thing. Some of the cousins rose then, even some of the wives, and even the workmen were moving around the pool's perimeter, then abruptly stopping and looking out over the water.

I don't know what might have happened had these new actions continued. Most of the talking had stopped, clusters of men and women in conversation had broken up, and there was an edginess in the way people were behaving. They were moving quickly, sometimes bumping into each other roughly as they passed, then abruptly stopping, looking out at the water, their heads jerking this way and that as they searched for a focus, then moving again, almost stalking, hungry and close to a kind of panic, and each of them solitary as they moved, their hands opening and closing, around the pool's perimeter.

I myself rose from the blanket then, surprised at the energy and speed with which I did so. I stood still at the blanket's fringe, looking down at the loose circle of children. I felt my body vibrating slightly as I fought against movement. Then I looked up at the crane's cab. The door was standing open, and Chen was out on the catwalk, his hands gripping the tubular railing as he leaned over, watching the frenetic movements below him. His cap was pulled down tight on his head, and I could not see his face, but the hash marks on his white jumper were distinct in the sun. I think he saw me, but he gave no sign. As I watched him, he pushed back at the railing, turning quickly and with urgency, and entered the cab again, quickly closing the thin metal door behind him.

Only a moment passed, then a shrill whistle sounded, a long blast, followed by a dozen or more shorter ones. The stalkers at the pool's edges stopped moving and lifted their eyes from the water to the crane. The crane's motor revved. Then Chen was halfway out the door again, waving his right arm and calling down.

I heard Benitez's name, then looked to where he was, poised and alone across the pool from me. He glanced up at the cab, clearly irritated at the interruption. I saw Donny in the corner of my vision. He'd begun to move again, then stopped short, his arms hanging at his sides. He was shaking his hands loosely at his wrists. Benitez jerked his head back toward the pool. Then I heard Chen call him again and saw his shoulders slump a little, the cords at the sides of his neck loosen. He pulled his head away from the pool's surface then, took a step one way, then another. Then he too was shaking his arms out. He brought the back of his right hand to his brow, as if clearing something away.

I glanced up at Chen—still at the cab's half-open door and looking down—then over at Benitez, who seemed back in himself now. He was moving, calling out, and I saw three other men move toward him, stop when they got to him. They shuffled their feet, watching the ground as he gave instructions. Then all four moved along the pool's perimeter. The crane's motor revved again, and when I looked up, the heavy boom was moving and Chen was back inside. I could see him through the picture window, his hands working at the tall levers. He had his cap tilted back a little on his head now. The boom swung over to poolside, to where the large stone slabs were stacked and Benitez and the other workers now waited. Then everyone was back on the blankets again, or clustered together near the pool's edges in small friendly gatherings, and Chen began the process of forming the upper layer.

Now he took his time, and a great deal of it, with each placement. But even though his work was methodical and slow, he was in no way in a perfect position to judge the placement of the slabs. His yellow cab was well back from the pool's bank, so that he, like the rest of us, had no more than a refracted image of the life he was creating. His methodical adjustments of the slabs over the surface seemed more a kind of ritual action than any understood preparation for what the result would be when they were lowered into the water.

Benitez and the workmen had removed the jaw that Chen had used to form the primal layer and had attached a hook to the end of the thick cable. They used equally heavy cable to form the netlike device that they adjusted around each slab. The device had a thick screw eye attached to it, one that the crane's hook could slip into and then out of again after a slab had been insinuated below the pool's surface.

Once a slab was secure, Chen would lift it, cranking the crane's boom upward until the cable was taut and shimmering in the sun, just a fraction above the ground on which the slab had rested. And then he would maneuver it out over the surface of the pool slowly. It would turn, massive and weighty, causing deep creaks in the cable and machinery, torquing the cable until the slab ground to a stop. Then it would rotate back a little, finally coming to rest in the air, no more than a yard above the still surface. The slabs' bulks would cut dark figured shadows, and depending upon one's position at poolside, these shadows would slice down into the water, bisecting the matrix of the rock-and-stone layer below, causing patterns to emerge again, new relationships, nodes of association in what had seemed before no more than a kinetic scatter of raw materials.

Then Chen might torque the cable slightly, turning the slab, then reposition the entire boom very slowly, getting the rough rectangle to the place he wanted. And when it came to rest again from its slight swaying, he would lower it slowly in.

As it entered, the water would swell up slightly around it, an almost imperceptible wash moving out and away from it, and the water level in the pool would rise up slightly, bringing us, the observers who circled the rough perimeter of the pool, in closer, though we were not moving. We had set up our chairs and blankets at what seemed a proper distance initially, but as the pool was filled with the rocks and slabs, we felt drawn into it until, about halfway through the day, I think, we all realized that we would wind up at the very brink of the water by the time Chen had finished.

Once during the day I made my way up the low embankment and climbed the steep metal ladder on the crane's side to Chen's cab. He was in the best of spirits. People had brought him beer and soda and plenty of food, and Donny had spread a small, colorful tablecloth over the motor housing so that Chen would have a place for his various paper plates. One was heaped with salad, plenty of avocado and cherry tomatoes. Another spilled over with pieces of fried chicken and chorizo. And there was a large one that his wife had prepared. It sat in the middle of his makeshift table and contained thinly sliced pieces of raw and cooked fish, slivers of beef, also raw, and an array of vegetables that had been carefully cut to resemble figures of some kind. I couldn't make them out, but they reminded me of the bones and dice the children were playing with on the blankets.

And the cabin itself had been made a home as well. Prints of various organic figures, natural and man-made landscapes, had been hung on the yellow metal walls beside the windows, as well as a photograph of Chen's parents, an old one, with the roller coaster at the long ago demolished Long Beach Pike in the background. On another wall, someone had put up a cork bulletin board, and pinned to it were other photographs of family members. And there was a lovely piece of carpeting on the metal floor, something with both geometric and flower figures on it.

Chen nibbled at a piece of fried chicken as I spoke to him. He had his cap back and cocked a little to the side, and his jumper flap lifted a little in the ribbon of breeze that came in through a slightly opened side window. I wanted to know if things were okay, if he was doing all right. He nodded emphatically, put the piece of chicken aside, and quickly lifted a heaping silver serving fork of coleslaw to his mouth, then took a good swig of Mexican beer from a quart bottle, still nodding almost madly. He was in the crane's chair but could reach everything he needed from it. He kept nodding, waving his left hand in my direction as he reached for one of the tall levers with his right. I stayed for a few moments, watching him manipulate the various levers, turn the small wheels beside them, then I left him to his task.

So Chen would let the slabs hang in the air, turning slowly, coming to rest and casting their fixed shadows. We would see him move around in the cab, see a bottle or fork at his mouth. He would come to the doorway at times, gaze out over the pool, scratch his forehead, adjust his San Diego Padres baseball cap. Once he even climbed the boom itself, clear to the end, and hung there looking down at the slab that drifted out over the water at the end of the cable, just above the surface.

When he made this trip, I heard laughter and talking from the next blanket, and when I looked over I saw his father pointing, nudging his mother. Chen's wife and her mother rocked back on the blanket, their hands in the air, gesturing and touching each other on the shoulders. All four were smiling and laughing, pointing to where Chen hung like a drunken sailor in some high rigging. Then, after these various sightings, he would go back inside, the crane would begin to hum, and he would lower the slab in. I had seen none of the drawings or photographs that he had taken, no evidence of his weeks of preparation, in the cab with him.

As the day moved slowly on and the large slabs formed their surface over the primal layer, I noticed what I can only name as a strange calm dignity beginning to emerge in the water-refracted images and shadows that became apparent. They were larger images, of course, less infernally complex and troublesome than those of the underlayer. But they seemed profoundly enigmatic as well. They were almost too simple in comparison, as if their weight and bulk, their simple shapes, provided a covering of modesty to that other, cruder underside.

And the growing calmness in the pool was reflected in the watchers and participants. I saw it first in Benitez and the men, the way they worked so easily with the massive slabs. Their motions were relaxed and seemed almost natural, as if they had done the job many times before. They were even able to talk with one another, joke lightly, as they hooked up the cable net, leaned against the heavy slabs' weights while Chen slowly lifted them above the ground. And then I began to see it in the others, in their postures on the blankets and in the chairs, the way they moved about, strolled, in fact, as if on an evening's walk after a good dinner. Conversation was quieter, less punctuated, as the sun began to fall and shadows lengthened. Only the children seemed untouched by all of it, but they had been that way since the beginning. It was something to wonder about, but I was growing too relaxed myself to be concerned with it. It was just that there seemed no layers in them, no distinction yet that could create such conflict.

But the underlayer in the pool showed through in places, in thin spaces where the slabs joined roughly, in shallow and extremely deep crevices where points and blades of under-rock protruded into dimly lit caverns. Yet it was that size and weight that introduced a dignified and settled feeling to the whole. It covered and hid the underlife with a complete and steady sureness, a calm and inviolable weight. What was there would never emerge, though glimpses of its existence were from certain vantage points available, evidence of a complex and unmindful richness that was finally banal in its insouciance. It was the larger slabs that covered it that held true mystery, not a mystery to be unraveled and understood, but one to push the adrenaline to the brink of some understanding. It was clear that it was simply mysterious, mystery was what it was, a certainty. I was sure that it could be watched, as Chen had wished, with a clear eye, but one with a slightly hazy focus at both pupil and periphery, that watchers could spill themselves out into it a little, not losing themselves but letting their cares flood out, all those cares that one might name in order to characterize their world.

"I think we might surely have to lose it altogether."

"What did you say?"

"The terrace, Jack, maybe out completely. What do you think?"

He was looking out at it, to the right of the pool and a good distance back in the direction of the freeway. It took me a little time to pull myself from the pool's shifting surface, to come back to him and the reason we were standing there.

"I wonder how many people will come out here, to look at the pool this way."

"Not many, I'd guess," Chen said. "But that's okay, isn't it? Pretty damn good pool, if I do say so myself."

"It is that," I said.

"What do you think? Should we lose it, Jack?"

"I still don't know," I said. "It's a trouble. To figure something else, I mean. Got to have something there, I think. But we can't mess with it for too much longer."

"Okay," Chen said. "Let's get back to the trailer. We can give it a few more days, maybe even a week or so, but that's it."

"You're right," I said. "Let's make it a week tops, then just make the fucking decision."

"Could work out for the best that way. Who knows?" He tapped his cane down into the wood slats that formed the little platform at the trail's end, and then he turned away from the pool and we started back.

Though it had been more than a week and the men had washed it down with cutting solvent, then with soap and water, the trailer still held the smell of gasoline and fire. There'd been a breeze up earlier, and I hadn't noticed, but it was one o'clock now, the haze had burned away, and the sky was clear and calm. Chen lifted his face a little, a mockery of scenting, then smiled and winked, looking back down at me as he struggled up the few steep steps to the narrow opening. The ridge of his Zapata scar was a raw red in the sunlight.

"Still stinks," Donny said, his face in the light at the trailer door as he reached out to help Chen up and in.

"Ah, memory," Chen said.

It felt much longer than it had been. Inside the trailer, things were pretty much the way we had left them on that day, though a different scatter of papers across the drafting table now, and when I looked back at the doorway, I could see the mark the wrench had made as the man had brought it up, a wide blue scratch and a little raw metal near the top hinge. Chen had brought me back to the trailer to talk about Uncle Edward's landscape painting, the Polaroid I'd left with him the night before. He said he knew something for sure now, that Donny had gotten books and maps for him.

"Don, could you take a hike? Jack and I have some things to go over. Maybe you could find Benitez, tell him I'll call him from the hospital tonight."

It was a little crowded in the trailer with the three of us, and Chen had some awkward maneuvering to do to get to the little side table where Donny had put the two thick books and the folds of maps.

"You don't wanna see him before you go?"

"No. That's okay. Tonight will be good enough."

Once Donny had gone and we had room, Chen pulled out one of the maps, a good-sized one, and hobbled back to the drafting table, where he opened it over the scatter of prints and other papers. He ran his palms along the creases and rolled the corners under, getting it flat and centered. Then he moved back from it just a little, scanned it, and then touched it, pressing his fingers down on it in four different places.

"Lesbos," he said. "I think this has to be it." He stepped to the side slightly, giving me room to move closer.

The island was shaped like a rough clover leaf, and while it was the only island pictured on the map, there was more land above and to the right side of its rendering.

"That's Turkey," Chen said. "See how the island tucks in there? You can see mainland from many points and directions on it, except seaward to the west, towns down on the coast. The Aegean Sea. It's a pretty big place. Some mountains, steep but not too high. That's Mytilene, or Mitilíni, the big city, maybe thirty thousand people or more. Pretty big place, but almost *all* the people are there. The rest of the place is mostly villages, small ones, little homesteads and such. Maybe some shepherds, olive growers. All kinds of olive trees here. You could call it a major industry."

"What makes you think it's here?"

"I've studied the picture some," he said. "Look here." He took the photo out of his shirt pocket and dropped it on the map's surface, adjusting it with his fingers.

"There. At the edge. Those are olive trees. With the glass you can see they're part of an orchard, a farm, or whatever they call such things. I figure they run out and down, in this direction. And over here"—he pointed with the tip of a pencil from the tray of drafting instruments—"you can see, again with the glass, it's starting to get verdant, very rich, as it moves down. As I said before, I figure it goes for a good distance. Probably down toward water. Even though the camera is pretty poor, and there's almost no good detail, it makes sense. Lesbos. The books say the high country tends to get quickly arid, low growth, like that in much of the painting, various kinds of scrub. But down in what you might call valleys, very verdant. Lush even. I haven't traced the causes. Could be weather, geography, even soil conditions. Something else entirely. I don't know. But the books are clear that it's often quite dramatic. I figure it is in the picture too."

I still had to wonder if the photograph was an accident. Polaroids had a way of sticking together that way. But why *this* picture? It was like what I had found in the paintings, in that context at least, messages. But none in the letters that I had found. It was hard to figure, and yet I had to take it that way. It seemed the only way to take it, at least if I wanted to try to make sense out of it.

"Why couldn't it be some other island?"

"Ah, ha!" he said. "It could. Most any of the Aegean chain. They'd all have at least some of what this has. It's a dilemma, isn't it? One would have to look around for a good long time. Unless one got lucky. Could take a little time."

It was another way Chen had of getting down to things, and he knew I knew about it. He wasn't teasing. Just enjoying his approach.

"So how could one possibly know that it's Lesbos? Why the choice of this one and not some other?"

"Couldn't be in the nature of any of the growths," he said. "Nor in geography."

"Must be something else entirely," I said.

"Indeed. It must be."

Chen touched the picture again, then turned and hobbled over in the direction of the smaller table, where Donny had put the two heavy books. As he moved, I saw his back darken, and when I looked to the small window above the table the heavy weight of dark clouds was moving in, and even as I watched them a few drops of rain hit against the glass, beading for a moment and then collapsing and running down it in slow serpentine paths.

"Rain," I began, but before I could go on or Chen could answer, we heard a scrape in the gravel near the trailer door. I think we both stiffened a little, remembering the last time we'd been together here, then relaxed our shoulders as we heard Donny's voice.

"Not alone," he said, and we heard a cough from someone else and then saw Donny's head coming up and into the doorway. There was someone behind him, and once he'd entered the trailer he stepped aside to let the other pass. He was someone I had never seen, but Chen knew him.

"Steps of investigation?" he said, hobbling back to the drafting table.

"No, not exactly." The man looked over at me and nodded, his eyes on my forehead and the cut line there. He was small, a Chicano, I thought. "Something like that though. It wasn't the union splinter group."

Chen introduced us. His name was Perez, Inspector Perez from the Long Beach Police. He had visited Chen in the hospital a few times and was heading the investigation. He had not been among the people I'd spoken to right after the incident.

"You're looking good," he said to Chen.

"He does, doesn't he," Donny said.

"Shut up, Don," Chen said, but he was smiling. "Who's the father here?"

We sat down where there was room. It was tight for four in the trailer, but Donny clearly wanted to get the story, and Chen didn't bother him. Donny and I unfolded a couple of chairs, and I ordered things a little on the drafting table.

"So, what do you mean, not union?" Chen said once we were settled in.

"Just that," Perez said. "It was not those maverick union people who hired those guys, nor were they from that group, at least not the one we have. We checked it out. He's got a good story."

"Who was it, then?" I asked.

Perez looked over at Donny, who was leaning forward, his chin cupped in his hands. "I wish I could tell you," he finally said. "What we know for certain is that we can't know that. But not union connected, for sure."

The one they had was hired in an anonymous way, a phone call and then a money drop and instructions before the thing. He'd been told to meet the other three only an hour before. Not their names or what they looked like. They found him in a motel parking lot. He didn't recognize them and they hadn't used names. They were tough guys, but he didn't figure them for the low-level professional he was. He thought they knew each other, but he couldn't be sure.

There'd been plea bargaining, Perez said, and he was sure the guy had told them all he knew.

He had done things that were union connected in the past, mostly in the East, small jobs of muscle work when it was needed.

Things not legal, but nothing they had gotten him on, not very serious. It was that and the calls that Chen and the men had gotten before the thing that had led the police astray. The guy couldn't figure why they'd needed him at all. He too had thought it was a union job, at least before he'd met the others. Then he'd thought it was something else.

"But this doesn't sound convincing," Chen said. "That it couldn't be that union splinter group."

"But it stands to reason," Perez said. "For other reasons. They've got that group by the balls on a job down in San Diego. A long-term investigation, undercover, but it was brought into the open, at least to the union officials, a good two weeks before you were hit here. The papers had ahold of it last week."

"I read that," Donny said.

"Just wouldn't make any sense at all for them to be the ones. They *knew* they were on the hot seat on the other thing, both from the outside and internally, from the union itself. It was something else. The guy is telling us the truth."

Perez had come to tell us this, but also to ask us if we might have other ideas, now that we knew the union connection was out. I had some, but I couldn't really believe them and didn't say anything. I guess I didn't want to open yet another door, that this could be connected up to Uncle Edward in some way. The idea was disorienting, but I knew I could make it stand to reason if I gave it a chance, even though the timing seemed all wrong. The problem was that I'd come to feel that almost anything could stand to reason.

Perez lingered awhile, even after it was clear that we could offer nothing, and I thought it was curious that he had time for that. I asked Chen about it once he'd gone. Donny went with him. Chen and I had decided to go for a late lunch and that I would then take him back to the hospital.

"Days of Little League," Chen said, when the two were gone. "Donny and his son on the same poor team. We had a few beers, talked baseball. When he learned about the thing, he found a way of getting into it."

Chen liked riding in the Porsche. By the time we'd climbed down from the trailer, it was two-fifteen, the little spurts of rain had quit.

It was clearing and there was sun, and he asked me a little sheepishly if I minded putting the top down. And so we hit the freeway with a breeze blowing in our hair. It was too noisy to talk, and Chen pointed out directions, touching me on the shoulder from time to time.

I knew it would be McDonald's, but he wanted a specific one, a good twenty minutes from the site but at least in the right direction, one that did not take us too far out of the way of the hospital.

"They've an outside Ronald McDonald playpen," he yelled over to me at one point. "You can see it clearly through the windows."

Chen had asked me to lug one of the heavy books along with us. I'd tucked the photograph and the tattoo illustration between the pages.

It was well past lunchtime, but still there were many children, with mothers watching and helping them negotiate the plastic slides, roll around among the large and brightly colored animals— a turtle, as I remember it, and a young, friendly bear. The glass was thick enough, and we could hear almost nothing through it. There were Ronald McDonald posters on the walls, a life-size cutout of that same neuter figure, and a stack of paper bibs and party hats on a counter near us.

"Festive, don't you think?" Chen said.

"Right," I said.

After we'd gotten our burgers, fries, and McNuggets and Chen had smacked away and washed it all down with a large Coke, I dumped our leavings in the closed trash container and got back in line for coffee. When I returned to our table, Chen had the tattoo rendering out from between the book's pages. His fingers touched the corners of the Xerox copy and he was looking down at it.

As I settled myself, he looked up at me and raised his hands.

"I can't make it," he said. "Just nothing I can figure."

"Nothing at all?" I said.

"Well, some things maybe. But relatively useless."

"So, what are they?"

"It's a detail. That's for sure," he said. "And it's not stylized, though it might look that way. I mean no stylized rendering of something else. It's enlarged a little, I think. But it's accurate. Almost as if a tracing. There's an original, then. Something it's taken directly from."

"That's something," I said.

"Yeah. But that's all."

"How about the rest?" I said.

A crowd of noisy teenagers came in, jostling each other to be the first in line. They feigned punches and pushed each other lightly for a few moments, then settled down, and when they got their food they took it outside. It was dry and pleasant now, and I could see them over Chen's shoulder, leaning toward each other, gossiping and gesturing as they opened their bags and spread their food out on one of the redwood picnic tables.

"Outside tables are a new innovation at McDonald's," Chen said, dragging the heavy book toward him from across the table. He took the garden painting photograph out and rested it carefully beside the open book, and then began flipping carefully through the pages. It was a thick book and pretty old, I judged. I could see glossy pages, photographs passing by, some renderings, and blocks of prose. I moved from my place across from Chen to a seat beside him, and then I could see they were pictures of gardens, mostly opulent ones, formal, with statuary, stone fountains, brick- and stone-lined terraces. I could see headings with what I took to be family and estate names in them, but it was all in Greek, and I could not read any of it as it passed by.

"Very old book," Chen said. "One might wonder about the relevance."

I started to speak, but he put his hand up and stopped me. He was searching now, moving back and forth in the book's middle, looking for something. He found it in his own casual way, then ran a finger down the crease, getting the pages to lie in place. What he had opened to was a rougher garden than the ones in most of the pictures, something worked into a hillside. I slid in closer and could see over his shoulder that the place was mostly in ruin. At a point very close to where the photographer had stood, pieces of stone lay on the ground, mostly indistinguishable. Yet it was clear that they had been fashioned at one time. Chen pointed with his index finger, placing it on the page and running it along.

"Ruined leg," he said, then reached down and tapped his cast, a dull, hollow sound. "Here is another one."

I looked down at his leg, but he had moved his finger back to the photograph in the book, had pointed out a piece of thigh, only the knee still attached, but enough to make the anatomy clear to me once he had pointed it out. There were pieces of arms too, and what I took to be the back of a head, its face half buried in the earth.

From the foreground of stone body parts, what had been the garden opened out and sloped down for a good distance, maybe four hundred yards, where it ended in a thin slice of water, the sea possibly. There seemed to be a cliff where the ground ended. Maybe a strip of beach between it and the water. But that was not visible, only the rock, some spiky bits of possibly once cultivated bushes of some kind growing right out of it, and then the water, slightly in shadow below the sun line, but rippled and as such identifiable.

Between the pieces of ruined statuary and the possible sea, out in both directions from left to right to where the framing of the picture ended there was a series of receding terraces, at least what seemed to have once been terraces, broad ones, moving gradually out and downward. It was impossible to tell accurately how deep the stepping down had been. The photograph held only their brinks, or what seemed to be that, an ending of now rough growth before each step and then a slightly tortured line, hazy and almost indistinguishable, of what I thought was stone or brick.

"Maybe there is a way," Chen said, "of doing it as in the Boy Scouts, how high a tree might be, for example."

We could survey it too, I thought. The only problem would be in finding it.

"Okay," I said. "Let's check the photograph," knowing that Chen had already done that, and thoroughly.

The two looked almost nothing alike. The photograph of the painting held no edge of sea, and while it did include terraces, they were distinctly different from those possible ones in the book.

"All right," Chen said. "Enough fooling around. Just look over here. In each one."

And there it was, a slight indentation and gradual curve in one of the terrace edges, a place where it had been made to meander a little, weave its way around a broad boulder, a kind of rock table that extended no more than two feet above the terrace surface, I guessed, but was quite large in diameter, maybe forty feet or so. In the photo in the book it had some character, a rougher surface than in Uncle Edward's painting. But it was clearly the same configuration. And what was even clearer was the curve of wall that dipped around it, interrupting the gradual, smooth arc of the terrace edge.

They were close to identical in each photograph, even though the painting had been made from a different angle. In both, I could see the stones in the terrace wall, the same kind and placement in both pictures.

"It's clear it's Lesbos," Chen said. "And because of where the sun is and the shadows, it must be on the south side. It can't be pinpointed from these renderings in a visual way, but then we don't need to do that. We've got the name of the town near it in the book, at least in 1820 or around there."

He moved the book to the side and with his finger centered the photograph on the plastic table, then lifted it and turned it over. He'd penciled in the name in block letters: THROTA.

"A common wealthy man," he said. "Of no real historical importance, I don't think. And yet he had the money to hire this guy, one of the better landscape people of the time."

I thought I recognized the name from somewhere back in my education. Not a major architect by any means, but one of sufficient note, enough at least to make it into a book such as this.

"Do you know what the entry says?"

"Not much," he said. "Only with dictionary. It's something about the elegance of the place in ruin. Not much historical fact, as far as I can tell. It's a rather romantic book. Does it make much difference to you? We can check it out."

"No," I said. "It doesn't really make any."

Chen sat back in his chair and shifted his thick white leg. "So there it is," he said. "What do you think?"

"I don't know what to think."

Chen had me wipe the table down with a napkin before we left, something to do, he said, with proper behavior in McDonald's. I protested jokingly while I did it, saying it could infringe upon the job description of one of the workers.

"All the same," he said.

It was four-thirty by the time I had Chen to the hospital, and I didn't linger there. I wanted to get home, call Aunt Waverly before it got too late in Congress Park. Driving back, we made a tentative plan. I left the top down, but we avoided the freeway because of the rush hour, drove more slowly, and could hear each other. We decided to meet at the site the next afternoon, around four. Donny was free and could bring him out again. Even though we'd said earlier that we could give it a couple of days or more, we were both itchy about the terrace and agreed there was really no reason to put it off. We decided to just make the final decision. I thought I'd better leave on the following day. He nodded, agreeing that was a good idea and then insisting that Donny drive me to the airport, even though I said I could rent a car.

"Cost too much," he said. "And besides, what's Donny got to do anyway? It'll be good for him, screwing his time away as he is."

I raised my eyebrows, and Chen laughed lightly, shifting for a better position in the seat beside me, banging his cast heavily against the door.

"I spoke in metaphor," he said. "This coming year he's taking off."

"How is it with grad school?"

"Looks like law," he said. "Which is okay. Depending."

"Landscaping?"

"Well, of course. Yes, indeed, that is possible still. His mother wouldn't mind that at all."

"It's been raining here." Her voice was distant but still intimate through the crackle. "Thunder and flashes of lightning through the day. A nice summer storm."

"Here too," I said. "I mean the rain. But it seems to be clearing up for good now."

She sounded all right to me, as much as I could get a sense of that in her far-off voice. I had been worried a little, though not that much, since leaving her there alone. She'd been alone, of course, for many years, and I suspected she could handle things. Still, there were all those loose ends and that faint yet real cause for worry, that the men with the ski masks might come at her after all. It seemed reasonable that they wouldn't though. Too much time had passed.

"Has anyone called?" I said.

"No. Nothing particular. Just two calls from the museum in Downers. People got wind that Edward's materials were there and had been calling them. I told him to forward anything written. To suggest that callers write."

"Good."

"And there's one other thing," she said, some hesitancy in her voice. "A notice in the newspaper."

"What is it?" I said.

"Just a small notice really. About that man McHale, at the Art Institute?"

He's dead, I thought.

"I'm afraid it's bad news, Jack. He died three days ago. Just a small notice. A heart attack. He was quite young."

"And nothing else?"

"Just the notice and a small obituary. Seems he'd been gone from work for a few days. They found him in his apartment."

Longer than a few, I thought. He was somewhere else for a while.

"I'll be coming back," I said. "The day after tomorrow. I'll get to the museum then and do what I can to get all the banking and other stuff straightened out for good."

It had been only nine days since the funeral, and I knew that other things would be coming in for a while. We might have to wait before we could wrap everything up. Still, there were some things that could be final.

She said she'd talked with a lawyer, someone at Ross's suggestion. He'd said he'd known him for years and that he was the right kind for such things. They'd be getting together tomorrow. She'd ask him about claims, how to find out about any there might be and how to take care of them. I thought about Angela and Dorit as she spoke. What kind of claims could there be there? There were things that might take much more time than she might think to resolve. But it was good to hear that she was taking some action on her own.

"Are you eating?" I asked.

"Oh, of course, Jack! Don't be silly. I can take care of myself."

"I know it," I said. "I just wanted to be sure."

"I'll be waiting for you to come back."

"Very soon, then," I said.

It was six by the time we finished our conversation. At least it was that time in Seal Beach. A good stiff breeze had blown the rain and humidity out for good, and it was uncharacteristically cool for August. I went to the porch of my house, sat in the cheap beach chair I kept out there, and sipped at the crisp martini I had made myself. The Porsche sat with its top still down at the curb, looking both serious and friendly at the same time. The gutter and sidewalk were empty of the palm fronds, just a few small leavings here and there. And there were no people passing, either. The rain and now the unseasonable temperature was keeping them away from the beach. The street was quiet, none of my neighbors were in sight. Not even an occasional car passing. There were still a few clouds, and the sun was softened by them. The early evening sun.

I sat and sipped the drink, feeling just then that I had all the time in the world. It was really the first occasion in a long while, or at least it felt like a long while, that I had time alone, with nothing or no one driving me. The news about McHale's death seemed more like a confirmation than a further difficulty. I felt a sadness for him. I'd grown to like him, even in that short time we'd had together. But his death wasn't troubling me, not the way Joan and Marilyn's had.

And the Dorit envelope was another thing. I'd not read what she'd written yet, but the fact that she'd written and the circumstances mentioned in Uncle Edward's last letter pushed me closer to Janes' implication, as had the bulletin board in his house.

I sat there for a good half hour, enjoying the quiet of the early evening. It was so quiet I could hear each ocean wave as it washed in and soaked the beach a block away. California, I thought, and watched the deepening shadows on the Porsche's hood. Why don't I have a woman of my own, I thought, and felt my stomach turn slightly in hunger. I'd only nibbled at a few McNuggets earlier, hadn't really eaten anything since morning. There was a good Mexican place I hadn't been to in a long time. I pushed myself up from the chair then and went inside to wash and change.

I COULD IMAGINE THE tips of his fingers burning as he touched them lightly along the lines of her writing. The whole thing, written in a careful hand, appeared copied out from an earlier source that may itself have been uncertain when taken down, but I couldn't know of that. Very direct, I thought, and thoughtful and without hesitation, the letters blocky, half printed, a ragged right-hand margin and no hyphens.

"When I was a child . . . ," the very first words an indictment. Might surely have been sitting, as I was, in a posture of some repose. To read some measure of his life there, written so that he could get on with it, so she could with hers. But accused by that beginning. And she had known that, though she had misread it, had followed the words up: "When I was a child (and I start to release you from any mistake or cause) . . . " But that wasn't it at all. It was not that he had turned her fundamentally. Surely she had not known herself either, but that would have counted for nothing. He would have thought that *he* should have known, a thing so basic as that, as he read her words, even these first ones, rendering his life inauthentic.

Could she have added that parenthetical? It could have been once again a measure of that uncertainty I had come to count on in her, realizing that the picture I had of her, though it grew more vivid, had its source in Uncle Edward, some of it in Joan, those who had been profoundly implicated, the former drifting in some way into what I was coming to see as a kind of myopia.

And I too was feeling the implication, hesitating, that picture of Janes' face, the way I'd constructed it, shaping itself over my own as I looked back at Dorit's first words, trying somehow to put myself into him to get part of what he might have come to in himself, the full power of that indictment, as she unwittingly forced him to answer for his very life.

The wind was up and blowing a little now, touching the edge of Dorit's journal, the tips of pages flicking against my wrist below the finger I had under her words. I went to the study window, pushed it down the few inches to the frame, and looked out into my backyard and the narrow alley running behind it. A few loose papers rolled and flattened against the cyclone fencing. The alley was a wind tunnel, a good measure of the ocean's stirrings a block away. Even with the window closed I could hear the distant dull and heavy thud of surf at night. It's not a storm, I thought. The sky was dark above the houses to the rear of mine, but I could see the faint clouds moving, not rain clouds but lighter, windblown ones. A few drops of errant rain hit against the window near my face. I thought of Janes' big yacht, rocking heavily at its mooring in Huntington Harbour, across the patio and boardwalk from his house. Tomorrow, I thought. There won't be much rain, and it'll end by then. I turned away from the window, and headed back to my desk.

When I was a child . . . men used to watch me. It was no sexual matter as I would dream of it. Standing in a place or sitting, never moving, and I would be hesitant, I suppose. I was a tall and awkward child, thought of myself as misshapen, and in the dreams there was really nothing, but I'd wake up suddenly and with a shudder, thinking of their eyes, large and vacant. Not that I would catch them really, there was nothing furtive about it; just them watching me, my awkwardness as I experienced it, in what I felt as an accusation.

And I start here because of what I didn't notice then, but have come, in looking back, to know is true. Women watched me too. And then, in a while, it was snowing. A muffled music to my ears. It came down over the great expanse of those gutted Indiana cornfields. Fall too had accused me, naked as myself then I suppose is the way I saw it, see it now at any rate. And when the snow came down, with no wind pushing it, it dressed even the delicate barren twigs, softened the fence posts, took the house itself away from its distinctive separateness and vulnerability, standing fragile the way it did, guarded only by stick trees. Until the snow came. We also were bundled up then. All our words were softened, a mute now in each instrument. We were mostly still, in heavy chairs and other places against the cold. And there was very little for the men to be watching. I was twelve that winter. It's clear why I remember it.

"She'll grow out of it," my uncle said to my aunt's clucking. But he didn't mean that coltlike gangliness and hesitation as some conventional term of adolescence. It was the twin deaths they thought about, no psychology but simple common sense. Him walking out when I was old enough to know it, and then my mother's death when she was short of thirty only a year later. So they took me in, both older than she had been, childless and unprepared. I'd been eight years old then. Growing out of it meant getting beyond it in time. You know all this, but what I know now is that he was wrong. It was something else altogether, and I refuse clinical interpretation, at least of that. That it has taken me all these years is another thing. I remain uncertain there, but am trying for something here.

Then it was summer and things had changed and turned retrograde at the same time. I came with spring out of those neuter winter coverings embarrassed. Filled out, they called it. But I didn't know how to carry it, and was even more awkard and uncertain than before. Like boys were at that age, almost never girls. That's why I suppose Ella's Tom and not Janice was my confidant. Once, and only for a weekend, but it still has the vividness of a year. It's the way the past, I've come to see, has little to do with time, the way it can shine in the mind. Like glowing nodes in the foreground, open and closed palms that are nuclei, around which the rest seems only matrix.

Anyway, it was planting time and a seeding party, relatives and close friends from miles around. Janice was my age and haughty. There were others there, and she steered clear of me. Tom and I fumbled with each other under an old shade tree. We were awkward about it, both being awkward, and in it we laughed a lot, so that when it was over, just a little touching, kissing, we were left with the laughter and without guilt. At least I'd felt for the first time a comfort in my clumsiness. Because he was clumsy too and could not look at me and accuse me.

And then it was evening, all the adults and children in the large living room, small groups in conversation, some games engaged in, dice and scraps of play money on rugs and bare floor. And Tom and I looking at each other from time to time, our smiles furtive now, occasional laughter at other things, then looks that let each other know what the laughter was really about. I saw Ella watching me. It was later, when I went to bed, that she came up to me, sat on the edge of the bed and looked at me.

"Are you all right?" she said. She was small and thin, a half-beaten woman, but with a flame of icy spirit at her core. Too much housework, cooking, care of children, still she burned coolly. I'd always seen it, and could see it clearly then in her concerned and yet reserved eyes.

"I guess," I said.

And then she reached between the pillow and my head, brought out my thick braid and laid it over the cover above my breast. She arranged the tassled end with her fingers, looking in my eyes and not at the braid.

"Very nice hair," she said, something sparking in her eyes, and then she leaned over and kissed the corner of my mouth.

"Just watch yourself," she said, her mouth close to my ear. I felt her breath, and then she was erect again, looking at me.

What I remember most was the comfort of it. Her words were enigmatic. There was even the edge of a possible threat in them. I didn't know what she meant by any of it (though I do now), but it didn't make a bit of difference at the time. She had been in no way awkward, and I had been passively handled. I'd only said one word of uncertainty. I'd known my braid as a pressure that would be there until I found a way to decide to turn over. But I didn't have to turn. I remember falling asleep on my back, no longer fetal, the way a grownup might, my braid of no weight at all, only a faint, thick shadow between my small new breasts.

And I remember now that time that I had a discharge, Mark. We had been trying for some time for pregnancy, and that got in the way of it. And you had sent me, with much care, through a colleague of yours to an ob-gyn man that neither of us knew. That was all right, but there'd been no success. And then there was that night that you decided to do it yourself. I think we both felt we were at ease with that, but we couldn't have been too at ease. Otherwise you might have done it earlier. It had been a few months, and I was getting no better.

I didn't know you had so much in the house. I mean the lights, speculums, all that other stuff in your bag. You even had a way of placing me on the bed, getting me there as if you'd done the thing many times before. I remember I was curious, hesitant. But then I always was that, and I remember too your kneeling down, that there seemed no difference in it from the way you knelt when you did that other thing, turned me at an angle on the cover, pulled me toward you with your hands at my spread thighs, the way I liked it, liked the force of being slid that way to the bed's edge, and then your slow and careful kneeling on the floor, watching my face, smiling, all of it in one smooth motion.

I always had to force up my head a little to watch you. Sometimes my braid got in the way. And handling that always kept me away from spontaneity, turned it all mechanical, but in a way I thought was a good way. Something to anticipate and think about, knowing each gesture, move, and mild difficulty distinctly, that could vivify the imagination, fantasy, thinking out its coming.

And it was all the same that time, and that was the problem. You didn't even tell me to put my head back, to relax. I could see the cool steel of the speculum in the spotlight, a brightness in my inner thigh before it drifted off into shadow out of the light's beam. You had my right leg over your shoulder as always, and though your smile was more subdued, even professional, it had the edge of that leer in it. And the thing was I was mildly excited by it all, and knew that you were too. Oh, not perversely, I don't mean that. It could have been simply the closeness to that other routine, there on our familiar bed. You were gentle, serious enough, and responsible about it all. I wasn't frightened, and my only discomfort was in my neck. I don't remember where my braid was, and there was no thought of the way you often grabbed and pulled it, forcing me in against your mouth at those other times.

I think I could have handled a little perversity; that would have been better. Not that it would have changed anything in a large way. This is just one thing, and there are others. But perversity would have marked it off, would have said this is very close, but not the same thing, a little weird to be doing this; that's sexy. But it was continuity, a matter of degree only, the way you knew women, knew me at least, or more important, the way I knew you, the way I know now I knew men, not many of them to be sure, and one in a different way, but something fundamental nonetheless.

An anatomy of women. You know that perfectly, know the inside at least, and something of certain parts of surface. The way they move under anesthetic, the finally simple workings of what you call, jokingly, their plumbing. Jokingly and gently, it's true, but as if they could be known importantly in that way at least a little, more than a little when that information is taken as integral.

And you cured me. You even took a scraping and checked that out. You gave me perfect drugs, no side effects. I was better in a week. I found ways to thank you. What a privilege, we both felt, in the private usefulness of such skill.

This is not an argument. That's nothing I would attempt with you. What you have to learn of and accept is my conviction. I'm stumbling to the source of it here, not again to argue but to describe. Conviction, what a surprising word to come from little hesitant Dorit. You called me Little Dorit, understandably, but I was never little, and in my clumsiness I took up space. But I'll not be coy and "feminine" about any of this. I don't feel that way anymore. I'm not the woman you were married to, though I now wear the mark of your last twisted and desperate effort, this tattoo. Possession was a part of it all along though, and I no longer wonder what you might have been thinking of. To have put that mark on me. It was something like the way librarians can own libraries, keep their really simple knowledge arcane, privileged, as if they knew the secrets *in* the books. You thought you knew of my body better than I did, and that you had the right to own it because of that knowledge. I mean knowing and owning as equivalents. You knew at least the source of its secrets. Would a woman urologist think the same? That's almost funny. I wonder if there are any. But that's consciousness-raising talk, another language entirely. This is different from that.

And so we went to London, and at one of those parties at the Harwoods', I met Joan and Edward. You met them too, but you were understandably full of the new job at Bart's, the door that opened for you there into the ownership of art. I'd press ownership and possession again, and knowledge too, but I won't presume to know such a thing about you. But you did study it all, came to more information than I could ever hope to gather. You gathered what you thought was taste from that, and possibly it was that. At any rate, we didn't come to share them, Joan and Edward. They may have been my first private friends while we were together, which may have quickened things, but I would have gotten to where I am sooner or later.

Did you know about Susan Harwood? She was the first one, and maybe you did know about it in a while, and maybe that accounts for the tattoo. There were just a few others, brief experiments. I guess as a way to drive it into my head. And then there was Joan and then Edward, and finally there was Angela. Not many at all, and only Susan and Joan while we were together, and with Joan only a few times, and only the first time as a secret from you. We were already close to separation then, were in that literal one when you went back to the States. When I look back, I can feel no guilt, betrayal, or shame.

Susan was the first, but I won't spend much time on that. First should have been special, but it wasn't what it might have been. It didn't make me certain, but I had to thank it for making me know I'd probably have to find out. I watched myself with her. I didn't really see her, but I saw enough to know that she was like me, physically, and that released me more purely to watch myself. For her, I think, she was in love with me before we began it, and a certain narcissism came with that love, a need for her to love herself in it, and so she watched herself too.

With Joan it got better, at least a little more efficient, I guess you'd have to say. It wasn't bad at all, I don't mean that. It was, I guess no better word than natural, I mean against hesitancy and awkwardness, the way a body can move insouciantly. It was fundamentally familiar, nothing on either side of it to mark it out as repetition, familiar in *that* way, the way it was with us. It spilled over, as events might into the given world of family. Even though it was only a few times, even though we hardly even knew each other, had no common history.

And I could speak more about it, say those things now that were in it that I felt I knew were at the very roots of women together, but it's better if I wait awhile, until Angela and all the rest of that, and if I speak now of how it was with Edward.

Of course I'm still with Edward, but in a different way, not the best of ways for him, or for me to be with him either. But there is nothing to be done about that, things being what they are. You know the facts, of course, at least up to the recent ones. I won't speak of them, but of myself as lover and model.

Edward looked at me. Not as those men had nor like a gynecologist, but with the eyes of the perfect painter that he is. He's always looked at me that way, even as the paintings changed, though ever so slightly. He too saw the hesitancy, and when I finally came to sit for him it was always as if I were not still and fixed there, in his eyes at least, as he moved them over me and painted. My sitting was a place between things, gestures, often decisions, even emotions. That's there in the paintings, but it's the quality of our exchange in the sitting sessions that I speak about. It was more intense, of course, but it was really no different from the first times he spoke to me at the Harwoods', elsewhere, what it was in me that he was considering.

It was never, even from the first, to read things that were somehow "deeper" than the physical in my posture. It was that he saw some grace, something active in the stationary, and that he saw its proximate cause only as of interest, an activity and a wholeness one might well call character, just below the skin. When he looked at me I felt elevated into myself, specific, who I was at that moment, things beyond judgment or correction, very much there. But foreign also, to him at least. He never once looked at himself looking, I don't think. I was there for the painting, for that kind of narcissistic mirror, to be translated there and in no way back into myself.

Ideas maybe, a worldview; he has those, I think, though when he speaks of them they go beyond me, maybe beyond him as well. Oh, he's obsessive, driven, after something beyond ideas, I think, or aside from them. It keeps him going. He's said he doesn't think he's ever made it, not yet.

But I was whole and therefore wholesome in his eyes, not energies out of faults, and though the ideas in the paintings can accuse me when I let them, the source of disapproval can only come from me, and that only out of some understanding of where I was then and am. It's for me only, beyond myself and reasonable now, to make judgment. That's because the paintings don't judge, not like most men's eyes. What they do is picture—to my eye, in elegance —what is. What I judge is changes, that movement from the then to now. This is not Edward's judgment. His is rooted only in salvage, to say this is a value, to paint it is to understand it, which means to show it, though translated into a way of seeing, his own, rooted in a larger vision of seeing. The paintings tell me what the past was, through his eyes and the work of capture, and the fixed and permanent results present its value: that it was, in its certain way, is dignity. It's human. Its value is that it was.

There's a world of such values, but in my case I needed Edward to render it. There are other ways, I think, beyond art. There should be medical ways, or at least human ways backed by the wisdom of medicine. That's something that might accuse you, Mark; I don't know; if you had them you never showed them to me. Still, I remember that evening of the lights, the speculum, and our postures. It's there that I think we came the closest to it, only to be turned away from it, for me to see it was impossible. I had to get that close, I guess, to recognize that it *might* be possible, to learn absolutely that it wasn't.

Then Edward stepped across that space to me, and I was ruined for a while by the seeming magic of that violation. I mean the space itself was violated, that tripart arena of our engagement: myself sitting, the canvas between us, Edward on the other side of it. When he came from behind it, I knew what was going to happen. It was thrilling. I was sitting in the posture he had put me in for the painting, one appropriate to sex as well, or gynecological examination if I opened a little. He kept the brush in his hand; I remember that. It was a wide brush, with long black bristles, and it was loaded with red paint. The paint glistened in the overhead lighting, heavy and unmixed pigment, which slid almost imperceptibly down from the brush tip to where clean bristles bunched at the root were as yet untouched. He held it straight up, away from his side, like a torch.

He was not smiling, nor did he watch my legs slacken, only stopping when they touched the upholstered sides of the chair arms. He looked at my face, my braid lying over my right shoulder to the side of my breast. I suspected he'd been painting the braid, and found myself wondering about the red brush. He lifted it higher as he came down to his knees. I could see the lines in his face, the fact of his age more pronounced after these hours of intense work on the painting. But his eyes were those of a younger man, even a child, in the clear freshness of the way he looked at me, not in any way categorizing. Getting closer to me now, seeing me in this circumstance in a new way.

I watched his head descend as he knelt, caught the slight shake of the brush in the air at a level with my face as he settled between my legs. A drop fell to my thigh, thick and cool, a high-domed circular dot, not running but sitting there, even when I moved slightly to adjust myself. Below the dot I could see the upper edge of my blue tattoo, and I remembered you, realizing that could well have been part of your purpose, knowing it wasn't. But could you have been so willfully insidious? Then his dark hair and cheek came in against me. I felt his day's growth on my flesh and forgot it.

I watched the top of his head, his thin strands at the crown. I watched the vacant back of the painting on the easel. The brush had settled to a gentle swaying where it stood in the air, held delicately between his thumb and finger. The way of his touch was as wise as anything I have ever experienced. It expected nothing. It kept giving, giving, and only when it reached me in that perfect way did I find myself giving back in return. It moved beyond anything that might have been delicious quickly, and I was soon there in the bright room, away from consideration, magic, purposefulness. It was like sitting for him, though more intense, because the painting was not between us. It was no longer translation. I was not watching myself, but I was spending time being myself. I was right there, in it, but I was somewhere else also, aware of that.

Andrew was born at the end of that cold winter in Muswell Hill, just a year ago as I write this to you. He came with the last ice storm of the season, one that turned the streets and sidewalks to glass, sheeted the windows until they had to be scraped to look out. It was beautiful really, trees like large crystal ornaments, the hill empty of most activity, quiet though strangely energized by the few hot bodies of blackbirds and pigeons constantly passing, flying low, searching for places to land. And because of it all, when the time came I gave birth in the studio. The doctor had managed to get there, but it was Edward and Angela who were his nurses.

Angela. She came at us so suddenly, as out of nowhere. We'd been to the Tate and were walking along a street a few blocks from it. I was just pregnant, but not really showing. I remember she looked at me, stared carefully at my stomach, then my face, a touch of a smile, cold, but in no way bitter or ironic.

I can't remember the specifics of Edward's first response, but that he was surely shaken. So much had passed, and she was there so suddenly and was too much to deal with, unclear and muddy emotion, some of it distant and needing time. I think it would have been hard even had the contact been in letters or prepared for and tentatively moved into on the telephone.

So neither one of them could enter into any of it just then, certainly not Edward, though Angela seemed to have clearer attitudes from the beginning. I remember they did touch each other, but in a slightly formal way, reserved and uncertain, everything overcome by the fact of their sudden meeting on that public street. I remember her frailness, its prominence as first impression. Soon enough that receded as I came to know her, but at first it was that and the visual hard core of resolve in her face that rendered the frailness brittle.

She looked at my stomach, and though for the rest of the minutes in which we stood there awkwardly she looked only at Edward, I could tell she had not forgotten me, that I was of some account in her first reckonings.

Edward had told me of her, not in any detail but the important things, those events and enigmatic attitudes he still carried with him, that came up in him at times. I don't know if they were a presence that was constant. He was mostly quite private about his past, clearly enough so it did not stand between us as withholding. As they talked and watched each other, I could tell in her manner that she assumed this, that we were together and therefore I would know about her. It gave me a presence in the meeting. In a way it was all three of us who were involved.

Then she was gone, and in the following few months we did not see her. I was getting occupied with myself, awaiting the beginning of final happenings in my body, those beyond the constant swelling I knew would be coming on. I was growing away from the idea of Andrew, into his presence. I'd had no thought of a child, as you once had, nothing against the idea of it really, but without fantasy or awareness of what such a thing might be. I was feeling him now, not so much the motion as the presence, and I was beginning to know myself as a mother, that age-old thing, natural and appropriate, nothing that had anything to do with decisions.

Edward spoke to her in those months. She would call, and I would see him gather himself around the phone box on the wall, the sound of his voice sometimes insistent. Short conversations mostly, but there were a couple in which they spoke for a long time. He told me he didn't want to bother me, that he had an idea, and that he would tell me when it was possible. I said he had to tell me, we didn't keep such things from each other. Then he did tell me. He was trying to get her to come and live with us. She was sick, he said. She wouldn't speak about it, but he thought it might be serious. It was shortly after he told me that that he told me Angela was close to giving in, that she said she would come, but that it had to be right for me. I said it was okay, and within a week she had moved in, bringing very little with her.

How the complex of our being together, Edward, the easel, and I, changed so importantly with Angela's coming to live with us was marked by no drama even as I now recall it. It had begun to change before that. I had Andrew in me, and when I started to show, Edward's attention shifted from me as sitter and lover to holder of a new life for him; he could be a father again, at his age, would have a second chance, this time to do it right. He went out into the fall and painted nature, differently now than he had done before: pictures without people or drama, but exquisite ones, careful renderings of barren trees in parks, finding the hidden life in them before it went dormant for winter. The rest of the time he tended me and watched my growth. His step quickened, those lines of severe attention faded from his face, he grew younger, those powers that had been a magnet to me in him turned in their mood, becoming sunnier, hotter, even as fall faded and winter set in.

So when Angela moved in and the ice storms began, our positions were already in transition, turning from one thing into what finally became another.

The ice brought Edward away from nature, and Angela brought him, for a while, away from painting. She was indeed frail, and in the first days of her arrival Edward turned to tending her. He turned away from me, at least a good part of his attention did, and there was no time for him to become ambivalent about that. From the beginning Angela came to me. We were invalids, all three of us, in our separate ways. The heat was faulty in the apartment, but for the studio, and we moved beds, wardrobes, and a hot plate into that large, expansive space. Fragile areas were set aside for each of us, then madras throws hung up from rods and ceiling along bedsides and washstands.

I think that Edward saw the obvious frailty of Angela as a recent thing and measured it as a father might against that other vision of her, the one he held from over twenty years before. An absurd thing, but he was a father, and had to be twisted also by the constantly apparent reminder, in me, that he would soon be a father again. That had been for him his second chance, but now he had another one, for Angela was back, sick, he thought, and he could also see that as she moved to me, tended me as Edward tended her, she might rise out of that frailness. I saw her eyes clear in the first few days, her mouth loosen, even as I saw Edward's posture slump again, back to what was appropriate for his age, though the new fire that had grown in him since my pregnancy became apparent remained.

"I am dying," Angela said to me at one point, and I knew that what she said was literal and true. And what of me? I was vessel and clock. To Edward I contained a part now of his second chance, but only a part, and even in our first few days together in that ice winter I could see an urgency in him, that if he was to tend Angela and cure her he had to do it before the child came. It was as if that would determine things in some way; it was an either/or. And when the child came, things would change, and he had to be somewhere by then, and Angela had to be there too.

"I am dying," she said. She had reached down from where she sat on my bedside. She had kissed the corner of my mouth. My braid was resting on the covers, and she had lifted it and moved it slightly and put her mouth near my ear. Then she had moved back, erect again, and lifted her hand deliberately and placed it on my stomach. Her eyes were bright and glistening, and I knew she meant something other in her words. For her I was a clock too. She awaited the child.

But she was not dying. Edward was curing her. It's true she had that disease, but there was her other condition, the one that had set in, begun setting in when she was no more than an adolescent, the one that Edward blamed himself for and was indeed a cause of, I think, that long-term condition of a wasted life. Drugs, sex, and alcohol, and not eating, never settled, victimized, those proximate causes. But the deeper cause, the one that set her on the way and kept her there, that was the one he was getting at, not through reason or guilt or analysis but through a pure concern for her. Whatever was between them, including all those years that could never be corrected, that pure concern was moving her. He did not ask for forgiveness, knew well, I think, that that was impossible, and though she remained tight with him, held the core of herself back, and even though I think he knew that she would never give that, something happened between them, and whatever it was, she was rising out of something that might have been impossible to rise out of without it.

And so Edward brought Angela away from waste to a kind of wholesomeness, and as the months of my pregnancy passed she became more and more efficient and centered in the tending of me. And Edward at the same time released his concern for my condition, seeing Angela's improvement had a term of caring for me in it. I don't know when it was that he gave the child up to us, when he saw this was necessary, but I do remember a time, a feeling in time, in the last few weeks before Andrew's birth, where Edward moved back a little, just a little, and I think assessed things.

The moving back was literal. He helped us move Angela's bed behind the madras screen that hid mine, he shifted his own to a far corner of the large studio, nearer to the hot plate and the small sink, his easel and his large wooden paint-spattered table defining the separation between us, and he watched us, coming to feel, I think, that once it was demanded, unspokenly, by Angela, there was nothing else for him to do. It was as if the moral terms of his failure, cruelty and passion, what he had traded in for his painting, were now presented to him. There had always been emotional cost, for both of them, but this was different, almost economic. It was now time to pay up, and if he didn't pay up he was lost.

And she was dying. But that was in the short term, and we could really know nothing about it. There'd been therapy, two years ago, in the States, I think, on public health, but it was back again. "Nothing to do about it now," she said. But in the long term, that span that was her life, she was in no way dying anymore. She was coming alive, had come alive fully with the birth of Andrew, and now the cancer came forth in her face and body purely, no longer masked by that other illness, and we both knew she had time, time enough, really, for anything.

It was in the seventh week of Andrew's life that I gave him to her. We were together behind our screen of fabric, she was sitting on the side of her bed that had been pulled up close to mine, I holding Andrew against my full breasts, nursing him. The windows behind her were thick with days of frozen ice; they threw faint colors into the room like stained glass. We could hear Edward scratching at a pad on his table, the quiet but insistent sound of Andrew's sucking. There was no other sound. It had stormed in the night, snowed again, and the streets were empty. A surprise to all of us, almost spring now and snowing.

I'm not sure if I gestured or gave a sign, but she moved to my bedside, smiled down at the two of us, put her hand on Andrew's bare bottom. From the beginning we had been together with him, and even as he nursed he felt her touch as familiar, pulled back from the nipple and turned his head, gazing wide-eyed, serious, and pleasantly at her. I touched the back of her hand. She moved it away, and Andrew turned back to my nipple. Then I saw her tears, no change in her face at all, just those few drops pushing out beside her nose and running to the corners of her mouth. She continued to look down at us, her hands pressed together in her lap now, a strand of black hair fallen from her tight bun, curling along her cheek and down under her chin. I saw a tightness in her neck and knew it was an effort for her to keep looking at us.

"That wasn't it," I said, reaching out to touch her hands in her lap, Andrew finishing and turning to lie on his back to the side of my breast as I did so. She touched my fingers, taking my hand between her own. Andrew's hands too were moving. He was satisfied and smiling now, at Angela, his arms reaching out to her. Her face turned curious, though still guarded, expectant. Then I took Andrew in my hands, holding him at the waist, and lifted him in the air above me. He wiggled slightly, his arms and legs moving, reaching out. "He's yours," I said. "Take him."

There was only one sound in the room, then Edward's scratching stopped abruptly. I heard a deep, quiet exhalation of breath from the other end of the room. She reached out and received him then, took him to her thin breast. Her face relaxed, losing all its care, and the cancer returned, peacefully, as well as a hint of that other quality, that core of profound hardness Edward could never have softened, but it held no resentment at all now, now that justice was done.

And so she took the child that was to be Edward's redemption, and through the act he *was* in a way redeemed, and could that act of mine have been no more than a fixed emblem, something we could mark, measure, and get to the other side of (could we have known it and then put it away behind us), his redemption might have been complete. But this was real life and purgatorial still.

We lived out the remaining weeks of the long winter in that big room together. Though I had given Andrew up to her, I was still nursing him, and so Angela moved closer to both of us. Soon her bed was up against my own. We kept him on the coverlet between us, and when we moved from behind our screen, took him to the window to glimpse more of the world he had entered, she would stay close to me, right up against my body as we stood. She remained gaunt and a little frail, that was her life's condition, though she took on strength, still, through Edward's now more distant tending and through that new life she had, this child, something she had wanted, she said she knew deep in herself, for over twenty years, almost ever since she had made the grave mistake of giving it up the first time, the daughter that she had lost completely.

Edward became a grandfather to his son, something Angela in her firm possession of him pushed him toward. He moved slowly back to his painting, things he would do, then wipe out, begin again. The intense hours of his old work time returned, and as the brutal winter passed, Angela and I began to take Andrew, bundled up, out into the world.

I must admit I never felt the loss of him in this. It was a sharing, and even when the nursing stopped, Angela did not separate herself and him from me. I didn't know the reason for this in the beginning, thought it a natural enough thing. He had come out of my body in Angela's presence, and somehow as a woman there seemed a ground that it would have been inconceivable to violate. And that *may* have been part of it. It was only after the larger thing happened, the largest thing that I will tell you about in this letter, that I looked back for motive. I never found any. Angela was hard then, that is true, but she was beyond such vindictiveness. She took me as she had taken Andrew, and since then she has softened a little, but there was no spite, even in her hardness, when she did it.

And neither was Edward crushed by it. Rather he settled into himself, his purgatorial self. I think he could see a kind of justice in this as well, and I think too that he relaxed a little in it, knew that there was really nothing else that could come. But he was wounded, finally and permanently, and he saw (he told me this) that all he had left now was watching us, that and his painting, two very large things, he said. He said he would partake of both things as thoroughly as possible.

And so he faded back to the brink of being that aging man he thought he had escaped in impregnating me and fathering Andrew. He fell into himself, then gathered his resources and pulled himself erect again, standing in his smock, the same red glutted brush in his hand, in front of the freshly sized and virgin canvases.

Only now that certain evening, fulcrum to her levering me beyond that doorway that had always stood open. Since Ella, that distant marker. "Watch yourself," she'd said. "Nice hair." I'd had the same braid, though complementary gray strands now, highlighting the slowly fading fire of red. The same paintbrush tuft at the end, she touched across my nipple, smiling down at me, and I did not watch myself, not exactly that.

It was the last ice storm after a day of sun, this one of thin glaze only, almost transparent on the streets, but enough residue of others left on the windows so they remained glittery and opaque. Almost midnight, Edward under a spotlight, a large canvas that hid him. We grinned at his activity, a sweet release for us; he had been grave and powerful all day, mixing paint, really into something now. And Andrew, asleep and quietly snoring between us in the narrow bed. There was enough light, a low gooseneck lamp on our makeshift end table, one of Edward's rough, square crates.

She lifted my braid in her small fist, slowly inserted its tuft between buttons and under her flannel nightshirt, to touch it against her own nipples there. She had small breasts, like mine before they grew for Andrew, and when she opened her shirt up completely and slipped it from her shoulder I fancied I could feel the touch of her in the brush end of my braid. But it wasn't that, but familiarity without modesty, the way she revealed herself as nothing new to me. Oh, she was new, in that strength that was no longer brittle below her permanent frailness, but I had seen her body's surfaces, there in the mirror every day of my life, had known their touch so well and often that I had forgotten, like involuntary breathing, what that touch was like. And through that touch now might come some other things, at first erotic, anticipating the unknown, but when we'd finished this first time, far richer than that could ever be, as we quickly got beyond suspense.

And gestures too. With the few men I'd known, with Edward, with you, there had been that erotic fervor, coming forth always in shock of renewed knowledge of difference, stunning and to be looked at carefully, when it did come, not always, but thought of as marker, that then it had been very good between us; validated by a day at least afterward, skin sensitivity, the ways we moved in each other's presence, in a kind of assumed concord. Wonderful. Stunned into awe even: that such distinct figures, almost racially so, could find a way into such fitted intimacy. And that was love, I thought, and treasured those few times even in which you pushed me, held back, then moved yourself with me, and we peaked together. It's only now that I see how we came against each other, into our separate solitudes, that the end of wonder I held to was about the mechanical, or the biblical, or those other inflated mythologies we've manufactured against desperation.

It was not the same with Edward; his heart wasn't in it in that way; a father. And for me it was his complete lack of demand, in the same way he asked nothing of me in his painting. He only gave there too. I felt privileged and have come to know that was not romance, in either case, and though I might now have betrayed him, that seems no term of our vocabulary. Neither is "pinnacle."

And gestures too. I have forgotten many moments of our first time together; they were not (none of it was) made up for memory's sake, and I think I only remember it at all because it was the first time and in that sense only new. It's a watershed for me, another reason, of course, to hold it in some way dear. They were women's gestures, in no way unlike ones I had made myself, but when I had made them, with you, with Edward, they had brought me to isolation. Not here though.

Together we lifted Andrew from his place between us. He woke a little into the pleasure of our touching, and before we moved him to Angela's bed, only an arm's reach away, we held him between our naked breasts, touched his body, brushed him gently with my braid. And we took our time with him, until our caresses put him back to sleep again, before we placed him under the other coverlet, very close, so that we could reach and tend him should he awaken again.

I remember the utter familiarity of her, not just her body but the way she moved and the way I knew what the effects of anything I did to her would be before I did them and knew the complex particulars of what she was feeling as I did things. There was no physical mystery in her at all, nor I was sure was there any of that for her with me. And because of that we moved to a more startling mystery, one I had never gotten to at all before. I found clearly who she was, her distinct person, that part that stood forever separate, that I could minister to, because we were a mirror image, all the way down to the roots of our hair and nails, our bowels, our common intuition.

And mirror is the wrong word for it, I think, as is narcissism, but that it be a narcissism of species. I didn't watch myself in it at all, and yet I saw and moved myself, totally beyond myself, in her. Paintings are dead things, and that image in the mirror is no more than a game for ideas. I remember holding her nipple, gently, between my teeth. My fingers were in her and she had hers in me. It was early on and we were anticipating our beginning, getting to know that we knew exactly what to do and when to do it. I could see my image in her eyes, and I remember her mouth beginning to move, getting ready to say something. I bit her gently, and her smile told me she knew she didn't have to speak or direct me. She moved her fingers in me, a simple message, unnecessary. She knew it was that, and I knew it too. We laughed quietly, then continued on. We both knew we were going into something that would open beyond this bed and occasion, be taken into the world of all the rest of our days. And this has happened, and already I can draw no firm line between us. It was never sex, though possibly sexuality. At least a crucial part of it. That we have come to recognition of each other, and in that to recognize our selves as well. It is the necessary condition, though it is not sufficient. But Andrew is.

He woke up to us in the middle of our lovemaking, his start of restless cooing entering into the meld of quiet sounds of our bodies and voices. And we turned and reached for him in the same motions we were involved in. Then he was in the bed with us, an elemental male, but with no learned maleness. There seemed no pause at all in our joining, as if our soothing and quieting of him were another aspect of the same ground of connection. Finally, as is the way with babies, he drifted into sleep again so gradually that there seemed not even a fine line between sleeping and awareness.

I should put a mark on the page here, something to separate what I have just said from this ending. And it must be an ending, Mark. There is just no possibility of anything else. I didn't start out to tell you this extended story. I know I've said too much, even though really there is much more to say. To begin to try to write some of this down can make you think, and the draw of possible articulation can be a seduction, that edgy possibility of maybe finding a way to say the importance of one's life. I've tried to say just enough to be clear, not cruel, to let you know why it is that you must give it up, give me up, stop trying and worrying it, as if something might still be possible between us. Nothing is. Believe it.

Andrew is now one year old. Edward is back into his painting firmly. The four of us live together in some satisfaction, and though we know as much as anyone can know that what we have is temporary, we move in it knowing it is what we have right now. I think we live it all out fully, and as a family, though possibly a strange one.

I won't continue on. To be hard about it, whatever else I could say is private; as with me now, it is simply not your business.

Give it up, Mark. Goodbye. Finally, goodbye.

Dorit

I WOKE EARLY IN THE morning, heavy with the enchiladas I'd eaten the night before. I hadn't been to the place for a while, a neighborhood bar called Chico's over near Santa Monica. It was a long drive for dinner alone, but it gave me a chance to work the Porsche a little.

As I moved along the freeway, it seemed that even in the short time I'd been gone the profiles of the tracks and towns I passed by had altered and become foreign. California had always been a difficult place to call home. The objects of one's past had a way of disappearing, buildings and streets, even remembered hill contours, terraced or completely cut away to make room for the fragile future of others.

Still, it had places of semipermanence, sections and byways that had remained essentially the same for almost a hundred years. Chicano places mostly, and many within a few blocks of missions, those still remaining structures that had tales to tell, violent and suppressive ones that trailed back to the beginnings.

Chico's was not near one of them, but it had been around as long as I had. I'd gotten a table in a dark corner, and the waitress, to my surprise, had remembered me. The enchiladas were the same, even though they were now listed among nouvelle nacho dishes on a slick, trendy menu.

Now it was 6:00 A.M. I settled for strong black coffee and a glass of juice, sat at the kitchen table, and thought about Dorit. I'd read her letter to Janes between ten and when I'd gone to bed, on a full stomach, and I knew I'd had troubled dreams, though I could remember nothing from them.

How could she be more than a shade to me? What I had was a strange composite: photographs of her from earlier years, those animated presences in Edward's paintings, his careful but egocentric talk of her, Joan's wistful recollections, and Janes' view through the eyes, memories, and motivations of others. And now I had her own words, those that completed the written record. They were words of implicit cruelty, like the ones Edward had written to Waverly. But his had attempted connection, while Dorit's aimed to present her life as an emblem, in order to free herself from Janes.

She moved through the pages of her letter with clarity and a certain grace that should have fixed her for me, and yet I had to constantly work to remember that she was almost forty when she'd written, would be five years older now, my age. Her letter was that of a cured virgin. Reading it, I'd felt far older than she, and I'd found myself thinking that mine was a falsely jaded view. The power of her discovery: that had surely passed me by completely, and I was an aging victim of my own virginity. Again I thought that I did not know a single woman. Then my thoughts turned to Aunt Waverly.

It was seven by the time I'd called the airline and made a reservation for the following day, a flight that would get me to Chicago in the late afternoon. I was still in my robe, hesitant about getting the day started. I had nothing at all to do until four, when I would meet Chen and Donny at the site.

I got another cup of coffee and went out the back door and stood in the yard, facing the alley. I could see between garages and house sides to the next street, could hear the distant sound of surf washing in. Cars were starting up, faint voices of people heading off to work. I'd seen and heard it all before, many times, but it seemed unfamiliar and foreign now, and not mine at all. I'll need a shave, I thought. And then I turned and went back into my house.

There was a six-block strip of land that separated the community of Huntington Harbour from the freeway. This island contained markets, gas stations, various shops and restaurants that served the community needs, keeping the winding streets of the Harbour itself free from any eyesores.

I parked in a lot that served both a high-tech stereo place and a 7 Eleven. It was ten in the morning by the time I got there, and though the stereo place wouldn't open until noon, there was a good turnover of traffic at the convenience store. I thought for sure that the rain was completely gone now. There were no clouds at all, and the temperature had settled back to what was appropriate for the month, warm and dry, with only a light, soft breeze coming in off the sea.

I'd dressed in sweats this time, a pair of tennis shoes, and a headband in my one back pocket. I'd brought my racket along as well, zipped in its vinyl sleeve, and a vinyl sports bag, into which I'd shoved a screwdriver, a pair of needle-nosed pliers, the small penlight Aunt Waverly had given me, and a good length of thin nylon line. It was an old bag, one that I used for lugging things around from time to time, and there were a few other things, loose in its bottom. I had no idea at all of what use the things I took along might be, but I couldn't think to go without anything. Breaking into a yacht was nothing I had ever done or thought of doing. I locked my wallet in the glove compartment of the Porsche and shoved the keys down into my back pocket, under the headband.

There weren't many people out on the Harbour's streets, a few joggers in designer outfits, and at the outer boundary of the community, where the houses were farthest from the water and a little cheaper, there were a few men and women working their own flower beds and trees. The farther I got into the place, the more Chicanos and Asians I saw. They were dressed mostly in dark uniforms, to keep them inconspicuous, I guessed, though dark colors would be bad in the sun's heat. They were silent and kept their heads down, cutting hedges back, kneeling at carefully ordered plantings, picking weeds from the rich, dark soil. I walked slowly along the curving sidewalks, but I didn't stroll. I wanted it to look as though I was headed somewhere, either to the courts or back home from them. Not in a hurry but sure about where I was going. The last time, I'd approached without care. I'd had no trouble, but I thought I might have been lucky. I didn't think it was wise to be so casual again.

After I'd passed Janes' descending drive, I continued on for a block or more, then came to a narrow pathway leading down to the inlet. The path opened onto the boardwalk, and I moved across it to the railing at a place reserved for visiting boats, those without private berths, and looked out across the water, glancing occasionally to left and right, along the line of slips, at least half of them empty. There was no one at all in sight.

Down the line of boats to my left, I could see what I knew was the stern of Janes' yacht. It was a good-sized craft, oceangoing, I thought, though I knew little about boating. Its stern extended, broad and graceful, a good twenty feet beyond any of those that flanked it. I took it for well over a hundred feet, but its size was hard to judge, flanked as it was by other sizable boats. The boardwalk remained empty, and though I hesitated, I knew it would be as good a time as any, and I finally pushed back from the railing and headed toward the yacht.

When I got to Janes' house, I passed it, then stopped and moved to the railing and looked down at the yacht in the slip beside his own. Then I looked back along the boardwalk. Still no one, but now I could hear water running, that same sound I'd heard when I'd gone and broken into Janes' house. The sound came from behind a patio wall a few houses back. I turned away from the rail and headed toward it, feeling the awkwardness of my racket handle hitting against my thigh, and when I came abreast of Janes' yacht, I dipped quickly in beside the bow. There was a narrow metal walkway there, and I trotted down it until I got amidships, where the ample wheelhouse rose up. I kept low, protected from view between the two boats.

There was a door, directly across the gunwale to my right, a mahogany portal. I passed the door, moving down the catwalk to its end, looking for someplace to conceal myself, where I could study the possibilities of entry, but there was nothing, only the lower cabin structure to the rear of the wheelhouse, a row of windows running along it, with shades drawn over them. I was too exposed. I knew I had to make some move or get out of there. The door seemed the best bet, and I'd just have to trust that there'd be no alarm.

I moved back up the catwalk, digging into the zipper compartment for the screwdriver as I went. I didn't know marine hardware, but it hadn't looked like a very serious lock. When I got to the door, I grabbed the railing and threw my legs over it, landing in a squat, and dropped my tennis bag and racket on the deck to the side of the door. Then I pushed the screwdriver blade between the frame and the handle, felt it hit metal, then pushed the handle down and levered the screwdriver in and to the left. The bolt slipped once, then caught, and I grabbed at the handle as the door gave inward. Still squatting, one hand on the frame, I tossed my tennis bag and racket inside, then followed them, pulling the door closed behind me. It clicked again, and I sat down on the deck. Then I pulled my bag and racket to my lap and leaned against the bulkhead. Here I am again, I thought, a common criminal.

Janes' boat was as carefully ordered as his house, everything in its place and a severe spareness of things in general. Though I had to keep on my hands and knees while in the wheelhouse, I was able to get the map drawers open, and by the look of things the boat was indeed fitted out for oceangoing cruises. There was a thorough gathering of maps for the entire Pacific coastline, even down to South and Central America, and I found a few too for points west. Most of the others, though, were for the Atlantic, Europe, and the group I was looking for, which covered just about everything in the Mediterranean. The Aegean was displayed in great detail, with sectional maps for most islands and sea lanes. I shuffled through them but couldn't find Lesbos.

Once I'd made my way belowdecks, it was easier to move around. It was dark down there, but the penlight was enough to get by with, and I could stand erect and not have to worry about being seen from the outside. I felt my way down a brief ladder to a passageway, and when my hand hit the edge of a doorframe I searched for the handle and found it.

Two small portholes in the outer bulkhead admitted light to the cabin I entered. Even though curtains were pulled over them, I could see without use of the penlight. The cabin had the same feel as Janes' study. There was even a shelf of medical journals above the small built-in desk at one of the paneled bulkheads. I opened the desk drawers and took the few things out that were in them. A legal pad, sheets of fresh stationery, some medical circulars, and a small box with paper clips and rubber bands inside. Then I went to the shallow closet in the corner, slid the door back, and fingered through the clothing: casual deck outfits, seersucker and light khaki. There was a dull click as I pushed the hangers along the wooden doweling, and something heavier than material struck the back of my hand. I reached out and gathered the fabric, feeling the outlines and bulk of something in a jacket's side pocket—a key, and a flat disk attached to it. I got it out and took it back to the desk and sat down in the swivel chair, then turned the penlight on again.

The disk was the size and thickness of a large brass coin, and the side that looked up at me was smooth and blank. I turned it over, the short thick chain twisting the key's edge up from the desk blotter. And there it was again, that system of intersecting lines, the same ones I had seen rendered in Uncle Edward's letter and had learned more about from Joan. I knew of its presence from Dorit too and could imagine it, think of a woman spreading her legs modestly to show it, those purple lines high up on the soft white flesh of her thigh.

I let the key and emblem sit on the blotter, put my face in my hands, and looked down at them. The key had complex ridges, and I guessed it was made for a fine lock. The emblem told me nothing I didn't already know. Then, as I watched them, they seemed to begin to vibrate. I brought my head up and noticed that the light had changed somehow, shadows had moved and thickened. Then I felt the cabin's decking shudder, vibration from a deep and distant source through the soles of my tennis shoes, a power like gearing down, and up front an almost imperceptible rumble. I started to rise up, to do something. Then I sank back. I knew we'd left the harbor then for the open sea and that I'd not be leaving the boat for a while at least.

I reached out for the key and emblem, and then I saw my hand light up, a small fresh cut beside my thumb. The cabin itself brightened, the light flickering, then coming on constant and strong. I reached to the gooseneck fixture above the desk and pushed the button, then I stumbled up to my feet and stepped over to the cabin door and threw the switch beside it. I headed quickly back to the desk, grabbed the key and disk, and shoved them into my back pocket. Then I opened the desk drawer and put what I had taken out back in. I got my bag and racket from the floor, then went to the small closet and climbed into it, sliding the door closed behind me. I had to push beyond the clothing, twist myself around. I worked my way into the tight corner, then slid the garments toward the door end. My shoulders touched the walls on both sides. I could smell fabric, mothballs, some dampness, but there was room enough to stretch my legs out under the clothing, to sit upright, even room for my bag and racket over my thighs and groin.

I sat still and waited, listening for what I thought was a long time. It struck me how strange an embarrassment it would be to be found there, hiding in a closet, discovered and then having to come out, in my sweat suit, carrying my bag and racket. The racket was no good weapon, but it was something. I could imagine using it, stumbling around the cabin against the rocking, swinging it, keeping those who were after me at bay. It was a ludicrous image. Then I thought about swimming and felt the weight of new perspiration in my sweat suit. I would have to get out of it, be almost naked. I had swum out from Seal Beach at times, beyond the shelf, and now remembered how the water had begun to cool there even at the height of summer. I was no swimmer, though I had done laps in pools from time to time. This would be different though, a long haul, rolling waves most probably, a mouth full of salt water and after a while darkness coming on. I wondered briefly if I could make it to the site in time to meet Chen at four.

I could turn myself over to them, whoever they were, just leave my racket and bag in the cabin and go up to where I figured they ought to be. Just be direct about it and see what happened. I could figure a story of some kind or, probably better, have no story at all. Just wait for questions, figure an approach as I went along. Maybe Janes himself was up there. That would be interesting, this man I knew through others' memories and words, an oncologist after all, a doctor of some prominence, a wealthy and civilized man. Nothing to fear. It seemed the right thing to do, even though I flinched from it, from the fact of my culpability, of being here, and from the real story, both absurd and very important to me, that I was here because I was suspicious of his private past. If I had any right to that, it came from a very complex and tortured set of associations, a long story, and even as I began to rehearse it, just noting some of the facts in it, I imagined how it might appear to him. Something quite impossible to explain, even absurd, but possibly very threatening.

When I got out into the cabin again, the light glow from the curtained portholes was almost gone. It was darker in the small, low-ceilinged space, but there was enough light left for me to see by, to make sure that everything was in order, nothing left behind to give me away.

Once I was satisfied, I put my bag and racket on the floor near the cabin's center and went to the porthole near the desk and spread the curtains slightly. The boat must have turned. I could see shoreline in the distance. The porthole was low in the cabin wall, and getting down on my haunches again and peering out, my sight line just a few yards above the level of the dark water, I saw heavy and rolling rises, but no foam at the curls. The swells got in the way as I looked out, but between them and above as they receded I could see a few lights, dim flickers, and the contours of low hills, no buildings that I could distinguish. I figured we were at least a mile offshore, but I was uncertain about the estimation.

I closed the curtains and adjusted them, then paused for a moment, picturing the yacht at its slip and my position when I'd entered it. We were heading south, along the coast toward San Diego. It was an easy calculation, but I needed to articulate it to myself, to begin to reason things out methodically. Then I went to the closet and adjusted the clothing on the hangers, got my bag and racket, and crossed to the door.

There were lights now in the narrow passage, dim bulbs in recessed ceiling fixtures, a small dome of crisscrossed wire bulging down no more than an inch from each of them. Very few lights and only every other one burning, and when I looked back toward the ladder that had brought me down, all I could see was the shadow of its railing.

I held my racket and bag in the same hand and shuffled along the dimly shining blond wood of the deck. It was a claustrophobic space. Even the brass door levers I passed by seemed to assault it, limit movement, as if one would have to go around them, though they were set back into recessed frames and were no real obstacle. The same was true of the wire domes that held the lights. I kept feeling I had to duck under to avoid them.

I touched the wall with my extended left hand as I moved along, fearing that I was leaving moist prints that would stay there, be distinctly apparent to anyone who came along behind me. I even stopped and looked back from time to time, imagining a pool of sweat puddling on the floor at my shoes. But if I left prints, they were not apparent on the slick shine of the wood, much of it glowing only dimly, half shadowed, as far back as I could see.

When I reached the passageway's end, I came to the railing of a descending ladder. There was a fixture in the ceiling there, but it wasn't burning. The floor at my feet was dark, but I could see its surface, some little light bleeding into the passageway behind me. Down the ladder was nothing but darkness, only the first two metal steps visible, and the ceiling seemed to curve down over the ladder, like a kind of tube or tunnel. I could hear, down that tunnel, a slight deepening and enriching of what I was sure was the engine's drone.

To the right of the ladder was a narrow door, set back a little into a small wooden alcove. I reached for its handle and heard the slight click of the bolt as it pushed inward. A small storage room: the shine of cans on shelves, the dull brass fittings on floor and walls. I closed the door and turned back to the ladder. The darkness was extreme, but I could see the gleam of the black tubular railings. I found the first metal step, and gripping my gear tight against my chest, I started down.

But it wasn't the engine room, though the drone increased noticeably when I opened the door. The dark passage down had been brief, ending at a tight platform, and the door entered onto a dim and narrow passage, a large cylindrical tube with a flat, cross-hatched metal catwalk running down its center. No railings, but those alternating dim lights in the curved ceiling. At the end, about fifty feet from the entrance, was a circular boiler-plate door with a spoked wheel at its center.

I could feel a continuous vibration through my tennis shoes and knew that the engine room was still beyond me. I looked down, and in the shallow space below the catwalk I saw a dim row of thickly wrapped cables, the shine of a few metal pipes running along with them, a few dark, bulkier objects, and some snakelike twists that I was unsure of.

I began to feel the vibration moving up my legs, almost soothing them, and I knew before the movement reached my hips, then my stomach, that I was very hungry, but that I was also very tired, exhausted. I wasn't sure of the hours that might have passed. It could be night now, but not too late, I thought. It was tension and the insistent deep vibration working on that tension, draining my edge away. I kept looking down, then I saw the vague images below me start to swim a little and had to jerk my head up. I was falling asleep standing there.

I moved to the lip of the catwalk's side, put my bag and racket down on the metal, then lowered myself to a sitting position, my legs hanging over the side, toes touching a cable. I could smell a faint burning now, something electrical. I took the catwalk's edge in my hands, pushed off, and lowered myself the few inches, stepping carefully down on the pipes and cables. Then I squatted and rested my back against the curve of wall and pulled my bag and racket onto my lap. My eyes, though swimming now, were growing accustomed to the lack of light, and I could see my way under the catwalk.

I had to move slowly. There was heat in some of the pipes that I could feel even through my shoes. I gripped the cables with my hands, feeling the surge of electricity in them. I thought vaguely about gloves. A slight smell of sulfur bit at my nostrils, as well as that scent of burning that was not fire.

I crawled up under the catwalk for a few feet. Then I reached the bulkier objects that I had seen from above. They were heavy oil-cloths of some kind, weighty pieces of impregnated canvas. I worked at them, and as I hunched to pull them, my back touched the bottom of the catwalk from time to time.

Then I had the best things I could manage, a thick fold of cloth opened over the cables and pipes and an end bunched into a hard pillow. I turned over on my back then, pulling my bag and racket up. I got the bag on my chest, the racket in my grip on top of it. I was looking up at the crosshatched metal and through it to the fixture on the curved ceiling. It was one of those that was not lit. I felt a sense of good fortune, thinking somewhere how I had never been able to fall asleep with the lights on.

I came back to myself with a lurch, knowing that my eyes had opened moments before their quick focus into consciousness, the awareness of potential pain, a familiar blinking and watering. A fleck of dirt on the iris, then the black ribbing of his sole, no more than a few inches from my nose. I remember an audible rattle as I sucked air in and the fear that I would be heard and discovered. Then another sole came into the side of my vision, more flecks, and I shook my head in quick, tight lurches, the dirt settling on my cheeks and brow. The soles shifted. I could see under the edge of a cuff, a curling of black hair near the roll at the lip of blue sock. Then he had stepped over my face and head, the crosshatched metal irons of the catwalk vibrating slightly, bringing back the electric hum and the smell of cordite or sulfur under me and along both sides of my body. I tilted my chin back as far as I could get it, not wanting to lose contact with his movements. The gesture pulled at my chest and stomach muscles. I felt my bowels roll, an emptiness and a hook of hunger, and quickly lost sight of him. Then I heard suction and a heavy smooth sliding and knew it was the door to the engine room opening. It didn't close, and I lay still, and before I could begin to think about my situation, it did close, a shuddering in the catwalk again, and then his large shadow as he walked over me.

I slid out from under the grating as soon as he'd gone, climbed to its surface, and made my way to the heavy circular door and opened it. Another brief ladder. Then another door, a metal rectangle, and beyond it the engine room and what I figured must be the end of the yacht, nothing but the heavy hull, maybe a void or two, then the sea.

There were three engines, roughly cylindrical in shape, like cylinders slightly flattened, running back into a distance that their sleek smoothness exaggerated, quitting near an arched bulkhead at the end of the room. No moving parts were visible, and the only fittings I could see were those perfectly spaced lines of heavy bolts running away down the sides of their upper surfaces, what I took to be valve and lifter covers. Each had a small silver nameplate attached at its nose: *M.A.N.*, that simply, and nothing else.

There were narrow catwalks between the three and broader ones running along either side at the walls. I could see down through them, a complex of things under the engines, what I took to be that system of hookups to drive shafts, differentials, and finally the screws themselves, what must have been massive props, driving the craft heavily as it plowed through the sea.

Hunger bit at me again, but I forced it back and moved my eyes slowly and methodically over the surfaces of the room. It didn't take long. The engines offered nothing, nor did that space under them. There was something though, the only thing, and I began to figure how I might deal with it.

To the rear of the narrow room, high up on the bulkheads on either side, there were circular gratings, coverings for what I thought might be air ducts of some kind. They were set in flush with the metal walls, and as I moved along the throbbing engine on my right, I could see the wing nuts. It should be an easy matter to loosen them, I thought, if I can get up there. I stretched my arm along the metal of the wall, finding the bottom curve of the nearer grate's lip a good eight inches above my fingertips. I lowered my arm and looked back along the length of gleaming engine cover. The circular door was still closed, but I knew that should it open, even slowly, I'd have no place to go.

I got the length of nylon line from my bag and tied the end of it to the graphite tubing of my racket, just above the grip. Then I snaked the other end through the fabric handle of my bag, until the long length was curled in a rough circle on the floor below the grate. Resting the bag on the floor, I stood the racket up against the wall, the end of the rubber grip pushed in tight against the ribs in the floor's crosshatched metal. Then I took the free end of the line in my teeth, put the toe of my sneaker on that brief curved ridge where the racket head rested against the wall, and thrust myself up carefully, getting my fingers into the wire mesh of the grate.

I straightened my leg with care, the racket held firm, and the wing nuts came loose with just a little effort. When I had them free,

I pulled at the grate, but it wouldn't free up. I jerked again, more firmly this time, and heard a faint squeak as the racket grip bit into the flooring, sending a slight vibration against my toe where it rested precariously. I stood still and gathered myself, then looked again at the grating. There was a pin of some kind at the bottom curve, and it came to me that pulling was the wrong thing. I hit the right side of the circle firmly with my fist. It came free and the whole thing rotated, like a damper in a chimney flue.

Only half of the circle was available to me now. I reached into the wall, feeling along the sides of the opening until I found something, a place where the shaft's floor had a sort of sloping hole in it. There was harder metal there, something ringlike, very thick and heavy. I got my right hand gathered in the ring, pushed off, and, gripping the rotated grate with my other hand, pulled myself up the slick metal bulkhead and into the wall.

I had to slide in a good three feet before there was room to turn. The hole where I had found the metal ring was deep, but it was filled with other interlocked rings, descending. My feet and ankles were still outside, extended beyond the opening into the air of the room and visible, and I didn't hesitate but snaked the rope up quickly, gathering its loops between my legs and stopping only when I felt firm resistance. Then I slowly lifted the bag and racket free of the floor. The racket clanged briefly against the metal when it fell, but the sound was swallowed up by the heavy drone of the engines.

By the time I had the racket and bag in my lap and had untied the rope, I found I could see pretty clearly in the dim light of the passage. The room lit the opening, but I could also see evidence of another source where the walls of the passage lightened percepti-bly at the sides of my head. I opened my legs and looked down between them, seeing the heavy links of the chain as it passed over the large pulley and descended, down to where the winch would be. I knew I'd been lucky. Choosing the other grate would have put me into the passage of an active anchor mechanism, and there wouldn't have been enough room for me there. Here the chain had been drawn back in, leaving the passage empty.

After I had pulled my feet in, bent forward, and then stretched out and seated the grate and attached the wing nuts, I twisted around again and began to crawl along the passage, pulling my bag and racket at my side. In ten yards the tube of the passage began to expand and to turn gradually, and I was able to pull myself to my knees. Then at the end of another ten yards the tube I was in straightened out and I could see the terminus. I kept crawling until I'd reached the outer bulkhead of the craft, and it was there that I came upon the early morning and the sea.

THE SEA CAME BY IN lazy swells, sea green and void of any kelp or other weed, deep, I thought, and clear a good way down, and yet the little puffs of foam that rose at times looked oily. My space was set low in the stern, a teardrop space, but high enough for unencumbered sight line to the shore, night light still in the few structures, miles of desert slope and low scrub between them. It was just dawning; misty shadows rubbed away distinction. I thought we must be a half mile off at least.

The space was large enough to curl up in. I could even sit up, get my legs straight out and pointing toward the stern. Space enough as well for racket and bag beside me. I had my fingers in the wire grate of the opening. It was wet, whether from simple morning mist or wind spray I couldn't tell, and in a while my face and hair were wet, my sweat suit and my socks. It was a cool, refreshing thing that pulled me up from hunger, but it didn't last. I found myself relaxing, as certain as I could be of safety, and then I slept.

In what I think now must have been the next two days, I set about the ordering of my life just then. It was a fitful time, one marked only by moments of clarity. The sea got to me in that first sleeping in my space. I think I must have relaxed too much after those many hours of tension, and when I woke up I was shaking in fever.

I slept again, a shallower sleep this time, hunger and fever keeping me half awake, and when I couldn't sleep I felt a little better, but very thirsty. I knew I must have made the mistake of touching my sea-dampened fingers against my lips. My mouth was salty now, and I knew I had to act, get something to eat and drink, before I drifted beyond my fever into another kind of sickness. So I made my first forage, urged to it quite physically, having to concentrate hard in order to hold back from foolishness, remembering to take the rope and racket with me.

I traveled only to the little storeroom that first time, found canned goods, a box of cereal, and a net bag to put them in. And I was careful to move things on the shelves, cover my tracks. I knew there were at least two of them aboard, someone always at the wheel, but I guessed at three. It was a large craft, and they would surely need that many. Timing was the only thing that could help me, and I went down in the night. Surely one or more would be asleep. I remembered the penlight, and it was sufficient.

I made my way down twice more in the next few days, once to the cabin closet I had hid in, where I found a heavy navy blanket on a shelf and risked taking the one tweed jacket that hung among the lighter summer wear. The second time, I went in search of an empty bottle. I'd been drinking the juice from canned fruit, but it had salt in it, and though it helped, I remained constantly thirsty, kept sleeping and waking up with thirst. I found an open cabin door, a small bathroom in it, wet towels balled up on sink and toilet seat, none of the neatness of the other place. And in the medicine cabinet I found unopened Tylenol and hydrogen peroxide bottles. I drained them in the toilet, rinsed them, and filled them with water from the tap. I remember a loud rush as the bowl emptied. It snapped me to clarity, and I hurried out and made my way back to the engine room, toward safety.

Maybe it was four days, even five. All I know is that there came a time when I was back in my mind again and back in my body too, though tentatively. I was sore across my shoulders, probably from hoisting myself up to the wall grate. I saw cuts on my fingers below a scum of grime, and my stomach felt impacted. I had urinated through the grate and into the sea, but I had not relieved my bowels as yet. Still, I could move with some comfort in my chamber, and though my aches surprised me often, I felt strong and agile.

Finally, I had a civilized dinner. I mean I planned for it, getting what I had ready, a can of peas, two palmfuls of cereal that I poured out on a fold of blanket, half a can of peaches for dessert. I rested a bottle of water against one of the cans. It was night, but there was a full moon, and light entered through the grate, throwing a screen of shadow across my legs, the cans and the blanket. I'd found two twisted cigarettes in a crushed pack in the bottom of my tennis bag and a book of matches. I'd never smoked, and I had no idea how they had gotten there. I straightened one and put it beside the matches on the blanket. Then I looked out on the moonlit sea and across to the land, still only dark silhouettes of low hills, but with more light glimmers this night, a delicate string of vague diamonds following the twisting shoreline.

I settled back against the curve of metal wall, lifted the can of peas and sipped at the juice, then munched at the peas, adding pinches of cereal to the chewing. I took my time, avoided looking at my filthy hands. A light breeze came in and drifted over me from the sea. When I was finished, I bent the cans and squeezed them through the grate, letting them fall down into the night, not hearing them hit. Then I took an edge of blanket and scoured it over my teeth, sipped at the water, took up the cigarette and smoked it. It was only a brief spark in the dark air when I cast it out through the grate. Then I felt my stomach turn, and welcomed it. There was something else I'd better manage now. I peeled strips of cardboard from the cereal box and used them to clean myself.

Some clouds came in over the moon, and I worked in the dark to get my stores into my bag. Then I got Janes' jacket folded and under my head, worked my way between folds of the blanket. In a while I curled up on my side and slept, without waking, until morning.

Morning came with fog, a heavy line of it obscuring the shoreline completely, and dark rain clouds in the sky, moving quickly in the same direction we were headed. I didn't know where we were headed, nor did anyone know where I was, though they were counting on me. Chen especially. Donny was to have taken me to the airport, and I hadn't shown up for that either. And then there was Waverly. She might have called. Or Chen might have called her, wondering about me, thinking I must have gone back to Congress Park on some emergency. And if he had called, that would be a concern for Aunt Waverly. But I knew he would have been guarded if he'd called, not wanting to intrude, being careful not to offend, cause difficulty of any kind.

I thought if I got ashore I could call her, then realized I didn't know her number. I had very little Spanish and was heading down to countries where they spoke that, and I wasn't sure I could manage the information operator. It would have to be Chen, then. If I could reach him. Where *were* we going? Was Janes on the boat? I really didn't think so. The cabin that was surely his had been too orderly, clearly unused for a while.

I spent the whole of that rainy day at work on the grate that separated my small chamber from the sea. The bolts, though galvanized, were rusted, and the work went slowly. But I made a space where I could squeeze through to my waist and tested it, hanging out from the yacht's side in the rain. Below me the sea rushed under at the hull, and my stomach turned as I imagined falling and being sucked back to the screws. But I'd made another way out for myself, a possible one at least.

The rain continued on for what I thought were three days, but I lost track of day and night and couldn't be sure. It was a heavy and constant rain, and it fell from a low, dark cloud cover. My little cell grew dank, and when I was not sleeping I busied myself with rigging a line for my blanket and Janes' jacket, with keeping my stores dry and in order. Then, finally, the rain stopped. It was very late at night, I thought, close to morning. The clouds lingered, but they had risen to a higher altitude and thinned out considerably. I could see the blink of a few faint stars. I got the line and racket then and prepared to leave my chamber.

I'd found the passageway on one of my forages, a cabin door like all the others, but one that opened into another stairwell, a steep metal ladder ascending into darkness, at the top of which was another door, a low one, no platform at the ladder's end. I couldn't see the door clearly, but I could feel its frame and its handle. It opened inward, and when I stepped carefully through I was standing on a narrow wooden catwalk lined by a waist-high pipe-metal railing. The catwalk was slightly above the main deck of the craft, about ten feet up, and there was a ladder about ten yards to my left, descending to that deck. To my right was a glow of lights bathing the railing, the edges of the glow slightly sparkling and diffused as it melded into a light mist drifting along the gunwale. Spray, I thought, coming up as the bow cuts in. The light came from the wheelhouse, where I knew the man was steering the yacht.

I thought I might go to the ladder and descend, reach the broader main deck and head aft. I had no good sense of the rear of the craft abovedeck. Maybe there were things and places I could use, and I felt too exposed standing where I was. Then I recognized it was because there was nothing but sky over my head. I had one foot back, holding the door open and pressed against the inner bulkhead of the stairwell, but I soon realized that the sea was loud enough to cover any slight noise the door's movements might make, and I released it and let it swing a little in the yacht's gentle rock.

I was out in the world for the first time in days, and I just stood there, both hands gripping the rail at my waist, and let the spray dampen my face and hair, the blinking of the few stars sharpen my vision. I was to seaside, and the swells moving out and away from the gunwale were as black as pitch. But there was the glow of the wheelhouse lights in them, and as I watched, the near horizon of the night began to give way to the beginning of dawn's, and in a while I could see a faint lightening in the distance.

I was facing west, but thought for a moment that it was the sun coming up there, rather than its first reflections as it touched the land and sea to the other side of the craft. I remember thinking that it would be day then in Congress Park and having a clear image of Aunt Waverly in her bathrobe, standing at the kitchen window across from my own old house. She was brewing coffee, and as I stood at the rail I could smell its richness in the air. I dropped my arms, shook them, then raised them up parallel to my shoulders, enjoying a freedom of body in space that I had been missing. Then I recognized that the smell was no longer in my imagination. It was coming down on the air to me from the wheelhouse. Someone had put the pot up, a strong and slightly bitter brew. I took a few more moments, turning my head to both sides, looking up into the sky above me, then out at the slowly materializing horizon. I heard a gull, then saw it, then another, both dropping down out of the fading darkness to ride on currents no more than twenty feet from the bow. Then I looked back toward the wheelhouse.

He had come out of it and was standing at the railing below me, standing as I was, looking out over the sea. He held a mug in his hand, wore a black watch cap and a dark slicker, the heavy folds of it blowing in the bow's spray. I saw his left arm come up and rest on the railing, the slicker sleeve blow back from it, baring it to the elbow. Then I could see the tattoo, that twisted, snakelike figure, running up from his heavy wrist. I looked down at him for a long time, remembering his bulk, the way he had moved. Then I turned from the rail, made my way down the steep metal ladder, and before long I was climbing into the wall again.

There seemed nothing left for me to do. I had my stores in order, and I spent as much time as I could making a mental list of those things I would set out for after what I judged to be midnight. I had a new piece of information now, but when I went over the possibilities of Janes' implications in the past and present I had constructed for myself, I could find no way to fit him into it.

One of those on the yacht had been at the trailer with Chen and me, at least one, and I knew now that things had started even before I'd received the telegram from Waverly. It was not the site, nor Chen, that they'd been after, and if they were the same ones who had approached me on that country road near Congress Park, it had not been to steal the paintings. It was me they'd wanted, wanted to stop or slow me or even, quite possibly, kill me. I went over that, trying again to tie Janes into it, but though the threat seemed very clear, I couldn't come to any certain reason behind it. At least Chen's safe, I thought, as is the site. I wasn't though, and I knew I had to be very careful from here on out.

The nights were cool, and they brought on chills. Sun had entered in the hot days, reflecting off the walls and curved ceiling of my enclosure, and I had gotten a light burn, somewhat severe along one side of my body; I found myself having to wear Janes' jacket on my forages, which made my passage awkward. But I managed to search the yacht belowdecks as thoroughly as I thought safe in the next few nights. There were locked cabins and what I thought were other storerooms that I could not enter, but I got into a few. Then on one of my trips I tried the key attached to the emblem in a lock. It fit, and soon I found it was a master key, and before long I felt satisfied that I had enough to verify what had been impression. Janes was not on the yacht. I felt sure of that. There was just too much evidence that he or someone had cleared out all important belongings sometime prior to setting forth. He was probably waiting at the craft's destination and had sent the men I'd seen to get it and take it to him. Two men only, though I still felt there was at least another on the yacht. I was slightly disappointed at my discovery, that the key had lost its mystery, but there was still the emblem.

It was near the end of a stormy morning, after the sun had broken through the dissipating clouds and the heavy rain-blown wind had settled back, that we steamed around a certain point and entered what I knew was the gulf, then came to anchor in the Bay of Panama.

We were still far offshore, but I could make out buildings in Panama City, sleek new modern ones and even those from near the turn of the century, constructed when the canal was still only an outrageous possibility in a few men's minds. I thought too that I could see edges of those ramshackle structures of the poor. And some palms and bits of color, and in the distance steep mountains rising in the clear air.

There were many boats in sight, all still and pacific, some very large ones, and I assumed there were others around us where I could not see. I couldn't find the canal's mouth, nor the first locks, but I thought I could figure the zone, a certain way in which the shoreline structures changed.

The morning passed, and shortly after what I judged was noon, a quick storm came up, a rainy deluge, which passed in no more than a half hour. The wind stayed stiffly up for a while after that, and then the sun came back with force, like hot iron in a still sky. Still we were far enough offshore to catch a sea breeze, and I was comfortable enough in my nakedness.

We were waiting our turn. At times I felt the engines start, our stern seat lower as the screws turned, and we moved to a new position, closer in, then came to anchor again. The day passed slowly, though I wished it ahead to night, and as I watched our movements and watched the land's structures grow into clearer delineations as we approached them, I knew my chance would be coming sooner than that and began to prepare myself for it.

I started by putting a small can of fruit in the toe of each of my socks, then tying the cuffs tightly together and securing the nylon line around the fabric knot. Then I took a little water from the hydrogen peroxide bottle, wet the socks, and got a lather up with the sliver of soap I'd taken on one of my forages. The sea at the hull was placid, and I could see thin trails of what I thought was oil or other wasted fuel, some kelp and thinner weed, drifting on the surface below me. I waited for a space of clearer water, then snaked my socks out where I'd loosened the grate and dunked them vigorously in the sea. They'll be salty, I thought, but fairly clean, and when I'd hoisted them back up into my chamber, I laced them through the grate where the sun washed over it and let them dry out. Then I rigged my underwear in a similar way and repeated the process. I couldn't chance washing my sweats, fearing that they might not dry in time. Then I organized my bag, deciding what I could leave behind.

It must have been close to four when our engines started up again and we moved in very close to land, then came about behind a craft that was much larger than we were. It looked heavy and industrial, and I couldn't see any men on its metal decks, but then I lost sight of it as we moved in behind it and our engines came to an idle. We sat still in the water for only a few minutes this time, then we were moving up into the mouth at the shore, and I could see buildings at the edge of Panama City, no more than a few hundred yards away.

The sun heated up again as we left the last remnants of Pacific breezes behind us, and though it was low and on the other side and behind me now, its heat still cooked in the metal grating. I could lace my fingers in it lightly as I looked out, but it was uncomfortably warm to the touch, and I couldn't keep them there for long. I saw people in shirtsleeves and shorts, businessmen in white suits and seersucker. And I could see heavy machinery, clean and newly painted, that hinted at the beginnings of the Canal Zone and the mechanisms of the canal itself.

The mouth we had entered closed in and narrowed much more quickly than I had thought it would. I had figured at first that I would try the deck, just go up where I had been before, then head aft and somehow negotiate whatever space there was between the yacht and the canal's machinery. Surely there would be people not from the yacht aboard or close by, a pilot of some sort, canal hands. But then I thought of my clothing. It was very hot out there, and in my sweats I couldn't help but be conspicuous. I decided then that I would go out through the grate, and that I would try it when we were in the locks, a time when there'd be plenty of activity.

We were paused again at idle, waiting, I guessed, for our entrance into the first lock, when the rain came on. It came without much warning. I'd gotten my racket in its vinyl sleeve and had tied it to my bag. Then I'd cut a loop of rope that was large enough to get over my head and secured it to the bag handles. I was making sure of the zippers when my space suddenly darkened, and when I looked out the clouds were thick, black and ominous, filling the whole space of sky that I could see. Then the rain started, full and torrential, and in moments it was bouncing off the grate, hitting against my brow and hands.

I pressed my face close to the metal, blinking in the quick flood, and could see just enough variation of color, brief spaces of gray in the clouds, to tell that it was a fast-moving storm, typically tropical, I thought, and I guessed that it would last for a while, but that it would pass and then be clear evening. I felt wet at the ankles and moved my feet and dry socks as far from the grate as I could get them. It was reflex action. I knew I'd be soaked through very soon, at least I hoped I would, that the rain would continue, a good cover for my leaving.

Then we were in the chamber of the lock and rising. There was a wall of concrete beyond the grate. It was a good twenty feet away, but then we shifted as we rose, turned at a slight angle, and I could see forward a little, pieces of the massive doors ahead of us, and the word *Miraflores* on a metal sign.

We moved in closer to the wall, got within a few yards of it. Then I heard an engine that was not on board and felt us shift again, come to the end of a tether, then straighten out. I could see a rise and slow boiling at the hull below me, the force of that deeper turbulence as the chamber was flooded. I didn't know how many chambers there would be. I would watch our progress in this one carefully, and would give it a try in the next.

The rain settled in and continued, coming down with even more force. The sky darkened perceptibly, and before we rose to the level of the next chamber the turbulence at hullside was lost in it, its riveting drops stirring up its own surface waves. Then I felt us moving forward, the drone of our engines again, the tethers that were holding us pulling and releasing, keeping us on a right line. I saw the massive doors slide by as we moved slowly forward. Then the engines cut back, and we were in the second chamber.

I got the grate bent back, then looked out through the driving rain and into the surface of the wall. It was at least ten feet away, and though the rain obscured it, I could see there was no good place at all for purchase. Then the wall seemed to be moving, descending. The lock chamber was slowly filling, and we were rising.

I reached my bag and trussed-up racket out through the grate and into the rain. Then I wedged myself through, feeling a sharp bite at my forehead when I bumped it against an edge of metal. I got through to my waist, hanging out at the yacht's side, instantly soaked. I felt a stickiness at the corner of my eye and leaned my head back a little to let the rain wash it away, and even in the torrent I could see drops of blood, some dotting my hand where I held the grate, washed clean, then spotted again. The same fucking cut, I thought, then I looked up into the rain again and saw the top edge of the wall, the beginnings of some painted machinery, slick in the downpour, cables and some tracks and a boxy enclosed engine of some kind moving on them. I could see a small house, windows and a dim light in them, but it was far enough forward so that the rain obscured it, coming in waves now, almost blotting it out completely.

Then we were no more than ten feet down from the wall's upper edge, but it was still too far from the hull. I lifted the bag out from my side, feeling the rope sling cut into my neck, as if that would do it, but it was impossible. We had stopped rising, and I recognized that I was too far below the deck, which was now at a level with the top of the wall, that we would rise up no farther, and that there was nothing left for me to do.

I let the bag and racket hang down again, then edged out beyond my waist until I found a purchase with my feet at the grate's edge, my left hand entwined in the crosshatched metal near the frame's top. I was completely outside then, leaning away from the yacht's hull. I waited, and the rain filled my sweat suit. My shoulder began to ache, and my hand where I gripped the grate drifted quickly into numbness. I kept waiting. There was nothing else to do. Then I saw the second set of massive doors ahead of me begin slowly to open, felt our stern dip down a little as we came into gear and the engine's drone deepened. We lurched forward, and I swayed in the rain. Then I felt a wave coming up from behind me, that wash as the water we were in flooded forward into the next chamber. The stern shifted, moving in toward the wall, and rose up in the wake.

I saw the edge of the wall coming down toward me. I squatted back toward the grate and brought my bag and racket down in a wide sweep until it touched the hull, the twine sling burning my neck. Then I looked up into the rain at the wall's edge, blinking to keep my eyes as clear as I could get them. The edge swam in my vision, but I could see variations in its textures now, pieces of rubber and what I took to be metal cleats along its final surface. We were just coming up to the curl of the heavy wave when I leapt up and out, swinging my bag ahead of me and opening my left hand to free it from the grate. My feet held their slick purchase and gave me a good thrust. The bag hit the wall's edge at the same time as I got my left hand over the top of it.

Then I was fighting against the deep pain in my shoulders and pulling myself up. I think I felt the hull of the yacht brush against my legs as I kicked out with them, but it could have been just the slap of soaked fabric grabbing my calves.

I got up to my waist, then collapsed on the wall and rolled over it. There was a shallow indentation running along its length beyond the first feet of timbers and concrete, and I slid down into it, the rain pouring in buckets along the length of my body. I had my elbows tucked in at my sides, my hands cupped and my face in them. I lay still as a dead man in the crease, my chest pushing down into some unyielding surface. Then I was fighting for air, inhaling the rain, bucking and coughing, and somewhere in my shoulders or thighs I recognized a certainty that congealed quickly into words. I'm too old for this, I thought. Then I was laughing, in my head at least. I couldn't manage it in the world beyond that and still get my breath at the same time.

I'M NOT SURE HOW LONG I stayed in the crease, but when I turned slightly and looked up, the heavy chamber doors ahead of me were closing and I could see the superstructure of the yacht rising, a figure standing back in the stern working with something—a line, I thought. I could also see a clearing in the sky beyond the craft, a gaping hole in the cloud cover, faint pink at the edges. It faded and was filled again with darkness as I watched it. The rain beat down, but not as heavily as it had, and I figured I'd better use what good cover was left of it to get beyond the immediate mechanisms of the canal. There'd be workmen out in the rain, and when it stopped there'd surely be officials. I had no wallet, let alone passport or visa, and even if I had had them, I could offer no good explanation for what I was doing there.

I got up, awkward and stiff and a little rubbery on my legs, then took a few moments to loosen the bits of line that I had secured my bag and racket with. The rain was gentle now, but when I looked up I felt a soreness at my brow and reached for it, my fingers coming away with a smear of blood. I felt a stickiness at my right ankle as well and saw that my sock was pink. Then I lifted my gear and stepped away from the chamber wall, crossed over the narrow track and made my way through a system of painted engine housings, huge exposed gears, cement walkways moving among them. The structures went on for a while. Most were squat and low, but they provided some cover, and in a few minutes I could see what I took to be the outer edges of the canal workings proper, a shoulder of carefully manicured plantings, then a road, and on the other side of the road a long, low structure with few windows. Storage of some kind, I thought.

I looked to both sides as I approached the road, but there was no one coming. I crossed then and headed down a brief stone drive, and when I reached the front of the long building, I looked up into the rain to where I saw wires attached at its corner to my left. They came from low poles along the road, and there were two rows of them. They were wet with rain, but as I traced them they began to shine, and when I turned and looked back toward the canal I could see that the sun had broken through, the remaining clouds were quickly passing, and there was a clear sky off in the direction of the Caribbean across the isthmus.

Even before I got to the end of the building the sun had reached me, and I could see the aura of steam rising up from my soaked sweat suit as the water in it began to evaporate. I thought I'd look for a door, maybe a window that was out of sight, but when I came around the building's end I knew I wouldn't have to consider that. A small, modern phone kiosk was right there, bolted to the building's side.

It took some time, something about busy circuits and bad connections, but the operator was easy to deal with. She'd obviously put through many calls to the States, and I didn't need my awkward Spanish. I had not spoken a word in a very long time, and my voice creaked a little and sounded unfamiliar. I had to slow down and work consciously at forming words. While I waited I ran my hands through my quickly drying hair and used the arm of my sweatshirt to dab at the newly opened old cut at my brow. It wouldn't stop bleeding, and I had to use my arm to apply some direct pressure. Then it did stop. My arm brushed my cheek as I brought it down, and when I put my hand there I could feel the thick bristles of beard. Almost a real beard, I thought.

Donny answered the phone. "Christ, Jack!" he yelled. "Is it you?" He didn't wait for an answer. I heard the mouthpiece muffle as he put his hand over it, then heard him dimly as he called out. There was a brief silence. Then I heard Chen's familiar voice on the line.

"You're in Panama," he said.

"That's right. How did you know?"

"Are you all right?"

"Yes," I said, though I had to wonder if I really was. "But how?"

"I figured it would be the boat," he said, "after I faked a call back east and you weren't there. Donny checked the slip. There are records for such things. But where are you?"

"At a phone," I said. "At the canal. How far did the records take you?"

"Just to Panama, a reservation for crossing. Do you know the yacht's name?"

It struck me that that was something I hadn't thought about, but I really didn't have a hard guess. *"Dorit?"* I said.

"That's right, just the one word."

"It figures, of course. But it's a little too much. One would have thought he'd have a little more control. Chen? How long does it take to go through? Eight hours, right?"

"That's right," he said. "Sometimes a little more, depending."

I could tell he was listening attentively, saving his words, making sure that I got what I needed.

"And what time is it there?"

"Two o'clock," he said. "You're three hours later. It's five where you are."

"Okay," I said. "One thing." I started to speak, but he told me to hold on. Again I heard muffled talk, then he was back on the line.

"Do you have a pencil?"

"No," I said. "Wait, just a minute, maybe I do." I let the phone dangle and squatted down, my thighs aching, and dug around in the bag. I *did* have a pencil, just a broken nub of one I'd found on the yacht.

"Go ahead," I said.

"It's Santos," he said. "Sylvan and Amanda Santos. And the town . . ." He waited as I wrote. "The town is Aransas. Aransas, do you have that? It's just outside the zone, as I remember it, a small place. Santos. Sylvan and Amanda. They don't have a phone. Amanda is daughter of my father's good friend, dead now, but they remain close to the family. Just tell them my name, if you can get there. Can you get there, Jack?"

"I'll get there," I said. "And, Chen?"

"Go ahead," he said. "Don't wait, just go ahead."

"Call my aunt for me, would you? Just tell her things are okay, but that I can't get back right now. Tell her something about the job. Anything. So long as she doesn't worry."

"It's done," he said.

"And one more thing. The site," I said.

"Go on, go on."

"I think we should definitely lose the terrace altogether. And my thought is that we replace it with a configuration of some kind, using the same stone and slab pieces that are in the pool. A kind of echo, but something without any motion in it. It could shift the eye back and forth. I think it'll work."

"Ah! Of course! Wonderful!"

"And, Chen. If you like the idea, after you think about it, *you* take it on. It would be yours anyway, given the pool. You'll get it right, and I don't need to be involved, to hold you up on it."

"Indeed and of course," he said. "When will you be coming back, then?"

"I can't tell, but I hope it won't be too long. I don't like to say. A week at least, maybe a little more. But I don't know. I have to—"

"Of course, of course," he cut in. "It's over three weeks yet until the opening. Things have been growing, Jack. It looks quite good."

"And how about your leg and the rest?"

"Shit. Everything's fine. I'm good on the cane now. Nothing to bother about."

"Okay," I said. "I'd better go now."

"Santos," he said. "You got it? And the town's Aransas."

"I got it, Chen. I'll try to keep you posted."

"As you can, Jack. Are you learning?"

"Just bits and pieces, I'm afraid, but I think more soon."

"Good enough," he said. "Little bits add up to big ones."

By the time we were into the last words of our conversation, I found I had to keep lifting my forearm to my brow to dab the sweat away. The sun had come back, even hotter than I had imagined it would, and my skin was soaked and clammy. The sweats were still damp from the rain, but that was being replaced by a saltier substance. The sweat ran down my legs and into my socks, and I could even feel it in a grittiness between my toes.

I hung up the phone, reached in my back pocket and got my headband and put it on. Then I turned away from the kiosk, looked back across the road toward the canal and then in the other direction, along the building's side and off into the gently rolling hills behind it. The hills were flooded with long grasses and wildflowers, and the sun beat down into them. They were low hills, no more than brief undulations in the otherwise flat land, and off in the distance beyond them, sun flashed off the roofs of occasional cars.

It took me longer than I'd thought it would to get to the road, and I was bitten severely by small insects before I was halfway. The road was public, but it was no highway, only a two-lane strip of winding blacktop.

The first car that came along picked me up, an old Ford, but very clean and carefully detailed out. The driver was a young soldier, in short-sleeved summer khaki. I noticed his PFC stripes, nothing much over his breast pocket. He was as clean and fit as his car was, razor creases and trim short haircut. The Ford's seat was vinyl covered, but he'd tucked a blue sheet carefully over it.

"You're a mess," he said, once I'd gotten in and settled.

"You're right. Some fool turned the court sprinklers on."

"Clay?" he said, getting the car carefully into gear and edging back off the shoulder. I nodded, not wanting to move further into the absurdity of the lie. He brought the Ford up to a slow speed. A couple of cars roared past us.

"I didn't know there'd be courts around here."

"A few," I said, then pushed him away from questions. "This is a very nice car."

He beamed at that and told me he hoped to take it back north. Only a few more months now. He was going to be transferred to the States.

He was headed to the other side of the isthmus, to Colón, where he was stationed. He'd had a two-day pass and had spent it in Panama City. I guessed women, some lowlife, and said, "That's right, it's Sunday."

He looked briefly over at me. "Wednesday," he said.

I tried to remember the day I'd gone to Janes' place and got aboard the yacht. I thought it had been a Wednesday, maybe a Tuesday, but I wasn't sure of it. I tried moving back to when I'd gone to Janes' office, knowing that had been Sunday, but I couldn't fill in the days following that in any sure way. I guessed that it had been a week or more since I'd boarded the yacht at Huntington Harbour.

"The library," he said. "My plans are engineering. I've been studying about the canal while I've been here. A real feat."

"I wonder if landscaping might have helped at all. I mean in the early days," I said. "Growth to hold the hills back, something to increase the angle of repose."

This got him started. He knew things, dates and conditions, almost by rote, and he seemed to lose all suspicion of me as he mentioned names and figures, politics, historical difficulties.

It took no more than a half hour for us to get to the turn that would take us to Aransas. There was no sign or other marking, nothing on the map he consulted as we sat at idle on the shoulder. Still, he seemed sure of the turnoff. It was a place he'd come across in his research, something to do with the canal just after the French gave up on it.

In the beginning he'd said he could let me off when we got there, but once he'd folded his map and tucked it back in the glove compartment, he said what the hell, it was only a few miles out of his way, he thought, and he could drive me.

At first the road was good, narrower than the other but with a smooth surface and tended shoulders. He drove slowly, glancing at the few signs we passed. Then in a while the road turned rougher, breaks and bumps in the asphalt and weeds growing among collapsed and cracked slabs of some kind at the verge. Then there were no signs at all. We'd left the zone, and I felt myself relaxing a little in that awareness. And with relaxation came a certain deep exhaustion. My edge went very quickly, and all the little aches and pains I had came up to the surface. I shifted in the seat, feeling each small bump in the ruined pavement. At least it had cooled down, and the new sweat that began to trickle from my forehead and chest as we slowed and lost the wind the car's motion had provided was a cool, almost clean sweat, and had something soothing in it.

H E LEFT ME AT THE MOUTH of a broad dirt street that had once been paved, but so long ago that dust now covered most of the cracked and dissolved slabs. The growths in the yards of the houses that fronted the street came right down to it, and there were places well out in it where weeds and even clusters of wildflowers were poking up.

Above and behind the houses I could see thicker growths, twisted palm trunks and the bulks of heavier ones I could not identify, a wild system of vines snaking and twisting among them, many as thick as a man's arm. And large leaves and bunches of fleshy flowers, blood red and a dark violet that looked like coagulated blood. It was a heavy, opaque surface of growth, and only in places could I see into it, and then only for a few feet, to places where fresh stalks and green tendrils were aggressively pushing forward, finding their own purchase, crowding up into the gaps. It was like jungle really, and it looked to be threatening to engulf the houses.

The street appeared to turn a few blocks down, but I could not see it do so. It seemed to end at a wall of growth like the ones coming up behind and over the houses on both sides. In places the house roofs were touched by heavy vines, long fingers reaching out from the growth wall, searching to take hold.

I started down the middle of the street, but after a few feet felt uncomfortable and exposed and moved to the right side. There was no sidewalk, just a growth-matted path, well worn, that ran where the sides of the street melded into the yards. I wondered at the street's broad width, then thought it must have been at one time a company town, a place for canal workers, possibly, and that the street could hold heavy traffic, supplies and machinery. But it was all useless now and had gone to ruin, though not the houses.

They were wood-frame houses, simple and alike, but with a touch here and there of some architectural concern, some grace at the cornice, porch rails that had care and specificity in their fashioning. Each house had a porch, a large one that was screened in from floor to overhanging roof on three sides. The screening was old, attached to wood and not aluminum, but it was well cared for and looked tight. No wonder, I thought, feeling again the bites along my legs and arms. Movement was an irritation to them, as was the lack of any significant breeze. It was very hot and close now, and I could see heat shimmer rising up for a few feet above the dusty, ruined blacktop.

There was no one in the yards, no movement on the porches that I noticed as I passed them. It must have been close to six o'clock, maybe later. Too late, I thought, for siesta, but it was still hot enough to explain the absence. Then I did see someone, an almost imperceptible movement, on a porch across the street, and I entered the dusty roadway once again and headed over there.

I called out as I reached the path that led up to the porch steps, *"Buenos días."* There was silence, then a wet and serious cough and the same words, guttural and half indistinct.

The man was black, very old, I thought, and small, and he was tucked into a rocking chair back in the porch's corner. He had a sheet draped over his knees, was naked above it, and I could see his thin, hard chest, sweaty and like polished wood, when I put my face up close to the screen door. He kept rocking. I said the name Santos, then mentioned their first names.

"*Sí*," he said, "*y Coco*. Across the street, third one up."

His English was quick and sure, and I was a little taken back by it. Then I heard a sound from inside the open door of the house, across from the screen. It was dark inside and hard to see, and I felt the presence of the other man in the doorway before I could focus on him. He stepped over the frame then, and I could see him. He was white and also old, but younger than the other man, and dressed in a white linen jumpsuit that hung loosely from his bony shoulders. His skin was pale but without blemish, and I thought I could tell he took some care with it. He smiled at me, then looked over at the other man.

"Okay?" he said.

"Yes," I said. "I just need some directions."

"There's no barber here," he said. The words might have been aggressive, a little nasty, but he was smiling, sharing the joke with me, reaching for a bit of intimacy.

"I could surely use one," I said, reaching my free hand up and touching my face. He saw the gesture, but was looking down at my other hand, my bag and racket.

"No courts either, sad to say. I used to play, you know."

I shifted at the screen, giving him what time he needed. The black man nodded, looking at me and then the other.

"But I'm afraid that's over now. A cool drink?"

It took me a moment to get the offer. "No," I said. "No, thank you. It's Santos. I need to find them."

"Of course," he said, then turned to the black man. "Did you tell him?"

"*Sí*," the black man said.

"Just up the street." He lifted his right arm and pointed.

The Santos house was on the other side and like all the others was fronted by a large screened-in porch and a shallow front yard that came right into the street. This yard seemed more orderly though. There were tended plantings lining the path that led up to the porch steps, and the perimeters on both sides were planted with leafy bushes that had been trimmed back. These, like most of the growths I'd seen so far, were unfamiliar to me. Tropical things that I had no experience with.

I could see up over the house as I approached it, some evidence of the jungle behind it threatening above the peak, but the wall of growth seemed well back from the house, and I guessed that there was an ample yard between the two.

When I got up the steps to the screen door, I knocked. There was little rattle. The door was set square and firm in its frame. I waited, heard some movement inside, well back in the house, then someone approaching. As with the other house, the front door beyond the porch was wide open, and when the stocky woman appeared in the frame I could see her clearly. She stood looking at me, then stepped out on the porch. I started to speak, then saw the intensity of her squinting change to a bright smile. Her arms came up in excitement, and she glanced over her shoulder, torn between calling back into the house and coming forward.

"I—"

"Jack! It's Jack!" She smiled, still struggling in both directions. She wore a simple housedress, much like those made from feed sacks in the Midwest many years ago, but she was more vibrant than her clothing. No little housewife. There was a subtle makeup at the corners of her eyes and an almost imperceptible wash on her lids. Her hair was short and would have been a little mannish if it weren't for a careful flip on one side, and her nails were painted a dark red. All of her presence came at me before she spoke my name, and when she did speak it I felt dizzy and knew I was sliding a little to the side. She saw this. Her face clouded a little, then brightened again as she followed her first impulse and stepped toward the door.

"The picture," she said as she opened the door and reached and took my arm. It was the side on which I held the racket and bag, and she felt the weight and looked down for a moment. "Chen sent it. A very good picture!"

She had me across the porch and into the room beyond it, seated in a white wicker chair, before I could speak again. It was a little dark inside. They'd not turned the lights on yet, though dusk was already here and deepening. I saw the picture on the wall across from where I was sitting. It hung over a wicker corner table. An eight-by-ten or larger, Chen and I standing beside each other, his shoulder touching my upper arm, both of us looking straight into the lens. I couldn't remember when it had been taken, but I could see something familiar behind us, a turn of path and a stone wall, a site, I thought, somewhere in Pasadena. At least four years ago.

It was odd to look at, almost eerie, as if the past had been transported, and I must have lost myself in looking.

The next thing I knew, she had entered the room again and I had a tall glass of some clear liquid in my hand. It had ice in it and was very cool, and I drank immediately, realizing just how thirsty I was. It had a bitter edge, like sugarless tonic, but with something else beside that in it, though nothing alcoholic. When I lowered the glass, the man was in the room with us.

He was very dark, almost black, but his features had a slightly Indian look about them, broad nose and smooth brow. They were close to the same size, about Chen's size, I thought, in their late fifties, and now that I had myself somewhat together again I saw that the woman's features were clearly Asian. Something about his father's family, Chen had said, and I guessed that she was mostly Chinese.

The room was spare, but neat and clean, an old rug on the floor, and when I looked around I could see that what money they must have had had gone into tight screening on the windows and a very serious and heavy fan that was standing waiting in a corner of the room.

I don't know why, but I told them the whole story, every single detail that I could remember. It must have been around six or later when I began it, and during the early parts I saw Amanda fidget a little. It was clear she wanted somehow to tend me. I knew I looked like hell, but once I'd started talking I couldn't stop. From the beginning, Sylvan seemed to understand. He settled back in his chair, ready to urge me with questions if I needed them. And in a while Amanda did the same.

It was something about the isolation of the place. At least I felt it as such. I recognized that it was the first place I'd been in in a very long time where I had no care about the implications for my listeners. The story couldn't hurt them, having it from me couldn't, and I just let it spill out of me, the facts of it, and at no point did I try to censor or understand. It was a long story with many digressions and byways, and I felt, telling it, that I was somehow going through it as I had when I had lived it. Oddly, I had lived very little of it myself, and if there was anything revealed to me in my telling,

it was that. It was not my story at all, and because of that it had no
external power over me. And the parts I had lived, I had asked for,
though with some exceptions, with a clear view of things. The
exceptions were important, possibly even crucial. But the real and
central power was a thing I'd brought to it. I needed it, as much as
I needed the telling of it then, and in the telling I was driven in the
same way that I had pursued the facts. I couldn't stop, not until I
reached the end of it. And the telling was not the end. It only
brought me back to the room I was sitting in with them, these two
unimplicated people, and I returned and started the extension beyond the story with a few questions.

"Yes," Sylvan said. "It's seven. You *do* have time. I'd figure
eleven-thirty, safely, probably an hour later. If we leave, you leave,
at ten-thirty, that will be plenty of time."

She fed me beans and threw a good piece of meat into the pot. It
was the first real meal I'd had in a week, and I had to take my time
with it. They ate with me, and Sylvan offered wine. I wanted some
badly, but I knew it wouldn't be a good idea and settled for more
of the slightly bitter drink that Amanda had brought me earlier.
The kitchen was behind the front room, what I thought were bedrooms off to the side, and behind the kitchen was another, though
smaller, screened porch, this one lined with thick and leafy plants,
and I couldn't see beyond it to what I knew must be the backyard.
There were things and structures out there, I thought, but I
couldn't make them out. Sylvan saw me looking.

"After dinner," he said. "We'll show you. Then maybe a bath?"

I nodded vigorously, my mouth full of food.

We only talked a little while we ate, and not about my story. I'd
told it in so much detail that there was little for them to ask, and I
think too that they saw how famished I was and didn't want to
keep me from the food. We talked about Chen and his wife, bits
about the old days, Chen's two boys and what they were up to
now.

"We came here after my father's death," Amanda said at one
point. "That's a good twenty years ago."

"Why here?"

"My idea," Sylvan said. "It seemed a good place for such as us."

I didn't quite get what he meant, but I was still eating and didn't
pursue it.

"And you have a child?" I said. "Coco?"

"How did you know that?" Amanda said, coming erect in her seat.

"Across the street. The two old men."

"Ah," Sylvan said. "Gordon and James. They're senior people on the street. They have been here much longer even than us."

"Coco," Amanda said. "She should be here soon."

"Does she work?" I said, though I couldn't quite imagine where work might be in this place.

"Yes, here. But she's off now making curtains."

I heard a sound from the rear of the house just then, and thought it was a bird.

"Here she is now," Sylvan said, and got up from his chair and went out to the porch. I heard the screen door squeak a little on its tight hinges, then heard Sylvan speak in a lilting tone. He was there for a few minutes, then stepped aside and let his daughter enter.

She came into the room boldly, though in no rush, but when she saw me she backed up a step and her mouth formed a little O. I was sure Sylvan had warned her that I was there, but I don't think she expected me to look so bad. She caught herself, pulled away from her shock quickly, and smiled and said hello. There was indeed something birdlike about her, and her voice had that flavor, a reedy lilt, raw and insouciant. Not a bird of prey exactly, but a primitive one, rare and a bit crude, not totally adapted, a holdover from some previous time. I was taken with her strongly and immediately, and I couldn't keep my eyes from her body as she moved to the vacant chair beside me and sat down, then leaned toward me, her elbows on the table.

"Yes, I do look like hell, don't I," I said. She laughed her birdlike laugh and sat back in her chair, dropping her arms to her sides. It was a strange gesture. It stretched her cotton dress across her body, revealing the lines, the sharp hipbones, slight moon curve of stomach, her small but distinct breasts. I looked at the wings of her clavicles and the small, exquisite cups running in toward her neck. Her pitch-black hair touched into them on both sides, tips licking in the hollows. She had a pointed nose, eyes like dark gulfs, and her cheekbones protruded and looked like slick armor plating, as if metal had been inserted under her skin there in some old ritual.

"You don't have much time," she said. Her mouth moved, but the rest of her face remained fixed. All the expression was in her words. The pupils of her eyes were almost as dark as her hair and very large, and they remained constant as she looked at me.

"He has a little," Sylvan said, and his voice entered into my consciousness from the side, as if coming from some other zone. She was small, like her parents, but much thinner. She had Sylvan's black skin, but the Asian broadness and teardrop eyes of her mother. I guessed her at around thirty, maybe a little older than that.

"You've been making curtains," I said, unable to find anything else to say just then. "Is that what you do?"

"You haven't shown him?" she said to her mother, but kept her eyes on my face, then moved them down my right arm, stopping where, I knew, there was a ring of dirt at my wrist. The day's heat had abated some with the sun's sinking, and though I still felt hot in my sweats, I was no longer drenched with perspiration.

"We've been eating," Amanda said. "But we're finished now. Jack, do you feel up to coming outside?"

I said I did, but when I tried to rise from the chair I had some trouble. It must have shown in my face. Coco was up in a moment, and I felt her bony fingers grip tightly, a little clawlike, both hands holding my right arm. She didn't pull up, but waited for me to gather myself and try again, and together we got my stiff and weary body to its feet and out to the back porch. After the first few steps I was steady again, and Coco released me and led the way out.

The fight against the wall of growth at the rear of the house seemed a constant one. The wall rose up, thick and aggressive, higher than any man at the perimeter's edge, and as it moved back a few feet it grew even higher, an ascending hill, I supposed, until it filled most of the darkened sky. I could see no place of passage into it. Even where its thick-trunked trees tried to take dominance, branches were gripped tightly in tangles of heavy vines, green and hard-skinned, some as large almost as the trunks themselves. The wall seemed to be pressing down into the yard even as I watched it, to be visible in its growing and pushing.

Where the yard ended and before the thick weight of the wall began, there was a broad beaten path, a six-foot strip of earth that had been pounded down to a dark hardness from years of walking. And at each end of the path, set out in the yard a little from neighbors' hedges on either side, there was a racklike structure, heavy stanchions and a crosspiece with large hooks screwed into it, supporting machetes. I counted eight in all, four on each rack, various in size and in the curve of steel blade. They held a vibrant shine, a sparkle at the cutting edge, and I saw that beside each rack was a small grinding wheel, an ancient-looking thing with a wooden stool built into it and a manual foot pedal for turning. Coco was behind me now and at my shoulder. She must have seen me looking.

"Very macho, no?" she said softly and with considerable irony, and when I glanced back to her face I saw she was looking at the wall of growth and not the racks and was smiling. Sylvan had moved back toward the growth wall, had quickly made his way along the path, clearly checking for intrusions. When he got to the end he turned, satisfied for the time being at least.

It would have been quite dark in the yard, but the wash of lights from the kitchen and those that had been turned on behind the porch screening and plants flooded out into it and were joined by four lanterns, set high on wooden poles, in a little from the yard's four corners. It had taken only a few moments for my eyes to adjust, to bring the growth wall, then the open shed that sat near the middle of the yard, into clear focus. Then I could see the rack-like wooden tables clearly as well. They were long and sturdy, lined up in a square around the shed, and all four of them were covered with various sizes and shapes of ceramic pots, some brightly colored and a good portion done in simple and rich earth tones. I looked for the kiln and found it a little behind me, near the corner of the rear of the house. The open shed in the middle covered three pottery wheels, cement tubs and crude wooden boxes and a stack of what I took to be raw clay bricks.

"So this is it," Amanda said. She was moving along one of the racks, touching the pots, and I saw her beckon to me with her chin. This and another of the racks had small awnings set stiffly over them, a few feet above the pots. Something against the rain when they're very raw, I guessed. The little awnings had mechanisms at various places, cords and pulleys to draw them back.

I went to Amanda, the colors on the pots deepening and becoming more vibrant in the dim lighting as I approached, and when I got to her she handed one of them to me, holding it up almost at her head level. I took it and turned it. It had a thick glazed surface, hard and slick, and I could feel another surface over that and knew it was hand painted. And when I turned it and looked at it I saw the line of dancing figures, men and women, some holding hands, involved in various kinds of dancing, some delirious and some frantic, others stately and removed. But they were all together on the pot's surface, old and young, and the great variety in the dress and motion seemed a unified enough thing. She handed me another, and I turned that also.

It was a small water jug of some kind, a repeated figure at four points, a small and dark young woman. Her hair was thick but tightly fixed, and fell in one huge braid behind her ears and below her neck. She held what looked like an instrument, tucked in at the crook of her arm at her left shoulder, her hand touching the strings, the instrument pressed into the side of her small, protruding breasts. Her right arm came up slightly from her side, palm open and facing outward at her hip, not offering or welcoming or in any clear way gesturing. Still, it was a gesture of some kind, not really ritualized but close to that. It said something, large and possibly universal, but nothing I could make out. The figure wore a robelike dress, cinctured at the waist. I looked down at Amanda. She shrugged and I handed the pot back to her and she replaced it carefully on the rack.

We spent a few more minutes looking at pots, both those that seemed finished and those still raw and just recently turned. Their shapes were graceful, and there was no question about the skill involved. And the glazes too were perfect, without blemish, some holding colors that I didn't think I'd seen before. But the real art was in the painting—not just in the execution of it but in the imagination that had created the figures and rendered expression and motion.

"So this is it," I said. We had paused at the end of one of the racks, all of us gathered together in a loose circle. I felt odd, being so much taller than the other three, but I was no longer self-conscious about my dress and appearance.

"It's a living," Sylvan said softly, and Coco laughed.

"Who does the painting?" I said.

"I do." It was Coco, and I was not surprised to hear it.

We left the yard and went back into the house. My body was tight and sore again. I was finding that if I paused, either standing or sitting, for even a short time, I would seize up a little. There'd be cramps then when I moved again, pain rising to the surface in various places.

"It's eight-fifteen," Sylvan said, when we had reached the kitchen. "A bath maybe?"

"Yes," I said. "That would be very good."

"Then I can help you," Coco said.

"Yes, yes! That would be good too," Amanda said. "Coco has good lotions and things."

"Anything," I said. "I do feel like I look."

"And that's again like hell," Sylvan said, laughing lightly.

Amanda took me into a small, dark bedroom and through it to a door set low in the back wall. I had to bend a little to get through, and when I raised my head I found myself in a dimly lit wooden room with a large barrel-like tub in the middle of it, its top set in flush with the wood floor. The tub took most of the space, but there was room for a thin pallet to one side and a small wooden bucket with a dipper in it, a low, square box full of various earthen containers, two water jugs, and a stack of dark-colored towels resting on the rough edge of flooring. Four candles were burning, fat ones, and I imagined that Coco had lit them, and there was a faint scent in the air that I could not place. Then I did place it. Up in the low eaves there was a space between the walls and the flat roof, and flower vines had been allowed to take hold there and come in. The vines snaked along the opening on all three sides. I could see the flesh of dark petals among them, and wondered what kind of flowers could grow in such darkness. Their scent was faint but not subtle, a definite presence with a slightly acrid bite in it. It reminded me of the bitter taste of the drink Amanda had brought me. This is something I could use in my work, I thought, but the thought drifted away as soon as it came to me.

It was strangely cool in the room, and the water that filled the large barrel was still, slight waves of a green scum forming a graceful abstract pattern on its surface.

Amanda spoke softly. "It's a kind of powder. You'll see when you get in."

I couldn't stand fully erect, and I felt awkward, large and soiled, as I stood hunched over at the barrel's side. Amanda was on the other side of it, watching me.

"Do you need help?" she said.

"No, no," I said, and reached down and untied my tennis shoes and pulled my socks off. Even in the dim light of the candles I could see the filth on my feet. I didn't hesitate, but pulled down

my sweat pants, then my underwear, then sat down on the wood
and swung my legs over and into the water. It was tepid at the
surface, but hotter deeper down, and as I slipped in I could see the
green powder catch in the hair on my legs, then change to a much
deeper and richer green as my legs went under the surface and the
water wet it.

Amanda was behind me, helping me to get my sweatshirt over
my head, and when my chest reached the water I kept going, up
to my neck, then turned in the barrel until I was facing up at her,
then submerged myself completely and stayed there for a long
moment, my arms moving slowly out to my sides, rotating a little
and keeping me down.

When I came to the surface she was gone. She had moved the
bucket closer to the pool's edge and had put a bar of hard-milled
soap and a washcloth beside it. And now there were two handles
coming up out of the bucket, the ladle and a brush. I reached for
the soap, but before I could bring it to the water and begin a lather,
the low door opened again, and Coco stepped through.

She had changed from her thin dress into a long robe, very much
like the one that the painted figure on the pot wore, and she had
gathered her hair back in a similar way. She was carrying a cloth
fold of some kind, and when she saw the soap in my hand she told
me to wait, came around to where I was hanging in the water,
knelt down at the barrel's edge, and took up one of the earthen
containers from the wooden box.

"Shampoo," she said. She had lowered her head close to mine,
and I could feel her breath on my cheek as she said the word. She
put her hand on top of my head and pushed down and I went
under the water completely again, then felt a brief tug at my hair
and rose up. Almost immediately a cool substance soaked through
my hair and down into my scalp, and then I felt her fingers, strong
and vigorous, a mix of massage and scrubbing. She dunked me
three times, and after the second time the liquid that she applied
was a different one, icy cold, and she told me I could open my eyes
as she lathered it in.

When she was finished with my hair, she had me stand up in
the tub and lift my arms and turn. The water rose up to my stomach
only, and she knelt at the pool's side and took the soap and wash-
cloth and scrubbed my back and chest. She held the hard bar in her
small fist and raised a rich lather in my armpits, and she inserted

the tip of the washcloth in my navel and cleaned that thoroughly as well. The soap was milder than I thought it would be, and silky.

We talked very softly as she moved and scrubbed me, her head always close to my own, almost in whispers, but what we said was only directions, questions about them, answers. "Okay?" I said, and "Like this?" and "Should I go under again?" And sometimes she would not answer back but would touch me, usually with the tips of her fingers, would turn me, press down at the point of my shoulder, pull at my hair gently.

After a time she got up to her feet and handed down the wash-cloth and the soap and turned away from me and went to a corner of the room, where she leaned down and ordered and moved objects that I could not see. I understood and took the soap and cloth and scrubbed thoroughly and carefully at my groin and the crease of my buttocks. I was struggling to get my foot up out of the water and in reach of my hands, when she returned and saw what I was doing and the obvious awkwardness in it, the way my stiff legs were refusing. I looked up at her, then laughed a little in frustration. She waved a finger, told me to wait again, then came and took the soap and cloth from me and went to the far edge of the tub. I leaned back, put my arms up along the surface of the floor, and raised my extended legs until my feet were resting near her hands at the tub's lip.

She took time with my feet. She had a pumice stone and a bone file of some kind and a pair of scissors. First she washed them, using the soap and cloth and a small stiff brush. Then she worked at the pads with the stone, using the file and scissors when her fingers hit a burr or an edge of ripped nail. When she began, I felt my calves tighten, some old involuntary desire to pull my feet away from her, to avoid the intimacy of the thing. She had been so matter-of-fact about it all up to then that I had felt no modesty at all as she washed me, but my feet seemed a different matter, and there was something about her concentration on them, as if there were in it a desire to know them in some private and complete way, that troubled me at first. She understood this, looking up from my feet in mock crossness. The joke in her look was even more intimate than the washing, and it let me relax back into it.

It took a long time, and as she washed and studied and reached for the stone or file, I began to feel a strong and powerful desire for her. It was not a sexual desire exactly, though it contained that, but more a need to get myself physically closer to her, to get my face close to hers again, feel her breath on my cheek as she spoke and directed me, know that birdlike voice touching against my ear. Whether she read this desire in me, in the very touch of my feet, I cannot say, but she did look up from her labors as I was feeling it.

"Soon," she said, "I'll be shaving you."

Her words seemed to take time to pass to me from the other side of the tub, and when they reached me I felt the muscles in my neck relax. I leaned my head back to the wood and stopped watching her and gazed up into the twisted vines and dark flowers that grew in at the eaves. Then in a while I felt light pressure on my soles, gave in to it, and my feet went under the water again, and I raised my head.

She got up from the pool's side and, lifting her instruments from the wood, went back to the room's dark corner. I heard a brief slap, and in a moment she had turned and come back, this time with a strap and a straight razor. She set them both down on the floor, and before I could imagine what it might be like, she had slipped her robe over her head and slid into the water beside me, her leg brushing against my knee as she settled on her feet. She reached the strap end out and hooked its metal clasp to a nub of wood set in at the pool's edge. She had leaned out near my shoulder to do it, and I watched the way her small breasts hung down and out above her rib cage, her dark nipples close to the still and greenish surface.

I could see no suds or dirt. It had all seemed to sink down under, and the water had a dark clarity still, as clean and fresh as it had been when I'd first entered it. I'd felt no turbulence of pump or filtration system, but I didn't wonder about it. I watched the long system of flat muscle running from under her shoulder, down from her armpit to where it dipped and found insertion at her hip. Then she pulled herself erect again, leaned back a little and extended the strap out over the surface, the end of it held in her fist at her shoulder, and began to strop the razor. The water was above her stomach, and I watched the tight strain in her arms and the way her still dry hair bounced lightly, the tips of it just brushing occasionally at her neck and shoulders. The stropping made a dull slapping sound, and even in the room's dim candlelight I could see the blade flashing as she moved it in long and easy strokes.

In a while she stopped and held the blade up in the air above the strap and looked at it, turned it, then brought it down near her wrist and moved it in a quick slicing motion, testing it on her forearm. Her hand still held the strap end near her shoulder, and once she'd made the pass she had only to move the blade a few inches to get it to her face. She shook it, and I thought I could see a faint powdering of hair fall from it.

She reached out and unhooked the strap then and threw it back on the wood floor. It hit with a click and slight slap. She moved up very close to me in the water and reached out beside my shoulder to the wooden box, and when her hand came back into my view I could see it held a glob of thick white cream. It looked like animal fat, but when she brought it to my face I could smell its herbal qualities. She smeared it along my cheeks, and I felt its coolness soaking into my thick whiskers. Then she reached to the box again and came back with an old shaving brush and began to lather me up.

I watched her eyes as she watched my face, carefully moving the brush over it in small, tight circles. She was where I wanted her now, close enough. I could feel her breath and smell her hair, and as I watched her watching me I imagined reaching out to her head, pulling her slowly to me, then kissing her, taking those thin and slightly twisted lips over my own, smearing her face with the thick lather. Then I was doing it, but without any intention that I could control, making the image real almost without knowing it. At least I reached up for her, had run my hand and fingers along her forearm to her shoulder.

She stopped the small circles, looked down into my eyes, then slowly over to her shoulder to where my hand now held her. She knew exactly what I was doing, and knew also, I think, that I did not really have it in my mind to do it. She didn't say, what are you doing, or ask me anything else. Nor had she stiffened at my touch. She accepted it, not in any way surprised by it, and when she did speak I felt no shame, nor that I had betrayed her trust in any way.

"But you don't understand," she said. "It's just a human thing. Just the two of us here. It's all right, all right, I'll take care of you."

Her words were in no way insistent, just matter-of-fact, and when I received them I recognized all of the truth in them, and recognized also that what I had wanted was not at all what I had imagined but that I wanted to tell her, physically, that I thanked her, that she was doing something very nice for me, that it was the kind of thing anyone ought to be doing for another, and that I was aware of some lack in myself in that I could not have imagined it, not in the way it was going, the textures of it, the impersonality that made it so powerfully human, that it didn't make much difference who we were. Just the two of us, she had said. Any two, I thought, and then I squeezed her shoulder gently and then released it, my hand slipping down again under the water. And then she shaved me and afterward massaged some thin liquid into my cheeks and the creases beside my nose.

When she was finished, she got up out of the pool, wrapped a towel around her hips, then reached down to give me a hand. I took it, but as I stepped up to the floor I realized that I didn't need it. All the aches and pains were gone, and I felt strong again and clean. She handed me a towel, but before I could take it and wrap it around me she pulled it back a little. She was looking at my chest and stomach, and she reached out and took my arm and pushed it. I turned around, and in a moment she spoke.

"These bites," she said. "There's something to do about them. Come over here."

I did what I was told, moved across the floor to the pallet that she now stood beside and lowered myself down onto it.

"On your back," she said, and I recognized that bird music in her voice again. It was now like a gathering of birds chirping at a feeder.

She knelt down beside me, and I watched as she opened the cloth fold that she had brought into the room with her. She spread it out on the floor beside the pallet, and I had to come up to my elbows to see what she was doing. The cloth opened to reveal a long, thin stick, much thinner than a pencil even, a small clear jar of dark-red liquid, and a piece of what looked like amber wax. She'd brought one of the candles and placed it on the floor beside the fold, and I watched as she broke off a bit of wax and stuck it onto the pointed end of the stick. It was a tiny piece, and she held it out over the candle flame for just a moment, then pulled it quickly away. I watched as it melted down into a teardrop, covered the end of the stick, then quickly hardened and became translucent. Then she removed the tiny cork from the bottle and dipped the wax-tipped stick down into the red liquid. She held it up and like a pencil, then smiled at me and told me to lie back.

I looked up at the ceiling again, knowing what she was doing

and not needing to watch it. The first touch came as a small surprise. There was a brief moment of intense pain. It was smaller
than a needle prick, so localized that the pain couldn't get beyond
it, and it was followed immediately by a quick numbing, gone itself
in a moment, then a brief drawing out and puckering, then nothing
at all, absolutely nothing, no awareness of bite or itching. It was an
immediate and piecemeal curing, and though I was not watching I
could see the progress of it with my skin.

She finished my chest, arms, and legs, and then got me to turn
over, and I felt the reenactment of the same thing on my back,
buttocks, and legs. I could feel what I thought was a cluster of bites
just above the base of my spine, felt the touch of the stick there,
the pain points, and thought I felt brief strokes of a kind of tracing.
Then in a while she was finished and I was up on my feet again. I
looked down at the front of my body and saw the numerous red
marks, little dots like a pox of some kind.

"That's the thing," she said. "They'll take a month or more to
fade."

I looked around for my clothing, but it wasn't there. Then I
remembered my bag and racket and wondered where they
might be.

"My mother's drying your things," Coco said. "Wait here. I'll go
see."

She was back in a few moments with my sweats, socks, and
underwear, holding them out to me, and in her free hand she held
the key and emblem.

"These will be hot," she said. "Maybe something else?"

"I don't think so," I said, taking the key and emblem from her
hand. "They may end up being just the thing."

She shrugged, then knelt down and helped me with my socks
and shoes. The white sneakers were still dirty and severely scuffed,
but they, like the clothing, had been cleaned as best they could be.
I could smell a remnant of soap in the sweats, and though I was
not yet wearing them, I knew they'd feel soft and clean against my
skin. She handed me a comb then and held up a small mirror, and
I combed my hair. I could see my smooth, white face in the glass,
without nick or red blemish, and I reached my free hand up and
stroked my chin dramatically, and she looked up at me and
laughed lightly. Then she removed the towel from her hips and
while I slipped into my sweats she lifted the robe over her head, let

it fall and settle, then tied the cincture. I didn't miss her nakedness when she did so, but I kept my eyes on her face, wanting to hold on to it for as long as was possible.

The four of us met again at the kitchen table, and even as we took our places I felt a quick cool breeze and in a moment heard a clap of thunder. Then it was raining, a sudden flood hammering down on the roof of the house.

"All the time," Sylvan said. "It'll pass in ten minutes."

It was ten o'clock, but I felt no rush. I had seen no car and had no idea how they planned to get me back to the canal, but for some reason I couldn't bring myself to ask them. I wanted to talk, to share something even if it was just talk. They had been so good to me, and I had never felt that they were doing it because of Chen and that relationship. It was as if I had just come along, had been in some trouble, and they had done what had to be done, and not out of any moral standard of some kind. It was far simpler than that, and I could not name it.

"Do you have a piece of clay?" I said. "Just a small piece?"

"Of course!" Amanda said, and got up from her chair and went out to the back porch. She was back in a moment, a gob of raw clay in her hand.

"There's something," I said, and reached into my back pocket and got the key and emblem out and put them on the table. Then I unfastened the chain, took the piece of clay and flattened it with the heel of my hand until it was a smooth, round disk. I took the emblem up and pressed it down into the clay. When I removed it, its image had transferred, very clear and sharp-edged. Coco got to her feet, as did Amanda, and Sylvan moved his chair over next to mine.

"Ah! That's something, isn't it," Sylvan said, and all three of them looked down intently at the system of curved and intersecting lines.

"I don't know it," Coco said. "But I *feel* I do. Not a logo, I don't think. What is it? Do you know what it is?"

"I'll be damned if I do," I said. "But it's the tattoo."

"Ah, ha!" Sylvan said. "The one in your story."

"Exactly," I said.

"Well, we thank you for it," Amanda said. "It will look very good on a trivet."

"Or on a flat weed pot," Coco said. "On anything really."

And it was something, and they were in no way humoring me or speaking in some appropriate fashion. They might have done that, even if they didn't value the thing as a thing, and that would have been all right. It would have been a gesture in front of the real gesture, an acceptance of my thanking them formally, which certainly seemed the right thing. But I could tell that they actually did like it, and I thought their pleasure had something to do with the story I had told them. I had not told it to Coco, but she seemed moved by the emblem in a way that was similar to the way I was involved with it. She meant it when she said she felt she knew it.

We spoke for a few more minutes, all three of them smiling at me and asking me to please give their strongest regards to Chen and his wife, to the older son, whom they all remembered, and even to Donny, about whom I had told them a few stories. They said they felt they knew him now, and I believed them.

"I hear them," Sylvan said after a while, and I listened for something but couldn't hear it.

"There!" Coco said.

Then I did hear it, the cough and catch of some motor, and as I listened it grew louder, and the rain stopped beating down on the roof as quickly as it had come.

"Gordon said they'd have to go to the pump first," Sylvan said. "We've got about ten minutes."

"The two old men?" I said.

"It's the only decent car on the street," Amanda said. "They were pleased at the prospect of getting out and around."

And in the time remaining, Amanda packed a tight little bag of food for me, and Coco leaned up to kiss my cheek. I started to speak to her, but she put her finger against my lips and shook her head.

"Come back," she said. "You'll see what we did with the emblem."

Then she turned and left the kitchen and went through the porch and out the back door. We heard a brief toot in front of the house, and Sylvan and Amanda walked on either side of me, each holding an arm as we moved back through the front room and out to the screened-in porch.

The car waited in front where the lawn entered the street. It was a large, dark Oldsmobile, about ten years old. Gordon was standing in a white suit beside it, leaning against the door, smoking a cigarette. He had a hat on now, white also, and his shoes, patent leather, were white and shiny. He gestured with his cigarette when he saw us come out on the porch, and I could see the dark figure of James in the corner of the back seat.

I heard voices and looked up the street through the porch side screening. I could see dark figures in the distance. The rain has cooled things, I thought. The residents have eaten and are out strolling. Sylvan and Amanda came in close beside me and began their final goodbyes. They spoke of Chen and his wife, said they hoped I'd be healthy and successful, thanked me again for the emblem imprint.

"There's the mail," Sylvan said. "It would be good to know how the story ends."

I said I would write, thanked them once again, and asked them to thank Coco again for me.

They stood close beside each other in the porch's open doorway as I descended the steps to the path. I had my racket and bag in one hand and the small packet of food Amanda had carefully prepared for me in the other. Though my legs felt ready and sure now, recent habit kept me from trusting them completely, and I watched each step as I went down. It was when I reached the path that the low lights came on. I thought at first that they came from behind me, and paused and turned back around. But Sylvan and Amanda were in shadow in the porch doorway, and I could not see their faces. I heard Amanda speak softly: "Something we've all done together." And then I turned back around again, toward the old and well-kept Oldsmobile and Gordon leaning against it. A wisp of smoke curled up from the tip of the cigarette in his mouth, and I could see the glint from his teeth as he smiled around the bite.

There were two low-set lights, no more than a foot from the ground, hidden slightly by shrubs at the street corners of Amanda and Sylvan's house, and as I looked up the street I could see that the houses on both sides each sent a similar glow out over the pathways that served as the street's sidewalks and well out into the dusty street itself. The rain had settled the dust into dark, hard-packed dirt, and there were people, in light and loose clothing, moving along the pathways and strolling out in the center of the street as well. They were mostly couples, a dozen or more, and as I watched them, slow and relaxed and gently intimate as they were, I could see that not one of them was mixed. It was men together and women together, and they were leaning against each other, some holding hands or with arms around each other's waists, speaking indistinctly, some pausing, even out in the street's center, to embrace gracefully, to kiss and hold each other close.

The low lights sent a dreamy wash along the whole street, and I felt it as the only street, as if the whole town were contained there, isolated, totally efficient, and without real care. Main Street, I thought, a barter economy. They would trade pots for curtains, the labor of sewing them for food. I could imagine them passing, carrying things from house to house, exchanging greetings and a multitude of objects, staying alive that way, both in spirit and in body.

The light reached only to the houses' eaves, where it diffused and became smoky, but I could still see the dark peaks of the roofs and over that the darker walls of organic growth, leaning in now like a graceful canopy along both sides. I knew it was growing and pushing in, even in the darkness, but I knew also that they had control of it, that there were racks and machetes ready behind each house, and that in the daylight they'd be vigilant enough to manage it. It was only natural too, after all, and though it would have swallowed and taken the street if left alone, they had a barter with it as well. The cutting kept it pruned and vibrantly alive, and in exchange it was both protection and reminder: a guarding canopy, a sure and insistent encroachment of an outer world.

Then across the street and up two houses on the other side, I saw the figure of a woman standing alone on the pathway. She was facing out into the street, obviously waiting for someone. Her hand came up as I watched her. She held something in it, a piece of raw fabric, I thought, and was now waving it or presenting it in some way. Then Coco moved out into the street and made her way slowly over to the woman, who now held the fabric out at arm's length. Coco took it from her when she reached her, held it up herself in her fingertips until it rippled in the almost imperceptible breeze. Then she lowered it and moved in close to the woman. They were touching each other's arms then, embracing and pressing against each other. Coco was a little smaller, and she stood on her toes, her face elevated slightly and pressed into the neck of the other.

I looked away and back to Gordon, and when he saw me looking at him he removed his cigarette from between his teeth and spoke.

"It's time to go," he said, and then gestured broadly over the dark roof of the car toward the passenger side. I turned back to the porch for a moment, lifting the tight packet of food up in the direction of the two dark figures in the doorframe. I could see their faces now, but not their expressions. Then Sylvan spoke a last time.

"It seemed the right place for us," he said, and I nodded to both of them in recognition. Then I turned back and started down the pathway toward the car.

Some of the couples out in the street paused, and I pulled up for a moment and looked up the street to where Coco and the other woman had been, but they were gone now. I lifted my bag and racket slightly as I moved past Gordon and went around the front of the car. There were two women standing directly across the street from me, and as I reached the door I saw a third move up out of the darkness behind them. She was tall and very thin, and her neck was a bright white column in the dim light. She stepped beyond the other two a little, coming out into the edge of the street. Then I could see she was getting ready to speak, and for a moment I thought she would address me. I watched her closely and soon saw that she was looking above and beyond me, past the car and the yard.

"Amanda," she called out softly but distinctly in the soft night air, then again, "Amanda."

I opened the door of the car, and as I dipped my head down to climb in I heard the porch door squeak a little, then a lightness of step. Then Gordon got in behind the wheel and we both closed our doors at the same time. I heard a wet cough behind me, then heard the engine catch as Gordon twisted the key.

"Here we go," James said. "Men and Metaxa, the baths of Colón."

GORDON DROVE SLOWLY and carefully and kept his eyes on the road. He was a good driver, but I guessed that he drove very little. The car was kept clean though and ready, and the few words that passed between him and James, names of bars and restaurants, bits of reminiscence, let me know that this was a trip made often enough.

The road was very good, well lit and maintained, and I was sure that it was the main passage crossing the isthmus from Panama City to Colón and the Caribbean mouth of the canal.

"We'll get off this when we get close," Gordon said after a half hour or more, and James spoke one word from the back seat, "Culebra," and I saw Gordon nod.

We'd climbed up into the hills near the Culebra Cut, that achievement of brutal engineering where whole mountains had been excavated for the canal's passage. From the car the hills seemed benign enough, but it was too dark beyond the roadway to see them clearly.

"Are we near the canal?" I said.

"Not far," Gordon said. "Closer sometimes than others."

I wanted to ask them both about the street, about Sylvan and Amanda, and of course Coco, but I wasn't sure quite how to begin. I was tired now, a peaceful tiredness. My body felt fine again, and my mind was clear and attentive. But I had a full belly, and my skin felt that relaxation of a normal late evening. I would have liked nothing better than a cup of tea, a book, and a soft chair in Seal Beach. Anticipation kept me from dozing off, and though I did rest my head back in the seat and close my eyes, my mind kept working, imagining the terms of reentrance to the yacht.

"Do you have any idea about a good place?" I asked. "You know what I have to do?"

"Yes," Gordon said. "You'll need luck."

"Gatún," James said distinctly from the back seat.

"That's right," Gordon said. "The locks. It's about the only good place. There will be light enough. And activity."

"Rain would be good," I said.

"Indeed, indeed," said James.

We came down from the hills and traveled on the flat for a while, then drove across a long, low bridge with just a slight bending curve in it. I could see out and beyond the lights at the open window, a wake of dark water continuing as far as I could see. And in the distance ahead of us, a brighter cluster of lights, with blinking ribbons of illumination extending out of it.

"It's Gatún Lake we're on now," Gordon said. "What you see up there? That's the locks, Gatún and Mindi, then far off is Colón."

Once we were past the lake the road rose up slightly, and Gordon slowed down. We had entered the zone again, into streets with houses and industrial buildings. After a few blocks, James called out.

"Up ahead there, Gordo. That's the turn, I think."

Gordon slowed and stopped at a traffic light, and when it changed he made a left turn and entered into a section where all the buildings were dark and industrial. Mostly storage buildings, I thought, high windows and nothing in the way of formal entrances, just doors set flush in the lines of walls.

The streets went on in a tight grid. Gordon made a few turns that I couldn't quite figure. I saw brighter lights in the distance, the rise of a crane boom, and thought I could hear a deep hum of machinery. We kept on for a while, Gordon driving very slowly now though there was little traffic, only a few cars passing us heading back the way we had come. Then the buildings ended, and after a block of empty fields the street itself ended, intersecting with a broader avenue. Gordon pulled over to the curb.

The car sat at idle, and Gordon reached over and turned the lights off. I could see the brighter lights more distinctly then, about two blocks ahead of us, unshielded lights, some of which glared out in our direction, but most of them directed the other way.

"The canal," James said after a while.

"It's as close as I can get," Gordon said. "And anyway, closer wouldn't make sense."

"I can see that," I said, and turned toward Gordon. He had reached his hand out, and I extended mine and took it, a brief firm shake. Then I turned in my seat and reached back toward James. His grip was weaker, and I thought I felt an edge of palsy in it.

"Good luck," he said. "Come back again."

I thanked them, then opened the door and got out, reaching back in to get my racket and bag and the sack of food. I heard Gordon speak as the door closed. I didn't catch his words, but I could tell they were rich with encouragement. Then the car moved ahead to the crossroad, and I saw the left blinker come on. He turned then, slowly, and moved away. I stood in the dark and watched the taillights until I could no longer see them. Then I started out toward the crossroad and over it and down into the flat field on the other side.

The cover of darkness lasted for only a few hundred yards, but where it ended I found myself once again among blocky covered mechanisms, some of which were large enough to protect me a little from the vision of anyone who might be watching. I came upon no one, but when I was close to a hundred yards from the bright lights, I could see figures moving along what I thought was the canal's brink. They were slightly above me. On the walls of the chambers themselves, I thought. The structures around me were more numerous and larger, and I could see a small rail car moving along, a lighted figure at the controls.

I reached in my back pocket for the headband. It wasn't there. I must have left it behind. I ran my hand through my hair and touched my face. I'm clean and in order, I thought, oddly dressed but in no way disreputable, so I moved ahead, walking straight for the lights, the machinery, and the working figures.

It was dry and there was a slight breeze, and I felt that the night was far cooler than the day had been. When I could see a few of the working figures distinctly, I saw they wore navy watch caps, dark work uniforms, and boots. When I reached the incline at the canal's brink, I started up without hesitation.

My head came over the brink and into the bright lights, and I was almost knocked back down by the blast of what I knew immediately after was a ship's horn. It sounded two more times, what felt like an absence of all air between each blast, and when I looked up and to my left, I saw the massive wedge of a high hull come into view. It had a bright emblem attached near the point of its bow, some Scandinavian name, and the broad wall of its hull was freshly painted a hard, stark white. Between blasts, I heard voices close up above me, then saw legs moving. Some of the figures were running, and a heavy motor started. Then lines were tossed up, and I heard a mechanical-sounding voice, almost as loud as the ship's horn had been, coming from somewhere up on the high deck. Everyone seemed busy, and I finished the last few feet of my climb and stood back on the broad walkway near the chamber wall.

The ship was almost as wide as the lock was, and as it drifted slowly ahead and loomed over me I felt that it would press up against the chamber's sides soon, keel over and crush everything for a good distance out, including myself. I thought it did lean a little, but it was the lights on the other side blocked out by its bulk as the many-storied cabins of its superstructure came into view above me. There was a deep rumble, then a quake in the timbers and cement at canalside. It rocked my legs and stomach. It was the engines backing, the screws reversing the direction of turbulence in the chamber behind it as the ship came to a stop, rolling just a little and rising up.

Men were moving, and I had to step back as one brushed past me. He glanced at me, a large Panamanian, dark as Sylvan, but larger and with a heavy mustache. He said something in Spanish that sounded friendly, then hurried along the lock side to the prow of the ship, where he went to work with a hand winch, a thin cable running from it up high in the air to the prow's point. There were other cables, some amidships and some well back at the stern, and I heard machines whining and saw wheels turning all along the chamber. Everyone I could see was busy, even the quickly moving figures high on the ship's deck, some running along the railing, others calling out, giving brief and authoritative directions. No one showed any interest in me at all.

I stayed where I was and watched the activity. Then I felt another deep motion coming up through the wood and concrete, and when I looked far back along the ship's hull, I saw the edges of the massive gate wall on my side begin to move out and into the water. It closed more quickly than I would have thought. I knew there was a gate on the other side, another thick wall, and that they would soon come together. I turned and moved along the chamber wall, and when I was nearing the ship's stern, I looked up and saw the second set of doors far in the distance. They had been opening, and now they stopped, parallel to the chamber's walls. The hull of the large ship was lowering at my shoulder now, and the prow of another ship moved into the chamber behind it. It was much smaller, was a boat really, a yacht, and it was only when I saw the two figures standing in the prow that I recognized it was Janes'. It's too early, I thought. I almost missed it. I stepped back then, feeling exposed.

The men in the prow were still a long distance away, but they were moving closer, and they were looking in my direction. I couldn't see their faces, but I recognized their postures and clothing. They were the two I'd seen, the one with the tattoo and the other, and as I watched them a third man came out of the wheelhouse and walked quickly toward them. It could have been Janes himself. He seemed the right size, the right age, but I wouldn't be sure of him even were he much closer. I had only an idea of what he might look like, and I had discounted his presence on the yacht a long time before. He must have called out then. The two others turned back toward him, and when they did so I stepped from the chamber side and went down the embankment again, turned when I reached the flat, and found a place for myself beside a tall metal shed where I could wait.

I was parallel to the large ship's stern and could still see it. Motors were grinding, cables slackened, became taut again. Then one of the heaviest cables fell away from where it was fixed near the ship's high rail, and I saw an arm come up as someone back on the deck cast it off. It fell down out of sight, curling back and over on itself. Then I felt the deep rumble of the screws again and saw the large craft begin to move slowly forward. The chamber came back into bright focus as the ship passed and the lights on the other side shone down brightly over it once more.

I kept waiting. It seemed a long time, but I knew that they were refilling the lock and that it would take some time. While I waited, I tried to visualize and then rehearse what I would have to do, what I thought was my only good course. The yacht was far narrower of beam than was the larger craft, whose hull, I figured, had itself been too far away from me to cover the space between the lock side and the deck, eight feet or more. I could only hope that the yacht would be close enough, that it would drift to my side of the chamber when it got in it. Possible, but not likely.

I could remember the place where I had stood, out of sight now and up the embankment above me. It was ten, maybe twelve feet wide, enough for a start, but not much of one. If the yacht hugged the other wall, I'd have no chance at all. I could swim for it, but I remembered that even my teardrop chamber was too high up on the hull's side for me to reach from the water. I thought of the length of line in my bag, but knew there was no way to use it. Then I heard that smooth heavy movement that I knew was the lock doors swinging open. It was time, and I gathered my belongings and climbed back up the embankment to the lock wall.

The yacht moved slowly into the chamber, and as its prow came at me I saw it was drifting toward the far wall. I looked back to the cable attached at its stern. It was taut, and I felt a pain in my temples as I realized that it was probably held taut on the other side as well and that it wouldn't come any closer. Then it was amidships to me, a good twenty-five feet from the edge of the wall I was standing on, and it came to a stop in the water and stayed there as the chamber doors at its stern began to close. It was too low a craft to block out the lights coming from the other side of the chamber, and I could see the wheelhouse clearly, the low lines of the aft cabin, even the folds in the drapes that covered the series of windows there. And behind that I saw my space, even the edge of the crosshatched screening where I had dismantled it.

Above it, someone stood in the stern, not one of the three but a man with an official-looking cap on. One man was in the wheelhouse, busy, and I could see one of the others leaning out over the railing at the prow.

I could do nothing but stand there. Soon the yacht would be descending in the chamber, and I would be out of luck completely. I suddenly felt very foolish, having come this far, having undergone and done what I had, only to lose it all now. At least Coco, I thought, the street in Aransas. Then to my left I heard the quiet whir of a small motor, and when I looked toward the source of the sound, I saw a narrow catwalk moving out on some pivot from the chamber's side.

It was long and fragile looking, with thin tubular railings, and as it moved out over the surface, I could see that it was swinging toward the yacht's stern. I looked there and saw the man with the cap poised at the railing, watching, waiting for the catwalk to reach him. I turned quickly and started along the chamber wall, heading for where the catwalk was connected on its pivot, and as I went I reached in my back pocket and got the emblem and key.

The end of the catwalk reached the stern of the yacht as I got to its foot, and I saw the man in the cap step over the railing and reach out for the catwalk's thinner one. He was watching his step, and kept doing so as he moved quickly along the narrow metal toward where I was standing.

I reached up with the emblem then and dug it into my forehead along the healing cut line. I dug deeply and twisted it and moved it from side to side. When I brought it away, my fingers and the emblem were drenched in fresh red blood and I could feel it, sticky, in my eyebrow. The man looked up as he reached the catwalk's end and saw me. He gripped the railings tighter and stopped.

"*Qué pasa?*" he said, looking above my eyes to my forehead. I held the emblem up briefly so he could see it. He reached out for it, involuntarily.

"No, no!" I said, raising my hand back up to my brow. "*Médico, médico!*" And I gestured with my chin toward the yacht's stern.

He stood for a moment, blocking my way at the catwalk's end. Then the curious look in his eyes changed to one of concern, and he stepped off the metal and moved to the side.

"*Muchas gracias!*" I said, and headed up the catwalk toward the yacht's stern. When I stepped over the railing I looked back. He was watching me, his cap off now and held at his brow, his thumb moving over his own forehead. I lifted the emblem up and waved. Then he turned and gestured down the chamber's side to his left. I then heard the quiet whirring again, and the catwalk moved out and away as the yacht's gearing engaged and it lurched forward.

A ND SO IT WAS THAT I found myself at each recent turn, both in the present and in those uncovered from the past, among the concerns and deep involvements of women, and felt more acutely the absence of one in my own life. I traced my simple path, my parents' death, myself set loose to wandering, those years in the service, the university, then Chen and I and what I thought of as my real life. It had all seemed very clear and simple but had grown opaque now, somehow inauthentic, and I couldn't shake the sense that I had manufactured its simplicity, had faked it all, and that what I was uncovering was the real thing.

I had had women over the years, of course, had them for their bodies but never one as a friend. And I thought now that I had experienced that as a freedom. It had never once been a trouble to me, and that is what I could not understand. But now I had many of them, some in relationships that I was still constructing, others, Aunt Waverly and even Coco, I thought, in the real world. I remembered Coco and what had happened in the bath, then thought of the image of that dimly lit street, a place that I could wish to be at peace in, feeling even as I longed for it that it was not for me. Maybe I'm a cold man, I thought, and a hollow one, as I considered the empty past I'd thought of as a clean, clear ordering that had gotten me where I was. It was colorless and vacant to me now, as the one I was constructing shone as a bright and vibrant parallel beside it.

There was Congress Park before my leaving at seventeen, then there was this time I was living in, the one that started with the telegram at Seal Beach. Between them there seemed nothing now but a slow fading, a dissolve of what had never had fixed substance in the first place, had been no more than a latticework of a life, dates, records, and sites, nothing to tell a good story about, but for those occasional ones since Chen and I had been together. But they would be his stories and not mine, generated in his purer attention and imagination.

There was a world of gardens, lawns, and terraces back behind me, but in California the growths we'd designed and planted now seemed monstrous to me, without a will of their own, easy to control. The flowers and plants in California had become lush servants, as had the malleable landscape. Anything was possible. It all grew too quickly, outside of a partnership, then soon looked permanent, as if it had always been there. There was no real living with it, no commonly shared struggle that brought it to fruition, no history.

I thought of Chen and knew he could find a way to live in Aransas. Then I thought of the growth walls, that powerful canopy, and of my father's garden in Congress Park, then of my own, that small childish space that Angela and I had worked and fashioned. Aunt Waverly could live on that street as well. It was a way of being at peace with oneself that would be necessary. Whatever else, she had that, as did Chen, and I wondered if I would ever find my own.

They'd been busy at the wheelhouse and the prow, and I hadn't stayed to watch the catwalk swing away. I'd seen the man in the cap continue to watch me, then had turned and made my way directly to the narrow side deck, down the dark ladder into the passage. I couldn't feel the yacht lowering in the lock chamber, but knew it was, and before I reached the engine room, I felt the craft move forward slowly, heard the engines come away from their idle. I was up into the wall quickly, and when I reached my small enclosure I ordered my belongings, then settled in to examine the food store Amanda had provided. It was bright in my chamber. The lock's lights washed over floor and curved walls, and I stayed well back from the grate.

I wondered about the smallness of the tight package, but soon found out how wise she had been. It was a long fold of linen cloth, and rolled up in it were thin strips of a kind of beef jerky, a dozen of them, and a dozen carrots and a careful pattern of dried tomatoes and mushrooms. There were other dried vegetables too, ones that I couldn't identify, and even pieces of sliced root or vine, the outer surface of which looked like the ones I'd seen thickly twisted in the growth wall. And at the end of the fold she'd placed a flattened piece of slick coated paper and a pair of thin wooden chopsticks. I lifted the stiff paper and saw that there were notches in it, and with just a little effort I got it together into a shallow square dish. There was a note in the packet too, a small slip of paper. *Just add water. Good luck!* It was signed by each of them. I looked at the note for a few moments, pleased and warmed by it, then balled it up and pushed it through the grate and let it fall down and out of sight.

I wanted to watch us leave the locks, enter Limon Bay, then head out into the Caribbean, but I couldn't stay with it. I was safe again now, and as tension drained away I grew tired. I noticed the light beyond the grate grow dimmer, heard our engines come up in thrust, felt the stern gutter down in the water. Then I turned my head on Janes' jacket and saw the twinkles of reflection on the curved metal ceiling of my enclosure, watched them phase out and diminish.

I'm not sure how long I slept, but it was a good sleep and dreamless. When I woke up it was still dark, though I could see a dim rose glow in the sky when I moved and peered out through the grate. I felt the sea air against my face and a slight stretching at my brow as I squinted to see out. I touched my forehead and felt the crusting; bits of dried blood came away in my fingernails.

The yacht was moving at a good pace, the distant hum of the engines constant and healthy. I could see the dark swells of waves.

The stars were bright, no apparent clouds, and out over the water's surface I could see occasional blinking lights that I thought for a moment must be the shore. Then I realized that they were colored and moving. Running lights, other ships in their passage. A busy sea lane, I thought. Far off at times I could see fixed lights, islands perhaps, or some mainland shore, but I couldn't be sure. The lights diminished as the faint red glow in the sky brightened. Day was coming. I didn't want to lose the night, the coolness and peace. So I moved back to my makeshift bed, curled up on my side, and went back to sleep.

In the early morning hours of what I took to be our third day out, I left my teardrop chamber and made my way up the dark metal ladder to the narrow elevated deck where I had stood before. I was growing bored again, feeling confined. I'd taken all the time I could manage, much longer than was necessary, in arranging everything that I had for what awaited me. But I had little and had so little idea of what I might find ahead that preparation became whimsical, hard to concentrate on, and in the middle of going over things for yet another time I quit in disgust, threw down my sweatpants, the cloth rope tie I'd been once again adjusting, and moved up close to the grate. I'd been sleeping too much as well, and was growing soft. I felt I was losing that edge I'd gained through Coco's minis- trations. I could still see her ointment-covered fingers. It was a strong, energizing image, and I hoped never to lose it. I could feel the pattern of red dots at the base of my spine.

The sky outside the grate was bright with stars, no moon, and I could see their sparkle in the dark swells of ocean for many yards beyond my enclosure. We'd been free of all sight of land for more than a day now, and I could imagine the swells' continuance into the darkness as if to infinity. There was a stiff but soft breeze blowing, and though it touched my brow as I pressed up against the grate, I wanted more of it, wanted to feel it in the hair on my naked chest, have it wash across my groin.

And so I dressed and made my way down through the wall and into the engine room, then crept along the corridors, past the closed doors of the dark cabins, and up the stairwell to the low portal, pulled the door carefully inward and stepped out again on the narrow deck. I could see the lights' glow from the wheelhouse ahead and to my left the narrow descending ladder. I leaned out over the railing and looked along the curve of the broader lower deck. Starlight gleamed in the wood. I had stowed my racket in the small storeroom this time. I was free and clear of any encumbrance, and I didn't hesitate for long, but made my way down the ladder and headed toward the stern.

It was a longer trip than I remembered, though I recognized that taking it before had been a thoughtless thing. I'd felt I had no time, exposed that way abovedeck in the locks, and had hurried along to get below without noticing the qualities of the route. But now I had time and what felt like expansive space.

I passed along the curtained windows of the lower rear cabin, keeping my body bent a little to stay below its upper level. I was shadowed by a suspended lifeboat on my right, and after that, where the stern was devoid of superstructure, there were various lashed-down crates and a low winch housing, for the anchor, I supposed, to keep me hidden. And yet I didn't practice great care. There was a gentle wind up now, a warm one that may only have been the result of our movement, and when I reached the broad curve of the stern's terminus and looked over and down I could see that the turbulence above the screws was only a low boil. We were pushing into a calm sea. The glow of the red and green of our running lights merged together a few yards behind us, and there the water folded in on itself and flattened out again, only that faint hint, ribbons of a slightly rocking wake unraveling out beyond the lights' dim colors and into darkness. There was only a little spray, and that occasionally, the thinnest mist coming back from far ahead at the plowing prow to gently wash my ears and neck and dampen the fabric of my sweatshirt.

I could have lingered there. Starlight hit the water at the stern as well as the colored glow, and though it was just a repetition in the interminable folds of sea, I found patterns in the light and was drawn to the edges, out to space where darkness overtook our emanations and the ocean became only itself again. I had to fight away from the railing, and once I'd turned and could see back up over the low cabin to the higher wheelhouse, I recognized that I might be visible, if only as a foreign shape, to anyone who might chance to look my way. There were two large windows in the aft wall of the wheelhouse, and through the one on the left I could see the shoulder and bare head of someone at the wheel. He was bathed in yellow, eerily so, light from a dim and naked bulb in the ceiling beside his head.

I moved among the bulks of crates and housings then, and near the railing on either side I found broad, shallow indentations in the deck's surface. They were just about the shape and size of a prone figure, smooth and oblong troughs that descended slightly and ended in half circles of firm steel grates at the stern's hull. I couldn't figure them for sure, but thought they might be drain channels of some kind, to siphon off the sea in storms, gutters for when the deck was flooded and swabbed. Both were open to the sky, but the one to port and above my small enclosure had crates and coils of rope near it. I chose that one and got down into it, and before I lay back and looked up, I pulled my sweats off, unlaced my tennis shoes, and removed them and my socks. Then I lay back, naked and as if in a shallow open coffin, my feet a little lower than my head, the entire length of my body just below the level of the deck. I was low enough that the spray no longer touched me, but an edge of damp, warm air curled over the gunwales and washed me with a thin wet film. I could feel it in my groin as I had wished for and in the hair on my legs and chest.

The sky was full of stars, distinct and colored in a way that I had never seen on shore, but I recognized that I had not looked up much while on land, had found no need for navigation with myself as a point of reference. I had lived as if the future were a concrete thing, out there, waiting for me to act properly for its welcoming. But now the figures in the sky looked down at me. I could pick out many constellations that I had no names for. But the real shapes were there, austere animals and gods, metallic objects, clearly useful in the proper circumstances and hands. And I felt the sky was pulling at me as if I were the crucial gear or pivot of the ship, was lifting me above the smooth wood of my tomblike trough, gravity of the stars' influence, and if I stayed put long enough I would be in tune with them, even in my skin, its hair follicles raised into their own patterns by the slow wet breeze that also was being steered by the stars, planets, after all, as powerful and complex as the one I was riding on.

I thought of Uncle Edward then. His too had been a way of breaching some limit, not earthbound, as mine seemed now, but of this earth, so that the objective stars could shine down on all of it commonly, and viewers could find the machine of earth in everything and then come to a meshing of it with the celestial. What a noble enterprise, I thought, naive and foolish, but so much richer than the plain safety of my engagements. But for Chen, I thought, the pool and his larger vision.

There was one star that pulled at me mightily, a distinct red glow that was larger than the others. It seemed closer, and was wavering slightly. Then, as I watched it, it darted down, what looked like smoke of a burning trail following it. A shooting star. But then my eyes pulled back into closer focus, and I recognized the cigarette tip. It was no more than a yard above me. He had removed the cigarette from his mouth, and it now dangled loosely between two fingers, his index and second one, along the dark leg of his pants.

He was standing just at the edge of my shallow identation, and when I turned my head carefully, I could see the toe of his heavy rubber-soled work shoe just inches from my face. I looked up his leg, past fingers and the red-tipped cigarette, to his forearm, where I thought I could see the dark snaking of his tattoo moving up under his folded-back shirt cuff. I could see his chin, the edge of his nose, and a darkness against the sky that was his brow. All he would have to do was look down slightly. He would see my white feet.

I turned my head slowly, resting it back against the wood again. I could see up the length of his body and, out and above the column of it, the night of objective stars. He lifted the cigarette from time to time, and its tip joined into the bright night sky, still a star to me, though the false one I knew it for. And the cigarette defamed what I now saw as my romantic ruminations. It was no fault of the bright night, but my own human failings, the egocentric judgments, placing myself even as significant witness of involvement.

But it was not true for him, and I relaxed then, felt tension drain from my neck and shoulders, knowing he would not see me, was intent on that other vision of a glorious night that he could count himself as part of. I lay naked and disillusioned at his feet. The air freshened a little, and a drier breeze came up and pulled at the damp hair in my groin. Then I was rising too, but just that part of me that might have risen to Coco in the tub. There's not much difference after all, I thought, recognizing our strange sharing, at least in the image of it, and I took my mind to the far gunwale to watch us: a man in rough clothing, standing still near the rail, watching a dark sea and smoking, and another man, erect also, naked at his feet. But it was only in the images of shared closeness that they were alike, and I had not risen up to Coco in such aggression. It was the pull of the wholeness of the night that had stirred me, as if nothing under the stars' canopy could be separate. But I knew I was that, both in my life and in my acute presence at his feet. Just let it pass, I thought. It will surely pass.

I felt the dry touch of ashes at my hip. He smoked and shifted quietly from foot to foot. Then, in a while, he raised his arm and sent the butt of his still glowing cigarette out into the night sky and over the railing. It was only a quick, weak spark as it went out of sight. He turned then, and I heard the deck creak as he walked away. I continued to lie there, looking up at the stars, and in a while I felt that utter peace return to me. I could then put the constellations into a proper perspective. They remained beautiful, ordered and clearly significant. But their importance was not mine. What I had to do was as real as they were, though, and though I did not yet know what it was, I still trusted it would get me to the only significance that could really matter. My own, I thought, and what else is there. I slept then, and only found myself awakening when dawn was distinctly coming. Then I dressed quickly and made my way back down to the anchor well.

IN THE COURSE OF THE next few days a storm came up, and the yacht began to feel fragile, its bulk and size no more than a weak figure at the sea's mercy. My space was flooded, waves rising up for a while continuously, washing through and over me. I'd find myself floating briefly in my teardrop enclosure and would have to reach to the grate, gather my fingers in it and hold tight. I thought for sure that the waves were washing down and into the engine room, and in a break in the storm I crawled back to the wall screen and checked it. It was dry there, and I could see that my space and the well where the chain descended were designed for drainage.

Everything I had was sodden, and there were times when I saw dried mushrooms floating and slowly swelling up in puddles, then draining back and sticking to the grate's squares. I ate some of them, and managed to keep my two water bottles from breaking open or washing away.

Then in a while the storm receded, though very slowly. I had been awake for more than a day and night by then, almost always moving in my space, fighting to hold to the grate and keep my belongings close to me and in some order. I managed to hug the blanket, my bag, and Janes' coat, to roll into them and press up against the grate and get some sleep. But I kept waking, feeling the sea bang into fabric and wrench at my spine. Then I didn't wake for a while, slept for what I felt was a long time, and when I awoke the storm was over, the sea placid again, the sun out.

I stripped myself of the heavy weight of my sodden sweat clothes, then knelt naked and urinated out through the grate. The sun had quickly dried the walls and floor of my enclosure, but everything I possessed was scattered about in sodden pools, heavy with sea water. Using the length of nylon cord, I rigged a line and found a way to attach my clothing and the blanket to it. Then I snaked the objects out through the grate opening and watched the breeze catch them. I'd knotted one end of the line into the grate, and as I held the other I could feel the strong tug as clothes and blanket billowed out, flapping, drying, as my mother's laundry had so many years ago in Congress Park.

I spent the remainder of the sunny day in cleaning the rust from my tools and zippers. It was a small job, but tedious, and I kept feeling myself nod off as I worked. The storm had taken me close to exhaustion, and before the sun set I had tucked myself into the now dry folds of blanket and sunk into a deep sleep.

I felt the force of the open sea diminish a good half day before we left it. It was evening, and we were once again plowing smoothly along, the water rising in low swells and only a distant and light cloud cover at the far horizon. It was the breeze that I first noticed had altered, not that it had softened or quickened, but that I could feel what I imagined was earth in it and a presence of mulchy fishiness. But I felt the change more than I could measure it. It was a simple quality of difference in the way it washed over me. It was no better than it had been, but I welcomed change, and that itself was better.

I moved up close to the grate but could see nothing, only the open sea. Then I looked down into the swells and thought I did see something, weed, deep down under the surface, at least some different quality of color below it. It was gone quickly. Then I looked up into the failing light and thought I saw something curve in the air, a bird maybe. I strained to see, but night was coming on too quickly, and even as I peered out, the horizon was losing its definition. I stayed at the grate for a long time, watching the night close in, and in a while I saw that the sea below my portal was once again lit dimly by our running lights. Not yet, I thought, but soon. Maybe tomorrow, before the sun sets again.

I stayed awake for as long as I could, even tried using the penlight to look over my gear again. But the light was almost useless now, and in a while it began to flicker. Then it died out completely. There was no moon, and the stars were faint, and I had to take time and care in ordering my bed in the dark. It would be the last time, I hoped, and I wanted it right, without lumps and comfortable. I could smell an organic, animal scent through the slight dampness that remained in Janes' wool jacket. It was a smell of earth, and I fell asleep thinking of it as a promise.

It was the sun that woke me, and not the morning sun. And once I'd stretched and gotten out from among the folds of blanket, I crawled up next to the grate and felt that taste of air that was like the one I'd gone to sleep with. It had salt in it, but mixed in too was a vague flower scent, oleander, and what I thought was olive. The sea was blue. The sun, high up already, was a light disk in the sky. There must have been some distant cover of mist or cloud, for I could see into the sun's edges plainly and didn't have to look away. Aegean blue, I thought. Dear Waverly, I've arrived.

I could see small islands off the bow ahead, and directly out from where I was, a closer one and then another well behind it rising up. And well back behind it all there was a broad expanse of shoreline that I thought must be Turkey. We're hugging along the coast, I thought, just out in Grecian waters. I was sure we were well past the largest island, Crete, and I thought Rhodes as well, but I had no clear idea of geography, no real sense of the journey left. We were not really in among the islands, I didn't think, but were plowing along some sea lane passage at a good speed. We could be getting there very soon, or it might take the day.

I watched the islands pass for a while, their lush lower headlands and the tough and arid hillsides that rose to a good height on some of them. We were too far off most of the time to see signs of life, and even when we did pass close I could only make out what I thought were a few villages, squat and indistinct buildings, places of cultivation. There were gently terraced hillsides that I knew must be olive groves, and at times white boxy structures climbed up out of the low villages to edge into them.

I gave up my watching after an hour or so, then laced my still damp underwear and socks into the grate and prepared my noon meal, the last one, I hoped, on board the yacht. It was two strips of jerky that I'd managed to salvage from the storm, a small can of pears and one of mushrooms, and a half bottle of water. I kept the hydrogen peroxide bottle full and to the side, figuring I might not be able to go down for more again. Then I ordered my clothing and bag. I decided against the blanket, but folded Janes' jacket again as a pillow, figuring I would take it with me. The few tools had dried, and I'd used oil from a can of sardines to coat them after I'd rubbed away the rust. They were serviceable again.

The day moved slowly, but I was no longer anxious for its ending. I cleaned my finger- and toenails, checked the still red dots where Coco had ministered to my bites. They had hardened and flattened out and were crusted over with a red slickness as shiny as fingernail polish. I felt at my lower spine, where there was a tight cluster, and fought against a mild urge to pick at it. Then I moved my body into various positions, stretching it, searching for aches and stiffness. I was able to get the deep bruise in my thigh to react, that old remnant of reminder of Chen and me at the trailer, but it was no real impairment anymore. Only the cut along my brow was still raw, but when I looked at it in the mirror of the small emblem it looked clean and seemed to be on its way to healing, bits of scab again at one end of it. The sun was sinking down by the time I'd finished, and seeing it near the horizon, I carefully packed my bag up. I left the few remaining canned goods out and rolled them tightly in the blanket and stowed it in a corner of my space. I packed only a small box of dry cereal. I left Janes' jacket out, and I didn't dress but unlaced my now dry socks and underwear from the grate and placed them on top of my folded sweats beside the racket and bag. Then I leaned back naked, my head on the folded jacket, and in a position in which I could stretch out fully and still see what there was to see through the grate.

It must have been past five o'clock when I heard our engines cut back a little and felt us bank in a gradual curve. I came to my knees and moved up close to the grate, where I could see along the turning bow ahead. The island was a hazy image at first. The sun was going down on the other side of the boat, and the way it washed into and over the shoreline and the ascending hills caused a bright reflection for a while. It was only when we had moved up close and the sun's light was deflected in its angle that I could see again clearly, hills of olive groves, a lushness of hibiscus, bougain-villea, and what I thought were fruit trees, fig, quince, and even pomegranate, down below them. No town or village, but a few white scattered houses, slightly above low cliffs near the shore. Where the hills reached their highest, and after the olives had given way to a narrow swath of cotton, there was an abrupt and arid change, pines only, then, and white and sandy rock formations climbing up. And as we got closer, I could see inlets, even a few docks, I thought, and in places a ramble of more buildings, both wood and stucco, tucked into rising crevices and small, thick clus-ters of chestnut trees. Then the yacht curved away, began a turn that would take it along the coast instead of directly toward shore, and the island was lost to me.

We moved at a slow speed for another hour or more. There was nothing for me now but the open sea out through the grate. It was still and placid, no more than a faint breeze coming off it. Then I heard the engines cut back, and we slowed even more and the yacht banked again. I looked out, but still could see only sea. We came to a stop in the water, and I saw our wash come up beside us, a low curl of soapy foam, and heard the sound of the anchor chain. There was a slight lurch as the anchor settled down and caught, then the idle of the engines stopped. I heard voices and movements, the sound of a smaller motor in the distance. I looked out the grate, could feel the yacht drifting, turning, and as I watched, the turning brought me back in sight of land again.

We had come to rest at the mouth of a small harbor, and through the grate I could see down the brief channel neck that protected it to where it opened, almost circular, the pacific blue-jade of the water in it moving out in the V of a gentle surface wave behind the small white power boat that was heading toward us. The boat passed by a cluster of large bare rocks that extended a good ten feet above the bay's surface, and I could see others, lower ones, at various places in the bay, an obvious reason for our distant anchoring.

I saw the terminal ends of the V wash quietly over the white sands at the shoreline as the boat came on, touching the perimeters of a crescent beach, protected in privacy on both sides by steeply climbing rock formations that ended fifty or more yards up from it in low scrub and patches of vividly colored wildflowers that I could not identify from my distance, rock roses and morning glory, I thought, the side hills leveling slightly above them in oak and plane, then a thick forest of chestnut running up to the crest.

Immediately above the crescent beach and running for most of its gentle curve was a broad swath of low cedars, and above that the first terrace of the garden started. I could see four terraces, deep and shadowed now in their steps, and ending high up in the lusher garden landscape. I couldn't see that broad flat rock that Chen had found in the photo of the painting, but I knew it would be there somewhere. My view was from another aspect, but I was sure of the terrace shapes, even though the size of the garden itself seemed now a monstrous extrapolation from what the photo had held.

Above the terraces, the garden encompassed the whole rise of the open hill, and I could see stone and what I judged were wooden walkways meandering down from the hill's crest into it. They were lost in places, stands of poplar and what Chen had identified as ilex. And oak and olive too, and black pine. There were tended hedges of bougainvillea, large circles of hibiscus, and in some places the paths seemed to enter under trellis awnings that extended down in curves for great distances, broad covered tunnel paths, emptying at rock and earth shelves where I thought I saw man-made structures, wooden chairs and tables tucked under the branches of trees, guarded and restful places with views out to the sea. The whole hill stepped back from the terraces in gentle crests, and I couldn't be sure of the nature of the garden's uppermost brink, but I could see the blocky towers and low rectangles of the house above it, what might have been a second story at least. They were white and looked like rough stucco, and the setting sun washed over them, defining their edges sharply against the darker chestnut forests to both sides and the sky, still blue, behind them. The sky was jagged and a little darker where it met the house's sharp lines. Another hill, I thought, running up behind the house to another crest.

I brought my eyes back down to the bay and saw that the boat was getting very close now. I could see, through its curved plastic windshield, a standing figure at the wheel, his head out in the air, tufts of hair waving, then saw the boat's prow lower and the wash come up from behind it and push it forward a little as its engines cut back. It was a larger craft than it had seemed from a distance, an inboard, and when it drifted to the side and floated toward us, its engines jumping, then cutting back, I saw the wooden housings of the twin diesels and that there was room enough for eight at least aboard. It was built for speed, I thought, and very expensive too.

There were voices calling down from above, and a rope flew out and past my grate. It had a small red buoy at the end of it, which bobbed on the sea, and I watched the man snag it with a long hook. Then he was pulling his smaller craft closer, and when I leaned my cheek against the grate and sighted down the hull, I saw a metal-and-wood ladder unfold and watched as he stepped to his gunwale and climbed up and out of sight. He was small and roughly clothed, and there was something about his gestures and the sureness of his movements that made me think that he was a resident of the island.

I sat back against my enclosure wall and waited. Now that the engines were off and we were still in the water, I could hear things, thuds and the sounds of feet moving along decking, both high above and somewhere in the body of the yacht. And chains and ropes being pulled, I thought, and sometimes voices calling out. The sun was sinking, and it soon left the rough geometry of the house and was only a dim glow in the trees and pathways of the garden. The steps of terrace darkened and receded and the white beach became gray. Then a slow breeze came up, hard and a little cold, and I moved from where I was leaning naked against Janes' jacket and dressed myself.

I could hear a knock and creak above me at the rail again, and when I looked along the hull I saw the legs of the boatman as he descended the ladder. He reached the deck of the smaller craft, then got ahold of the rope and pulled his boat in tight against the hull. I watched as the three others came down, each hanging out on the ladder for a moment as he descended, dropping a heavy duffel ahead to the boatman. They gathered together behind the windshield, looking in toward the shore. Then the diesels caught and rumbled, and in a moment they had banked away from the yacht's side. The boat moved slowly until it straightened out, then the motors revved and they were heading in at full throttle toward the dusky beach, and I had the whole yacht to myself.

Once I'd gathered my belongings and climbed down out of the engine room wall, I went straight up to the wheelhouse, but carefully, listening for the presence of someone, though I was sure that I was alone. There were a few packed boxes resting on the enclosed deck, and I saw they'd hooked a small loop of rope around the wheel spoke and secured it. Ahead, through the windows and at the prow, I could see neat circles of rope on the deck and what I took to be a forward anchor chain running through a low pulley from a hand winch.

I started in the wheelhouse itself, then moved aft to the long cabin behind it. The key fit every lock. The cabin was indeed a lounge, a fairly spartan one, with built-in leather couches, a few tables, and a simple bar. It was neat and orderly and hadn't recently been used. Behind it I found a small dining room and the galley. I opened every door and drawer but found nothing. Then I made my way through the rest of the craft, but I could find nothing there either, only more storage spaces and bedrooms. I went back up to the deck then, and stood at the rail.

There were lights in the distance now, a few high up in the almost indistinguishable contours of the house, and, lower down, dim rows of them lining the garden pathways. And there was one, vaguely yellow at this distance, down close to the water where I guessed the dock was. There was just a bit of glow left from the setting sun, and as I looked out from the rail and watched it fade, I saw another one, way up at the hill's crest. It brightened as the other left, and before too long the moon appeared, a bright crescent, and lit up the house and the hill again and shone out over the water of the small harbor. Then the little wind died down. I could see the rock figures in the bay clearly, still and ominous, and the whole expanse of flat water, sparkling in the moonlight. I pushed back from the rail then, and went around the wheelhouse.

The trip down the harbor must have taken me a half hour or more, and when I reached the looming cluster of rocks I was still a good three hundred yards offshore. I'd found the rubber lifeboat, taken it from its metal housing, inflated it, and got it over the side. I'd used my length of line to get myself and my gear down into it. It was a four-man boat, and there were hinged oars in the housing with it.

It was night now, only the moon and the dim light at the dock to guide me. I pulled in behind the rock cluster, bumping against a mossy surface, and maneuvered the rubber boat to a place where I could see between the rocks. Then I scanned the shoreline in both directions and looked above the dock, where I could now see the smaller craft tied up, and watched the strip of cedar forest and above it the terraces. I stayed still for ten minutes or more, dipping my oars and watching closely. The lights far above burned dim but constant where I knew the house was, and the lamps lining the garden's paths were unflickering. There was no motion at all, and in a while I headed around the rock cluster and pushed in toward shore. The breeze had come up lightly again. I could feel it on the backs of my hands as I worked the oars and hear it moving across the hills in a wash in the trees' leaves and branches.

I beached the boat at dockside, struggling to get its prow up on the sand, then searched in the dark to find the plug and pulled it, letting the air hiss quietly out. Then I dragged it over the beach to the brink of the trees and dug a hole in the sand and buried it, together with the oars. I went back then and used my racket head to cover my tracks.

There was a cut in the cedars and a wooden stairway running up steeply from the beach behind the dock where the boat rested, tied up against the pilings, and I moved along the tree line and headed for it. The steps turned slightly after a few feet, and when I looked back the beach was gone and I was in a dark forest, the branches of the cedars hanging in over the wooden pathway. It creaked a little, and I spread my feet to keep them over the runners and made my way gradually upward until the path turned again and I could see the branch-covered archway where the cedars ended, a glow of faint light beyond it.

At the archway's mouth I found I was standing facing into a steeply ascending wall, the first step of terrace. It was buttressed in places with heavy timbers, and there were dim, hooded lights at knee level, marking the pathway of gravel that fronted it. I stepped out and moved along the wall and the forest's limit, and in a few feet found the break, a carefully fashioned stone stairway cut into the wall and lined with timbers. It was narrow and went up steeply, room enough only for one person's passage, and when I approached the top of it I paused again.

My head was at a level with the second step, grass now and low ground cover and not gravel, and it was a broader step, and a few yards to the left was another cut. The wall was higher than the one below, and I couldn't see over its brink to the next terrace, nor higher to where the garden proper started.

I didn't like my situation, the narrowness and angle of ascent. I felt below everything, and felt that if anyone came upon me I wouldn't have much of a chance. So I stepped up to the horizontal verge, avoided the next cut, and made my way along the second step, staying close under the wall, and heading for what I thought would be the terrace boundary. It was a long walk and the wall curved a little as I moved along it, and I came upon its ending abruptly, a slope of raw hillside. It was tall, twenty feet or so of face, but the rock jutted out in many places and I didn't need the rope.

I was standing among brush and stone at the outer edge of the terrace when I got up. Two more massive steps ascended above me, but from where I was I could see the beginnings of the garden taking shape. The house was invisible to me now, but I thought I saw a brighter glow of lights above those dimmer ones that illuminated the garden's pathways. They came over the high crest above me, a wash of light only, but they brightened the tree tips up the hill. I didn't hesitate for long, but stepped up the slope, passed the next two terraces, then came up parallel to the garden itself.

Even off to the side in the moonlight I could make out the complexity of the thing, something of the logic of its fashioning, though that seemed strangely aborted from my angle. Seen from the sea, the garden's expansive face had seemed more gentle, but from where I was its profile had a more warped character. Its slopes and the indentations where the paths cut in contained a kind of steep violence, and the few shelves I could make out jutted aggressively in their overhangs. I could see the edges of low tile roofs breaking the grace of oak and chestnut stands; garden storage sheds, I thought, but they seemed too large for that somehow, extensive and well made. It was too dark to make out flowers, though I was sure of the curves of bougainvillea, the trellis-covered pathways I had seen from my grate. They stepped abruptly down in places, and I was sure that ground had been cut away to accommodate their lushness. And I could see other cuts as well, places where clustered growths and pathways' turns had been accomplished by serious earth movings, without regard for what had been there. I could only see halfway across the garden, and up above, a sharp slope cut off my view, but I could see enough to know it was not my kind of landscaping, nor could I figure it as the one I had seen in the photo of Uncle Edward's painting.

There was too much in the way of terrain alteration. It seemed to keep the general shape of the hill in mind, but it violated the uncultivated ground on which I was standing and I suspected did the same on the other side. It was not site specific in any way, and even from my grate out on the sea, where its contours had been softer, it had been too large and stagy.

I remembered Uncle Edward's letter, his entrance into the harbor and the sight of the dock and building where that Greek art show had been held where he'd first seen Dorit. It could have been that, I thought, a wish for a healing gesture, to bring her to a place of some similarity. But the analogue seemed monstrous to me, the similarity only pushing the contrast. Then I remembered that the terraces and garden had been built over an ancestor, the one Chen had showed me in the book. That helped take it away from a simple matter of context. What was here now was fashioned over a history of landscape, itself fashioned. And by a rich man, I thought, one who had undoubtedly exploited people and had thought nothing about doing the same thing to the land. It was hard to tell if this new garden was a further exploitation or a softening of the former one. It could be either, but it was the latter that made more sense to me. It fitted better with what I thought I knew of Uncle Edward. Still, it was a very large indulgence, and as I thought of his painting of it, it seemed to me that the work had attempted to reduce it, to bring its overwhelming size into some gracefulness, and to point up a beauty that was not of landscaping but of nature, textures in specific growths and their shapes and colors against others.

I was standing at the brink of the garden, and the moonlight was bright enough so I could see some things, but I couldn't make even a tentative guess as to where Uncle Edward might have stood and looked out as he painted. Chen and I had decided on one possibility, but when I looked up there, near the middle and facing away from the sea, nothing seemed right. It just didn't appear to be the same place at all. Then it struck me that there was yet another possibility, another history, and that this was not the same garden that Uncle Edward had painted, but yet another one fashioned over it. Nothing that Uncle Edward could have made though. I thought I was sure of that, though the thought could get me nowhere. I pushed it all back down and away from confusion and continued to make my way up the steep, rocky hillside at the garden's perimeter.

I climbed for a long time. The hillside grew steeper, and the stones became large boulders, with sharp and gnarled bushes growing among them. And the hill climbed up higher at the garden's edge, a steep cliff to my right, and I paused often to get my breath and to look out over the garden's expanse now that I was getting up above it. I wasn't too far up. The cliff rose twenty feet or so and remained at that height. But I was higher now than any growth, and could see to where the garden crested before it continued down on the other side. I took it in but could not raise much of an interest in it. Only the size seemed impressive now. For the rest, it seemed monotonous and without any overall form. A few curves of path had beauty, and when I looked behind me at the descending terraces there was plenty of grace there. Those, I thought, are salvaged from the original, but someone had worked hard to undo that. Then I climbed up over a brief crest of boulders, and the tiled roofs and rectangles of the house came into view. Ahead of me the slope continued to rise and in a while became the dark chestnut forest I had seen from the yacht.

I moved back a few feet, to a place where the boulders were head high, and put my bag and racket down and studied the house and the broad stone drive that curved between it and the garden's upper entrance. The house itself was curved slightly, two gently concave wings running out to either side of an open tile porch that led into an entranceway. The porch roof had a slightly higher elevation than the wings and looked templelike. I could make out carving in its eaves, and there were pieces of broken statuary, a head, I thought, and a torso, on pedestals to the sides of the broad porch opening. Above the wings and behind them were the edges of peaks of what I took to be other roofs, rooms running back a little, but not too far, and above them the quick rise of a steep wooded hill. There was a car parked near the entranceway, a large, dark, blocky thing, and I recognized without shock that it was like the one I had seen through Dorit's knee in Edward's painting, a British Rover. There were lights in a few windows in the house's rectangles, and I could see the glow coming from other lights over the front roofs to the rear of the house. I counted what I thought were four rooms in each wing, a total of three with lights burning. Then there were those on the other side. At least ten rooms in the house, but there could have been many more.

One of the lights burned in the corner of the rectangle on my side, and I made my way carefully along the upper edge of the rock face until I was just above it. The roof was no more than forty feet away. There was the brief rock face at my feet, the width of gravel drive that extended out below me from its base, then the wing's end. I looked up the drive to where it turned and disappeared, heading up the hill, then I began to look for a way down. The face descended for fifteen feet or more, and I didn't want to risk jumping.

It took a while. The moonlight tricked my vision, and seemingly firm and sturdy branches and roots pulled away easily. Then I found a loop of root, a secure one that curved up almost like a handle from the ground. I got the line out, lowered my bag and racket, then slipped the end through the root. I backed up to the cliff's edge, leaned out with a length of line in each hand, and stepped down the cliff face, hanging out almost horizontal in the air, until I could reach the gravel of the drive.

It was dark enough when I got there, the cliff face cutting off the moonlight, and after I had pulled the line loop down from the root and untied my bag and racket, I put the line back in the bag and made my way across the stone drive toward the low window where the light glowed out. There was only a narrow grass path between it and the drive itself, but when I got there I felt safe enough. The overhanging eaves cut off the moonlight as the rock face had. It was dark, and I only hoped I'd hear if a car was coming. I looked back toward the rear of the house, figuring that was the way I'd have to head. It was even darker there, a cluster of heavy oaks where the peaked roof descended. I settled my bag and racket on the path a few feet from me. Then I moved along the stucco to the edge of the window. It was at chest level, and I only had to squat down a little as I brought my head around the edge of the frame.

I was looking into the face of Dorit, and I pulled my head back quickly, the afterimage of her angular features still before my eyes. I thought she must have seen me, and I pressed my shoulder against the rough stucco and waited. There was no sound at all from the house, just a faint and distant rustling in the trees behind me and high up on the hill. I gave it a long minute, recognizing that I didn't want to look in again, even feeling that I might have been mistaken, that it hadn't been she, yet knowing that it was. I've come so far, I thought, but this is too sudden, too soon. I wasn't ready to lose the story I'd constructed in a real present. Paintings, I thought, and letters, and only Janes' old photographs beyond translation, memory, and passion, and those too received in a context that was part of the story, or at least I'd made it so, a construction like a fiction, the faces and lives of people put together egocentrically. I'd be a pivot at the end somehow, and to look back through the window was to break a membrane, to begin that engagement. But mostly I feared the loss of luminosity, that she would now be just another woman, free of Edward, of Janes, but of me mostly, in there beyond the window in her own right, no longer a game of manipulation in my mind. The breeze flowed down the hillside and lifted the hair at my collar. I squatted and moved under the sill and looked again through the window, this time from the other side.

She was sitting in a heavy upholstered chair on the far side of the large room, looking in my direction, but I could tell by the tilt of her head that her eyes were focused on something below the sill line. Her hands were in her lap, her knees parted and touching the insides of the chair arms. Then I saw her hands come up and gesture and her mouth moved and the small head of the child appeared just a few feet from me as he moved out from the wall.

He was thin and sturdy, his shoulders angular like hers, and he moved toward her with grace and a sure step. And when he reached her chair her arms opened and took him in. He climbed up in her lap, and she brought her left hand to the side of his head and stroked his cheek and short red hair. His face was turned toward me now, and I saw he had her nose and mouth, but a shorter neck and a chin that was not so pointed as hers was. There was a faint darkness at the edges of his lips. He had her vulnerable brows, and I saw a dark place, a scab, I thought, on one of his bare knees. Dorit looked down at him, then raised her head and looked to a place that I could not see and moved her mouth in speech again.

I could her hear talking now, but only distant rhythms and punctuations. Her braid slid over her shoulder and extended down along her small right breast. It was thick and tufted at the end in the way I had seen it so often in photographs and paintings, but it didn't have that fiery luster that I remembered, and I recognized again that she was my age now and thought I could make out gray strands. But the deep lines in her face that exaggerated the angles and hollows did not seem a part of age, nor did the darkness above her prominent cheekbones. I was not close enough to tell, but I thought too that her green eyes had lost their luster, that quality that Edward had spoken of and painted. All the milkiness of her eyes seemed still there, but what I'd come to think of as a lime's tartness wasn't sparking through.

There was something careless in the way she moved her head and arms, no hint of hesitancy at all, and something else too, as if she had gotten beyond some sickness or depression and into a resignation the other side of any hope. Nothing now of any choice to be hesitant about. I felt a certain containment, even in the nature of her movements, felt that she had moved back into some free space, not much of it, but a space in which she had complete control. I recognized that I was trying to construct her while I watched her, almost as if she were not there but still that figure I had made up for myself. She was there though, and I tried hard to let her go and become herself.

Her hair was tightly pulled back from her face and very neat, and she was dressed in thin cotton, a quiet geometric print that seemed sexless and ready and without pretension. I could see her sharp hipbones under it, the shape of her small breasts, the column of her white neck rising above her small collar. She held the child casually and not tightly, and though she took her braid in her fist and brushed its tufted tip over his forehead, she was not teasing or lightly playing. And the child knew this and sprawled out on her lap, one relaxed leg dangling along her own, the toe of his sandal touching the floor beside her foot. Her toenails were cut straight across, and I could see no shine on them. Then I saw her smile. Her thin lips pulled back from her almost transparent teeth, but the rest of her face didn't change much. Even her vulnerable brows remained fixed, but I thought I saw that lime-green spark in her eyes. Then I saw Angela.

The room had a certain familiarity about it, something I could associate with Uncle Edward far more easily than I could the garden and the house itself. There were frayed, earth-toned rugs over the brown tile floor, and most of the furniture looked hand made, wicker and rattan. And I could see what looked like a very fine tapestry hanging on one of the walls and on another a modern print, a detailed, quiet landscape, possibly a watercolor, not Edward's but something I thought he would have liked, a hillside of bare winter trees, rich in subtle gradations of color.

But Angela was not colorful, though she moved with a certain comfort past the print and seemed very much at home, as Dorit did, in the room. She had her hair pulled back tight along her head also, but it was black and thicker, and I thought by its slick shine that she had oiled or greased it. It looked sculptured, and though I could see no tie, it gathered in behind her ears and hung down in a broad bunch to where it was cut off straight below her shoulder line. The bunch looked like a small log and had a texture like bark. She was wearing a brown robe, cinctured with a rope at her waist. It was like the one that Coco had worn, slightly religious, almost monklike. I couldn't see her face full on as she crossed the room and came to Dorit's chair, but I could see her cheek and the deep hollow of her eye, her thin arm and the edge of some cluster of blemishes running up under her sleeve. Her step was sure but a little stiff, and it struck me that she was very ill but was living with it. Angela, I thought. Still alive, Waverly. But who knows for how long.

She reached the chair and leaned down and put one of her hands on the arm and with the other reached out and stroked the child's wrist. Then she leaned down and kissed Dorit on the forehead, a long kiss, and in a while Dorit's head bent back and Angela's lips slid down over her eye and found her mouth. They kissed deeply then, and Angela's hand moved from the boy's arm and held Dorit's face, her thumb moving back and forth along her cheekbone. The boy leaned back into Dorit's breast and looked up and watched them.

I watched also, and when in a while their mouths separated and Angela's head moved back a little, I could see the moisture on

Dorit's lips. Their faces were close together, and I could not see Angela's, but I could see Dorit's mouth moving again, her hand running absently along the boy's arm. There was something beyond time and expectation in the tableau of the three of them. Even the boy, Andrew, I thought, was at ease in the long conversation. He made no move to get up, just languished there, waiting for nothing at all.

I moved away from the window, feeling a tightness in my neck, and reached up and rubbed it with my fingers, then brought my hand around to my face and rubbed my eyes. I looked along the building to the back of the house. It seemed darker there, and when I looked up into the sky, I could see a high cloud cover above the eaves, the moon now in shadow. I started to turn around, to look back at the broad stone drive and the garden beyond it, but before I could I heard a sound beyond the window and moved up to the edge again and looked back in.

Angela was standing straight now beside Dorit's chair, her arms hanging down at her sides. Her back was to me, and over her shoulder, to the side of her loglike hair, I saw the head and shoulders of a man entering the room from a small alcove. His head was down, but he lifted it as he came into full view. He was dressed in tan chinos and a dark-brown canvas shirt, and I was sure he was Janes. There was something familiar about him, the way he moved. I could just see the edge of his face beyond Angela, and it struck me how powerful the talk and writing about him must have been, through Joan, Dorit, and Edward. Though I had not seen him, except for those possible small figures in the background on the street passing in Uncle Edward's paintings, I had put things together from that and the talk, and I could recognize him. Then he moved up to the back of the chair and put his hands on the broad curve of fabric. They were large hands, the fingers thick. And his torso and arms were too heavy and thick. I knew it was not Janes even before I looked up to his face and recognized that I had not placed the familiarity because I could not imagine it here. It was Joel Fitz, of Fitz Cement in Milwaukee, Angela's husband.

I felt myself quaking at the sill and had to reach up and grip it with my fingers. This is quite mad, I thought, but as I watched Fitz turn his head to look at Angela, saw his smile and the cool look in his eyes, the fact of their real engagement, I began to recognize that the madness came only from me, that the problem was in the complex web of possibilities I'd been spinning out now for so long. I thought I'd covered everything that reached out to the unknown, but Fitz had never been in the accounting in any way. At least not in this way, whatever it was.

I recognized the same demeanor as when I had sat across the table from him in the crude new restaurant near his place. His way of movement and gesturing were familiar, but there was something different in his face, a hard puffiness in the cheeks and a sharper series of angles in his look. He turned his head from Angela's face and looked down over Dorit's shoulder at Andrew. Then he must have said something, for I saw Andrew responding. He nodded his head almost imperceptibly and there was a tightening in his calf as his foot moved.

Then Fitz came around to the front of the chair and reached his hand out. I saw Angela's hand flex a little at her side, then Dorit's slip from the boy's arm. She looked up at Fitz, her face set and with no expression that I could understand in it. Then Andrew raised his arm up a little, but not much, and Fitz had to reach down to take his hand. He pulled the boy carefully to his feet and away from Dorit, and the two started around the chair and headed for the alcove where I knew the door must be. Dorit rested her head back into the fabric of the chair when they had gone by her and out of sight. Angela stood where she was and watched their backs. They held hands, Fitz bending to the side slightly, speaking down to the boy, who didn't look up at him.

They were gone out of my sight then, and I saw Angela turn her head and look at Dorit. Dorit's hands came up from her lap again, opened out, and Angela slowly slid down to her lap, where Andrew had been, and put her head against Dorit's shoulder. They faced each other for a moment, but I could not see them speak. Then Dorit rested her head back against the chair again and looked up at the ceiling.

I watched them for a long time, but they didn't move, and in a while Dorit's eyes closed. They just stayed in the chair together, Angela's light body in the other's arms. Dorit's arm rested along the chair's arm, and Angela had her hands in her lap now, her fingers tucked between her knees. I kept watching, but there was no movement in them. Their still bodies seemed drained of all activity and even its potential. I could not find even a movement of breathing in their backs and shoulders.

In a while I began to feel that I was violating some privacy in them, and I released the sill, ducked down and moved under it, then got my bag and racket and headed for the rear of the house. I couldn't guess at the time, but I thought I'd stood at the window for a long while and that it must be close to midnight.

THE DRIVE TURNED BACK behind the house, went to the other end of it, then turned sharply again and started up the steep, wooded hill in what I thought must be a series of switchbacks to the top. One of the roofs I'd seen from the garden side belonged to a large garage, room enough for a couple of cars, I guessed, and light equipment. Cloud cover lingered, and I found a place along the garage's far wall, a small dead-end alleyway between it and the house's other rear extension, what looked like a newer structure. It was dark there, and I put my bag and racket on the ground and sat down and leaned against the building.

I didn't know what to think, and once I'd gone back and examined my conversation with Joel Fitz in Milwaukee, then tried to piece together something from Waverly's comments about him, my thoughts turned to Janes again. Could it be that he was here too, that they were together in some way?

Fitz could make some sense, I thought, but I didn't know what.

He, like Janes, had a past that went back all the way to the beginning. There was one thing, his and Angela's daughter. Her name
was Saphia, and I remembered the sound of his son's voice on the
phone, its guarded quality. But it was just another fact to me, with
no answers in it. The first thing, the only way I could see right
then, was through the women. There was a story in the way they'd
behaved with each other, with the child, Andrew, and with Fitz
when he'd come into the room. And it was after all why I had come
here, or been brought here, to get that story and in so doing understand my own. But not tonight, I thought. I'll have to find a place
for myself, one where I can hide even in sunlight, and after I'd
thought about it awhile I decided on the hill that had brought me
to the house, up in the thick chestnut forest I had seen from the
yacht. I regretted that I'd slipped the length of rope out of the root's
loop. Now I'd have to go down through the garden until the slope
decreased, then back up again. I got up from the ground and lifted
my bag and racket and looked into the vacant stucco wall across
from me. It was something else, and I thought I'd better check it
before leaving.

I moved out from the narrow alleyway and stepped carefully
along the building's rear wall. The stucco was bright and still had
sharp edges I could feel when I touched it. I could see what I
thought was fairly fresh wood where the tiled eaves met the soffits.
The two sides I'd seen had been windowless, but as I approached
its far corner I saw a wash of dim light touching into a tended privet
hedge beyond it. I was careful as I edged up to the corner, and
when I got there I paused and listened, then eased my head out
and looked around it.

The light was yellowish and came from a high row of windows
set in just under the eaves and the rain gutter, and I could now see
that the new wing had been attached at the very end of the one I'd
seen to the right of the entranceway out front. The dimly lit windows faced into the hillside, which was close to identical to the one
I'd come down, but there was no steep wall of stone on this side,
and I saw I could get up there, be at the windows' level without
much trouble. I stepped away from the building then, went around
the privet hedge and up the hill, and when I'd reached the first
crest the windows were across from me, about forty yards away,
the light coming from them washing into the hillside below my

feet. The eaves hung over too far, and even when I squatted, then lay prone on the ground and looked across, I couldn't see under them.

I stood up again. I was at a level with the roof line, and I could see the row of skylights set into it, four very large ones, with only a few feet between them. There was no door in the wall below the row of windows, and I hadn't passed one coming around the building. The only entrance seemed to be from the house's front wing, unless I had missed something. I ran my eye along the roof's eave, and at the building's corner where I'd passed moments ago I found the dark downspout descending. It ran down close to the far right window frame, and it looked firm enough, metal, I thought, but not aluminum, and I decided to climb back down and try it. I could see no other lights at all now, only a dim wash of moonlight touching the roof tiles. The clouds had thinned out a little, though their cover still extended into the dark night's horizons, and I could see the moon through them, a faint gray crescent well back in the layers.

Getting up was no problem. I left my gear under the privet at the hill's foot and stepped over to the building and tested the brackets. The spout was set out a little from the wall, and there were steel brackets every two feet or so and enough room to get my foot behind the pipe and on them. I climbed carefully, found a good footing near the top, and reached my left arm up and got a grip on the gutter that was comfortable. Then I dipped down a little and got my head under the eave and looked through the glass.

The room was broad and rectangular. The only door I could find was at the far end of it, and it was over that door that a bare yellow bulb was burning, source of the dim wash of light that I had seen from below. The door was flush to the wall in its frame, a square window set in the upper half of it, and I judged that there'd be another room beyond it, a narrow one, before the addition came to the house proper.

All the walls were white, and when I crouched and looked up, I could see the peak of the white plaster ceiling, most of the skylight borders, and a row of heavy industrial track lighting across from them, six floods aimed down toward the wall on the far side. Set out from that wall were three large and heavy easels, a good six feet between them. They all seemed to be supporting a large rectangle, eighteen feet by ten at least. I was sure it was a stretched canvas, though I could not see its surface. It was draped over with a piece of thin white fabric, the edge of which flowed jagged against the easels' legs.

Near the room's center, facing the canvas, were two sawhorses holding up a large piece of Formica-covered plywood, and in a cluster on one side of that surface I saw a gathering of jars with brush handles sticking up out of them and various tubes and cans of paint. Most of the rest of the surface had thick swirls of color on it, broad brush strokes, and there was a place near the right end where I saw careful dots of color in neat rows, quarter-sized circles that gleamed even in the dim lighting.

There was little else in the room: a wooden chair beside an old floor lamp, the edge of a heavy couch off in a corner where I could not see all of it, and behind the canvas and leaning against the wall what I took to be more canvases, possibly four or more. They were of the same size as the other, draped in white cloth also, but tightly. Either new and ready, I thought, or already painted.

The floor of the room was white tile and held no shine at all. And running across it between the table and the canvas was what looked like a set of tracks of some kind, its source somewhere off to the right of where I could see, and its terminus, after a slight curve, out in the room a good ten feet from the bare, bulb-lit door. There was a small metal-and-wood affair bolted to the floor where the tracks ended, reminiscent of a spur's terminus at a railroad siding in miniature.

I changed my grip on the gutter and swung out a little, trying to get an angle back beyond the low window frame to my right, but it was darker there, and all I could make out was the edge of something gleaming, something very large and resting on a structure that I thought had wheels. I started to swing back to my place, then noticed something else. It was nothing I could see clearly, a system of rods and levers and a cable, and when I squatted and looked up toward the ceiling I saw more tracks, thinner and more delicate, four at least, and followed their way across the ceiling, where they were screwed in along the track lighting fixture. I studied them as best I could, but a pain had come up in my shoulder, and after a few moments I had to move back in against the building's side, shift my foot on the downspout bracket. My shoulder pain eased then, and I dipped down a little and flexed my thigh and calf to keep them from cramping. Then I let my eyes move over the room's interior again.

I was sure it was Uncle Edward's studio, and was sure too that he had set himself up here a good while ago. The place had a worn and worked-in feel about it, places where the walls were marked, and I thought I could see smudging on the doorframe and around the light switch beside it.

So he had been here for a while and had been working too. It explained some things, the mail and banking business in Muswell Hill. That would have been five years ago now, and they might all have been here since then, would have come shortly after Andrew's birth. But why the secrecy, I thought, and did he die here, or had he gone back to London for some reason? Questions again, and no good answers, but there was Joel Fitz now, and that was certainly something, a huge fact that kept coming back to me freshly, a powerful torquing of the matrix I'd been building, a constant disorientation, one that caused me to sway out away from the building's dark side again, to adjust my grip on the gutter.

I struggled back to my place and looked in once more, figuring I'd better get the room into my mind as thoroughly as possible. I could see no use for it at all, but then there were other things that had seemed useless too, until I'd used them. And in a while I thought I had it. Then I pulled my hand free of the gutter, flexed my fingers, and started down. I was stiff now and a little shaky in my arms and legs, and I climbed down slowly, finding each bracket.

I reached the ground and started toward the privet hedge where I had left my bag and racket, and then the bush lit up brightly and I could see them plainly, tucked up under it. For a moment I didn't understand what I was seeing. Then I turned quickly and looked up and saw the bright light flooding out at the row of windows I had just left. I looked around, then back up at the windows, then at the house proper. The house was still dark, and the bright light, though it washed over the hillside to my left, stopped short of it. I looked at the studio's roof and could see light flooding out into the air above it. I too was in the light, as was the building side. Still, I knew I had to go back. I stepped to the privet and took my bag and racket around to the other side and tucked them in again. It was dark enough there. Then I went back and climbed the drainpipe.

The door at the far end of the room was standing open, the bare bulb set in the wall above it turned off now. But the switch had been thrown, and the whole room was lit up brightly by the floods in the ceiling tracks. There was no one in the room, and as I shifted for other sight lines it was the paint-splotched table and the broad, covered canvas on the easels that kept demanding focus, like an empty stage set waiting for something. I could see into the space beyond the open door, the edge of a single bed, a chair, table, and lamp, and a white sink with a mirror over it. A very small room, I thought. The lamp was lit with a weak light, the glow washing over a dark carpet.

Then I saw a movement, an edge of shadow at first, then a figure, small, its back hunched as it leaned down over the bed's edge and gathered something. Cloth rippled, and the figure came erect and moved toward me through the doorway, arms in the air, then hands poking from sleeve cuffs as it slipped what I now saw was a white smock down over its head and arms to settle on its shoulders. I saw the top of his head then, thin black hair, gray-streaked, and then his face came up and into my view, and I knew he was Uncle Edward.

I let myself swing back on the gutter when I saw him, not really recognizing him, a way of taking on the force of that first vision. There was nothing forceful in him at all, reason stood against him, but I knew that he was Uncle Edward even before he turned toward the table and the covered canvas and I saw the blue markings behind his ear. He reached the table, his back to me now, and I saw his hands come out, checking brush handles and paint cans. He even touched a paint spot on the surface with his index finger. He was old and he seemed frail, his arms like sticks, a clear knottiness at his knuckles and elbows. He moved slowly and with care, but there was a certain focused intensity in his gestures, nothing tentative, and as I watched he moved around the table to the easels and began pulling the covering away from the canvas, gathering its folds in his arms.

I could see his face in profile as he moved along the rectangle, his broad nose and thin lips, the way his chin protruded, and I tried to place his face in memory, but it was useless. Even in those

old photographs Aunt Waverly had shown me he'd been an occasional presence only, something vague in backgrounds. I even tried
for his expression when he'd held on to me when I was seventeen
and learned of my parents' death. Something seemed to be there,
getting to me, but I could not be certain if I was finding it in him or
making it up, placing a skin of strange nostalgia over his present
image. All I knew was that he was not foreign but very present,
and that all the implications of his living that flooded up in me
were not really touching me, not in my own past life yet. He was
there, a few yards away, and it was that I had and not the past's
construction anymore. Then he had the covering pulled away, and
it was the painting that drew my attention, though I kept trying to
place him, to force him into some context. He came around the
table and looked over it at the broad canvas, and I was behind and
above him, looking also, over his shoulder.

The three life-size figures stood facing us. Andrew was in the
middle, and the two women, Angela and Dorit, flanked him,
not closely but a few yards away, each in her own space. They
stood in what I knew was the garden, on a stone pathway, the
hill moving up behind them until in the far background and at
the painting's top the house appeared, not all of it, just roof
angles and upper wall planes, but sharply delineated in a wash
of sun.

It was late afternoon, and where they stood was darker, long
shadows falling from their figures, forming dark, coffinlike ob-
longs, set off at slight angles on the earth behind them, as if they
had each shed a rigid covering of dead skin, their new bodies in
strong relief. And there were flowers, oleander, begonia, morning
glory, and nut and fruit trees, pistachio, I thought, and almond,
fig, quince, and lemon, all running from their feet and up to cover
the whole hill behind them, each carefully rendered and vibrant in
the way that I had seen things rendered in those other paintings,
but here somehow fresher, even more accurate and detailed. They
were looking not down the hill toward the sea but straight out from
the canvas and into our eyes.

Andrew was focal, but only, I thought, because he was at a
symmetrical center. His thin chest was bare, as were his long mus-
cular legs, childish muscle really, rounded and immature, but getting there. He wore sandals, the same ones I thought that I had
seen on him in the room, and dark short pants, but he was

younger, possibly four, and his posture suggested posing and being tired of it, as a child might. He seemed on the brink of movement. It was not that his limbs seemed ready. They were in repose, his hip slung slightly, both feet firm on the ground. It was something in the rendering of his neck and his expression, as if he would turn his head, then follow his new attention and gaze and run away. But not to Dorit and not to Angela either. Nor would he run forward, into the arms of the viewer or to someone else one might imagine, behind where he stood or off to the side. It was as if his movement would be off into a kind of pure freedom, as if he existed one way in the painting, a way that was his life, but only for the moment, and when he ran out of it he would enter into another life, one that had nothing to do with the painting, painter, or observer. His hair had been ordered by someone, but a breeze had come up and disassembled that action, and his hair had settled into a more natural arrangement, and there was now a difficult and painful edge between it and the way his face and neck looked. It had been realized, and they were still potential, a little agonized, forced back from catching up.

I caught a motion, and I pulled my eyes away from Andrew's hair and face and saw Uncle Edward move around the table toward the canvas. He had a long, thin brush in his hand now, and I watched as he squatted down with some effort and dabbed at the stones near Andrew's feet. Those must be last touches, I thought. The entire canvas was covered with paint, and the refinement was what I had come to expect in the paintings I'd seen, though this one was different from the others. Not just in size. It had a boldness that they did not have, a master's hand. The colors were more basic and vivid, and though Uncle Edward's painting had always been very sure of itself, it was even more sure here, I thought. He dabbed, then he struggled to his feet and walked along the length of the painting, looking down at the foreground, the literal ground at the figures' feet, and when he got to the feet of Dorit he paused and went to work again.

Dorit's feet were shod in sandals also, but ones with thin strips of leather at her ankles. They were wide apart, firm on the earth, and she was not, like Andrew, hip slung. I looked up along her legs, smooth white towers without much surface muscle definition, thin but with a slick hardness to the skin that seemed to go down very deep, textures without fat to the bone. Her knees had a sharper anatomy, and I could see the bone and tendon beside them and imagine the thick cord running down behind. She wore a short, severe skirt, leather, I thought, or thin sheets of copper, like a piece of aggressive uniform, scalloped edges cutting across high on her thighs, and the rest of her was naked, the smooth narrow torso and small breasts I remembered, and her braid again a fiery thick rope coming over her shoulder, its brush tuft resting along her sternum, hair pulled back tightly around her head so that her face was stretched taut.

But she was different too. There were fine lines of age at the corners of her eyes, and the high arch of her cheekbones had taken on a severity that could not be accounted for by the pull of her tight hair. It was almost skeletal now, still elegant but no longer a term of surprised hesitancy. Nor did her eyes hold that. They were vulnerable as they had been. Her brows still refused in their wispy thinness to fix and define them, and they were still green. But the milkiness was gone, the green had become hard and gemlike, and they were fixed firmly where they were looking, intently, and beyond that old ambiguity of choice. They would look ahead forever, or if they did change and choose something else, they'd be a direct follower of that choice, and one would see nothing of the workings of hard decision in them.

She had her hands on her hips, her chest and face pushed almost imperceptibly forward, and her neck, like Andrew's, was on the edge of activity. But in her case it was not of motion but of speech, I thought. She was on the brink of saying something, a thing she was certain about. It would be a warning away, a protective thing, a matter of closure of her self in it. It would isolate her from the viewer. She could never, not in her previous embodiments in the paintings, nor in the letters, not even, I thought, in the one she had sent to Janes, have behaved or stood this way. It was a different Dorit, but it was not that that was crucial. What was shocking was that it was the same painter. It was not technique that was at issue, though that had altered too, but the place of the painter as observer. It was that that was now frustrated, where before frustration had been in the painting. She was now an invulnerable surface, and Uncle Edward could not get under her skin. There was a faint halo of light around her head and face. Her shoulders were above any shadows, and there was a small olive tree growing on the slope of the garden's hillside behind her that was off slightly in perspective. It seemed at times to be a kind of crown or headdress for her.

Uncle Edward rose up again, turned, and came back around the table holding the pointed brush out before him. I swung out a little, changing my grip on the gutter and shifting my other hand on the downspout. He stood and looked at the painting, and I watched the back of his head and the slope of his old shoulders. Then I looked up at the remaining figure, at Angela, and tried to make some sense out of her.

She was dressed in the same kind of robelike garment I had seen her wearing when I'd looked through the other window, and her hair had the same sculptured quality, barklike and oiled or greased. I could see the edge of the descending log shape at her ear and neck. Even her arm hung down at her side as it had when she'd seen Fitz approaching, but now her palm was open and facing out, and she held something high up against her breast in the crook of her other arm. It was a wooden instrument of some kind, almost square, with a few vertical strings, and a carved post at the top. The post was near her cheek, and I recognized her face as both younger and older than she really was. There was something in her expression, in the slight tilt of her head and in the way her mouth curled up a little at the corners, not a smile exactly but a look of satisfaction after anticipation, that brought her to me as the child I had known when I too was a child in Congress Park, and when I looked at the instrument's post near her cheek, I thought I recognized that too. It was a miniature rendering of the carved head of the stair post near the bottom landing in my own old house across from Waverly's. How could he remember that, I thought, and why? Then I recognized that I too remembered it, vividly, as I saw it there. More to the point, I thought, and found myself drifting away from the window, hanging back out in the air a little from the gutter. I caught myself and tightened my forearm and pulled back into the glass again.

The older thing was in her face as well as in the certain repose in her body. She stood with her feet together, her legs straight, and she had the instrument propped on her hip as if it were a part of her. She held it like an old master, that complete artist whose tool has become completely habitual. There was a certainty beyond all arrogance or show in her, and the lines and expression in her face gathered age as experience into that limited knowledge that is wisdom. And that against the remembered child in her made her vibrant, though in a very reserved way. There may have been sickness in the way he'd painted her. The knowledge that she *was* sick could alter the way her posture and expression were taken. Still, I couldn't see it. She seemed at peace, but not naively so, had that small, contained portion of peace that only the experienced know is possible.

I had moved my gaze to the background of the painting, to the garden's ascending hillside and the house above it, when I was pulled away from that by Uncle Edward's movements. He stepped back from the table, lifted his arms from his sides and ran them down his chest, then dropped them again and shook them along his thighs. Then he turned and moved off to the right and went out of sight and into that dark end of the room that I couldn't see from where I was hanging. He was gone and it was quiet for a few moments, then I felt a faint rumbling, and when I looked to the floor at the edge of my window frame, I saw the low, wheeled structure begin to come into view, the wheels turning slowly as they moved along on the tracks. Then I saw Uncle Edward's back, the smock stretched tight across his bony shoulders. He was pulling something out from the wall and working to turn it. It was as if his hands were in pantomime for a few moments, then I realized that I was seeing through the object and not at it, and the huge circle of the magnifying lens turned and slid into view.

It was much taller than he was, probably ten feet in diameter and very thick, and it was held in a broad band of metal with a thick pipe post at the bottom. The post went into a sleeve of some kind in the low wheeled car that moved on the tracks, and once he'd turned it and worked it along for a few feet it slid more easily. He got it out until it was near the painting's edge. Then he went back out of sight again, and in a few more moments I saw him backing up, his hands over his head. He was pulling a system of rods and cables out and along the other track line, the one in the ceiling. His hands gripped handles, and once he'd maneuvered it up and over the disk's curve, his hands came down to his waist and he slid the system all the way to the other end of the canvas, beyond the figure of Dorit, to where the ceiling tracks ended. It was a complex system that he was moving. It looked collapsed into itself somehow, rods hanging down from twisted wires that slipped through pulleys close to the ceiling. He let it hang in the room's air like a sort of collapsed mobile, then went back behind the paint table and moved to the lens. There was a handhold molded into the band near his shoulder, and he gripped it and slid the huge circle along easily on its tracks until he got it in front of the figure of Dorit. Then he moved behind it, reached out to the handle with the tips of his fingers, and adjusted the disk until we could both see through it and into the painting.

The lens showed a circle that covered the whole section of the painting where Dorit stood, her entire body and the stone path at her feet, the garden to her sides and climbing up the hill above her, and at the top a piece of the left wing of the house. I saw at once that the painting contained in the circle was not the same one that I could still see to the right of the lens curve, but another one that was under it, slightly below the surface of skin and bark, leaves and the needles of bushes and shrubs that surrounded Dorit's figure, and even the stucco of the section of house that entered under the upper edge of the glass.

It was all something I had seen before, but the attack was more aggressive and wholesale here, and I looked away to the rendering of Andrew, to fix some sense of the outer surface before I allowed myself to go deeper. Uncle Edward was behind the table again and was bent down working over something that his figure blocked from my view. I looked back into the image that the lens contained and began with the complex to the figure's sides, the way the veins in the leaves were human capillaries, the twigs epidermal, with twists of ligament and tendon winding through them. Even the stones at her feet seemed to be coursing with mucus, wet and pulsing a little. I looked to the section of house that was visible above her, but it was too far in the distance, and I couldn't make it out. Then I moved to Dorit herself, starting with her limbs and moving in and up.

I could see the sap at her wrists and elbows, the way the now displayed anatomy along her thighs was constructed of oozing woody strips, tendon and muscle sheaths fashioned like harsh, weather-torqued surfaces of bare mountain trees. I moved in across her stomach and breasts, finding the same things, then up to her pointed shoulders, the column of her neck, and when I reached her head and the vague aura around it I began to see a difference.

Her face pushed out from the canvas even more aggressively now, and though I could see through the tight skin at her cheekbones to that vegetable anatomy, the surface above it now seemed impenetrable, like some transparent metal that I might see under but could never really get through. I looked down from her face to her short skirt, to the now clearly apparent scalloped layers of pounded copper and what I thought was thin lead, and brass too, all bonded together into a shieldlike surface, and when I looked back to her face I saw that the layer just under her skin was actually metal too, also an armoring. It was still Dorit's angular face that looked out at me, but it now had a certainty in it, and unlike the other paintings I had seen, the underlayer was no joining into a peacefulness in some pantheistic vision below the tortured uncertainty of her humanity. It was the other way around. Her aspect was utterly certain. It was the deeper layer, just under the armoring, that was vulnerable, without logic, and wild.

I traced the surface of her red braid down from the side of her neck to where it ended in its bright tuft between her breasts. Once again he'd made it a spine, one that I saw was not human this time but a copy. It was a metal replica of a spine. Even the hair, which was now transparent, was thin red metal wires. It seemed perfect, each vertebra rendered in that exquisite detail that I had come to know and so close to its human model that I had to keep refocusing to see it as it really was. It was perfectly frustrated, so close to what it copied and yet in its materials impossible. I looked back to the skin of her armored face, then down to the nipples beside her braid tuft. They were made of metal as well, dark polished ovals of bronze, like rivets on a shield. Then I looked to the sheathing of her stomach and to her skirt. I knew her sex was up there under it, actually there, that he had painted it, then encased it, taking it away from himself forever. I looked back to the tuft at the end of the metal spine, recognized again that it was a braid, layers upon layers. My eyes swam, and I moved back from the glass a little, then swung back in and focused. I was looking for other things now, beginning to realize that there was even more there than I'd been seeing.

The figures in the knee came back to me, as well as the fingernails and their message. I started to look deeper, then saw Uncle

Edward move and stand erect behind the table. He turned slightly toward me and held something up in his hand and looked at it. It was a long, thin piece of wood, no more than the thickness of a toothpick, and he held it delicately up and out from his shoulder and moved to where the collapsed system of rods and wires hung down from the ceiling tracks. I saw him affix the stick to a holder of some kind, then reach up and grip one of the hanging handles. He squeezed it or turned it in some way, and then the hanging system began to unfold and expand and become rigid in the air. He gripped another handle, and the rod with the stick holder in the end of it extended out like a pointer. He let the whole thing hang there and then went back to the table and returned with a small, dark vessel, a little open jar. With his free hand he took the handle again and turned it. The pointer swung slowly around until the stick was in view in its holder at the edge of the lens. I could see through it now, to the rigid black hair sticking out from the stick's tip.

Uncle Edward looked through the lens too, then moved up to it, and I saw him reach the small vessel around the edge and hold it up near the tip of the hair until the hair came over the rim, and when he brought it away it was wet and glossy. Again he went back to the table, put the vessel down, and placed a lid over it. Then he went between the table and the lens and began working the handles. The stick at the end of the rod moved up above Dorit's head, slowly coming into position near the canvas. Then it was touching the canvas, and he was painting.

What had seemed a halo surrounding her head still seemed like that, but as I watched the movement of the thin brush I could see that there were trails moving out of the halo in various directions and places and that he was working, extending one of them. The hair at the end of the stick moved close to the surface, leaving a luminous trail. I suddenly realized that it was the air that he was painting, and I began to see flecks of minute airborne dust, tiny amoeba shapes, things that one would never be able to see in any conventional reality, but could see only through a strong lens, like this one, or a microscope.

It struck me that there was something completely mad in the act, obsession driven through to some insane limit. Who would ever see it, I thought, but then recognized that it could be seen, that like the surface of Dorit's face, the visible air without the lens revelation was the life surface of the painting and that this exquisite attention to the underlayers would only harden it and push it forward. I looked away from the lens and the moving brush and studied the air around Andrew's and Angela's heads, and I thought I could see it, a dance in a stillness, an invisible activity where there was none.

He returned again and again, getting the small vessel, opening it, loading the brush, and in a while I stopped watching him paint and went back to search out other things. The knee and the nails were fresh in my mind again now, and when I brought my eyes to Dorit's stomach I found what I was looking for immediately, those structures under the underlayers, images I could now see through all the folds of vegetable anatomy and metal sheathing. I thought it was clear that they were at the final limit, that there was nothing but a returning to the surface from them.

There was a level of air above her stomach, what I thought must be heat waves or currents. Then the stomach's taut skin, and just under the surface a kind of gestalt of folds of thin copper and lead sheets, but veined through with leaf capillaries and sappy tendon and muscle sheaths, transparent, then a sky at first, then clouds, cirrus and wispy, and down through that an oval. It was Congress Park, the oval of the park lined again with those Dutch elm trees that had been decimated and lost to disease after my leaving. And to the right of the park's oval, a house, but with the roof gone, partitions of a second story, the rise and square turn of an ascending stairway. Then I saw my mother's bedroom, my mother in her chair at her vanity. She was dressed in a thin nightgown. Her arm was up. She was applying something to her face. And there was a small figure on the floor at her feet, a child in a white diaper. It was me. There were other rooms, and I found my own, with a crib in it, a small mobile. My father was nowhere in evidence, but there was a light in another room, in another roofless house to the side of mine, Angela's room, but the figure standing at the window was not she, but Uncle Edward himself.

And there were objects and events depicted in places under every surface that I looked into, filmy openings in the interstices of tissue and leaf folds, around corners, open windows, even in the bark of pistachio trees and the skins of pomegranates. And there was something even under the stucco of the section of house near the painting's top, though it was too far away and I could not make it out. Would he need an even stronger lens for that, I thought, or is it that I would see it were I down in the room with him? I couldn't be sure, but I knew that while I wanted to climb down and find some way in, I couldn't in reason do so. It was too soon, too soon. I needed more of the story. I still needed time. So I continued to hang at the gutter and look in.

He was still painting, still moving that thin brush in its system. He's painting the air, I thought again, and when I looked there I could see nothing through it. Like Dorit's braid, her sex under her metal skirt, her nipples, and her face, it had a finality that he was not breaching. All the rest had another layer, and the point of it all came to me as I moved my eyes slowly over the emerging structures again, how it was all such a strange and ironic result of the force that had driven him, one that had been both a life's work and a life work to him. It had all started before Dorit. I knew that from his letters. But it was in her that it had taken on specific shape and a direction that he had translated into an operation, a skillful refinement and a series of tasks to be taken up. It had been reality that he'd been after, and without arrogance, and purely that. And maybe he had come close to getting hold of it, of seeing it at least, in those paintings of Dorit's uncertainty, things in her look, posture, and frozen gestures that captured a deeper activity, a motion in stillness that was lifelike in a real sense.

But his desire had told him that the source was not there, at the surface, but below it, and he had gone down under there and come to things. But they were not finally the things he was after, and he had gone deeper. He must have been learning to do it for a long time, I thought. I'd seen its beginnings in that tree painting and in renderings of Dorit's limbs. By the time he'd altered those paintings, sent out the messages in knee and nails, he had almost had it. That couldn't have been too long ago, but he had pushed through from that, or at least extended it. He had all the tools then, and what he came to find was indeed reality, his memory, the very things that he had walked away from in order to get to what he wanted. It had trailed him in part because he couldn't let it go, all those letters to Waverly, messages in paintings, then Angela herself coming literally out of his past to change his present, and his future.

Now he was painting his autobiography. Everything I could find had something to do with that: Congress Park, renderings of furniture, his studio and illustration implements, Waverly standing in a doorway, old clothing, anatomy illustrations, my father's small garden across the fence. But nothing from Angela, and though she was here now and he didn't need her that way, to reconstruct the memory of her, I still wondered about that and wondered too at my mother at her vanity and me in my diaper on the floor.

But I had the final irony, and felt I had it in myself somehow as well. He had gotten through to the primal layer, but he had found that it was a mirror, that there would always be that screen of memory through which he must see things, and so he had painted the screen itself, in all its nostalgia, melodrama, and authentic emotion. But the resulting power was not there. It was back on the surface, in the way the underlayers fought to come up and couldn't get there. It was in the embodiments of Andrew and Angela to the side of the powerful lens, seen clearly without it, a surface that was exquisitely dignified and human precisely because it could not be penetrated.

And it all had a story, one that I knew pretty well now, events in his life in the real world. And he was excluded from them, from his own painting, it seemed to me, from the surface that guarded the lives of those three people at least. And so he had gone under the surface only to create it, to display that image of his leaving coming back to haunt and then call him to account for it. I could pull my eyes to the surface of Dorit's body and see it, the way she stood with her hands on her hips, the thrust of her hard face at the brink of speech. She wouldn't say "keep back" because he would already know that, had presented his recognition of it in her. I knew I'd see the same things were the lens to be moved to Angela, though I was not sure about Andrew.

I moved my head to where the thin brush was moving in the air beside Dorit's head. My neck was stiffening, but Uncle Edward was still painting, and I couldn't think to climb down from my place until he finished or something else happened. His motion and the life in him there kept coming up to me. Whose was the body? It had had the tattoo, and as Edward moved I could see the authentic one behind his ear at times, faded out a little but distinct. I leaned back and looked up over the eaves and saw that the crescent moon had moved down at the roof's peak, only half of it visible to me now, but brighter, the cloud cover dissipated. My shoulder ached, and I could feel a numbness in the ball of my foot on the bracket through my tennis shoe. I shifted and swung out a little and looked down the side of the stucco building, rotating my stiff neck on my shoulders, then dipped back under again and looked in.

He was standing to the side of the lens now, to Andrew's side, and I saw him reach to the thick grip in the band and lean back a little. Then the lens was sliding along the track again. It had turned a fraction, and as it passed over the figures of Andrew and Angela I could see nothing in focus through it. He went out of sight. Then the lens itself disappeared, sliding slowly beyond the window frame. He was back in a few moments, bent over a little, and he looked tired from his concentration. Then he went to the wire and rod system, took the handles again, and I watched as it slowly collapsed. He didn't slide it back along the ceiling track but left it hanging in the air to the left of the canvas and went and got the pile of white drapes. He covered Angela and Andrew quickly, but took some time and care with draping Dorit. It had been a very thin glaze, I guessed, and would be almost dry already.

I wanted a last glimpse of his face, to have a chance to find something in his eyes, but he didn't turn in my direction, and I could only watch his stooped back as he walked stiffly toward the door in the far end of the room, reached up to the switch on the wall when he got there, and threw it. The room darkened and the yellow light above the door came on at the same time. I saw the edge of the bed, the glow of the dim lamp as he passed through. Then he closed the door behind him, and I was alone at the window.

I knew I couldn't get back up the stone wall I had roped down and that I would have to enter the garden. It was only the broad stone drive in front of the house that I was unsure of. But it was very late now, close to two o'clock, I thought, possibly even three, and when I reached the edge of the house's wing and looked around it, all the windows were dark. I didn't hesitate but walked out into the drive and across it, then down into the stone pathway where the garden started.

The garden went out almost on a level for a hundred feet or

more, only slowly descending. When I reached the first crest, the
path began a gentle curve to the right, and I followed it until it cut
back the other way, then left it and headed among dark trees and
shrubbery toward the slope I had climbed up earlier. The moon
was bright and fully visible again. It lit my way, and I was soon at
the garden's edge and up the steep embankment.

I climbed back up for fifty yards or so until I found a crest that
moved off into the darkness and away from the garden's side, and
before I headed along it I turned back and looked down at the bay.
It was visible in the moonlight now, though the sea far out beyond
the neck and mouth was still in complete darkness. I could see the
yacht, very white and placid in the moonlight, the dark shape of
the rocks out in the water, but I could not see back under to where
the dock was, the smaller boat and the sandy beach. It was a lovely
sight, the moon's silver shimmer in the water, but it was too quiet
somehow, and I slumped a little as I watched it. I recognized how
tired I was, and before I gave in to the urge to sit down among the
bushes and stones at my feet, to lean back and watch the bay, I
gripped my bag and racket and set off along the ridge.

It stayed out in the open for a while, then as I got higher it
entered into the chestnut forest. There were no pathways, but the
trees were spaced widely enough, and I was able to pass among
them with no trouble. I went on for only a few minutes, then the
forest ended. It had clearly been cut away. There was twenty or
more feet of clearing, nothing at all growing in it, then a high metal
fence, barbed wire along its top and those small white cylinders
that told me it was electrified. On the other side of the fence, the
cleared space continued for a long way, then the forest started
again. I moved out into the space and looked up the cut, then
turned and looked down it. It continued for a good distance, then
dissolved in darkness, and I guessed that it lined the whole perimeter of the land that the house ruled. I looked in both directions
again, then felt that slumping in my shoulders, my lids slipping,
and so I turned and went back into the forest.

Again I moved upslope, but this time slowly, keeping my eyes
wide in the darkness, and in only a few minutes I found a cluster
of boulders among the chestnuts and some flat ground. I lowered
my bag and propped my racket on its side against one of the rocks.
Then I got down on my knees and felt in the bag for Janes' jacket.
My fingers hit against the box of cereal, and for a moment I thought

about eating. I was hungry, but I knew it was sleep I really needed. So I pulled the jacket free, then folded it carefully and put it down on the ground, stretched out on my back, and pulled the bag over and tucked it between my legs. I settled my head into Janes' jacket, then got my racket too, and rested it under my folded hands over my chest. I looked up into the trees' branches above me. There was some moonlight filtering through, but the branches were thick and leafy, and there wasn't much.

I WOKE WITH THE FEEL of warm sun on my face, and when I opened my eyes I could see bright leaves up through the branches where the moonlight had filtered through the night before. I smelled the chestnuts and recognized that I was in among them. There was another faint smell, distant and fishy and present in the breeze that washed over my arms. It came and went, and I guessed it must be sardines, remembering something about such commerce as I came back to myself. Then I struggled up to a sitting position, my racket falling to my hips, and leaned back against a rock. My shoulder was tight, and I rotated it a little, feeling some pain but no impairment of motion. My bag was still tucked tight between my legs, and I got it out and to the side, then got to my feet and stretched and walked around in small circles among the boulders and trees.

I was okay, but hungry and thirsty, and before I considered anything else I got the box of cereal out and the hydrogen peroxide bottle and ate and drank. I thought from the sun's position that it must be late, certainly well into the morning if not noon already. Things were coming back to me: Uncle Edward, Fitz, and the women. The shock of it all was coming back, and I had to force myself away from consideration. It was Dorit and Angela that I had to try to reach somehow. There were things I'd have to do.

Then I heard something, a bright echo and then the sound itself, like hammering, then the distant whine of a power tool. It came from far away and though faint had a clarity to it. It was something to begin with, and once I'd stashed my bag and racket and gone to the clearing and the fence and screwed a stick into the ground as a marker, I went back into the forest and started down the hill again, angling away from the fence and in the direction of the garden.

I got to the brink of the woods but stayed in among the trees until I found a place beyond them, a shallow cut in the hillside that led down to the first major crest. It was deep enough to keep me out of sight. I could see the edge of the garden now, a good hundred yards to my left, and knew I'd be able to see it even better when I got down to the crest.

The cut ended at a rocky brink where I could stand and still be concealed. I could see much of the garden now and the first two descending terraces, but there were still crests below me, and I couldn't see the beach or dock. But I could see out to the rock clusters in the harbor, wet and bright in the sun, and beyond them the yacht at the harbor's mouth. I thought it was closer than it had been, that they'd brought it in a little, though not much, just enough so that it was in the neck now and away from the open sea. The echo came again. The yacht was still broadside, and I thought I could see figures moving on the deck, two, maybe three.

Then I saw a piece of railing flash in the sun, turn a little, and be lifted away from the gunwale and carried back. There was someone on the roof of the wheelhouse, and I saw movement there also, then heard the distant thud and echo again and saw what I thought was a long plank being handed down. They're dismantling her, I thought, at least the superstructure, and it was then that the absence of Janes began to feel ominous. They may be rendering the yacht absent as well, I thought. I kept watching the distant deck, trying to pick out movement, then I heard the sound of those twin diesels again and saw the small white craft come out from under the crests below me.

I saw it was heavily laden as it cut its straight V in the water and headed out to the larger boat at mooring. I could see lumber, what I thought was a window frame, and metal tubing. I watched it until it slowed and banked and drifted in broadside toward the yacht's hull, but before it got there, I saw something else, a flash of color and movement off to my left. It had come from the garden, and I looked over the edge of the rock pile beside me and waited for it to appear again. Then I saw it, a figure come out from under a stand of olive trees, pass through an open space of stone path, then enter under a leafy awning of growth, one of those trellised tunnelways that I had seen from the sea. Then two more figures, one very small, and I knew it was the three of them. I was too far away to make them out distinctly, but I could see they were carrying things, what looked like baskets, towels possibly, blankets or pieces of clothing. I looked back to the yacht again and saw that the smaller boat was now tied up against the hull and that they were unloading it. Then I stepped back from the crest and looked for a good way to get to the garden.

I was there in ten minutes. There hadn't been much cover, but I was low enough down to be out of sight of all but the roof lines of the house, and I figured that a good number of whoever was here was occupied with the yacht. Fitz wouldn't be, I guessed, but I couldn't get much worry up about him. What if he did find me? At least some things would get clear.

The place of entrance into the trellis tunnel was marked off by a certain awkward formality. There was a stone pedestal to either side of it, and these held broken shards of statuary like the ones Chen had shown me in the old landscape book, an almost indistinguishable torso on one, and on the other, two arms, each from a different statue, laid out in a banal gesture of prayer, broken fingers and a sliced-away palm. It was all too small in proportion to the base and looked pathetic.

I'd come over the edge and gotten quickly down among the trees of a small orchard, lemon smell and almond, and when I'd left that I'd stayed close to a heavy wall of bougainvillea, on a stone pathway that curved with it. The path had ended in a small, circular clearing of oleander, the tunnel mouth across from it, an actual wood-trellis archway grown over with flower vines that were unfamiliar to me. After the first few feet, the trellis ended and the vines themselves took over. I could see places at first where they had been trimmed and cut back, but then it was too dark, only a faint filtering of sun through the crosshatched matrix of growth above me.

The tunnel went straight for a while, but just when the earth underfoot was getting spongy and I could hardly see the sides and arch of the passage, it turned in a gradual curve, and I could see an archway of light ahead. I thought I could hear voices, but there were small birds nesting and chirping above my head, and I couldn't be sure. I went slowly, and when I got a few feet from the tunnel's end, I paused and listened.

I could hear water running, just a light bubble and trickle, some twitter of bird song, but that was all. Then I moved to the tunnel's end and eased out into another clearing, this one hanging with hibiscus and morning glory. A narrow path, with wooden steps set into the earth, moved steeply up across from me, turning and going out of sight after an incline of ten feet or so, and when I looked up to where it turned I saw through the branches of plane trees, nothing but open sky on the other side.

I crossed the space, got up the wooden steps, and reached the turning. The treads ascended steeply, almost a staircase, for another twenty feet or so, and when I reached the top I was standing on a flat dirt path among the plane trees. The path went straight before me for only a few yards, then opened out into a shelf of stone, on the other side of which was the sky, then the far side of the hills that extended to form the harbor's oval. I heard the bubble and lap of water, a metal click, then a woman's voice, and I left the path and moved among the tree trunks. There was a low hedge ahead of me at the shelf edge. Dwarf oak, I thought, and some pine too, and I was able to get up to it, to squat beside it on the ground and see through its branches.

The clearing held a rough wooden table and four chairs, and while the garden side of it was lined by a low stone wall, its seaside lip, a shelf that seemed to hang out over the air, held only four heavy planters as a border. Each had a small fruit tree in it, fig and quince, and beyond them there was only sky and an open view of the harbor down below. I was back and off to the side, but I knew that the yacht would be visible from the lip, the whole mouth and neck of the harbor and a good way out to the sea beyond that. In the middle of the flagstone clearing, a low circular fountain bubbled, a geometric rock figure, new, I thought, but made to look old, nothing out of any history at all, too modern for this place.

I was looking at Dorit again. She sat in one of the chairs near the low back wall, a straw basket on the stone floor beside her. On the table to her right were a plastic cooler bag and a canvas one, towels, and an open bottle of mineral water. She had her head back, her face taking the sun in, and I could again see the bones of her sharp shoulders, the thrust of her clavicles through the thin cotton of her dress. Her braid ran along her arm, the bushy end resting in the crook of her elbow. She wore no makeup at all, and though her eyes were closed and she was resting, her face still looked tight and severe, lines to the sides of her nose and at the corners of her eyes.

Then I heard a rustle in the trees to the other side of the clearing and saw Angela and Andrew enter from a path below it. He was carrying a piece of wood, gnarled and weathered. It was white and looked petrified, like marble, and he was testing it as a staff. Angela was watching him, her hand reaching out to his shoulder as he took it and showed it to Dorit. Angela wore a dress now too, and she had loosened her hair, no longer that barklike surface, no luster at all now. It hung straight until it brushed her shoulders. Then they were talking, casually, and Angela was taking glasses and containers of food out of the two bags. I saw a bottle of wine and a metal corkscrew, plastic bowls and silverware. The bubble of the fountain masked their talk, and though I could hear words, sometimes whole phrases, I couldn't get much of the content.

Again I was the voyeur, and for a while I couldn't bear to break into their tight commerce, their talk and preparations. Dorit rose from her chair and was helping, and even Andrew was laying napkins over the light-blue tablecloth that Dorit had spread on the table. Then the food came out and into bowls. There was a salad of some kind, pieces of chicken, raw vegetables, fruit. And I saw white wine splash into glass goblets. I could smell some of it, and I felt my stomach turn. I'd eaten the cereal and was not really hungry. It was the quality of the meal that was getting to me, and it may have been that more than anything else that got me moving.

Andrew had finished his work and had gone out to the lip near the tree tubs, testing his stick again, leaning down into it as he walked. Then he'd started around the hedge perimeter, poking the stick down into the earth where the stone floor ended. He was coming closer to where I sat, and I reached up and spread the branches so that he'd be able to see me.

He was standing just across from me, no more than three feet away, looking down at the earth where he was poking his stick in. I shook the branches a little, and he glanced up at the motion and sound. Then he was looking straight at me, blinking. I didn't hesitate but spoke to him before he could understand or gather into some shock or turn away. The fountain bubbled between us and the women, and I knew that they would not hear us.

"Andrew," I said. "You're Andrew." I had spoken in a whisper, and he looked seriously at me and then nodded gravely.

"I'm your cousin," I said. "I'm Jack, Jackie." It came out of me from nowhere, but I thought as I said it that in a way it might be true. The look on his face changed a little, but I could not read it. Then his head turned back toward the table, and I spoke again.

"Would you go tell Angela?" I said. "Tell her that her cousin Jackie is here?"

He kept looking at me, then in a few moments he nodded again.

"And, Andrew, whisper it to her," I said. "And don't point."

He was already half turned when I spoke the last words, and I thought I heard him say something, but his back was to me and I couldn't see his lips, and he was moving toward the table and the women.

Dorit was bent over, searching for something in the straw bag beside her chair, and he moved to the side of Angela, who was laying the last plate on the table. He reached up and touched her elbow, and she looked down at him, then bent over and put her ear near his mouth. He spoke, and I saw him glance fleetingly toward where I was hidden. Then Angela pulled suddenly away from him and came erect, her left hand at her breast, then moving to her throat. She looked over to where I was, then quickly away. Then she reached down and touched Andrew's shoulder and spoke to him, then moved to where Dorit was rummaging in her bag.

The two of them stood close together and spoke intently for a few moments. I saw Angela pull at Dorit's sleeve as her head started to come up. Then Dorit moved to the table, taking her straw bag with her, and began ordering bowls and glasses, straightening silver over napkins. Andrew helped her, and Angela moved past the fountain to the lip, looked out over the harbor, then made her way slowly along the hedge line until she was standing near me. I heard her voice over my head in a sharp whisper. It seemed to come to me from a much greater distance, out of my past.

"Christ, Jackie! Can it be you?"

"Or you," I said, and saw her hands tighten across her stomach through the screen of branches. She turned then and faced back toward the table, then spoke again, her voice a little fainter.

"How in the world?" she said. "But it's no good. He'll be watching. Or someone could."

"Go back," I said. "We can wait a little, be careful."

She went back to the table then and served up plates of salad and chicken. Dorit filled the glasses, and I saw her take a bottle of mineral water and a foil-wrapped packet and put them in a paper bag. It was Andrew's job to get it to me, and he chose to put it on the stone wall, then get his stick, go back to it, and work his way to the narrow path that cut through the plane trees. He edged it into the passage with his foot, then made his way back to the table.

I sat cross-legged on the ground, the foil in my lap and the bottle of water at my knee, and ate and watched them. They were eating too, though slowly and sparingly, while I tore at the chicken with my teeth and swallowed long gulps of the water. We were at a strange distance in our meal together, but I had made contact with them and was no longer the voyeur, and I tried hard to pull my sense of the circumstance back again and to get outside of it. It was no good, though. I watched them, but I could not thrust Dorit's gestures, nor her expression nor Angela's, back into any construction I had made of them. They're just two women, I thought, even relatives. I'm beyond the surface now, and I can't get back to it.

We finished eating, and I put the foil on the ground beside the bottle, then watched as they wrapped the remaining food and put the containers back into the insulated bag. Then Angela filled their glasses, and they got up from the table. Dorit took one of the chairs and moved it to the shelf lip, a few feet back, between the fruit trees, and stood beside it, her back to me now, and Angela moved a chair into the middle of the space, beside the fountain and a good six feet from the hedge, but close enough, I thought, so that we could hear each other. Andrew had taken up his stick again and was moving its tip, outlining stones' edges in the shelf floor. I moved in closer to the hedge, feeling now like a priest in a confessional, the screen of branches slightly obscuring my vision.

"The yacht," I said. "Is it still there?"

Dorit stepped from the chair side, closer to the lip.

"Yes," she said. "And the little boat too."

"It's Janes'," I said. "Did you know that?"

I saw her stiffen, start to turn, then catch herself.

They didn't know it, didn't even know that Janes had a yacht, nor had they seen him or had contact with him, not since Dorit had written her letter, a long time before. She'd thought that was the end of it. He hadn't written back, and she figured that he was convinced.

"I read it," I said, and this time she did turn, then pulled her chair back a few feet and sat down in it.

I told them about Huntington Harbour, how I'd gotten into Janes' house and seen the photographs and taken the letter, then how I'd found myself on the yacht and come here. I spoke of Panama, but nothing in detail about Aransas. I could see Angela's face, her desire to speak but also to listen. There was wonder in it, but an almost passive one. Andrew had come to sit on the wooden arm of her chair, and he had his hand on her shoulder.

The telling seemed to make some difference, to me at least. It was a way of placing myself there, being with Angela again after so many years. I wasn't sure what it did for her.

"I can't imagine," Dorit said. "That he would come here after me. What's *wrong* with the man?"

Her question wanted no specific answer. There was a recognition in it, I thought, that there was indeed something wrong with him, or there had been, and that there was nothing to be done about it.

"Tell me," I said, "about Uncle Edward."

"Who's that?" Andrew said, looking toward Dorit's back.

"Daddy," she said faintly. "This man, he could be your cousin."

"Cousin Jackie," Angela said wistfully, but with an edge of final resignation.

It came out piecemeal, but without much hesitation or considering. They'd gone through it all before, I thought, turned and troubled it for a while, then let it become hard fact, a given and a closure. It was almost as if they spoke of some other people now, that it was a story, and that there was nothing in it that could change things as they were.

Angela did most of the talking, but Dorit added things and prompted her, her voice coming to me more faintly as she faced away from me and it was masked by the fountain's bubble. At first I had a strong desire to see that face I had known now in so many other ways, but that soon left me. Early on, I saw, it was Uncle Edward that kept them here, that without him they might have found a way. I had questions, and I asked some of them, but even when they'd drained themselves there was still more to learn.

They hadn't spoken to Edward in close to a year, not since shortly after Fitz had come. They saw him though, but always at a distance, and they didn't think he'd seen them at all.

Edward had gone to Mytilene for a shipment of paint supplies, and when he came back Fitz and those other two were in the car with him. Fitz said it was their daughter, that she was ill and failing. Angela remembered that he said her name, Saphia, with a hardness in his voice. The other two had taken Edward inside the house, and Fitz only used the excuse until he was gone. Then he took the three of them inside and sat them down and told them how things would be from then on. He included Andrew in the talk, though he was only three then and didn't understand what was going on. Angela thought that it was then that he decided he would take Andrew, and he did. They didn't see him for close to a month. When he brought him back to them, he was weak and sickly, and he told them from then on they'd have him on a sched-ule, when he wanted it, and he'd have him the rest of the time. In the beginning they saw Edward, and early on the three of them made a plan, but Fitz found out about it and took Edward away permanently. He made sure they saw him from time to time, at a distance, so they'd know he was still there, and captive.

"We tried it a few more times," Dorit said. "Without Edward. But then he began to watch us more closely, to keep us separated, and the threats got more serious. He said he'd do away with him, or any one of us left behind. They watch us, probably right now, in fact."

"Your mother thinks he's dead," I said.

It seemed as good a time as any to get it out, and I waited afterward, in a long silence. She was pulling herself together, and I thought she might begin to speak, to talk about her leaving twenty years before, maybe to talk about her daughter and what leaving her had been like, a retarded child. The silence lingered, and at the end of it she said, "Go on."

And so I told them about the body, the crates of paintings, and the letters, and about Joan and her stories of London, the tattoo, and her death, and that of McHale as well. And I got to Fitz and our talk in Milwaukee, reliving it as I went through it, trying to find some clue in what he'd said then and the way he'd behaved. It came to me that he had been a perfect liar, almost too good at it, as if he too had believed what he had told me. At the end of it all, I told them about Waverly.

They took it all in without speaking. I saw Dorit's leg move when I mentioned Joan and the tattoo. I recognized something of my own expression in Angela's face, remnants of a common past, I thought, and felt a little bit of Congress Park in her as I spoke of it.

"She's all right," I said. "All right. There's been me, and Edward's good agent, and help from other places. She didn't take it all that hard really. He'd been effectively dead for her for a long time, and she'd made a life for herself without him. Without you too, Angela." I knew it was a cruel thing to say, but it was out before I could pull it back.

"But why didn't she write back?" Angela said. "Didn't she care at all? We waited. We even had a trip planned, all of us to go back to see her."

There was a sadness in her voice, but a complicated one. She knew she'd been culpable for a long time and could expect nothing. But there was still a daughter's angry resentment in her, though one that was tempered by maturity and knowledge. She knew she had no right to expect anything, but she felt it nonetheless. I thought about my own parents then and recognized for the first time, I think, a strong resentment of them. It rose up in my throat as bile, so bitter that I imagined it had been sticky and pooled somewhere down in my stomach since I was seventeen. Why did you have to do that! I thought. My eyes clouded over, and I had to blink to clear them. Christ, I thought, can't we give our parents their lives, let them have them to themselves?

"She didn't open them," I said. "I did. Just a few weeks ago," and I heard a breath as she let it go and fancied that even at her distance from me I could smell a deeply bitter scent in it.

"How long?" I said.

She understood immediately. "It's been a long time, years now. He sees to the medicine, but it isn't helping much anymore. I can't really tell, but I think it's in my stomach now. This puffiness. I'm really very thin under it."

She meant around her eyes and in her cheeks. Not much at all really, as if she had been sitting in the sun too long. I heard the distant sound of a motor and saw Dorit get up from her chair and move to the shelf lip again. There was a breeze out there, cutting along the garden face, and her thin dress rippled at her knees.

"How many are there?" I said.

"Just one," she said. "The small Greek. They've got the whole cabin down, and the back one too."

"Is there anything in the boat but him?"

"No. Nothing. It's all out on the yacht. They're still working."

She turned then and came back to her chair, but she didn't sit down. She was facing toward me now but looking over at Angela. I thought she would speak, but it was Angela who did.

"You know, he's completely crazy. He comes and then he goes. Then when he comes back he acts as if he's been here all along. And he behaves strangely with Andrew, acts like a divorced father or something. On a family visit. He gives him useless presents, has his age all wrong, and talks to him like an adult. And from the first he's been having the garden worked on. Look at this fucking fountain. Edward was restoring it all. But Joel has been pouring money into it. Big machinery. He has no fucking taste at all. He says it's his place now. Everything is his."

"Your daughter?" I said. She moved her head, and I saw her face tighten, but she was in the anger of what she was saying, and she continued on in bitterness, but one that seemed to have no real power to wish for change in it.

"That's another thing. There was that fire. Just after I sent her to him. He keeps telling me that. Brings it up at the oddest times, when it has nothing to do with anything. He even sometimes says he needs to talk to me about something. Then sits me down and runs through it all, describing her scars in detail, some trouble with her arm, that she has to wear a wig because her scalp is scarred. Over and fucking over. The same things, as if he'd written them down and memorized them. He tells it coldly, and he watches me coldly. I don't think he feels a thing for her really. Not anymore. But he wants me to."

So the seriousness of the fire had been another of Fitz's lies. Her voice broke on the last few words. She *did* feel something, guilt, regret, and anger, I thought, all mixed up together. Fitz had gotten to her with Saphia, and in a very evil way, I thought. I couldn't say that there was no justice in it, in the fact of her suffering at least. If suffering can be a kind of justice. They'd made Edward suffer too, after all. Still, I didn't feel that I was there to judge them, though I found myself doing so.

"And retarded as well," I said.

"What do you mean?" she said. "Who?" She had been looking out toward the lip, but now her head turned to face me.

"Why, Saphia," I said.

"That's another lie," she said. "But you should know that. From my mother."

It hit me then how cruel he had really been. A cruelty without clear focus. He had had no reason to treat Aunt Waverly in that way, none at all in any rational world.

"She never saw her," I said. "She doesn't even know that she exists."

Angela got to her feet then and moved slowly to the lip. She stood with her back to us, looking out over the bay. I could see a tightness in her shoulders and along her arms. I think that Dorit saw it too. Neither of us spoke, nor did Dorit go to her. She needed time, and we gave it to her. Then Andrew got up from the chair's arm, took his stick, and went to the lip and stood beside her, a good two feet away, and looked out at the bay also. They both stood there for a few moments, then Angela reached out to him and put her hand on his shoulder. In a while they both returned to the chair, and I thought I could see something of a new resolve in her expression.

"He's very dangerous," I said. "I'm sure he killed Joan or had her killed, and he killed at least two other people as well. I'm beginning to think he killed Janes too."

Dorit blinked, her mouth twisting slightly. "Mark? How can that be?"

I told them I figured that Janes had come here looking for Dorit, that Fitz had been exposed in whatever it was that he was doing, or at least that he had felt that way, and that he had killed Janes and then sent him back as Edward. He'd had him tattooed as well, I thought. And now they'd got his yacht and were refitting it to keep from getting caught with it, probably to sell it. I said I didn't understand just why they'd risked that, taking the yacht. Maybe they needed money. It would certainly bring a lot. But I was sure

of two of the men who had been aboard, that they'd been implicated in all this. There was one other, whom I hadn't recognized.

"That's Condra," Angela said. "The other two are Blankenship
and Greeley. They've been gone awhile. Joel's been here for a few
weeks now. They don't come close to us, just watch."

"How many are there altogether?"

"Those three," Dorit said. "And Joel and two more, the one in
the boat and one other, both Greeks."

"Look again," I said. "How many can you see out there?"

She went back to the lip, looked out over the edge, and then
spoke.

"All four."

"It's a big payroll," I said, and waited, but neither of them had
any answer to that.

"What time is it?" I said.

Angela looked at her watch. "It's three."

"Can you see the dock from there?"

"Yes," Dorit said, moving back to the lip and looking over. We
had lost much of our guile, and when she turned back she was
looking directly into the hedge where I was hidden. But I knew
now that there would be only Fitz and the man coming in on the
boat.

"He's just tying up now. He'll pass close on his way up."

"But he won't come here, will he?"

"Oh, no," Angela said. "They never do."

"Okay," I said. "We're leaving right from here. And in that boat.
I'll go back to the house and get Edward. It should take a half hour,
no more than that. But you must be ready sooner, be waiting here
for us. There's a way down from here, isn't there?"

All three of them nodded.

I had no idea at all how I might accomplish the thing. They didn't
know that though, and I saw a slight rise of anticipation in both of
them, and in Andrew too. It was not something that I had seen at
all in them before. They'd been resigned completely under everything. They'd tried their escapes in the past and had been
thwarted, and then the costs of trying had gotten much more serious, and they'd had to give up on it. That had been a while ago,
and they'd slipped into a kind of resignation. But now their bodies
and expressions had that edge of tautness I had seen in Uncle

Edward's paintings, even in the large one that he'd been working on the night before. I was at least a new element, something to interrupt the predictable.

"Yes," Angela said, pulling erect in her chair. Andrew got off the wooden arm and stood beside her, then turned and went to get his stick. Dorit crossed from the lip to the fountain.

"Easy," I said. "Easy. You have time. Just keep a watch on it. And don't take anything."

I saw Andrew grip his stick tighter.

"But the stick," I said. "Be sure to take the stick."

I left them standing beside their chairs, their glasses in their hands. I had made them go to the table and get them, then lift them in a toast, but a secret one that anyone watching wouldn't notice. I'd drunk from the plastic bottle. It was a toast to our success in leaving, and I made Andrew drink to it too. They'd come a little away from their resignation, but I thought I needed some new optimism, and thought that a toast might help. Dorit had even laughed a little at the idea of it, and when I left them standing there I felt better about our chances.

I went back along the tunnel and started up through the garden. We'd heard the footsteps of the man coming up from the boat, and it was shortly after he'd passed us that I started out, figuring that his going ahead could hide me. Attention would be on his open progress and not my secret one. I thought only briefly about my bag and racket. There was no time, and it was too far. I touched my back pocket and felt the outlines of the key and emblem.

I stayed off the paths, moving among fruit and olive trees. I could hear the man at times, and twice I saw his head and shoulders bobbing as he zigzagged along the pathways. He was a good hundred yards ahead of me, and I slowed at times to keep him that far out. Then I saw him dip over what I thought was the uppermost crest, and I hurried up and into a stand of oak at the crest's edge.

He was moving on the flat now, and as I watched he stepped out of the garden and into the stone of the broad drive. The Rover was sitting where it had been, and I saw Fitz standing on the top step at the entranceway, his hands on his hips. He was flanked by the pedestals holding those sad human shards, and he was dressed in a dark suit and wore a tie. He was obviously waiting for the man to get there, impatiently, and his posture reminded me of that of a sulky child.

The man reached the porch, and Fitz dropped his hands from his hips and spoke to him. He spoke again, and the man went past him and deep into the entranceway, and I thought I could see a door opening there. Fitz turned to follow him with his eyes, and in a moment the man came out again, carrying things, what looked like a small card table and a wooden chair. He moved to the Rover's trunk and put them down in the gravel. Then he pulled at the table's legs, adjusted them in the stones, and fussed with the chair, until he had them both steady. He went to the Rover's trunk lid then and opened it.

I looked back to where Fitz had been, but he wasn't there. Then I saw him again. He came out to the edge of the entrance, slowly and not alone. Uncle Edward was with him, dressed casually as I had seen him in his studio. His step faltered slightly, but it was because Fitz had him by the arm and was pulling him out to the steps. He wasn't fighting it, but the pulling was working against his rhythm, and I saw him stumble. Fitz pulled up and looked over at him. It was almost as if he'd been unaware that he was there, had somehow forgotten that he had him by the arm. They came down the steps, and Fitz steered Uncle Edward to the table and sat him down. Then he looked to the man and gestured, and I saw the man nod his head and then turn and go back into the house.

The sun was bright out in the open there, and a shadow fell across Uncle Edward's brow and I couldn't see his face. Fitz looked up for a moment, then went to the open trunk and reached into it, and when he rose up again I saw that he held a hat in his hand, a baseball cap. He took it back to the table and started to put it on Uncle Edward's head, as one might put a hat on a child, and I saw Edward's hand come up and jerk in the air. Fitz stepped back, then reached the hat out to him, and he took it and settled it on his head, pulling at the bill. He looked ludicrous, and I felt a rage welling up in me and pushed closer to the edge of the tree cover.

Fitz went back to the car trunk, and this time he returned to the table with what looked like a large artist's folder. He put it down and adjusted it. His back was to me now. It was broad and heavy, the suit coat stretched tight over it, and Uncle Edward was lost to my view. Then Fitz went to the trunk once again and returned this time with a small box of some kind. He put it on the table beside the sheaf of papers that he had taken from the folder, and then stood back to the side and watched Edward.

He just sat there for a moment. Then I saw Fitz gesture insistently, even heard his voice, and Uncle Edward opened the box and took something out of it. He was bent down over the sheaf of papers then and working at it in some way, and Fitz was watching him carefully.

I was still close to a hundred yards away from them, more garden and then the broad stone drive between us. I could go around, I thought. But I couldn't judge how long whatever they were doing might take. Fitz was dressed for travel, and by the time I came at them from the house it might be too late. They might be gone, and I had no idea what I might do then. The other man was nowhere in sight, but he could be close. Still, I couldn't think that I would find a better circumstance, and I stepped out from the tree line and started across the final yards of garden. There was no cover at all now, and though I moved out in a crouch I soon came up from it, and my only concern was in being careful where I stepped. Fitz was intent enough in watching Edward as he worked at the sheets. He seemed unaware of anything else, and as I got closer to them I saw that Uncle Edward was signing the papers. I couldn't see their surfaces, but I guessed they were works of art, watercolors or, more likely, drawings of some kind. Why he was doing it out in the sun at the car's trunk was beyond me. Something about Fitz himself, I thought, not a thing to be reasoned out.

I reached the garden's edge and stood there for a moment, no more than forty yards from them now. Then I stepped out into the stones and walked toward them.

Fitz heard the sound of the crunching gravel before I had gone ten feet. His head came up, and he looked back toward the porch, then he turned and saw me coming. His hand came quickly to his brow, to shield his eyes from the sun, and he leaned forward a little and peered at me. He hadn't recognized me yet, and I kept coming, walking toward them quickly, but with as much casual ease as I could manage.

I was only twenty yards away when his hand came down and into a fist at his chest. Uncle Edward was looking at me too now, and I saw his hand flatten out on the table as he started to rise. I couldn't think there was any possibility at all that he could know me, but then he spoke.

"Jackie?" he said. "Jackie?"

I couldn't see his eyes under the cap brim, but the corners of his thin lips had pulled up a little, and he was beginning to smile.

"You!" Fitz said, looking quickly at Edward as he got to his feet, then back at me. He said it loudly, and I saw both hands come into fists as he took a step toward me. There was so much force and rage in the word and gesture that they stopped me. I was ten feet away now, standing among the stones in my sweat suit, waiting for his next move. He made it, coming at me, his heavy forearms in the air, and I could do nothing but step forward and engage him.

He hit into me with his shoulders and chest, and I was driven back, struggling to keep my feet. Then I went down under him, my head banging hard into the stones, and before I could get my arms free he had me by the throat, his thumbs digging down into my windpipe. He was far more powerful than I was, and I knew I had no chance with him at all.

It was all happening too quickly. I could feel myself going away. I looked up into his face, his cheeks red and strained in his effort. His eyes were wide open and focused clearly, but he seemed to be looking through my head and down into the stones. His mouth was moving. He was speaking, but not to me. Then his image was swimming and fading. I heard a dull thud somewhere, then felt his breath wash out and across my face. My eyes drew back into focus, and I felt his grip slacken, his body begin to fall to the side. His mouth was wide open now, in a kind of wonder. Then I saw Uncle Edward in his cap standing over us, the tire iron in his hand.

I pushed Fitz as he fell away, and rolled and struggled to my feet. He was on his hands and knees beside me, his head hanging down and shaking. There was a sharp crack, and a spray of stones bounced up from the drive and hit against my arms and chest. I was moving to Uncle Edward, stumbling, but I turned and saw the small man standing a few feet away at the porch edge, the rifle in his hands. Uncle Edward looked up at me from under his brim, and for a moment I could see deep into his eyes. There was a dull vacancy at the surface, but something powerful and sure under that, a focus of vision.

The man raised the rifle up and trained it at us. I wanted to say something, answer the word of my old name that he had spoken, tell him that I was all right now. But Uncle Edward looked away from me, stepped between us, and headed for him. I could hear

Fitz grunting on the ground behind me. The man said a foreign word, and I saw him shake the rifle. Then Uncle Edward reached him. He had a hold on the gun barrel then, and the man was shaking it to get it free. I heard Fitz behind me and turned to face him. He was up to one knee now, and I thought to hit him. But he was looking beyond me at the other two.

"No! No!" he called out, his voice weak and dry. Then I heard the muffled sound of the rifle and Fitz's voice a fraction after: "This one! This one! Not him!"

I turned and saw Uncle Edward step back, a dark, rich circle of blood forming on the back of his white shirt. He still gripped the rifle barrel near the end, and the man was jerking at it, trying to get it free. Uncle Edward's body lurched forward as the man pulled, and I headed for them, hearing Fitz come to his feet behind me in the stones.

As I got to them, the rifle jerked free of Uncle Edward's grip and flew up in the air. He was falling to the side, almost as if he intended it, to get out of my way, and before the small man could pull the weapon back down again I hit him solidly between the eyes, the blow rocking in my elbow, then hit him again, just above the ear as he fell. The rifle clattered in the stones.

Uncle Edward was on his knees, his hands gripping his chest, and I reached down and grabbed his thin upper arm and pulled him to his feet. He seemed as light as air, and I had him up in my arms like a child, with no effort at all. The man was rolling on the ground at the porch steps, his hand over his face, and I turned from him and looked for Fitz.

He was on his feet again and coming at us. But he was weaving, his eyes glazed and unfocused. I started to bend, to put Uncle Edward down and get ready for him. But then he was stumbling, falling. He came to his knees six feet from us, but he kept coming, crawling now, and I saw his hand reach out for my leg. I stepped back then and for a moment watched him, his hand opening and closing in the air. Then I turned and started across the drive, the stones pressing hard into the soles of my tennis shoes, and when I reached the garden's brink I turned Uncle Edward in my arms and slipped him over my shoulder. There were voices now, guttural and with moans in them, behind me, and I could feel a wet stickiness on my shoulder and back.

. . .

They were ready and waiting when I got through the tunnel again and up to the ledge. I'd had to shift Uncle Edward into my arms again to get him through the vine-covered space, and when they saw us they started toward us across the stone floor. Angela's hands were up and she was reaching for him.

"No!" I said. "We have to hurry!"

"Is he hurt?" Dorit said, still moving toward us.

I lifted him up in my arms, gesturing with his body toward the other side of the ledge.

"Go on!" I said. "I can feel him! Hurry!"

My insistence was enough, and Angela reached to Dorit's arm and they both turned, Angela leading the way, and stepped down into the path. Andrew had his stick in his hand, and he went behind them, and I followed.

We moved quickly down the pathway. It was steep and twisting and had not been tended for a long time. Scrub pine and oak extended their branches in over it, and we had to turn to the side to get through in places and push at the branches. One branch hit against my forehead, and I waited for the wetness at the cut line, but it didn't come. My stomach was wet though, and when I looked down I could see my sweatshirt sticking to Uncle Edward's white one, a glue of blood. His face was ashen, but I could see his nostrils and lips were moving.

Soon we reached the swath of cedar forest, Angela moving quickly along its verge well out ahead of us, until she found the stairway. She stopped and waited beside it, and when we got there I slipped by her and took the lead. Her hand came out as I passed, touching Uncle Edward's brow. We came to the turn in a few moments. Then I could see down through the trees' archway to the narrow beach and the edge of the dock, the boat resting in the placid water beside it.

I stepped quickly down the remaining wooden steps to the beach, then out into the soft sand, hefting and adjusting Uncle Edward in my arms.

I hadn't hot-wired a car since I was a kid in Congress Park, and never a boat, but I thought I remembered the process and only hoped I could get up under the dash to the wires easily. I wished I had a free hand, could get to the key and emblem, have them ready if I needed them to jump the spark.

I hit the wood of the dock and moved quickly up it to the boat's side, then turned and waited. They were close behind me, and when Angela reached me I lifted Uncle Edward up a little.

"He's light," I said. "Can you hold him?"

She didn't speak, but she reached out and took him from me, her face tightening a little, then relaxing when she found how light he actually was. She held him easily, and I turned and stepped to the boat's gunwale and down behind the curve of plastic wind-shield to the wheel. I saw the single key poking out of the ignition beside the starter button and knew he'd catch hell for that.

"A boat on the water!" It was Dorit, and when I looked back toward her, I saw her standing with the stern rope in her hand. She had freed it from the mooring and was looking out to the harbor behind me. I turned and saw the small outboard. It was coming in toward us, but slowly, three men standing in the prow. They were lost behind the rocks for a moment, but then came around them, and I could see the weapons in their hands.

I stepped to the gunwale and put my other foot on the dock. Dorit was moving to the prow line now, and I reached up as she passed behind Angela, touching her arm, and took Uncle Edward from her. Then I stepped back down into the slightly rocking boat, spread my feet apart to get my legs. Andrew had climbed into the stern, and I moved toward him. He was sitting in the middle of the long wooden bench in front of the engine housing, and when he saw me coming he moved to the far side. I rested his father beside him on the bench, put his feet up and his head in Andrew's lap. Then I winked at Andrew, who looked gravely up at me, and turned and moved back to the wheel. The women were both in the boat now, moving back to Edward and Andrew.

I turned the key and hit the starter button. The starter motor ground, but the diesels refused to catch. Then I saw the black choke handle, pulled it, and hit the button again. The engines coughed once, came up quickly to a roar. I pulled the throttle back, and hit the gear lever. We lurched ahead a little. I turned around and made sure that we were clear of the dock. Dorit and Angela were sitting down on the deck at Andrew's feet, leaning over, working at Uncle Edward. Angela had ripped a piece of her dress away and was using it to press down on his wound. I could see that Andrew still held his petrified stick. Dorit had her hand on Uncle Edward's brow. I turned back then and pulled down on the throttle.

The boat roared away from the dock, the front end coming up high and quickly. It was much more powerful than I had imagined, and I was about to ease back on the handle, when the bow settled down again and we came to a plane. I could see the outboard clearly now, and the men standing in it, no more than a hundred yards out and heading for us. Fitz must have had a way to contact them, or else they had heard the shots.

They had their rifles up, and I ducked down behind the wheel and looked through its spokes and headed directly at them. I heard a shot, then another, then saw their weapons come down. We were getting close to them and moving at a terrific speed. We would hit dead into them if they didn't turn. Then I saw them moving, stumbling back toward the stern, and the boat banked away.

I twisted the wheel to the left as we passed them. They were in the stern now, their weapons up again and firing. There was a thud in the wood of the hull behind me, and I looked back at the others. Andrew was leaning over now, his head close to Uncle Edward's chest, and Dorit had her hand pressed on Andrew's shoulder. All four were below the motor housings. I cranked the wheel the other way and cut in behind the rocks and straightened out and headed for the harbor's mouth.

I saw the yacht far out in the distance. It rested broadside in the neck, but there was room enough at its stern, and I cut left a little and headed for the passage. There was a figure at the rail, and as we approached I saw his hands gripping it as he looked out at us. The superstructure of the new cabins was up, though still raw, and the yacht looked different to me. But as we approached I could see the grate at my teardrop space, the familiar hull below it. The man pushed back from the rail, started to turn, to head for the anchor, I guessed, to do something. Then he paused. We were coming toward him very quickly, and he must have seen that he had no chance. He turned back and took the rail in his hands then, and just watched us approaching.

Then we were roaring under the shadow of the yacht's stern. I looked up and saw the name *Dorit*, very distinct for a moment, shining down at us from its inset metal plaque. The neck's shore was close to us on the other side, and I was suddenly amazed by the sight of four wild horses moving in a line through rocks and what I thought was wild tobacco. They stopped and turned their heads and looked at us as we moved past them, and I lifted my arm up and waved.

"Look! Look!" I heard Andrew call out, his words lost quickly in the stiff breeze and the engine's roar. Then we passed the yacht and the horses and the neck's end as well, and there was a new sharp slapping at the prow as we got beyond the harbor's mouth and out into the open sea.

I cut back on the throttle, banked to starboard, and brought the boat perpendicular to the neck. I could see into the harbor now, and I looked back to the stern, and Angela nodded and pointed beyond me in the direction that I was heading. The yacht was under way now and moving in, and I wondered how far it would get before it came to ground. Beyond the rocks, the outboard had reached the dock, and I thought I saw Fitz there, among the other men. But I knew I was just imagining him. They were only anonymous figures now, too far away to see distinctly.

The garden was bright and aggressive in its colors and textures in the late afternoon sun above them, and there was a light also on the house's geometry. It looked two-dimensional, a flat facade. I brought the boat back up to full throttle again, and we passed beyond the edge of the neck. Then our view of the whole thing was lost to us.

U NCLE E DWARD DIED IN A small hospital not far from the harbor in Mytilene. The place was near the end of a narrow street that began at the waterfront, then rose up until it looked down over the city, and from the broad front porch of the hospital one could see out beyond the breakwater. The building was really no different from the houses to the side and across from it, but inside was a small open ward with tall windows and filmy white cotton curtains blowing in the room's air.

He died without ever waking, and both Dorit and Angela were at his bedside when he gave it up. They wept for him, pure tears, I could tell, ones beyond all that complexity that they at least had managed to put behind them for a while. It was Dorit herself who came to the porch where I was waiting with Andrew and told me. I had looked into his face earlier. It had been in complete repose in his coma, and if there was anything left, it was guarding it like the skin of a stone statue. Seeing him finally up close and still, I had recognized him, something left in his cheeks and brows, that image of him looking down as he held me, hysterical beyond desperation at my parents' death. But that was all. The rest that I saw seemed foreign, nothing I could connect firmly to the letters and paintings and the construction I had made from them. "He's gone," she said. And Andrew had risen from his seat beside me and moved to her, his thin shoulders shaking, not for the loss of his father but at the expression in his mother's eyes.

They'd caught Fitz in Mithimna as he was trying to board the boat to Athens. He'd parked the Rover at the pier, and they were looking for the car, an uncommon enough one on the island, and had found him, it, and the sheaf of signed drawings in the trunk. They were studies for the larger paintings, detailed ones that I suspected contained much information about technique that led to the final works.

And they'd gotten to the harbor in time as well. The yacht had run aground, and they'd caught the men as they were loading what they could carry into another car, all but the small one with the rifle, but they knew of him and had the ports guarded, and they didn't think he'd be on the loose for long.

We stayed in Mytilene for a week, in a small hotel near the hospital and harbor. I called Chen and Waverly, then had a long and detailed talk with Uncle Edward's agent. I told Aunt Waverly that I had found Angela and that we were coming back, but I didn't tell her about Edward or the other things. Ross said he would do that for me, and I could tell that he was taking notes as I spoke with him, getting down my exact words. The information had to be given face to face, and he seemed a very good one to be passing it to her. Nothing had really changed since I'd left Congress Park, though Ross said he was close to finishing with his inventory and the financial tangle. There'll be more, I told him, a complex of things from here. He said he had a better sense now, and that things were worth even more than we had figured. That doesn't make much difference either, I thought.

Uncle Edward hung on for three days, and while the women were sitting with him, I spent time at the police station with Andrew. They'd assigned a detective to us, a bright young man in his thirties who had gone to college at Occidental in Los Angeles and then had worked for the force in Burbank. He'd gotten his priorities straight after a while and had come back home. His name was

Axiotis. He'd seen to the impounding of the house and the entire garden and harbor complex, and by the end of the second day he'd had the house and the yacht carefully searched and the materials boxed and brought down. He put me in a bare room with a large wooden table, a chair, and a gooseneck lamp, and had a secretary who spoke some English take Andrew for a walk and some food. Then he sat in a chair across from me and watched me go through the materials.

Fitz had been in the middle of a title transfer. There were blank legal forms that Uncle Edward had signed, and I found a piece of correspondence between Fitz and a lawyer, which I pushed across the table to Axiotis. In another packet, held together with a large rubber band, were bills and receipts for work on the garden. They spanned a period of over a year, and some of the figures almost astounded me, huge sums of money for planting and earth moving, carpentry and stone work. They added up to half of what Chen and I had spent for materials at the California site. I felt a sense of desperation in them, that he had come quickly to want the whole thing, to change and put his mark on it. It had to have been a good garden before he'd started, at least a finished one. The receipts were not about maintenance but about aesthetic change, if one could call it that. I thought of all the men and the payroll again as I went through them, and in another packet I found sheets of figures and bills that related to Fitz Cement in Milwaukee. I was no accountant, but I could see that the business was small and in deep trouble. And the fact that he'd brought the materials to Lesbos seemed to say something too. Figures were added again and again, crossed out, then tabulated in other ways. Then I came to a thick manila folder, opened it, and spread its contents out in front of me.

It contained sheets with the names of art works, both drawings and paintings, scraps of paper with proper names and phone numbers and addresses on them. The lists were not unlike the one I'd received in Uncle Edward's belongings in Congress Park, columns of names of works, dates, addresses, and dollar figures to the right. They were very large figures, and they were dated up to the last few weeks. Some of the final figures had question marks beside them, and I guessed that they were recent sales to be negotiated finally. The names and addresses were mostly from Europe and England, but there were some from the States as well. He'd been selling Uncle Edward's paintings, and in the end he'd been selling them after Uncle Edward's supposed death. The numbers in the last figures were quickly larger, but the fact that he hadn't waited, given it a little time for the death to settle in and have a stronger effect on the market, made his desperation clear. He was in need of huge sums of money, and he couldn't wait. It was clear to me now that he'd stolen the yacht for that reason.

There was a name that kept appearing, on scraps of paper, penciled in at the top of the lists, and I slid one of the sheets that held it across the table to Axiotis. He blinked at the name, then nodded and smiled.

"It thickens," he said, and wrote the name down on the yellow pad he was using for his notes.

Fitz had been in far too deeply. He couldn't have known of markets or individuals. There were others involved, at least in the commerce of the paintings. And in the rest of it too, I soon found out.

There was a letter from a doctor in London, a name that appeared also in the lists of painting accountings. I found it among the labeled contents of a small desk drawer. It was written in veiled language, but the intent was clear, especially when I put it together with the rest of the things: various utility and rent receipt books, fresh bank checks and statements.

The letter was concluding a deal of some kind, and I was sure that the doctor's name was the same one I had seen on the death certificate in Congress Park, though why Fitz had kept it and the drawer's contents was beyond me. Only some twist in his madness could account for it.

They'd faked Uncle Edward's dying in London and his living there in recent years. It was a diversionary tactic, but an impetuous one, maybe even desperate. Fitz had had no plan, I thought, just awkward attempts to cover up once things had happened. He'd needed money. Then Janes had come and he'd taken the opportunity. He'd probably figured that Waverly was too old to be a trouble, and he'd sent the papers and paintings to make it all look real, to satisfy her and keep her from looking into things.

He couldn't have accounted for the messages that Uncle Edward had put in the paintings, nor was I convinced that Edward himself thought of them that way. *Find Angela* could have been a message to himself, and the rendering of the Rover and the ski-masked men in the knee simply a record of that important event. They had accosted him on a road in Lesbos, and the fact that they had stopped me in a similar way, in Illinois, was no more than coincidence. As in the last painting I'd seen, he might only have been rendering his own life there. But I would never know, and there was no reason now to be troubling the thought.

It must have come to Fitz at some point that I might get involved, and he'd sent his men to get me at the trailer, to injure me and keep me from going back east. That hadn't worked, and he'd sent them to get me on the road. Then, when that had failed too, he'd gotten desperate. He'd had Joan and Marilyn killed, probably McHale. I'd been getting closer all the time, though I hadn't really known it. I slid the doctor's letter across the desk to Axiotis, telling him I thought it was another important thing.

"And the yacht?" he said, pointing to another box.

But there was nothing in it, just scraps of blank paper and the other things that I had seen on the boat. I'd told him the details of the story about Janes, just enough of the past to make it coherent, and he had already put in a call to Long Beach and another to Huntington Harbour. He'd also started to work on the exhumation request, and he told me it would probably take a week, maybe more. I'd made arrangements for them to hold Uncle Edward's body until we got back to Congress Park and sent for it. All the paintings and drawings would have to be held back in impoundment. For a while, he thought. Until the whole thing was straightened out.

It was three days after Uncle Edward's death, and we were sitting outside at a small café near the waterfront. A breeze came in off the water, cooling us in the August sun. We sat at a large table under an umbrella, and I could see the short sleeve of Dorit's new dress rippling against her arm. All three of them wore new clothes, as did I, a pair of loose, baggy chinos and a fine cotton shirt. I had gotten rid of everything and had bought real shoes of soft leather. I had nothing in my pockets but the key and emblem, some folded cash, and the thin laminated identity card that Axiotis had gotten for each of us. He'd helped us work out flight tickets through American Express, the card would serve as a temporary passport, and he had given me a thick fold of cash that they'd found among Fitz's belongings. I'd signed a receipt for it. He'd been a real help to us in many ways.

We'd shopped, all of us together, and the women and even Andrew had taken some pleasure in it. A pure pleasure of choice, I thought, unencumbered by any care or implication. They'd gotten bright dresses, different from one another. Dorit's was severe in its cut, very thin silk, blue with geometric figures in red and lime green. Angela's was cotton, narrow stripes, chocolate and beige, vertical on an off-white background. They had new shoes, real ones, not sandals, as did Andrew, who now wore long pants. It had all cost quite a bit, and we had enjoyed the extravagance of the thing, almost as if we were buying presents for our new selves. It had been a kind of ritual, putting the dead behind us, and the raw grief of each one of them was gone now. There'll be more, I thought, for each of them, but reasonable and in time. I didn't know if there was any left at all for me.

There were fishing boats in the harbor, and we watched as some of them steamed out beyond the breakwater, while others headed back in. Andrew sat with his stick resting against his leg, the tip between bricks near his chair. Dorit had bought him a box of colored clay, and he was forming enigmatic figures with it on the tabletop. We were speaking about the recent dead.

"Why did you come here in the first place?" I said. "From London."

"Well, Edward was sick of it," Dorit said. "And he had earned enough by then. But I think it was a return as well, to where he'd first seen me, at that show. As if he could undo it all. I don't mean he was adamant or hopeful. More of nostalgia, and that he'd had enough of London. He'd been working it all out in his paintings, at least we thought so. That we were all pretty much at peace with the situation, though it was new and fragile. But there seemed some balance."

"Then he built that studio," Angela said, and Dorit looked over at her.

"Yes. And he showed it to us. And showed us that lens. Then he started to withdraw from us. Just spending so many hours painting. And when we were together he was silent. Even with Andrew. He had no time, or at least it felt that way."

"But he did paint the garden once. He was outside and we

watched him and even talked with him while he did it. And he always kept things in order." There was something a little desperate in Angela's voice.

"Of course, of course. But you know as well as I do that age and other things were getting to him." There was nothing cruel in what Dorit said. She was being honest though, and I heard Angela make a sound in her throat, perhaps surrendering a piece of her denial.

"The garden," I said.

"It was really quite something," Dorit said. "Before Joel got to it. Very old. And even though others had altered it, built things over it, it still came through. It had a feel of history in it. Edward loved it, actually. I think he saw it like his paintings. As you know, those places under the surface that he was after. It was like that."

"And your father," Angela said. "Something of that too, I think. You remember the garden he helped us with? In Congress Park?"

"I remember it," I said. "We were some gardeners."

Angela laughed at that, remembering.

"How about you, Andrew?" I said.

He had a piece of clay in his hands and was pressing it down on the table. He looked up at me and blinked, then nodded.

"Something," he said. "He taught me how to paint."

The women talked about him in his presence, but they had a way of doing it that seemed appropriate. They had taken him away from Uncle Edward, and when they spoke of the two of them and their relationship it was as if they were speaking of another life. But I could find no guilt at all in the things they said. They seemed to have accepted what they had done as justice, and I could not fault them for that. A cost of the artist's life, I thought, at least this one, that brutal egocentricity. He'd had to pay for it. But he'd had his art.

"Why did you steal those things from me?" I tried to say it brightly and with a joke in my voice, to lighten the conversation. "We found them, Waverly and I. Just a few weeks ago."

"Well!" Angela said, blushing, knowing right away what I was referring to.

It was really just the story of an old domestic difficulty, and she spoke about it literally and without psychology. She had felt that Uncle Edward had wanted me, a son, and not her, and she had taken them to hurt me. Then, once she had them, they were possessions in a kind of payoff or trade.

"We were just children," she said.

It was more than that though. Her simple words contained a weighty power, that he had wanted me and not her. And I believed that was the crux of it for her. There were the details of her going away, Fitz then, and women. Drugs too, though I wasn't sure anymore that I could trust that part. But her father was at the heart of it all, I thought, and I thought too that it could never be really known now. It was just too long ago, and it was not about facts in the world at all. It was about nuances, old needs, and privacy, and it was not my business, even though it accounted in a large part for my being there.

It was a similar kind of thing when I asked Dorit about Janes. Though she'd been surprised at the pictures on the wall, that story, she could reason it into what she already knew, the tattoo especially. It was something general finally, about women and men, and he was only an exaggeration of that. It had to do with possession, ideas of manliness, that kind of thing, and she didn't think that much more could be made of it, that there was any mystery.

"Mark had no taste," she said. "Not really. He had a literal mind, and I don't think he could feel much. Or at least know what it was. He was a collector."

"They collected *us*," Angela said. "Joel, even my father."

"True enough," Dorit said. "I could have written, made something out of myself, but I was a model, for both of them. They were only interested from the skin down, how the inside manifested itself there. I guess it was partly my fault too, but I could have had some power out in the world, beyond myself. I had skills. I could have done something."

"I have, you know," Angela said, turning to me. "I'm a medical technologist, and a very good one. I've worked at that for many years. I know things. Lab work, even x-ray. Time in a pharmacy. I made a living for myself. Now maybe we can begin to do things."

She had turned her head back toward Dorit, and I recognized that I too had been seeing them over all this time as only women, just as the other men had. I had not thought of them as fragile necessarily but as purely sexual, as if they were their sex and nothing more, nothing out in the world at all. Janes had been a doctor, Fitz had his cement company, and Uncle Edward had been a painter, had had his art. But these women had been taken up by all of us as self-contained objects, very intricate and complex ones, needing constant tuning and revision, but objects nonetheless. They'd had no power out in the world for us, no skills or professions. They'd *been* their professions, women only, and we'd treated them as if their surfaces could only lead inward.

It had taken a man to bring them out, literally, from that island, and even though I knew I'd had much luck in the matter, I wanted to bring that into the open, argue it with them in some way. But there was still enough of those older images in my mind that I couldn't yet figure the terms of doing so, fearing that I might insult them in some way, offend their sensibilities. I knew I wouldn't have felt that way at all had they been men, or even Coco or Waverly, but I wasn't as yet ready to get into such things. Both of them were looking at me now, as if waiting.

"The tattoo has some beauty," I said. "This emblem." I took it out of my pocket and put it on the table in front of me.

"Oh, that," Dorit said. "Yes, yes. He showed some imagination there, all right. But I don't think he got the real point of it. It was no scarlet letter to us."

"You know about it?" I said. "Edward didn't think so. I mean in his letters."

"Of course!" Dorit said. "We both do. Mark told me shortly after he'd made me get it. It was that, really, that was the strange part. His telling me, I mean. I didn't think it right to tell Edward, not after he had it put on himself. Now Mark has it back, I guess. I wonder if that could be called justice."

I looked across the table at Angela, and she raised her hand up. Then she moved her shoulder strap to the side and lowered the bodice of her dress a little. The tattoo was there, just a little larger than the emblem itself, at the rise of her small breast, the delicate blue lines hard-edged against her dark flesh.

I looked over at Andrew, and he grinned and shook his head, and both Dorit and Angela laughed.

It was just a short walk from the café to the small park. The afternoon had passed with our talking, and while there was still some glow left from the sun, lights blinked dimly on the boats out in the harbor and a few lit windows glowed in the houses that we passed by. We were on a boardwalk, not too far from the harbor's landing dock, when Dorit raised her arm up and pointed to the park's entrance just a few feet ahead.

The park was small and walled in, the walls a good ten feet high and grown over with green leafy vines and hibiscus and bougain-villea. Behind the statue that stood on a high cylindrical pedestal near the back of the square space, I could see the arched windows and the tile roof of the second story of what I thought was a church. Small ferns grew in a plot around the statue's base, but there was a narrow walkway that could get us to it.

It was a small statue, almost life-size, a woman holding a lyre or another stringed instrument, and I saw immediately that she was dressed in the way I had seen both Angela and Coco dressed, a robed gown with a rope cincture at the waist, folds of marble bil-lowing slightly over it. And her hair was gathered in the same way as Angela's had been, a loglike roll running down behind her ear and below her shoulders. She held the instrument up at her neck, her hand on the strings, and her other arm was bent slightly at the elbow along her side, her palm open and facing out to us at her hip.

It was a gesture that I had seen before, but it was enigmatic here. It was sure and passive at the same time. It welcomed something, but I couldn't tell just what. She had the beginning of a smile on her face, and her eyes looked straight out into space high above us, either vacantly or in concentration.

"She's Sappho," Angela said softly at my shoulder. Dorit was turned to the side, her hand in the shopping bag we had brought with us, and Andrew had taken his stick and was poking into the overgrown wall at the square's side.

"It's no great statue at all," Angela said. "But I guess we have claimed it, claimed her, I mean. Isn't she lovely?"

She was small, compact, and unlovely in any conventional way. But I knew that the woman she represented had been strong and probably brilliant, and, in a hard time for that, tough and brilliant at the same time. She was sexual, but uncompromised. The sculptor had gotten that. Then Dorit's hand came out of the shopping bag with a piece of Andrew's clay in it, the color of putty, and she held it up and motioned to Angela, and they both went around the narrow path to the statue's base.

I watched them, and when I saw what they were about to do, I started to move toward them, to go around the fern plot to help them. But Angela saw me and waved her hand at me, and I stayed where I was.

Dorit knelt down on one knee at the base and made a cup of her hands. Then Angela stepped into it and held to the base's upper lip as Dorit lifted her. I could tell she wasn't heavy. Dorit had no trouble at all hoisting her up. Her hands came all the way to her shoulders, so that Angela could step from them to the base's surface.

She moved carefully to the side, holding to the statue's waist. They were close to the same size. I saw the clay fly up in the air as Dorit tossed it. Angela caught it with ease, then edged to the front of the statue, still holding on to it like a lover.

She was facing it now, embracing it, and I saw her hand reach down to the stone's open palm and press the clay into it, shaping it deep in above the fingers. She pressed it in with her own fingers, then in a few moments took the edge of its flattened curve and peeled it away. She turned then on the narrow lip, her hand holding to the loglike roll of hair, and leaned out and away from the statue and looked down and across the fern plot to where I was standing.

"Here. Catch!" she said.

She spun the flattened disk of clay out in the air and across the fern plot. It was a good throw, and I caught it in my left hand at my shoulder. Then I brought it down and turned it and saw Sappho's palm lines, her life lines, formed into the emblem and tattoo figure. Finally, it had a quality of life that was specific, and when I looked up Angela was smiling down at me from Sappho's side.

To come back after a long history of absence and to find one's old house essentially unchanged, the same shingles and siding, windows where they had been, holding the same glass . . . It's an odd and can seem a wondrous thing, especially in America, that ethic of achievement and its equivalent in change always present. My grandmother went on a long trip to Boston, but her mind was somehow greedy, which was out of character for her, and she came back with more than she could carry or remember. It was enough to fill her house in the woods to overflowing, and she left things on the trail leading up to it. She had no real desire or need for them, but they were hers now, and in America that meant responsibility. Later, she would go out into the clearing and count them where they stood, linked together in a line that had no real logic, save for the one that could join them, but only in memory.

"My grandmother went to Boston," Angela said, and I was

shocked to hear it. But when I looked quickly at her, she was smiling, though weakly. I'd been thinking of Capability Brown, those landscapes he'd planned in England. Not to be realized for four generations, an attitude of continuity that had no place in America, especially in California.

She was as nervous as she could be, and I looked behind me where she was looking, to Andrew and Dorit, then down to the others, their suitcases and liquor cartons, hats and carved staffs, a small model of the Parthenon, a plastic statue and a jigsaw puzzle in a bright green box, souvenirs of a Greek journey, linked together in a way I could have worked with in that game. Now they were coming home, and maybe I was too. I had my own trail, of people though, the three of them standing behind me in the customs line.

I smiled at Angela in an old recognition. She gripped Andrew's hand, and Dorit was pushing up against him from behind, her own hand touching his hair occasionally. He held his staff, and he seemed bright-eyed and ready. We were close to the counter, carrying very little, and we'd be through it very soon.

"It'll be all right," I said. "Don't worry."

And there *was* nothing to worry about. I had a thought that when Aunt Waverly saw us she'd have to make a choice. We were both coming home after all. I'd been gone a long time too. It felt much longer than actual time. So much had happened. I was no longer so ignorant, and that seemed the largest change, the thing that separated me profoundly from the one who had left Congress Park after my returning, really only a short time ago. But nothing to worry about.

I saw her through the glass wall, tall and still straight and in a light cotton dress, but a fashionable one, a pleated skirt and a high yoke, her hair recently cut and combed, short but with that flare to one side, a wave riding out above the gleam of her small earring. She had her hand up and was waving and smiling. Her eyes glistened. I waved back, then reached behind me and took Angela's arm and brought her out to my side. There was no choice for Aunt Waverly at all. They would get to all the years and complexities later.

"It'll take a while," Waverly said. "I can't really imagine."

"I know," I said. "There's a lot to it. Things that'll always be confused but are maybe quite simple at the bottom. Just men and women. Though saying it doesn't get you very far."

"And what will you do, Jack?"

"I don't know. I'll have to go home soon though."

"This could be it," she said, "your home." But I didn't think so.

I was exhausted from the flight and the arrival, but I couldn't think to let her stay up alone. She was energized by it all, though I could hear a tiredness in her voice now too. We were sitting in the dark in the living room, a light from the hallway seeping in dimly over the carpet. I could see her face and expression, the pattern on her teacup.

"It was his mind," she said. "Something in it."''

"Complex," I said. "But it did come out in his painting, maybe the only fruit of this whole thing."

"No," she said, raising her hand and shaking her fingers at me. "You came back. And now you've brought back Angela."

We sat still and silent for a while, both realizing, I think, that if we got started we might talk the night through. She'd had a dinner ready, Swiss steak and potatoes, a large green salad, and home-made ice cream for dessert. They'd been tentative with each other after their initial acceptance at the airport, but not at all resentful. They just couldn't figure how to get started. It was Dorit and Andrew who helped them, doing it through that matrix of family that they now were. Andrew accepted Aunt Waverly into it immediately, and I could see that would do it, after a while at least. It was looking through the house then, showing them both her old room, the backyard, objects and places that she remembered. Some reminiscence of childhood then that even I participated in, and once they had reached the beginning of a fragile order, they were able to give in to their exhaustion and go to bed. We set up a cot in the guest room for Andrew, between the two single beds.

"I'll call tomorrow," I said. "To Milwaukee. I guess I'd better leave on the next day. What is it?"

"Wednesday," she said.

Saphia was in my mind, a part of the story yet to unfold, something I'd have to learn about later. Angela had decided not to tell her mother right away, not until she herself had made contact. There was no way of knowing what that might be like.

"Then I'll come back again. The body, of course, will be here next Monday. I'll call. You can let me know about the exhumation, whenever that gets straightened out."

My head was full of the few details that were left. I kept looking for more of them, missing all that I'd had to deal with in the recent past.

"Ross has most everything in order now," she said.

"That's good. It will be a while before things over there can be gotten at, straightened out and all."

"Won't they know things?" she said. "Angela and Dorit?" And she turned her head and looked out into the hall.

"Not much. But something, I guess. They can help."

Her face came back into the light, where I could see it. She was smiling, thinking of them asleep in their room in her house. And I thought I was excluded from her look and felt a pain under my sternum. I looked over her shoulder, out through the hall to the dining room and through its window to where the edge of my old house shone dimly in what starlight there was. She saw where I was looking and she caught a memory, her mouth forming an O.

"Oh, I forgot!" she said, and got up quickly and left the room. I heard her moving in the kitchen, and then in a few moments she was back and handing something to me, a key on a ring.

"They were going away," she said. "And when I knew you were coming back, I asked them if you could look through the place, your old house. Just for old times' sake."

"Oh," I said. "Yes, I think I would like to do that." I reached out and took the key from her hand.

I slept in Angela's room that night, slept late and without dreaming, but only after I'd unfolded the quilt Aunt Waverly had made for me. She'd put it at the foot of the bed and had placed a blue card in a blue envelope on top of it: *Jack, this is something for you. Love, Waverly.*

It was not a crazy quilt but a piece of careful symmetry, and after I'd read the card, I opened it up fully, thinking at first that it was made for a single bed, then finding the last fold, so that half of it hung over the bedside, down to the floor. I remembered getting the small nails for her, her look as she stood beside the wooden rack above me in the attic.

The quilt was made of squares of faded color, each one different in texture, many vaguely familiar. I imagined ragbags in the attic, swatches of clothing and other fabric, things saved and put away because they were the only tangible remnants of what had passed. Photographs were not that but an analogue, as were paintings.

I leaned down and touched a blue velvet square to my face, only knowing it was a piece of something I had worn as a child when I felt and smelled it. I saw the color of a dress my mother had worn, a piece cut from a shirt of my father's, squares that were only slightly familiar, ones that may have been from Waverly's clothing, Uncle Edward's and Angela's. There were no seams or collars, no cuffs or places for buttons. Each square had been cut away from all action. All specifics of their history were gone now, unless history was just this, smells and the sight and touch of things, that provocative pull of the senses, all that really remained in the body from what had gone before.

I thought of my grandmother, the one who had gone to Boston, and how that game had been a joining of the memories of all the players. I'd been good at it. I had a method, a forest in which all arbitrary objects had been joined in a narrative, a way of remembrance. I remembered stories about the pioneers, how, as they headed west into increasing change and difficulty, they had left belongings at the dusty trailside. At first the choices had been easy —a grandmother's crude, heavy bureau, a chest of everyday dishes. Then, as the trek became more awkward, they had to make hard choices—a certain child's toy, a dead uncle's hand-carved table. The trail was like my forest, with its holdings of memory measured in a line of objects. But in the pioneers' case, a history of values could be read in the leavings, their progress from the past a jettisoning, until they could come, lean, changed, and prepared, into their new selves in the future. I'd gone west too, but I had left everything at my beginning. All had been unresolved behind me, and I had not moved forward by changing.

The quilt was not at all like Uncle Edward's paintings. It was a lifting of the actual from the past and a joining of that actuality into an abstract pattern. His had been narrative, however twisted, as had the unfolding of the story I'd been after.

Every square of the quilt seemed to move in toward the center, as if a beginning, some core, could be found there. But at that center was a vacant, white square. I touched and smelled it. It was smooth and impenetrable, empty of all color, and it had no scent. I could see it as the source of the story, gone now, irretrievable. But even as I thought these things, I recognized that I was once again constructing some order, another story.

I stepped back and looked down at the quilt then. It was beautiful in its careful symmetry and sewing. The point was that Aunt Waverly had made it for me, that she'd been working and thinking of me while I'd been gone. The point was that there was room for two people under it. That made me smile. She had me thinking ahead into the future now, not back as I had before.

In the morning Aunt Waverly prepared a large breakfast, eggs and sausage, pancakes, orange juice, and plenty of coffee. We ate at the big table in the kitchen. It was a beautiful Tuesday, a soft sun and low humidity, and a light breeze ruffled the yellow curtains at the open window. We talked about the weather, how the air differed from that in both London and Lesbos, steered clear of serious matters, though when I mentioned I'd be calling Milwaukee, I saw Angela's face darken for a moment and Dorit reach out and touch her elbow. She'll have to get to that before long, I thought. But not just yet.

They both wore the dresses they had bought in Mytilene, their only clothing now, and Aunt Waverly spoke of shopping, of the mall out in Oakbrook. Then the Brookfield Zoo came up, Angela remembering how we had gone there as children. Andrew had never been to a zoo, and it was decided that they would all go. It was Tuesday and it shouldn't be crowded and it wasn't far at all, and afterward they could go out to Oakbrook and shop. Somewhere in the morning's conversation I managed to thank Aunt Waverly for the quilt. She smiled at me, her eyes bright and clear.

They came together in the planning, and before long Dorit and Aunt Waverly were talking, about painting, shows Waverly had seen, her tastes in the matter, and Dorit bringing up artists she had known in London. It was talk that was very close to more serious matters between them. They were letting down their guard. She had been with both Waverly's husband and her daughter, but they weren't thinking of that, not as some idea that could be troublesome. On the other hand, I thought, it might be something that spoke to a likeness in them. A strange idea, but one that didn't seem so odd just then.

I said I wouldn't go with them. I had things to do, calls to make, and I thought I might go through some papers again, put things in whatever final order I could before I left. They didn't seem to mind much, which seemed appropriate to me right then, and when they were ready I stood at the door and watched them drive away.

I called the police in Milwaukee then and spoke to the man Axiotis had told me to contact, not someone he knew but someone he knew of. There was nothing for me to do. They were investigating Fitz Cement. The police in Brookfield were doing the same about Joan and Marilyn, and in Chicago they were looking into the death of McHale again. They'd be considering extradition, he thought, but there were things to be dealt with in Greece too, and it might take a good long while. Not even Waverly knew that I had been in the house after Joan and Marilyn had died, and he could see no reason for me to stay around. Maybe if there was a trial, then I might have to come back. But, really, he doubted that it would ever come to that. I asked him about Fitz's children.

"Just the boy," he said. "A teenager. That's taken care of. The daughter is in her early twenties and on her own."

Saphia, I thought. One cause or victim of it all. But that was for Angela and not me. I hung up, then lifted the receiver again and made a flight reservation. Then I called Chen. He answered immediately, and I had a quick and warming thought that he'd been waiting right by the phone.

"My good man!" he said. "I was just thinking about you, when you'd be getting in touch. How the hell are you?"

"I'm fine now, Chen, fine. It's over and I'm coming back."

"All in order, then?"

"Not all of it," I said. "But as much as can be right now."

"And Aransas? How was Aransas?"

"That was something," I said. "They all send their best. Things we can talk about."

"Very good," he said.

"What about the site?"

"Friday's the day! Mucho hoopla, streamers and shit like that. They want us to wear suits."

"Means you'll have to rent one," I said.

"Still the comic? Donny's got a nice one that fits me."

"The cast is off, then?"

"A thin and smaller one now. Every other limb in perfect working order." I reached up to my forehead and felt the scab flaking away. There was only a bit of ridge under it, dry now.

"Come on back," he said. "Donny will pick you up."

After we'd spoken, I went back to Uncle Edward's study, figuring that I would call Ross and the museum in Downers Grove later. That would be it then, though I kept thinking that I had forgotten something.

The study was bright in the sunlight, and there was almost nothing in it, just the table and chair and the chest against the far wall. I went to the chest, thinking I would look at the box of magnifiers. They weren't there, and I remembered that I'd left them at the Downers Grove museum. Then I went back to the table.

There were those folders of papers in the cardboard box, the receipts and records, and I sat down and fingered through them for a few minutes, reading bills and canceled checks. But the story was over now as far as I was concerned, and they seemed no more than dead scraps, no longer shards and remnants of something that had once been alive for me to piece together in some way.

I could hear the sounds of voices toward the front of the house, children playing in the same park I had played in so many years ago. It was not the same though. The Dutch elms were gone, and the old patriotic landscaping around the war plaque had been changed utterly, only the sturdiest of growths now, things needing no tending, and no remnants of the plaque, either, all the names of the dead listed on it gone back now into the privacy of family.

I shifted in the chair and reached to put the papers in the box, then felt the shape of the key press into my leg through my pants pocket. I got up and headed through the house to the front door.

There were no children in the park now and no one on the sidewalks either. I went down the steps, crossed the few feet of sidewalk, then stepped up to the porch of my own old house and put the key into the lock.

Everything had changed. They had put dark paneling up over the white plaster. The ceiling had been dropped a few feet, and when I made my way up the staircase, I saw that the treads were new and had been carpeted and that the banister and square post at the bottom had been torn out or swallowed up under painted Sheetrock.

And the rooms upstairs were altered. There were partitions now, a bathroom where I thought my parents' bed had been, though I couldn't visualize it there, and they had put a narrow hallway in, running a few feet out from the wall adjacent to Aunt Waverly's house. The window across from Angela's was still there, but as I stood in front of it and looked across, I recognized that looking in from the other side, imagining my small room, I'd been looking into a dark wall only, just the narrow space of passage, with nothing in it where I was now standing.

They'd done the same thing on the ground floor, and what I'd thought was the kitchen, where I had imagined the shadow of my mother passing, was only a small pantry now, unused, shelves stacked with castoffs, cardboard boxes, and broken-down appliances. I thought of Uncle Edward's painting as I stood there, all the objects that had shown themselves through the enlightening lens, my mother at her vanity, I in my diaper on the floor. Could there have been something between them? Could he have wanted a son that badly? I'd never know. It had only been alive in his memory, and in mine, I knew, now. Even the room itself was gone.

I went through the kitchen to the small back porch and looked out into the yard, lawn chairs and trees grown up where my father's garden and mine had been, oak trees, thick and substantial at their bases, looking as though they'd been there forever.

I turned and went back to the living room then and sat down on the couch and leaned back into it and took it all in. Not a curve or an angle, not even a quality of shadow coming in at the windows, that I remembered or could manufacture some feeling about. They're gone, I thought. Completely now. And it was never really my life that they left behind, but their very own.

It was right then that I gave them back their lives, recognizing even as I did so that they had never been mine to have or give. Goodbye, I thought, goodbye.

Then I got up and went back out into the soft sunlight, walked the few feet of sidewalk to Aunt Waverly's house. It was no place for me either, but for one more night, until I could head back home.

Donny met me at the airport and drove me to Seal Beach. It was one of those fine California days. It had rained and wind had blown the smog out, and we could see the mountains in the distance. We kept the windows open, but the traffic was light on the freeway, and we could hear each other.

"They seem to be all ready," Donny said. "They put a tent up, in the parking lot, food and drink and a whole crew of executives."

"Should be great fun," I said. "How's your father handling it?"

"Well, he looks good in my suit."

We laughed at that, both picturing Chen in a tie, then looked over at each other and grinned.

Donny said Chen had asked if I could meet him at the site. For a last look at it together.

"At six, if that's okay. We got the Porsche."

"How?" I said.

426 / DORIT IN LESBOS

"Dad figured it. A set of keys at your gas station. Don't you remember?"

I did then, but only vaguely, at a time when I was having frequent trouble with the thing. "Quite efficient," I said.

"You know Dad."

The Porsche was sitting at the curb in front of the house. It had been washed, even the wheel rims were shining, and I found the keys on the floor just inside the door, where Donny had pushed them through the mail slot. The house was bright but a little stale, and I opened windows and adjusted screens, then had a long shower. I checked the two suits that I had. One was still in a plastic bag from the cleaners. I couldn't remember when I had last worn it. When I ripped the bag away, I saw that it was creased slightly from long hanging but that it would be okay. Then I dressed and went through the house again, even out to the garage and up to the study, just looking at things, touching them, getting myself familiar with the place again. It's a nice house, I thought, everything in its place.

I went to the front porch and looked out into the street. All the dead fronds had been cut away from the tall palms. They looked skinny and a little pathetic at their heads, but green and healthy. Occasional people passed on the sidewalk, carrying blankets and umbrellas, heading for the beach a block away. I could hear the surf washing in, as they could, and some of them looked over to where I stood and smiled. I left the porch then and went down to the street and put the Porsche's top down, got in, and headed for the freeway.

Chen was waiting in the parking lot, perched up on the fender of his old Buick and facing out over the site. He heard the crunch of the Porsche in the gravel, turned and waved when he saw me, and started to climb down as I pulled up. The open tent was set up to the side of his car, long folding tables in rows under it and a heavy wooden podium at one end. Speeches too, I thought, and climbed out of the Porsche and went over to where he was standing at his fender. He took my hand, then gripped my arm, then gave me a good hard whack on the shoulder.

"Ah, ha!" he said. "Ah, ha!"

"You look great, Chen," I said. "Really fine." That old quickness was back in his step and movement, and when I looked his face over, I could see no remnant at all of the injuries, but for that one line of scarring. He looked up at my brow and smiled.

"Fit as two fiddles," he said. "Maybe it didn't happen?"

We both laughed at that. Then he winked and took my arm and pulled me over to the edge of the gravel lot. I couldn't see him limp at all, though I knew he still had some kind of cast. He saw me looking at his leg.

"Not there," he said. "There!"

It was finished. All the berms, contours, and gentle slopes were covered with new grass now, and the various cluster plantings that I could see had taken root. There may still have been places of raw ground, but the sun was sinking, and if they were there I couldn't see them. All the pathways had been filled with stone and raked level, and the heads were now in place on the low lanterns that lined them. I could see, off at the freeway's verge, the low rise of a geometric figure, the slabs leaning against each other where the terrace had been. It looked good from where we were, but I knew I'd have to go down to the pool to be sure of it. Even at this distance and in the failing light there was something familiar about it, and Chen must have seen the question in my eyes.

"The tattoo figure," he said. "Standing up. It grew on me as something special, and I used its line curves as a frame, a kind of skeleton."

"They'll be using it in Aransas too," I said. "A trivet, or a pot."

"Oh, my!" he said. "You've surely gotten it around!"

"Sappho's palm," I said. "Probably in more places than we know."

He looked at me, but he didn't say anything, because he was Chen. He couldn't have understood what I meant, but for him that wasn't the point. Only that I did mean something, and his look was about the quality of the circumstance in which I'd said it. He was measuring that, and when I didn't speak again, he just smiled up at me.

We stood for a long time, looking the place over. Chen pointed things out, how the beach grass was coming in strongly and holding, ways in which the evening shadows softened particular hillsides, the muted colors of bougainvillea and yellow roses and how they'd be brighter in the sun. "When the place is up and ready for business."

"I can't find anything significantly wrong with it," he said after a while. "Can you?"

It was a serious question, and I took my time in scanning over it, measuring it both in pieces and as a whole.

"No, nothing," I said finally, then turned and looked at him. I had something to say, but he spoke it before I could get it out. He was smiling, almost sheepishly, but I knew he was faking that.

"I sure as hell wouldn't want to go through this shit again," he said. "And I don't mean the trailer business either." He laughed, and winked at me again, and I looked down at him and spoke.

"You said it. It's fine, you know, but in the end who needs it?"

"Except for the pool," he said. "That was something to do."

"And all the business with that terrace and what's out there now. That was interesting."

We both laughed at the way we were making our excuses. Then Chen touched me on the elbow, turned back a little, and pulled at my sleeve.

"But look at this," he said.

I turned back around with him. We were facing across the parking lot and looking up at the central administration building on its rise. Heavy shadows fell across its face now, but I knew there was something seriously wrong with it, though I couldn't see quite what.

"Up there," he said.

The windows were gone, the ones the workers would see the pool through. They'd filled the whole row of them in, cemented and painted, and there was nothing left up on the second story but a bright, narrow rectangle of solid white wall.

"They're on the other side now," Chen said. "Discussion of distraction, the sun coming in. The bosses made a choice for business, fine-tuned efficiency. What we all need."

"And the pool?" I said.

"For only the chosen few now, the gardeners, visiting executives if they have time, maybe some wanderers."

He shrugged, and then he laughed. He was free of it, as I knew I was. We'd drink a few cocktails, maybe pick up a home job or two. I might even meet a woman. But no more of this kind of thing. We'd thought it a step up, but it hadn't been that at all.

"Some food?" he said.

"Shit, yes," I said. "Of course. But first I want to go down to the pool, to see the slabs from there."

"You go," he said. "A place for private contemplation. I've had enough of it for today. I'll wait in the Porsche."

I moved to the edge of the parking lot then and stepped over the curbing. Then I made my way carefully on the new grass to where the path I wanted curved down at its edge. I moved through shallow cuts, then around the low hill we'd provided, and stepped to the wooden platform overlooking the pool. The ground rose up behind me now, guarding me from anyone's view, and I felt comfortably alone and safe.

I looked down at the pool's flat surface, then out to the distance where the slabs rose up and leaned against each other in their dark geometry at the freeway's edge. Cars passed behind them, then came into sight again, but they were of no consequence to my focus, only uncertain and dim sparks, transparent trails like the ones Uncle Edward had made, painting the air. I looked back to the pool then, and I could see that we'd found an answer to be satisfied with. It wasn't the only answer, and that itself had interest. Neither was Sappho's life lines.

It was getting on to eight. The sun was only a pink, milky wash across the landscape now, and there were large shadows resting on the pool's surface. But I could still see down into the water and through it to another surface, the large slabs of that dignified and centered mind, luminous below my feet, and in places I could see through at the edges, the small dark voids of entrance into the underlayer, where nothing at all could be that certain.

But the slabs' weight, then the pool's surface, then the shadows resting on it, all gave a certain integrity that was unbreachable. It was something that Uncle Edward might have liked, not really too far at all from what he'd been after, the surface of the world where all beauty resides.

The shadows thickened and lengthened across the pool. It was as if the mind was ready for sleep now, that a night shade was being drawn over it. I felt myself sinking down into it all, through shadows and water, down to the large slabs, but not beyond them. Then I looked up and focused again on the sharp and lovely outlines of the distant configuration at the freeway's verge. Just what it's supposed to do, I thought, take me back to the world.

I turned away and moved from the small promontory then, and followed the pathway back up toward the parking lot. The lights that lined it had not been lit yet, but there was a sparkle from the almost dead sun still in the stones, and it was easy going. I was thinking of Panama, and Aransas. Now that the job was finished, I might take a little trip for myself.

I reached the Porsche and climbed in and settled myself on the cool leather. Chen turned toward me, a look of mock expectancy on his face.

"So, where should we eat, then?" he asked.

I tried hard not to smile.

"Why, McDonald's, of course! This is America," I said. "Where else?"

We laughed all the way there, wind in our hair.

Toby Olson was born in Illinois in 1937, but has spent most of his life in California and New York City. The recipient of National Endowment for the Arts, Guggenheim, and Rockefeller fellowships, he has published numerous books of poetry, most recently *We Are the Fire*, and four previous novels, *The Life of Jesus*, *The Woman Who Escaped From Shame*, *Utah*, and *Seaview*, which received the PEN/Faulkner award in 1983. He currently lives in Philadelphia and Cape Cod with his wife, Miriam, and teaches English at Temple University.